MW00618432

SET THE TERMS

BOOK THREE OF THE RISE OF THE
PEACEMAKERS

Edited by
Mia R. Kleve and Kevin Ikenberry

Seventh Seal Press
Virginia Beach, VA

Copyright © 2020 by Mia R. Kleve and Kevin Ikenberry.

All rights reserved. No part of this publication may be reproduced, distributed or transmitted in any form or by any means, including photocopying, recording, or other electronic or mechanical methods, without the prior written permission of the publisher, except in the case of brief quotations embodied in critical reviews and certain other noncommercial uses permitted by copyright law.

Chris Kennedy/Seventh Seal Press
2052 Bierce Dr., Virginia Beach, VA 23454
http://chriskennedypublishing.com/

Publisher's Note: This is a work of fiction. Names, characters, places, and incidents are a product of the author's imagination. Locales and public names are sometimes used for atmospheric purposes. Any resemblance to actual people, living or dead, or to businesses, companies, events, institutions, or locales is completely coincidental.

The stories and articles contained herein have never been previously published. They are copyrighted as follows:

THAT THEY TOO SHALL KNOW PEACE by Mark Wandrey © 2020 by Mark Wandrey
WHEN PIGS FLY by Terry Mixon © 2020 by Terry Mixon
RECOVERY by Casey Moores © 2020 by Casey Moores
UNFORCED ERRORS by Marisa Wolf © 2020 by Marisa Wolf
JURISDICTION by Jon R. Osborne © 2020 by Jon R. Osborne
STARS OR BARS by Jamie Ibson © 2020 by Jamie Ibson
A NATURAL SELECTION by Kevin Ikenberry & Peter J. Aldin © 2020 Kevin Ikenberry & Peter J. Aldin
GUMBO by Matt Novotny © 2020 by Matt Novotny
HOW TO TRAIN YOUR CANAVAR by Marie Whittaker © 2020 by Marie Whittaker
SHADOWS IN THE KEY OF FEAR by William Alan Webb © 2020 by William Alan Webb
TANGENT ORANGE by Mark Stallings © 2020 by Mark Stallings
CURIOSITY KILLED THE PUSHTAL by Chris Kennedy © 2020 by Chris Kennedy
WE ARE NOT HEROES by Quincy J. Allen © 2020 by Quincy J. Allen
LAST by Kevin Steverson © 2020 by Kevin Steverson

Set the Terms/Mia R. Kleve and Kevin Ikenberry -- 1st ed.
ISBN 978-1648550300

Foreword by Kacey Ezell

What Price Peace

This is a question that has haunted humankind since the first of us clashed with members of neighboring families. Violence, for better or for worse, seems to be an essential component of the Human experience. We are creatures of will, and when our will conflicts with the will of another, we fight. That is, after all, the basis of the Four Horsemen Universe (4HU). It is this capacity to fight that made us useful and interesting to the denizens of the Galactic Union. Violence makes us valuable.

And yet, as a species, we have a long, distinguished history of striving *not* to fight. How many quests, how many crusades have begun in the name of establishing peace? How many times have people allowed themselves to be slowly subjugated, all because some despot promised peace and delivered only control? We long for peace; we yearn for it.

In what has to be one of the best ironic twists of all time, we Humans often find ourselves fighting…for peace.

So, as we make our way in a galaxy that values the ability to make war, how can anyone ever know peace?

Enter the Peacemakers.

When Mark Wandrey and Chris Kennedy first invited other writers into their universe, the concept of the Peacemaker Guild was by far the most popular. I think Chris told me once that no less than four authors pitched stories about this tiny guild that travels the galaxy and enforces the few ironclad laws in existence. I know that I was one of them, but Chris told me Kevin Ikenberry had gotten there first with his brilliant story "Stand on It." So, I focused on felinoid alien assassins, and Kevin gave us Jessica Francis.

Jessica Francis is by far one of my favorite characters in the Four Horsemen Universe. Neither Mark, Chris, nor Kevin is into pandering (nor is anyone else published in the 4HU, for that matter!) to any particular demographic, but I really feel as if she could have been written just for me. Jessica is a tough girl with a brilliant, complicated mind and complex emotions. She's unapologetically feminine, and yet is at home with hard core tough guys of all species. She'll make her mission happen come hell or high water, but she's going to do it her way, all the way. For all of these reasons, she resonates with me to my core. Jessica could be any one of my sisters-in-arms. I read her story, and I feel seen, which honestly isn't the case for most "strong female characters" in fiction.

And Jessica isn't alone! Over the course of her books, Jessica pulls together a team that is as much family as anything else. Much like the way the 4HU has developed, honestly. Jessica and her Peacemaker (and non-Peacemaker!) family have shaped the story of the Galactic Union in a myriad of ways. And now, Kevin has opened the guild doors to let us see deeper into this most mysterious of guilds.

Whether you're a longstanding fan of the series or a newcomer to the 4HU, you'll find that the Peacemakers in this volume have the eternal task of answering the question: What price, peace? And you'll find that though their answers vary, they're always accompanied by a damn good story.

So welcome, I hope you enjoy your visit to the guild.

Kacey Ezell
February 2020

Contents

* * * * *

That They Too Shall Know Peace by Mark Wandrey

Chapter 1

You couldn't escape the smell of corruption, no matter where you went. It permeated the streets, the bars, the restaurants, and the hospitals. The last two were abandoned or choked to overflowing. Jondar was in the first establishment, a bar within a kilometer of the starport just managing to stay in business. They even had some food, if you didn't think too hard about where it might have come from. Being an omnivore capable of consuming a wide variety of proteins and carbohydrates often had its own advantages.

"Do you want another portion?"

Jondar's antenna lifted at the voice, spoken in his own language. The bar's AI was smart enough to tell what race a patron was and speak in its own language, of course. Feesta had once been the crown jewel of the Cimaron, one of the galaxy's top five trading worlds and arguably the most beautiful to behold. Many came just to see the architectural and natural wonders.

But those times were gone. Gone forever.

He used his Mesh to check his account balance then clicked his mandibles in consternation. The service bot waited patiently. There were only three other customers, and two of them appeared unconscious. The last was greedily consuming a tube cake, the only substantial protein still on the menu.

"Yes," he said finally.

The bot beeped in understanding and a serving pipette extruded from the bar pouring 50 milliliters of greenish fluid into his glass. Jondar's taste receptors suggested it was based on a fungus of some kind. The taste wasn't unpleasant, not that a bad taste would have stopped him from going for the alcohol content. The feeling of the drink entering his bloodstream dulled the impact of another 200 RC gone. He shrugged his middle arms.

"What difference? Republic coin is worthless soon anyway."

"Party while you can, yes, Altar?"

Jondar's tiny black refractory eyes realigned toward the voice at the same time his off hand grasped the tiny laser derringer he kept in a tool belt. It was good for four shots, max. Better than empty hands.

"There is no need for weapons." The stranger was a TriRusk, and a big one, too. Jondar's strained Mesh said the being's build suggested male. He had a huge head that came to an armored beak and terminated in a short horn at the end. Large eyes were heavily shielded by a bone crest, which sloped back over its shoulders. He held up both hands to show he wasn't armed.

As if he would need a weapon. Jondar took his hand away from the gun. He could fire all four shots into the newcomer's open mouth and probably just piss him off. "I am not partying," he said.

"I was passing, saw the bar was still serving. I was amazed, so I came in." The TriRusk turned his huge head and examined the other patrons.

"It is a free bar, help yourself." Jondar doubted the massive herbivore would find anything appealing from the limited selection.

"To my knowledge, I am the only one of my kind on Feesta. The planet is divided, starving, and angry." He spread his powerful arms. "Our people have no quarrel of which I am aware?"

"No," Jondar agreed, sipping his drink. "The Altar and TriRusk were both citizens of the Republic, not servitors."

"Yes, yes!" the TriRusk happily agreed.

The alien who'd been chewing on the tube cake at the other side of the bar stopped and his furry head came up. Jondar silently cursed. He hadn't realized it was a Pushtal. Fantastic.

"What is your problem with a servitor, bug?" the feline growled.

Jondar's Mesh again responded sluggishly, only rendering the Pushtal's words into Altar after Jondar forced a manual operation. Since the Failing, nothing worked correctly anymore.

"Just that we were not slaves, like you," the newcomer said.

"I don't share his words," Jondar said, but his comment was swallowed up by the angry, hissing roar from the Pushtal.

"We were not *slaves!* We served the Kahraman proudly."

"Enjoyed the caress of their Genomancers, didn't you Pushtal. Or shouldn't it be PusSha?"

That did it, the felinoid uncoiled from the chair and leaped at the TriRusk in one incredibly fluid motion. Jondar marveled at the movement even as he realized he should be taking cover, especially since he was between the two. The power and grace of the Pushtal were in full display and showed why the Kahraman enjoyed using them in urban combat environments.

The Pushtal was halfway through its leap when the TriRusk took a long, booming step forward and caught it in one massive, gloved hand. The blade the Pushtal had been drawing fumbled in his grasp and fell onto the bar, shattering part of the glass top.

"No violence, please!" the bar's robotic voice cried out. "I will summon peacekeepers!"

"Gahk!" the Pushtal cried in alarm as the TriRusk swung him sideways, away from Jondar, who was incredibly grateful. The Pushtal had long, sharp claws on all four limbs, and Altar were neither armored, nor possessed thick fur to protect them. His skin was a light chiton. It didn't cut or puncture, it broke. His partially open circulatory system didn't help such wounds much either. His people had evolved to burrow and climb trees, not fight other predators for food.

"There are a still a few hundred of these *Pekah* controlling the industrial sector like little cat warlords," the TriRusk said to Jondar. "They're stealing what they can, killing, and generally skulking around hoping their Kahraman masters come back."

The Pushtal was clawing at the TriRusk's arm in vain. Clearly the armored limb was far too tough, even for the feline's claws. The TriRusk looked back at the Pushtal and laughed in his booming laugh. "Your time is up." With a grunt, he crushed the Pushtal's neck.

Jondar cringed at the sound of crunching bone. The Pushtal's eyes bugged out, and, despite the grip, a squeal still escaped its throat before it was completely crushed. With a grunt of contempt, the TriRusk tossed the not-quite-dead Pushtal into a heap by the door where it jerked and slowly died. Jondar looked in horror at the dead Pushtal then at the TriRusk.

The TriRusk noticed some blood on his big pawlike hands and rubbed them on his jacket. "Well, my Altar friend, I'm hungry."

The bar's operating system, likely once a capable AI, was trying to deal with the homicide which had just occurred within. Jondar could see several of its service bots and tentacled working units mov-

to extracting. A couple weeks ago, my lifter develops a problem. So, I have to leave and come talk to a Dusman servitor coordinator, see about having the repair parts fabricated. Only a Pushtal strike team found the moon and my lifter." He pointed at the dead Pushtal and smashed the table with a hand. "Boom! and Qorr don't own no lifter no more."

He shrugged and gobbled his last tube cake, washing it down with the drink. "Was it him? Probably not...but maybe." He shrugged again. "I spent the end of the war in my little shuttle trying to get a ride out and not get killed. Then the war was over. The Failing happened, and I landed here."

"Sorry about your lifter," Jondar said.

"You still have your ship?"

"Yes," he admitted. "My F11 is shot, though. I might make it one jump, but with the screwed up jump speeds, how far could I get? I can't even find out if my world still exists."

"You Altar have colonies?"

"Only little ones. Almost all of us live on our home world."

"Well, little one, I hope it still lives."

Jondar ended up exchanging contact codes with the TriRusk. He didn't think the alien would be of any help to him. He partly did it just in case a peacekeeper showed up at his ship asking about a dead Pushtal.

* * *

Chapter 2

Jondar was almost caught up in a riot on the way back to his ship. At least a thousand Skeshu were screaming, throwing rocks, and setting fire to everything. The part he found ironic was that the Skeshu owned the planet, granted to them as Dusman servitors.

He would normally not have been intimidated by the likes of Skeshu. It's hard to be afraid of a felinoid smaller than even the Altar's short stature. Their four eyes and antenna were strange and the lack of body hair wasn't something he usually noticed, since his insectile species didn't have any, either.

When he turned the corner and was confronted by the riot, he immediately altered his course. The huge crowd was assaulting a merchant's district, also operated by Skeshu. Since the race wasn't a warrior race, the riot didn't involve true combat, though it didn't stop the clumsy employment of a few lasers on either side. But the disturbance was enough that he added several blocks to his trip.

Finally, he was back at the starport. The perimeter fence, once manned by the deadly squat Dusman warbots, was now abandoned. When the war ended and the belligerents fled, all the instruments of war either stopped or were stolen by various opportunists and combatants. A few of the warbots remained, though they were nothing more than shells. One lay near the gate, its chest open, wires wadded and dangling like the entrails of a fallen warrior.

Like the warbots, the starport was scattered with the fallen refuse of the war's end. Thirty of the massive Dusman materiel transport ships were grounded twenty kilometers away. They'd arrived just before the end and never unloaded. Jondar knew there'd been fighting over the contents and wondered if his new "friend" Qorr had his horn into it.

Besides the transports, a hundred or more other ships were grounded. Many would never leave again. As he walked past, he took a different route than he had each time before. He was systematically noting the various ships' conditions. Many were damaged, some horribly. Either on the way in or from continuous fighting over Feesta. The fighting had been going continuously for half a year when he'd arrived with his load.

He didn't bother spending time looking at the hulks. The ones with moderate damage, though, he always took the excuse to spend an extra minute. He would slowly wander past the engineering support section and, if nobody was about, saunter over and touch the fill-point status select. This time it was a bulk transport, bigger and uglier than his. The status display was also uglier than his. Jondar left the other stranded ship behind and finished the walk to his own.

Grand Za had been his for ten years now. He'd used profits from a trading venture in the Tolo arm, far away from the war, and bought the ship. He'd made a good living until he'd been scooped up by a Dusman blockade and conscripted into service. The AI the Dusman had installed in his computer had carefully tabulated all the runs he'd made for the war. It didn't add up to a fortune, but he'd be able to pay for repairs and some upgrades afterwards. Only, like every other AI he knew about, it was no longer working, and along with it went all those records.

It's not like there are any Dusman anywhere about to pay me, anyway. One of the little native scavengers ran past and he kicked at it out of frustration. He missed, and it hissed at him as it fled. At least it was a sunny day. It almost made up for the ever-increasing putrid stench.

His ship was an Izlian design with modular configuration. It could be made bulbous with room for lots of cargo in space, then rearranged as it was now to land and take off more easily.

Grand Za squatted at the very edge of the starport, where he'd been ordered to land upon arrival. As a commandeered merchant-man, he'd been carrying war materials. They'd loaded him two weeks ago with cases of ammunition and sent him here. He knew Feesta was a major battleground and wondered if this was his last mission. But when he'd come out of hyperspace, there was no battle, no Kahraman, and most importantly, no damned Dusman.

He used his Mesh to code into *Grand Za* and rode the little lift up to the crew deck, all the way in the nose. As a product of commerce and now war, she had an observation lounge just aft of the bridge. He got himself some food from his autochef which, thankfully, had been filled just before coming to Feesta, and went to the observation lounge to eat.

He didn't know why he kept coming there to look at the scene, it wasn't anything he would normally have considered view worthy. When he'd landed, there were a dozen Dusman fire-control bases only meters away, just outside the starport. He would have unloaded his munitions to them, except as he landed, they were leaving. It had almost looked like they were running. Only, the Dusman didn't run. Ever. From anything.

Not knowing what to do, he had sat in *Grand Za* for a day and wondered what horrors were coming, what was frightening enough to scare away the iron spine of the Republic. Kilometers away stood an unknown number of what had made the Dusman so powerful; Raknar. They had stood ever since, unmoving. Nobody dared go near the living embodiment of their power. A couple of them could

Jondar used his Mesh for a minute, trying to tease out a correlation on the design. After sending a dozen inquiries to the city's AI and getting no response, he abandoned the effort.

"I need to dust off my programming training and see if I can work on the ship's computer." Other ship captains had removed their ships' dependencies on AI, bringing them back to a simpler working order. He was loath to give up the automation. It had been the AI which allowed a single person to operate a ship the size of *Grand Za*. Only, without the AI to handle all the necessary tasks, what would happen if something went wrong?

His eyes strayed to the distant resting place of the crashed transport and silently wondered. Meanwhile, the corvette slowed to a near stop, lowered its insect-like legs, and landed perfectly about halfway between *Grand Za* and the now-worthless starport facilities. "If you're hoping for supplies, you will be sadly disappointed."

The new ship was too far away to see what race its occupants might have been. A disabled bulk freighter and a cruiser which had burned after landing were between him and it. Jondar considered going out to investigate, but the encounter with Qorr was too fresh in his mind. Instead, he finished his meal and went back to the bridge.

He dug out some chips on programming and loaded them into his Mesh. He studied for maybe an hour, enough time to remember how difficult programming was, before giving up and turning in for the night. Tomorrow was another day.

* * *

Chapter 3

Jondar wandered by the corvette three times in the intervening week. He'd gotten no closer than a dozen meters before noticing the ship had a bevy of small automated anti-personnel laser turrets which not only appeared operational, but which actively tracked him as he approached. Nothing said "mind your own business" better than a megawatt of coherent light. He got the message and kept clear.

The ship was in excellent condition. In fact, it looked new. The anti-personnel turrets weren't its only weapons either. He was sure it sported a centrally mounted missile rack and probably a spinal-mount weapon of some kind, but standing on the ground staring at it didn't provide enough details to be sure. What he did know was that the ship probably had F11.

In town, he ran into another ship captain who'd been stuck on Feesta longer. His ship was a blockade runner, equipped with hyperspace shunts, which specialized in getting behind enemy lines. A simian race, Bugitar were common as spacers and were well-known as amoral tricksters. He'd gotten caught by the Dusman trying to smuggle in assets to the Kahraman. They'd put a lockout on his ship's hyperspace generator. Unlike every other AI which up and died during the Failing, and might have unlocked the ship, whatever they'd done to his ship had stayed done.

"You see that corvette?" the captain, Greep, asked. Like most simian races, he was constantly in motion and covered in hair. His long arms were always moving, grabbing stuff, twitching, scratching. It was like watching a broken bot spasming around.

"Yeah, it landed a few days ago," Jondar said. He'd run into Greep outside one of the little bazaars which had sprung up around the starport. Shipmasters desperate for parts traded with locals desperate for food. Unlike the old days, everyone appeared armed these days. Since the riot, he'd noticed any Skeshu he encountered were armed more often than not. The city was feeling more and more unsafe. Jondar had traded his little laser derringer for a proper pistol and two extra magazines. He never thought he'd miss peacekeepers.

"Have you seen the corvette's master?" Greep asked, clearly hoping Jondar could provide information.

"No. Have you?"

"No," he admitted. "The ship is beautiful. I could have made mountains of coin with such a craft!"

"You said you did make mountains of coin," Jondar reminded him.

"Yeah, but now who's going to pay my vouchers?" They walked along the edge of the bazaar, not so much walking together as both going in the same direction. "Oh, did you hear K'ka is back?"

"No," Jondar said, now genuinely interested. K'ka was a well-known and -liked Caroon trader who'd been stuck like the rest of them. There wasn't a ship in space those days who hadn't been low on F11. The majority of it went to the warring factions. They often paid in the precious fuel, allowing just enough out to keep you going, but not enough to let you look for other work. K'ka had left Feesta two weeks ago, saying he had enough F11 to make it to an outpost he'd heard about. When he hadn't returned, they figured the Caroon trader had made it. "Where is he?"

"Still in space," Greep said. "His reactor is in emergency mode."

"He didn't find the outpost?"

"Oh, he said he found it, only it was shot to hell and looted. It shook him, so he came back here. Said this place is better. Only, the trip took 170 hours each way!"

"No! Again?" Of all the stories he'd heard, the one about hyperspace travel being wrecked was the most disturbing. Sure, only the Dusman could access the fabled "Short Hop"; a quick 72-hour transit. Rumor had it, they possessed a way to make instantaneous travel, though it was as big a legend as the Arsenals. Faster hyperspace travel, though, was a fact.

Huge transports pinching coin used the slow routes, 170 hours and only a thousand light years each trip. If you weren't in any hurry. Everyone else went with the 120-hour, five to ten thousand-light year trips. The rich or desperate got the 100-hour, twenty-five thousand-light year route. You could get those as part of a deal hauling for the Dusman, too. Only now, rumor said it was 170 hours or nothing.

"What did the stargate operators say?"

"He said there are only Sumatozou in the gates now, and they offered no explanation or apology."

"Are they trying to extort coin?"

"K'ka said no attempt was made. The fee was unchanged—250 RC."

"I heard someone say they went 15,000 light years in 170 hours," a passing captain said. He was a Maki, looking a little like Greep. The Maki had been Dusman servitors, though.

"Ridiculous," Greep snorted. "Go find a Dusman backside to clean."

The Maki made a rude gesture and moved off, but Jondar wondered if it were true. Then he remembered K'ka again. "How is K'ka

position, and he could clearly see the accursed Altok gaining on him, chittering and whooping in their mammalian babble.

Hoping to gain some distance, he used his right mid-hand to grab the laser pistol from his equipment belt and fire a shot back at them, just to scare them and show he wasn't going to be an easy mark. His luck proved consistent for the day. His hit the leader of the group behind him directly in the face, killing him instantly.

"Well that's torn it," he moaned. He was a terrible shot; what were the odds he'd get a kill shot? Too high, apparently. He unleashed several more pulses toward his pursuers. Naturally, now that he was aiming, he missed every one of them. He clipped the gun back in place and concentrated on moving.

Jondar never even saw the Altok who hit him from the side alley; he just felt the impact and tried to roll into a ball. Being built with a head, thorax, and slightly elongated abdomen and segmented joints between body parts didn't lend to a flexible rolling design. He crashed through an abandoned storefront and into a pile of discarded old clothing.

He was lucky enough, the main impact was on his abdomen, which was flexible. If he'd hit the window head-first, it probably would have broken or cracked his antenna or even crushed his head. As it was, he managed to recover into a crouch and had his laser pistol in hand. *By the gods, if they mean to have me, I'll take as many with me as I can!*

The Altok who'd tackled him rushed up to the window. Jondar shot it through the torso, the energy of the beam igniting its fur. The being thrashed and screamed, causing his fellows to slow just outside the window. Jondar fired twice more at the others, making them dodge out of his view. Jondar swapped magazines even though the one in the gun still had four shots. Now he had ten in the gun, ten more in another magazine, and four in the original. Twenty-four shots against who knew how many pissed off little mammals.

One of the furry devils poked its head around the ruined window; he shot at it and missed, of course. He wondered if he shouldn't aim. It worked the first time. The whole thing was tiring.

"Come on you scum," he yelled. "Come see what Altar are made of!" He could hear them chattering to each other and hoped he didn't sound as terrified as he was. *Survive a galactic war and get killed by little simians,* he thought.

A sudden roar caught Jondar completely by surprise. It was utterly unlike the Altok vocalization, and sounded ten times their size. Whatever it was, the Altok immediately opened fire on it and were the recipients of a massive amount of return fire. Jondar skittered to the side and found some overturned metal shelving to shield behind as guns blazed. The white-hot beam of a particle weapon burned through the shelving just above his antenna, making Jondar scream in alarm. *A peacekeeper?* It wasn't possible, was it? The AI were all inoperable, and without AI they would remain that way.

Another particle beam didn't burn him in half, for which he was immensely grateful. As the sounds of Altok gunfire fell off, the cracking of the particle weapon became more evident. It was further away than he expected. Then it was over.

Jondar crawled slowly out from behind the clutter, letting just the tips of his antenna poke over the edge of the window he'd crashed through. The basic image they gave him was of a slaughter. A few of the Altok still moved, but none were going to survive.

The same roar echoed toward him. The sound receptors carried it clearly this time, and he used his Mesh to find a translation. It wasn't a common language, which he'd expected by the strange sound. Almost a minute later he finally found it.

"Who's in there?" By the time he had the correct translation matrix loaded, the speaker sounded pissed.

"I was just caught in the crossfire!" he yelled back, without exposing himself.

"Altaran?" the stranger asked. "You are a long way from home."

"You are nowhere near your home either, Equiri."

"You have a point. You may come out."

"No offense, noble, but I value my carapace."

A laugh came back in reply. "No offense, either. However if I wanted your carapace, it would be mine."

Fair enough, Jondar thought and stood. The Equiri was 50 meters away, at the corner of a nearby street. His Mesh said the alien was female, and she was cradling a very nasty looking particle rifle of a design Jondar had never seen before. The weapons were rare enough outside of peacekeepers, anyway. He'd seen a Dusman with one, once.

"May I go about my business?" he asked, keeping all four hands where the equine alien could see them.

"I was actually looking for someone."

"Who?"

"Why, you, of course." Jondar cocked his head in confusion. "A TriRusk named Qorr said you had a ship and wanted off this world."

Jondar was too surprised to do more than nod. The Equiri smiled. Even from 50 meters, the sharp predator's teeth were not a happy sight.

* * *

Chapter 4

The Equiri's name was Lossh. She wore an interesting design of armor he'd never seen before, obviously custom manufactured to fit her massive bipedal frame. He'd never seen or met an Equiri, but knew they'd fought for the Kahraman. Not as servitors, though somewhat faithfully if he remembered correctly. He believed they'd evolved the way she appeared before him, over two meters tall, decidedly equine in appearance, nearly hairless except a long flowing mane which Lossh had braided to fall over her dark green armor. The red-tinged eyes and sharp carnivore teeth made her a formidable being.

The Equiri led Jondar through the streets, which were now choked with rioting Altok and Skeshu. As night was approaching the two groups were escalating their warfare. If Jondar had been alone, he doubted he would have made it a block. With the towering Equiri leading him, he barely got a sidelong glance.

He wasn't surprised when they approached the bar where he'd met Qorr. The TriRusk was waiting when they arrived. He raised a big hand in greeting. Jondar waved back; Lossh just nodded. He sat far off to one side. As they entered, Jondar couldn't help looking to where the Pushtal's body had been. He was glad the glitchy bar's computer had removed the corpse, though he wondered what had become of it.

"I see Lossh found you!" Qorr said, shaking his big head happily.

"She saved me, actually," Jondar said as he took a seat with the two. "Though I now wonder why?"

"She was looking for transport off the planet, and I mentioned you had one of the best ships."

Jondar considered for a minute, then decided his fate wasn't as bad as some. "K'ka's ship is better, and he would work for next to nothing." He looked at the Equiri. "Assuming you have something of value to trade?"

Lossh reached into a pocket of the vest she wore, removed a small vial, and set it on the table. It was a blueish crystalline vial with unbroken seal. A vial of pure F11. "I have this, and more. But the Caroon is not available."

"Did he get another job?" Jondar wondered.

"He is dead," Lossh said. "His ship was destroyed by Pushtal pirates three days ago, when I arrived."

"Pushtals," Qorr spat. Lossh nodded.

"That is unfortunate," Jondar said. He used the little terminal on the bar and found they still had alcoholics he could drink, so he ordered one. Lossh produced a card of some sort and interfaced it with the bar.

"Your drink is on me, Altaran." He glanced at Qorr. "You as well."

"My thanks," Qorr said.

"Yes, I thank you, but I cannot promise help."

"Will you listen to my offer?"

"Of course," Jondar said. A bot delivered their drinks. Qorr's smelled a little like beer while Lossh's looked suspiciously like blood.

"I am here looking for a war criminal."

Both Qorr and Jondar stared at the Equiri, unsure how to respond. Jondar recovered first. "Doesn't a war criminal suggest some sort of justice system? Is the Republic regaining control?"

"There is no more Republic," Lossh said. Jondar and Qorr looked at each other. They weren't surprised, but it wasn't what they expected to hear.

"How can it just be gone?" Jondar asked.

"Call it suicide," Lossh said.

Jondar wanted to ask more, push for details, but something about the Equiri suggested she wasn't interested in telling stories.

"Who has charged you with hunting criminals then?"

"The Dusman's and the Kahramans' departure has created a power vacuum," Lossh explained. "Something always fills a vacuum."

"What is it called?" Jondar asked.

"It doesn't really have a name yet. But some races have begun talking instead of fighting. There is peace in places, and it's growing. Slowly."

"So, you *do* have someone behind you?" Qorr asked. Lossh nodded her long head and took a drink. She considered the half-empty glass, judging, then shrugged.

"If I help you, where are we going?" asked Jondar.

"I cannot say until we leave Feesta," she replied. "After I have completed my mission, you will drop me on another world, and you can be on your way."

Jondar held up the vial, examining how the bar's light shone through its rare contents. "How much?"

"As much as you need."

"How do you have F11?" Jondar asked.

"Does it matter?"

Qorr shrugged.

"What's in this for you?" he asked the TriRusk.

"My finder's fee is a ride off this rock."

"Sounds like she doesn't know where we're going, or at least she's not talking."

The TriRusk shrugged again. "Have you looked around? It doesn't matter; this place is going to burn."

Outside there was a flash of light and the sound of an explosion rolled over the bar. Jondar couldn't have asked for a clearer signal. "Okay, we have a deal."

* * *

The next morning, Jondar was back at *Grand Za,* finishing preparations to depart. He'd not bothered to have the ship in trim for flight since he'd landed. An amazing amount of stuff was just lying around. Once he'd secured everything, he reconfigured the forward compartment for two additional state-rooms. It cost him half his observation deck, but he was able to keep the cargo hold intact. It was still full of ammunition he'd never delivered. Maybe it would be worth something to someone.

He was on the bridge, going over his ship's power condition, when he saw a small cargo truck making its way across the huge open starport picking its way between ships. It had to be his Equiri and TriRusk passengers. So, he checked the power situation one more time. The reactor reported stable at 2% output, sufficient to keep the ship's basic systems working. F11 was at 97.5% saturation. If he increased power by even 1%, the fusion core would begin to heat up. He hoped the Equiri had more than the few milliliters of F11 she'd shown off.

By the time Jondar reached the main lock at ground level, the cargo truck was pulling to a stop. Qorr was driving the vehicle, which held four beings, not two. The Equiri was first out, a huge duffel bag over one shoulder.

"I don't have room for four," Jondar said as soon as the Equiri was close enough.

"These are my associates," Lossh explained. "They aren't coming with us."

Jondar saw they were unloading the truck. One was an Oogar, a race he'd only seen once before. A simply massive ursine race with improbably purple hair color. The other was smaller, a Cochkala. It examined Jondar with beady eyes over its black-and-white-striped facial fur. What Jondar found most interesting was that they both had the same highly polished and well-engineered green tinted body armor. They were both armed, as well, and carried themselves with confidence.

He watched the Oogar and Cochkala unload a standard container module, a cubic meter on a side with regular interlock points and a surprisingly high-tech locked interface. The Cochkala keyed something into the interface and nodded to the Oogar who simply picked up the module and carried it to the ship.

"Where do I put this?" he growled at Jondar.

Jondar opened the cargo door and indicated a free section of floor. The Oogar grunted and set the module in place, then expertly secured it. He'd apparently worked in the cargo section of a ship before, which itself was unusual. In most civilized corners of the galaxy, such work was done by bots. Jondar had four nearly new cargo bots himself, which were now useless with the dead AI.

The Oogar barely glanced at Jondar as he went back outside and talked with the Cochkala and Lossh. Afterward, they closed their eyes and lowered their heads.

What's this, some religious ritual? For a moment, Jondar wondered if Lossh was part of a church. He didn't consider a religious government moving in after the Republic to be an improvement. His race hadn't gone in for superstitions since their dark ages.

After a moment, they looked up and nodded to each other. In a moment of clarity Jondar realized they were communicating with their Mesh. He was surprised because the AI was no longer working, which meant communicating that way was many times more difficult.

The Oogar and Cochkala got back in the truck and drove away, leaving Lossh and Qorr with their bags standing outside *Grand Za*. "We are ready to go," Lossh said.

"I need the F11," Jondar reminded the Equiri.

"May I access your engineering systems?"

"Of course," Jondar said and led the Equiri inside.

The alien left her bag by the lock and followed Jondar to the engineering control system where he opened a Tri-V screen and entered his captain's code, something he would have done with his Mesh before. Lossh examined the controls for a moment before grunting and working through the controls.

"You have written manual controls," she noted. "Albeit rather badly."

"I haven't done any programming since school," he admitted.

"I will help you improve them," Qorr said, "if you wish. It will be a small repayment for your hospitality."

"I would appreciate it. You are a pilot, yes?" The TriRusk nodded.

"As am I," Lossh said.

"Good, I'll need the help flying *Grand Za*."

"No problem." Lossh finished with the computer. "Your F11 is at 97.5% saturation."

"That sounds correct."

She took a fluid transfer cable and attached it to the container she'd brought. Confirming Jondar's theory, the Equiri activated the container without using manual input. F11 flowed into his ship which automatically processed it. In five minutes, he was up to 15% F11. Before everything went to oblivion it would have been enough to get him halfway across the galaxy. Now, who knew?

"Sufficient?" Lossh asked.

"Yes," Jondar said, then glanced at the container. If it were full it would contain a thousand liters of F11. His mandibles clicked excitedly.

"It is all yours," Lossh said, then put a hand on it. "When we are done."

"Then let's get started."

* * *

Chapter 5

Leaving Feesta was both a moment of great relief and sorrow. The only thing the planet still had plenty of was reaction mass. Jondar had tanked up as soon as he landed, even before he realized the magnitude of what was happening.

The entire forward section of *Grand Za* was reconfigured for his two passengers, including the formerly tiny bridge. Now there were three workstations and both of his guests quickly made themselves at home with a familiarity you only saw among experienced spacers.

"Flying ships is going to be complicated now," Qorr said, "unless the AIs start working again."

"I'd just get used to it," Lossh said.

Jondar didn't like the sound of her statement, though he suspected there was a lot of truth in it. Since *Grand Za* was his ship, Jondar piloted. Lossh handled the ascent engines while Qorr managed their navigation. The entire process felt unnatural and left him feeling even more trepidatious about the future of space travel. What happened when a hundred ships were all vying for takeoff and landing positions at a busy starport? He rode the controls with white-knuckled intensity, missing the ability to simply tell *Grand Za* to land or takeoff.

"Clear of the field," Qorr announced.

Jondar took a moment to look back toward the starport now falling away behind them. The field of battle was hundreds of kilometers wide and long, a collection of burned and devastated lands pockmarked with dead Raknar and Canavar. It was a tableau frozen in time and would forever be his memory of Feesta.

He took one last look at the starport city. Fires were visible in many places; the riots had steadily increased in intensity as the last of the food was consumed and desperation overtook anger. He wondered if anyone would be alive on the former paradise world in a year. Then clouds swallowed the view.

"We have escape velocity," Qorr said.

"Reactor and ascent engine power are both nominal," Lossh said. Her businesslike demeanor reminded Jondar of how the computer once sounded.

It took an extra burn to circularize their orbit then another to set course for the system's stargate. Finally, they were coasting through the void, and Jondar had time to take in the space around Feesta. As he'd heard, the near orbit was cluttered with dead ships, though not as many as he'd expected. The Dusman and Kahraman had fought over the system for many months. All functional warships were long gone, and those which remained were little more than gutted hulks. A fortune in future salvage if anyone remained to claim it.

Passage through the stargate was more routine, though he had to manually talk with the gate master and transfer the required coin. Lossh took care of programming the hyperspace computer, the first of the promised modifications to *Grand Za* she would do.

The first leg of their trip took three hyperspace jumps, each lasting 120 hours. Jondar was curious about the 170-hour shorter range jumps he'd heard about, as was Qorr. However, Lossh wasn't interested in explaining, merely saying the interruption of AIs had many secondary consequences.

"What about those AI?" Qorr wondered during one meal session. Along with F11, Lossh had brought replenishments for the autochef, yet another handy provision for the trip.

"The Dusman developed all the AI technology," Lossh said. "They kept such innovations carefully secret. When the war ended, they took their technology with them."

"How was this even possible?" Jondar wondered.

"The Dusman were jealous masters," Lossh said. "They did not go gently from the stage." She was unwilling to share anymore, so the trip continued.

The two systems they passed through were horrors. The first had been a prosperous mining system with hundreds of asteroid bases where vast wealth flowed. There was no sign of life as *Grand Za* transited between emergence point and stargate. Likewise, there was no sign of what had happened to those who'd once lived there.

The second system left no doubt to the former residents. A single planet had once been home to billions of beings, its surface covered in life and blue waters. Only a shattered ring remained. One of the many worlds killed in the long, senseless war. Of the life it had once harbored, there remained no traces. A few ships occupied the system, but none approached or contacted them.

At the end of the third jump, they arrived in a strange non-viable star system. Jondar had never been in anything like it. An ancient red giant occupied the center of the system. There might have once been habitable planets, millions of years ago. Now there was only a trio of charred rocks slowly orbiting. Of asteroids there were only a small scattering. However, a space station orbited one planetoid, there was a stargate, and a considerable number of ships coming and going.

"What is this place?" Jondar asked.

"A forward operations base for my movement. From here we search for war criminals and try to aid rebuilding."

"Rebuilding what?" Qorr wondered.

"Whatever comes next," Lossh explained.

They docked with the space station, but Jondar and Qorr weren't allowed off. All the ships they could see were modern and in good repair. They were mostly small, though a few might have been the size of cruisers. The signs of organized activity somehow gave Jondar confidence. The entire galaxy hadn't slipped into a morass. They were fighting against, what? Decay? Oblivion? Entropy?

Lossh left the ship and returned with several of her fellows, all dressed in the same fancy green armor. One was another Equiri, and the other an insectoid like himself, though of a race he'd never seen before. The two newcomers examined the cargo on *Grand Za*. They seemed excited by what they found, and Jondar thought they would take it.

"No," Lossh said, "but we will pay you for it." Payment offered was two full modules of nutrient solution for his autochef. Enough food to last him years. Since he had no use for a cargo hold full of ammunition, it was a no-brainer.

"When do they offload it?"

"Not here," Jondar said. "At our next stop."

"How many more stops?"

"Just one."

Just before they left, Qorr announced he was leaving. "These people have offered me some work, so I took them up on the offer."

"I wish you well," Jondar said to the TriRusk. Despite the violent nature of their meeting, he'd come to like the big alien.

"Maybe we'll meet again."

"Could be."

Hours later, *Grand Za* pushed back from the space station and headed for the stargate.

"The stargate is not new," Jondar noted to his now-sole passenger.

"No, it is not."

"Who used it before? The design is strange."

"This is one of the repositories of the Kut'oja," she said. "One of hundreds across the galaxy."

"I've never heard of that race," Jondar said. He manually searched his Mesh and found no reference.

"No, you would not have. They were one of the Dusman's tools. One which ultimately turned on them and gave birth to my order. Though not intentionally, of course."

"I do not understand."

"You are not meant to."

Jondar fumed at being treated like an ignorant grub. However, he had no way of rectifying it. Lossh and her fellows were organized and rich, at least in the meaning of rich in the new galaxy he found himself in. So, he went where he was ordered.

Lossh had written an entire series of automation programs for *Grand Za*. They were elegant and worked so well Jondar almost didn't miss the AI. He still had to manually instruct the ship but did not have to control every system. She programmed as well as any AI he'd ever seen. The ship was running so well Jondar was nervous as they made what she'd promised would be their final jump. After all, what assurance did he have she wouldn't just shoot him when it was all over? The answer was none, of course.

Only 70 hours into the jump his computer summoned them to the bridge. Jondar was shocked as he floated into the bridge and found Lossh waiting there, floating at her station, eyes closed.

"Are we arriving?"

"Yes," she said without opening her eyes. For the first time he noticed she had some kind of implant at the base of her neck, under the bright mane of fur.

"A 72-hour jump?" She nodded. "How do you know how to do those?"

She opened her red eyes and stared at him. Jondar felt his chiton itch on the inside and shuddered. *What have I brought onto my ship?* he wondered. He went to his pilot's station and tried to log into the computer, only to find he was blocked. "What happened to the computer?"

"I am the computer now," Lossh responded, not from her mouth, but through the computer interface.

Jondar shuddered. If Lossh had linked with his computer, it only meant one thing: she had an AI. There was no other way to accomplish such an act. "W-what are you?"

"Quiet," she ordered. *"We are emerging from hyperspace."*

The telltale falling sensation announced the return to normal space. Jondar checked and saw he could still use regular instruments, it was only drive, nav, and comms he had no control over. He examined the data on the system they'd emerged into and his concern over Lossh taking over the ship's computer turned to horror. There was no star, no planets, no station, and, most importantly, no stargate. The horror of any spacer, a dead-end star system.

"You've killed us!" he howled in rage and reached for the laser pistol he'd carried since being attacked on Feesta.

"Kill me and you will never leave here alive."

"We can't leave, regardless. *Grand Za* doesn't have shunts!" The barrel of the laser pistol was centered on Lossh's big forehead. A kilogram of pressure and the strange alien would cease to exist.

Lossh pointed, and the Tri-V came on. There *was* something nearby after all.

Jondar glanced at the image, his antennae waving in alarm, unable to decide if he should kill the Equiri or not. He slowly sighed and put the weapon away. "It matters not," he said. However, his gaze was drawn back to the Tri-V. Was it a space station? No, it was bigger. Not a planetoid, it was artificial, an irregular triangular shape several kilometers on a side, spinning on one axis. "What is it?"

"The secret of the Dusman's might."

"No," Jondar said, shaking his head. "They don't exist."

The ship's engines came alive and they moved toward the construct. From what little Jondar could tell, they were lightyears from the nearest star, in a rift between two of the galactic arms. Voids where there were few stars. *An ideal location for it.*

As they approached, Jondar noticed the radio was transmitting. Lossh was speaking to the construct. Seconds later, a pair of incredibly fast drones raced alongside, scanning *Grand Za*. In particular, the cargo hold. Whatever they were scanning for, they must have been satisfied. Jondar was sure they were armed, but they didn't attack; they just flew off.

They headed for the construct.

* * *

A bay big enough to devour a hundred *Grand Za*'s opened to admit them. Lossh expertly piloted the ship into the bay, oriented with the direction of rotation, and settled against the gravity side. There were a pair of heavy Dusman transports docked not far away, identical to the ones sitting abandoned back on Feesta. As soon as they were down, Lossh disengaged from the computer and left the bridge.

"Where are you going?"

"To enact justice," she said.

"What does that mean?" She didn't answer. Jondar cursed at the retreating Equiri. Cursed the Dusman, cursed the Kahraman, and, most particularly, cursed the fates which put him there at that moment. Better to be taken by the slow, cruel entropy of the galaxy than the turn his life had taken. The bridge indicators said Lossh was opening the cargo doors. With another curse, Jondar headed aft.

He was halfway to the cargo hold when he heard the gunfire and broke into a run. At the cargo door he found two ruined Dusman peacekeeper bots. The tall striding figure of Lossh was already at the far end of the bay, her handheld particle rifle held at hip level, gunning down peacekeeper bots as they appeared.

"She's crazy!" Jondar said. "They're going to kill her." But just as he spoke a peacekeeper fired a laser at the Equiri which was stopped by the flash of a force field. Lossh had a personal force field, something only the Dusman possessed.

He didn't know why he followed Lossh, he just had. Even though the Equiri quickly outpaced him, Jondar was able to follow using the dead bots left in her wake. The further he followed her, the fewer peacekeeper bots there were. Jondar saw maintenance and cargo handling bots of all kinds. It appeared whoever was handling the response was sending everything they had. What he didn't see was anything living.

The structure was massive, but the majority was not easily accessible. Lossh seemed to know exactly where she was going and Jondar caught up with her after about a kilometer of walking. She was at an armored door placing charges.

"What is this place?" Jondar asked.

She glanced over her shoulder at him and grunted. "You know what it is: a Dusman Arsenal."

"Nobody really believed they existed."

"Where do you think all the ships, Raknar, and other instruments of war were made? Weapons infrastructure on a planet is vulnerable. They moved it all to these mobile manufactories shortly after the war's start. This way, no matter how many worlds, no matter how many trillions of their servitors were slaughtered, the war machine ground on. These are the worst war crimes imaginable, moving the means to make war out of reach of the very war they were waging."

"When would it have ended?" Jondar asked.

"It would never have ended. These Arsenals would have continued to churn out weapons as long as supplies were delivered. Even then, they had reserves enough for years. The only way to end it was to end them and the ones who built these things."

"Who made them?" Jondar asked, his voice a whisper.

"Do you really want to know?"

He nodded.

The Equiri's lips peeled back from her teeth in a feral smile. "Then find out." She backed away from the door and walked to him. He flinched as the tingling force field moved over him. The explosives detonated. He watched the shield shimmer as the blast effect and shrapnel hit it. There was a hole in the door.

Inside was a command center designed for no more than a tiny handful of beings. A few configurable chairs were scattered around, all empty save one. The being stared at them with unmitigated hatred, its big eyes full of an inner rage Jondar would have recognized even if he didn't know what race it was. "Simian," he said.

"Yes, this is a Biruda. They were the ones who made the engines of genocide for the Dusman."

The Biruda spoke. "We did as we were asked." Jondar's Mesh immediately translated the voice, which was speaking in Dusman. "We merely used our talents to help our allies."

"Helped your allies murder trillions," Lossh said, stepping into the command center.

Jondar stayed close behind so he remained within Lossh's force field. Who knew what wondrous means of murder the Biruda would have at its disposal?

"The Masters were cleansing a filth from the galaxy." It pointed a hairless finger at Lossh. "You will be cleansed for your treason."

"Biruda, you have been judged guilty of war crimes." Lossh went to the nearest wall and attached a cube to it. The device stuck where it was placed with no obvious means of attachment. "In the name of the Peacemaker, you and your *creations* are sentenced to entropy." She turned and walked back to the shattered door.

"You and your Peacemaker cannot stop us. Nothing can stop us!" Jondar rushed to keep up. A few steps outside the command center, a brilliant white light consumed it. Jondar covered his eyes and looked away. The force field shuddered, and he felt heat through it.

"Shit!" Jondar yelled and tried to run.

"Do not leave the shield," Lossh warned, catching Jondar by a limb and restraining him. The white-hot blast washed around them, then dissipated. "It is done."

"W-what now?" Jondar asked.

"I continue my search for the others."

"How many of these were there?"

"As many as a hundred or more," Lossh said.

Jondar shook his head in disbelief. They walked back toward the landing bay. Soon Lossh told him it was safe to leave the shield. As they approached the bay Jondar could finally speak again.

"What is the Peacemaker?"

"The head of my order. We couldn't stand by and let the Dusman and Kahraman end all life in the galaxy. Something had to be done."

"*You* stopped the war? How many Peacemakers are there?"

"Just one, originally," Lossh said. "The Peacemaker, we call it. Now there are hundreds. We've taken the name for ourselves, Peacemakers. Not like the Dusman's bots keeping the peace, their peace. No, we *make* peace. Someday there will be thousands of us, spreading peace throughout the galaxy."

"How could one being stop a galaxy wide war?"

"Do you *really* want to know?" Jondar nodded. "The only way to find out, is to become a Peacemaker. I've watched you, Jondar. You have the proper heart, and an anger at the destruction. Do you want to make it your life?"

"I don't know," he admitted. "What do I have to do? What will it cost?"

"Anything which needs to be done, and it will cost you everything. But it means thinking beyond your own hide. It means you must learn to honor the threat to all life, and in the end, when it all comes down to one thing, you must stand or fall. Defeat it or be defeated."

They'd reached the landing bay where *Grand Za* waited. He'd worked his entire life to earn the ship and used it to make a modest living. Yet, to what end if such forces existed which could, for their own desires, extinguish all life? Wasn't it more important to fight against this evil?

"Qorr already joined, didn't he?"

"Yes, it is why he stayed behind, to help another Peacemaker mission."

"Okay, I will do it," Jondar said. "I will be a Peacemaker, too."

"Very well," Lossh said, and she put a hand on his shoulder. "Come, Peacemaker, we will install shunts on your ship so we can get out of here. There is much work to be done."

* * * * *

Mark Wandrey Bio

Living life as a full-time RV traveler with his wife Joy, Mark Wandrey is a bestselling author who has been creating new worlds since he was old enough to write. A three-time Dragon Award finalist, Mark has written dozens of books and short stories, and is working on more all the time. A prolific world builder, he created the wildly popular Four Horsemen Universe as well as the Earth Song series and Turning Point, a zombie apocalypse series. His favorite medium is military sci-fi, but he is always up to a new challenge.

Sign up on his mailing list and get free stuff and updates! http://www.worldmaker.us/news-flash-sign-up-page/

# # # # #

When Pigs Fly by Terry Mixon

Elgar Xarbon settled into his seat as the shuttle made its final approach to their destination on Jukus. Sadly, the cushions weren't made for Gtandan posteriors, but that particular discomfort was something he'd grown used to over the years.

His friend and fellow Peacemaker, Hetok Hosmir, had his face glued to the viewport, drinking in his home world. He'd been that way ever since they'd begun their descent.

Staring out a viewport had never appealed to Elgar. Like all Gtandans, his eyesight was poor, which made sightseeing a futile pastime. Beyond a short distance, his vision was basically useless without technical enhancement.

Gtandus was a world of deep forests, and his people had evolved to live under those constraints. Beneath the massive canopy, light was scarce. Even if there had been illumination, no straight line went more than a few dozen meters without one of the massive trees blocking what lay beyond it.

In recompense for their weak eyes, evolution had blessed them with better hearing and an exceptional sense of smell. Elgar didn't have his father's eidetic olfactory senses, so he couldn't remember people years after they'd met, but even with his eyes closed, he could tally which species were represented aboard the shuttle with no difficulty at all.

Sadly, that also meant he could never escape the flat, recycled air on ships and shuttles. At least someone had done the necessary maintenance on the shuttle, and it didn't have the faint sour note that was all too often present.

With his observational skills thus limited, Elgar focused on his friend's excitement. Like all Juks, Hetok was small and slight of frame. Whereas a Gtandan male stood over two meters tall and was quite muscular, his people were about a quarter that size and perhaps a tenth the mass.

Their species had full-body fur that ran the gamut from silver to black. Hetok's was faded, the brown of his youth replaced by the gray of age.

It saddened him that Juks did not live as long as Gtandans, even with the full support of Union medical tech. Hetok was about Elgar's father's age, and already growing somewhat infirm. Not that that seemed to bother the ever-cheerful Juk. He was apparently content with the life that he'd lived.

The shuttle slowed, coming in softly for a landing. Once it was down, Elgar relaxed. Flying wasn't one of his favorite things, and he was glad to be on solid ground again. Heights had always been a particular challenge for him.

"Are you excited to be here for the selection?" Elgar asked as he undid his restraints and rose to his feet. "Or simply because you're home?"

Hetok grinned at him, showing sharp pointed teeth. "Both, of course, though I'm more interested in the selection at the moment. It always excites me to see a prospective Peacemaker taking the first steps on their journey.

"It's only great luck that my grandnephew is competing this year. I don't know if you've heard, but Hak-Chet is overseeing the competition."

As the main selector, it seemed something of a coincidence that the Sidar was on Jukus, but Hak-Chet had known Hetok for decades, so Elgar wagered it was no coincidence at all.

"It will be good to see him again," Elgar said as the hatch opened, and the crew began extending the ramp. "It's been a while since my own selection, but I recall him with more fondness than irritation. After all, he had to put up with quite a lot from me."

Hetok slid out of his seat, landed lightly on the shuttle floor, and started toward the exit. "Since it took you three times to make it through the selection process, I'm quite certain that he feels some mixed emotions as well. He's remarked on several occasions that you're remarkably stubborn. I don't know if he saw that as positive or negative, though."

"I'll take it as a compliment," Elgar rumbled, suppressing a laugh. "I was certainly determined to make it into the Peacemakers, and he was quite helpful in pointing out the areas where I fell short so that I could adjust my training regimen. I honestly think that's what allowed me to do so well at the Academy, once I finally made it."

"Three times," Hetok repeated with a shake of his head. "While that's not unheard of, it *is* unusual. Perhaps it speaks more to your determination than your brilliance."

Elgar grunted at his friend's needling. His grades had been excellent, though Hetok was correct in that no one had ever accused him of brilliance. He'd simply refused to give up when confronted by an obstacle.

He'd refused to fail at the Academy because he'd had to make up for the sins of his father.

Elgar's father had betrayed a mercenary company in his employ, who'd all been subsequently killed. Elgar's uncle—Peacemaker Enforcer Jardis Xarbon—had uncovered the crime and then arrested his own older brother.

To say that that had made family gatherings somewhat tense ever since was something of an understatement.

Elgar—a pudgy adolescent at the time—hadn't known anything more than the basics after Uncle Jardis had arrested his father, and visiting his father in prison had proven less than enlightening. The man had insisted that he was innocent, despite the incriminating files he'd had in his slate.

In the beginning, Elgar had believed him. It had taken several years before he'd spoken to his uncle at all, only then allowing him to explain what he could of the situation. It took even more time to accept the truth of what he'd been told.

With that acceptance came a determination to change the course of his life. A drive to bring criminals like his father to justice brought Elgar the competition to be selected for the Peacemaker Academy on his home world.

As Hetok enjoyed reminding him, his first attempt had been a dismal failure, at least from his point of view. Hak-Chet had, thankfully, disagreed and encouraged him to work harder before returning for another try.

The next time he'd ended up a finalist, but still failed.

That would've been the point where most people gave up, convinced that they didn't have what it took to be a Peacemaker. For Elgar, it only made him strive harder, and as the Humans said, the "third time was the charm."

He supposed that was better than "three strikes and you're out." He'd had to look up the latter saying to understand that it related to some sort of athletic competition. It amused him how the two sayings were so diametrically opposed.

How very much like humanity itself.

What had mattered then was that Hak-Chet had believed in him. That confidence and his own refusal to give up, no matter the obstacles he had to overcome, had been enough for him to finally achieve selection.

That in turn had given him the chance to use his intelligence and skill to make it through the Peacemaker Academy. The knowledge that he could count on himself had stood him in good stead ever since.

Elgar realized that he'd been lost in thought and forced his attention back to his friend.

Hetok was watching him closely, his expression one that Elgar knew from experience meant the Juk was feeling somber.

"I'm sorry to have sent your thoughts back to your father. I allowed my ebullience to carry me away."

"Don't trouble yourself," Elgar said with more cheer than he felt. "You're not responsible for the sins of my father, any more than I am. His crimes brought him into conflict with Uncle Jardis, and that was a contest he never had a chance of winning."

Hetok nodded. "Enforcer Jardis is *very* easy to underestimate. The two of you are quite alike, you know."

"I wish we were similar enough that I could've taken the training to become an Enforcer after I graduated from the Academy," Elgar grumbled. "Uncle Jardis is…formidable."

"We each serve the Union in our own way," Hetok assured him as they finally exited the shuttle. "Don't crave another's path. Forge your own destiny."

As soon as they'd exited the shuttle, a strong breeze washed over Elgar. He braced his lighter companion, which made him laugh.

"Fear not for me," Hetok chided him. "This is my home, and I can handle what it gives me."

"Why is it so windy?"

"For that, we'll need to step over to the right at about sixty degrees."

Here, in the wide open, Elgar's poor vision was of little help in seeing his surroundings, but he could tell that the pad was more than wide enough to comfortably fit two shuttles. That meant he could see out to the rails at the edges, but everything beyond was a blur.

He could tell they were in the open because the wind was gusting and whistling past him. The landing pad must be on a hill.

That impression was bolstered by the scent of nature on the breeze. He stood for a moment, trying to catalog all the smells— without success—and just generally enjoyed the fresh, unrecycled air.

"You'll want to put on your glasses for this," Hetok insisted. "And hold onto them so that the wind doesn't blow them off your face."

Grumbling to himself, Elgar fished out the glasses provided for Peacemakers and slid them over his eyes, making sure to keep his free hand on them. That brought the railing and the clear sky beyond it into clear focus as Hetok guided them to a specific spot.

When they stopped next to the railing, Hetok took hold of it, leaving Elgar free to look at their surroundings. There was open space, as far as the eye could see.

Including down.

Elgar only avoided stepping back in horror because he was frozen in place. Beyond the railing, there was a great forest spread out about five hundred meters below. His stomach lurched and he gripped the railing hard.

"This is…ah, unexpected," he muttered. "I thought your people were tree gliders."

His friend clapped him on the hip, thankfully not moving him one centimeter closer to the deadly edge. "We *evolved* as tree gliders, but my world is filled with these tall spires of rock created by ancient volcanic activity and erosion. Once we'd begun the trek to sentience, we flocked to them. As an advanced people, our centers of government are located in places like this." He smiled wickedly up at Elgar. "You sound disturbed. Is something the matter?"

"You know how I feel about heights," Elgar grumbled.

"Where's your sense of adventure, my young friend?" Hetok asked as he tugged Elgar toward the wide doorway leading into the spire that towered above them.

He hadn't seen the remaining part of the stone formation he was standing on because of his poor eyesight, but with his glasses in place, he now noted that it went up another several hundred meters.

It was impressive and more than a bit horrifying to be on.

At least from this point forward, they could stay within the spire, using mundane methods to get where they needed to go. He wouldn't have to look out at the steep drop again.

As if reading his thoughts, Hetok gestured to their left. "The selection area and our quarters are going to be in the adjacent spire, but don't worry, it's only going to take us a few minutes to glide between the two."

Elgar turned in the indicated direction, even as a wash of cold went through his system. There was indeed a very similar spire of stone about two hundred meters off the other side of the shuttle pad.

Not waiting for his friend to say anything more, Elgar stepped over to the railing on that side and looked down. The split between the two pieces of stone took place about one-third of the way up from the forest below.

"There will be elevators to take us down to where they join," Elgar disagreed sternly. "I'm quite certain that your people don't expect everyone to fly between these things."

Even as he said that, Elgar saw that that might not be completely true. There was a steady stream of Juks flowing between the two spires, and they weren't alone.

There were larger gliders—obviously mechanical in nature—that carried other species across the gap. He couldn't tell if the units were powered or not, but that hardly mattered. Some people were crazy enough to try anything.

"You need not worry, my friend," Hetok said as he clapped a hand on Elgar's waist. "The glider units are completely safe. Computers control every aspect of flight and no one is in any danger. Just think of it as an adventure."

Another Human saying immediately popped into his mind. Considering the slight resemblance Gtandans had to terrestrial swine, it was both insulting and ironically appropriate.

"When pigs fly," Elgar said firmly.

His friend laughed and then insisted on taking him to see the damned gliders, as if there was any chance at all that he'd agree to the madman's plan. There was a station with the devices a short distance from the shuttle pad, so he'd have had to walk right past them in any case.

There were a wide variety of sizes and configurations, as befitted the diversity of the Union races. They ranged in size from smaller than Hetok to even larger than Elgar.

"This one here is the one that you'd use," his friend said with exaggerated cheerfulness. "See the broad green stripe with the number three? That's suitable for Gtandans. I looked it up, just to be sure."

"I'm *not* jumping off a perfectly good mountain," Elgar said as repressively as he could.

Hetok ignored his objection and continued to explain the controls. "The harness securing you in is Union standard, so you'll have no issues with it."

"I'll have no issues because there is no way that I'm flying in this deathtrap."

"Gliding," Hetok corrected primly. "And you'll note the controls are easily grasped—both physically and mentally—by the user. If you feel inspired, you can control the trip manually. The computers won't allow anything dangerous unless properly overridden.

"Or you can let the glider handle everything by selecting your destination and allowing the glider to get you there. You'll note the goggles hanging on this other rack. Those should allow you to see everything with the *utmost* clarity."

"Not happening," Elgar said with a shudder that wasn't at all theatrical. "Let's get inside before I throw you off this thing and make my own way over."

Hetok roared with laughter and followed closely behind him. "You're so predictable, my young friend. Perhaps by the end of your stay I'll have worn you down enough to try. Remember that each level of the spires has a station just like this if you change your mind."

* * *

They took an elevator down, walked through a tunnel to reach the other spire, and then ascended again. Hetok chided him every step along the way, too.

Elgar felt no guilt about not taking his friend up on his outrageous offer to glide across together. While he was certainly willing to take risks in the course of his duties, he wasn't going to be suicidal while on vacation.

It only took them a few minutes to get their key cards and find their quarters. Elgar closed the door behind him, leaning against it to clear his head and just breathe. The last few minutes had been unexpectedly harrowing.

Once he'd restored some of his usual normality, he quickly confirmed that his luggage had arrived safely and was laid out across his bed, ready for his attention.

The small suite would suit him well, he thought. It had three rooms and a balcony. He wouldn't be using the latter, but the bath attached to the bedroom would be nice.

He closed his eyes and took a deep breath. The air in the room was clean, with just a hint of something pleasant. There were no plants in sight, so that would be an air freshener, most likely.

Elgar approved of the light touch. Most species wouldn't even have consciously detected it, while someone with his sensitivity wasn't overwhelmed. It was well done.

Satisfied everything was in order, he moved to rejoin Hetok. His friend was just leaving his suite down the hall when Elgar stepped out.

"Aren't these halls and rooms rather large for your people?" Elgar asked as they made their way back to the elevator.

"Indeed. This particular set of spires was renovated specifically to house other species. Most of the rest are crafted to hold my people, so you wouldn't fit. I'm grateful we have elevators because climbing up the exterior at my age might be a bit challenging."

They had to ask for directions, but finally found themselves in a large hall that Elgar suspected was normally used for banquets and such. And since he considered it large, he was certain Hetok and his people felt it was huge indeed.

He took a moment to put his glasses on so he could see the room in more detail. There were no tables, but someone had left seats in a visitor's section to one side of the room. It was filled with Juks observing the selection.

As a Peacemaker who had gone through the process three times under Hak-Chet, Elgar was intimately familiar with what was happening. In fact, he remembered going through what these candidates were doing quite clearly.

They were assembling modular furniture.

While that sounded mundane, the task had hidden complexity. First, the end product wasn't sized for their species. Elgar could tell that at a glance because the parts were very large. He was also certain that Hak-Chet hadn't provided any assembly instructions, either.

The purpose of this particular test was to see how good the candidates' reasoning skills were. This wouldn't be a timed affair, though he doubted the competitors were aware of that fact. It wasn't who finished first that mattered the most to Hak-Chet.

This exercise judged the manner in which they chose to complete the task. There was a time for haste and a time for meticulous thinking. One had to be able to tell one from the other and judge when each needed to be applied.

Selector Hak-Chet walked among the candidates. The long-beaked Sidar noted their arrival and came to meet them.

"It pleases me to see you here, old friend," Hak-Chet said to Hetok. "It's been far too long. Tell me, are you looking forward to retirement?"

Hetok grinned even more widely than he had earlier. "Deeply. After so many years traveling throughout the Union, it's good to see my home world again and know that I'm settling in for good.

"I've enjoyed my time as a Peacemaker, but the years are wearing on me. I long to relax and spend time with my clan."

"Your rest is well deserved," Hak-Chet said before turning his attention to Elgar.

"And how about you my young friend? Are you finding the view invigorating?"

There was a flash of humor in the Sidar's eyes at that last question.

"Invigorating isn't the word I'd use, Selector," Elgar said dryly. "Terrifying seems more apt."

Hak-Chet chuckled. "You've always had an almost unhealthy respect for heights. I suppose it isn't that surprising. Still, it's a weakness you should address. One never knows when a case will come up that requires you to face your greatest fear. Such a challenge should be addressed *before* one's life or mission are on the line."

Elgar stood his ground. "Distances and heights might be problematic for me, but I make up for it in other ways. Still, your advice is well taken. I'll look into what remedial training I can undertake to mitigate those weaknesses."

Eventually.

"Enough about this mass of wiry hair and thick skin," Hetok said firmly. "Tell me of my grandnephew. How's he doing?"

Elgar saw that Hetok was staring at one of the competitors. The young Juk had fur of the lightest brown. He worked with calm precision, examining all the pieces arrayed in front of him.

Each was laid out so that he could see it clearly. He'd obviously given great thought to what needed to fit where during the assembly process.

This was a difficult test, Elgar knew, but without knowing the features and shape of the intended species, it could fool you at the last moment.

For that matter, it could fool you at the beginning as well.

If this was anything like the challenge he'd faced, no one candidate had all the parts needed to complete the task. They'd need to convince one of their competitors to trade something before either of them could finish. The negotiation was a hidden part of the challenge.

"He's doing quite well," Hak-Chet said. "While I'm not prepared to say that he's the best in the room, he's certainly well positioned to be a finalist. With work and focus, he may still beat out his competitors. As you both know, the final tests are quite challenging."

As he said that, Hak-Chet looked straight at Elgar. If Gtandans had been prone to blushing, he might have done so under the scrutiny. Since they weren't, he merely smiled in return.

"If this follows the schedule I recall, you're looking at several more days for the selection process, are you not?" Elgar asked.

Hak-Chet nodded. "Indeed. This particular test will finish in about an hour. As you well know, it isn't timed, but if they take too long, I'll stop them. There's a difference between being meticulous and being slow."

"Perhaps we should return to our rooms, change out of our traveling clothes, and relax before we have something to eat," Hetok suggested. "We'd be pleased if you could join us, Hak-Chet."

The selector nodded his assent. "Nothing would please me more. Shall we meet in ninety minutes? I'll send you information on a restaurant I favor. It's somewhat out-of-the-way but quite good."

"I like the sound of that," Elgar admitted. "I'm hungry."

The two of them said their goodbyes and made their way back toward their rooms. They walked in silence and Elgar could tell that his friend was pleased at how well his grandnephew was doing. That was certain to be a topic of discussion as they ate.

At Elgar's door, they parted ways. Rather than entering his bedroom, Elgar stepped over to the clear barrier between his suite and the balcony. There was an inset door that he now opened to step out into the dangerous space.

The balcony had doors to the main room and his bedroom, and it also held several chairs and a table. Those with better eyesight probably enjoyed this as a comfortable place to relax and take in the view.

The wind wasn't too strong, so he steeled his will and put his glasses on. They revealed the clever baffles that someone had installed to keep the worst of the wind at bay. It also revealed more open space than he was comfortable with and showed him just how high up he really was.

His room was very near the top of the spire, so the trees were basically a green carpet over seven hundred meters below. He gripped the rail hard, his heart pounding in his chest as he took in the chilling vista.

No being should be so high off the ground when not safely enclosed in a shuttle. It was unnatural, he thought.

He was still considering that when an explosion violently knocked him off his feet, almost hurling him off the balcony. Half dazed, he clutched the railing even harder to keep from toppling over it.

The blast was strong enough to disrupt his equilibrium and his ears were ringing. That was one of the problems with having excellent hearing.

He gathered himself and raced into the hall, looking for the source of the explosion. Flames and smoke billowed from a shattered doorway close by.

Cold dread filled him. It led to Hetok's suite.

* * *

The flames were already dying down as Elgar rushed forward. A disassociated and shocked part of his brain couldn't believe that the fire suppression system was still functioning. It couldn't have been designed to withstand a blast like that.

Choking smoke still poured from the room, but he threw his arm across his snout and rushed inside. While the calculating part of his brain doubted his friend could have survived anything like this explosion, he had to try to save him.

The sight that greeted him only a few steps inside the room proved that he'd been too late the moment the explosives detonated. Hetok's body lay against one of the walls, scorched, bloody, and shredded.

His friend literally lay in pieces.

Holding his breath and blinking rapidly tearing eyes, he saw that the blast had been centered on the bed, where scraps of what had once been luggage lay blown apart and still burned weakly.

He noted the suite of rooms—identical to his own—were designed for non-Juk, but his friend had wanted to stay on the same floor as Elgar. While he was sure his small friend wouldn't have been comfortable on the large bed, it was easier to stay close so they could do things together.

Things they would now never do.

The damage to the room was more contained than he'd expected, based on the strength of the blast. It had blown out the door and shattered the barrier to the balcony, as well as having lit many of the furnishings on fire.

Yet none of the walls had blown out. The pressure wave had only been great enough to kill Hetok. The occupants in the rooms to either side of the suite might have been deafened, but they hadn't been in serious danger.

Someone had calculated the force required to build a device that was limited enough in scope to do the job without creating a mass casualty event.

The smoke and the stench of roasted flesh finally became too much to bear and he started to turn away when he saw something glinting just under the edge of the bed. He crouched lower and found his friend's badge. It must've been ripped away from him in the explosion.

Like all Peacemaker badges, it showed the stylized logo of a tree. In this case, it was undoubtedly one from his friend's home world, for each Peacemaker designed their own image.

Elgar pocketed the badge and fled the room. He'd have to return once the worst of the smoke had cleared out to oversee the gathering of evidence.

Outside, a crowd had gathered, mostly filling the hall. They were primarily other guests, but several XenSha in what were obviously security uniforms were pushing through the gawkers, their tentacles waving.

When the first of them got to him, Elgar held up a hand. "No one may enter this room until I say so."

"Please move aside, sir," the small security officer said, his voice hard. "I need to check for injured. Are you injured?"

"The room's occupant is dead," Elgar said grimly as he reached into his jacket and pulled out his Peacemaker badge, its logo resembling one of the massive trees on his home world. "This is a crime scene, and I am declaring it sealed under my authority as a Peacemaker."

He could see the XenSha wanted to argue, but he contained himself, stepped back, and nodded. "I'll summon my superior at once, Peacemaker. I'd be surprised if he wasn't already on his way. Can you tell me what happened? I'm going to have to write up a report and some details would be helpful."

"The occupant of the room was Peacemaker Hetok," Elgar said flatly. "The explosion seems to have been centered on his bed where his luggage was."

"A Peacemaker has been killed?" the XenSha asked in a strangled whisper. From his expression, he was already imagining the level of trouble that was coming, and the vision didn't appeal to him.

Elgar nodded. "Seal off this floor and begin questioning everyone who might have seen anyone going into his rooms. If there is surveillance video, I want it secured, as well. I'll be examining it in close detail as soon as my support team arrives."

The XenSha turned and began directing his people to start clearing the area of gawkers. Even as he was doing that, Hak-Chet pushed his way past the security line and walked up to Elgar.

"Hetok's room?" he asked quietly.

"There was something in his luggage," Elgar confirmed, sagging a little. "He was gone before he had a chance to realize that he was dead."

"That's a blessing," the Sidar said solemnly. "Perhaps the only one better is to die asleep in one's bed. Neither of those outcomes is typically the case for Peacemakers, sadly."

To Elgar, it looked as if his friend had aged fifty years in the space of just fifteen minutes. Even though he'd known Hetok for five years, Hak-Chet had known him far longer.

"Are you aware of any events that would prompt someone to attack Hetok?" Elgar asked. "Did he have any enemies that thirsted for his death?"

Hak-Chet made a gesture of uncertainty. "Like any other Peacemaker, he's undoubtedly made countless enemies over the course of his service. I'd wager many of them will rejoice in his death, but I know of no one in specific who knew he was returning home. Only his closest friends knew he intended to retire."

"That's something I'll have to examine in closer detail," Elgar said, rubbing his snout and unintentionally smearing soot across his face. "What about here on Jukus? Does his family or anyone he associated with hold a grudge worthy of killing him?"

"Juks are made up of clans," Hak-Chet said, fluttering his wings slightly. "Hetok was a member of Clan Ress. Once he left the Guild, his name would've reverted to Hetok Ress Hosmir. It's a very large and powerful clan, at least in a local sense. I fear that's the extent of my knowledge."

That wasn't an unexpected revelation. There was no reason for Hak-Chet—or any other Peacemaker—to know about Hetok's relationship with his clan or the people of his home world.

He had thought that he was going to enjoy a relaxing vacation, but now he would be spending his time on Jukus pursuing his friend's murderer with everything he could bring to bear.

While there were certainly far more heinous crimes the Peacemaker Guild dealt with, they reserved a special zeal in avenging their own. Whoever had killed his friend would deeply regret it before Elgar was through.

For now, he needed to get someone he trusted to go over the evidence. On a regular mission, his team would have been with him. But because he was technically off duty, he would have to pull something together.

Jukus was an advanced world that had strong trade ties and exported fine woods that were both highly sought after and fetched a tidy profit, or so Hetok had once said. Elgar had no doubt there was a Peacemaker office on the planet. They could provide trustworthy people to assist him.

He was lucky he had his communicator on him because he wouldn't be going back into his own rooms until they had been cleared. Whoever had killed Hetok might have wanted to eliminate more than one Peacemaker. As Jessica—the first Human Peacemaker—had once told him, "in for a penny, in for a pound."

"You need to stay away from your rooms," he told Hak-Chet firmly. "They'll need to be searched before you can use them again."

The Sidar blinked twice and then nodded. "You suspect that we're all targets? I've been here for weeks already. If they wanted me dead, they'd have already had a good chance to make it happen."

"I doubt they were after you," Elgar admitted. "But I'm not assuming anything at this point. Not until I have a suspect or suspects to start analyzing motives."

A disturbance up the hall captured their attention. A Juk with red-tinged brown fur was stalking through the security line toward them. She wore a necklace supporting a medallion that vigorously bounced off her vest as she stalked forward, her face a mask of grim fury.

"It looks like the first real challenge to your investigation has arrived, Peacemaker," Hak-Chet murmured. "That's Pitaw Ress Hosmir, Hetok's niece, head of Clan Ress, and the owner of this spire. She's also the mother of the boy Hetok came to see."

Elgar sighed. With the death of her uncle, he knew this was going to go badly. Sadly, there was no helping that. He'd just have to do the best he could for her.

* * *

Clan Leader Pitaw advanced so aggressively, it almost seemed as if she were gliding across the floor. She ignored Elgar and confronted Hak-Chet.

"I heard an explosion. What happened?"

Hak-Chet bowed his head. "I deeply regret that your uncle has been killed, Clan Leader. The circumstances are unclear, and you'll have to consult with Peacemaker Xarbon about the details of the investigation."

Pitaw blinked and stared at Hak-Chet, her mouth hanging slightly open. "What?"

Elgar took that moment to step forward. "Allow me to add my regrets, Clan Leader Hosmir. Your uncle was my friend, and I will do everything within my power to find out who's responsible and see that they face justice."

She stood there for a few seconds, seemingly unable to process what he'd said. Then she shook herself and stepped toward the smoldering room. "I need to see him."

Elgar stepped between her and the door. "I'm afraid this is a crime scene, Clan Leader, and now a matter for the Peacemaker Guild to investigate. I think it's best if we go somewhere we can talk more privately."

The woman sagged. "Of course. This is going to take some time to adjust to. Who could possibly have wanted to harm my uncle?"

"That's one of the things we're going to have to discuss. What can you tell me about his relationship with the people on your world?"

Pitaw walked slowly down the hallway with him, forcing him to shorten his steps drastically so he didn't leave her behind. Hetok had always been so full of energy that Elgar had never needed to slow down. Now he felt as if he were moving through molasses.

"Uncle Hetok was deeply respected on Jukus. His older brother was my father and clan leader before me. My uncle was revered and loved. I can't think of a single person who had ill will toward him. Surely this must have had something to do with his duties as a Peacemaker."

Even though he privately doubted it, Elgar shrugged slightly. "I'm going to investigate that possibility very thoroughly. Whoever did this, they haven't had time to get far. If they're from off world, we'll do everything possible to make sure they don't get away.

"It's my understanding that Clan Ress owns this spire. I'm going to need access to any and all recordings of public areas. While I'm certain you don't have anything inside your uncle's room, if there is a recording of this hallway, it might be crucial in determining what happened."

Pitaw sighed and shook her head. "Every floor has external access for Juks to arrive and leave via the air. Most also have artificial gliders for other guests.

"Sadly, the individual hallways aren't monitored. There are so many places that people can enter and exit the spire it never seemed worthwhile to monitor them. Now, I wish I'd chosen differently, but it's far too late for that."

The two of them reached the end of the hall and stood in front of a transparent barrier with a clear door, blocking off a wide balcony overlooking the breathtaking drop to the forest below.

There was only a short railing separating the paved area from the vast space beyond, but he supposed that made sense since people would be arriving and leaving by going *over* it. It wasn't there to prevent a fall. It was more of a demarcation line between the ground and sky.

While most of the balcony was clear, the right side had racks of the ubiquitous mechanical gliders for those visitors who couldn't themselves fly. Elgar still didn't understand why anyone could possibly want to do that, but there was no accounting for the relative sanity of other species.

He opened his mouth to continue with his questioning but paused. Now that he was away from the smoke and horror of Hetok's suite, his sense of smell had returned and brought with it a mystery.

Just at the edge of his senses, that same delicate scent that he'd smelled in his room was back.

He turned his head slightly, squinting in confusion. There was no sign of fragrance dispensers anywhere around them. Where was the scent coming from?

Elgar inhaled deeply and tried to determine more about the odor. It wasn't perfume. No, it had a more organic texture. It was *definitely* the same one that had been present in his room, though. Only now, it was stronger, though still subtle.

"Peacemaker Xarbon?" Pitaw asked. "Are you all right?"

"I'm sorry," he said with a wave of his hand. "I must still be a little muddled from the explosion. If I could have a moment?"

Elgar allowed his senses to dwell on the area around him, closing his eyes and giving himself over fully to his sense of smell. While it might not be the best that Gtandus had ever produced, it was far from the worst.

His unlamented father had seen to that via rigorous training. In business, being able to smell one's competitors and then interpret how they felt about something during negotiations was a key advantage Gtandans had, and his father had been determined Elgar would excel at it.

After a few deep breaths, he became certain the smell came from Clan Leader Pitaw.

He opened his eyes, retrieved his glasses, and considered her. After a few moment's reflection, he realized that the scent had to be coming from the medallion resting on her chest. It was wood and was about four centimeters across, suspended by what looked to be a silver chain around her neck.

It sported the carved image of a great tree. The same tree that had been on Hetok's Peacemaker badge, unless he was gravely mistaken.

"Do you mind if I ask what your medallion is made out of?" he asked.

She blinked at the apparent non sequitur, and then looked down at her chest. "It's our clan leadership sigil. It's carved from one of the ducia trees that we export. It's been the mark of leadership in Clan Ress for centuries."

"Is the wood rare?"

She shrugged slightly. "Not precisely rare, but it is *very* expensive."

He nodded. "Is it exported by many other clans, private individuals, or corporations?"

"No. It's a genetic hybrid created by Clan Ress about five centuries ago. To say that we're somewhat jealous about controlling access to the supply would be an understatement. Only Clan Ress as a whole, and certain individuals within the clan, are allowed to grow or sell ducia wood."

"Do others in your clan favor medallions or other body wear that uses ducia?"

Her eyes narrowed. "No. Why do you ask?"

He smiled slightly. "I'll explain in a moment. Did your uncle own any ducia trees?"

Her jaw clenched before she made an obvious effort to relax it. "Before he joined the Peacemakers, Uncle Hetok inherited one of the largest private holdings of ducia trees in the clan from my grandfather."

Elgar nodded slowly. The pieces were falling into place.

"And what happens to those trees now that he's dead? Who inherits them?"

"As he never married or sired children, they go to the clan," she said, her eyes hard. "I really don't see where this line of questioning is going. Does it have something to do with my uncle's death or are you just curious?"

"I believe it's relevant," he said serenely. "You see, I smelled the scent of that wood in my room earlier. If I were a betting sentient, I'd wager that there's an explosive device in my luggage right now. Whoever killed your uncle, they were in my room, and they had ducia wood on their person."

"Impossible. No one else would have this kind of wood on them, and even if they did, the scent is very subtle. I believe your imagination is playing tricks on you, Peacemaker."

"With any other species, you might be right. Let's just say that my sense of smell is significantly better than average.

"Whoever planted the explosives also probably didn't realize that residue from the devices is going to be on their person. My investigators will be here shortly. If there is one, they'll recover the bomb from my luggage. Then we can take any suspects into custody before they have an opportunity to clean themselves and prove beyond a shadow of a doubt that they murdered your uncle.

"So, I'm going to have to ask you to remain right here until such time as we can clear you of any suspicion in your uncle's death, Clan Leader. I'm sure you understand the necessity."

He was already certain they'd find explosive residue on her hands and fur. She hadn't counted on the events around her uncle's death unraveling so quickly, and she wouldn't have had time to thoroughly clean herself.

Elgar had no doubt that he'd found Hetok's murderer.

While he was still smugly congratulating himself, she ducked through the door to the balcony and used it to block his arm as he lunged for her. She raced across the stone with him right behind her. He almost managed to grab her but missed by centimeters as she threw herself into the sky.

Dumbfounded, he stared as his friend's killer glided away from him.

He couldn't let her get away, but the only way to capture her before she made it into the deep forest below was to pursue her right now, and that meant doing the unthinkable.

* * *

Elgar yanked his communicator out and called Hak-Chet, even as he searched for and found a glider with a green stripe and the number three. He spoke quickly as soon as his friend answered.

"Pitaw is the killer. She's gliding away from the spire right now, and I'm going after her. Send backup to home in on my communicator."

"You're doing *what?*"

With no time to discuss his actions, Elgar killed the connection, pocketed his communicator, and quickly strapped the glider on. He was grateful that Hetok had explained its operation in such gruesome detail, because now he at least had a chance at making this crazy plan work.

The harness was Union standard and bore a striking resemblance to those used in some military craft. That allowed him to quickly secure himself and bring the glider's computer online.

The small screen was positioned in front of his face in such a way that it would not obscure his field-of-view unless he tilted his head up. He imagined when the glider was oriented correctly, it would be above the panoramic view of the ground below.

The glider immediately prompted him to select a destination from a list or to visually mark one. Uncertain if it would work, he designated Pitaw as she fled through the open sky.

She was already small in the distance, gliding in a wide circle as she shed altitude and headed for the forest below. Even his specialized glasses were going to quickly lose track of her. He needed to begin pursuit.

The glider accepted her as his destination. Under other circumstances, achieving that level of success would have delighted him, but now it only pre-staged doing something suicidal.

Before he could think too hard about what he was doing, Elgar threw himself off the balcony.

The glider promptly adjusted its wings so they bit into the wind and stopped his precipitous descent and pulled him upward. The wind ripped his glasses off of his face. His already poor vision instantly became virtually unusable.

He made a mental note that if he was ever so stupid as to try this again, to grab a pair of goggles.

On the other hand, not being able to see what was below him did allow him to focus without the terror he *should* have been feeling. Small blessings, as they said.

Now that he was committed, he had to admit he was utterly terrified of what he'd done. Hak-Chet had been correct. He should have dealt with this fear a long time ago.

He watched the screen closely, observing the diminishing range between himself and Pitaw. Since her course hadn't greatly changed, he believed she was unaware of his looming presence.

Of course she was not. What kind of idiot would throw himself off a perfectly good mountain to chase after her?

A warning flashed on his screen telling him he was less than two hundred meters above the treetops. Since all he remembered seeing from the shuttle pad was an unbroken swath of forest, that meant he was going to crash. The only variable in the impending disaster was whether or not he caught his target before he did so.

He suppressed his fear and focused on the moment.

When he got within thirty meters of Pitaw, another notification popped up on his screen that warned he was too close to his target. The glider slowed slightly as the wings opened and slowed his descent. He had to override the setting, or it would keep him from catching up with her.

Overcoming this problem required going through several screens and affirming his desire to turn off the safety feature. The glider promptly lowered its nose and picked up speed again.

He supposed the only reason the feature could be disabled at all was for morons who liked performing aerial acrobatics.

Morons like him, apparently.

Pitaw veered to the right when he was almost on top of her. She must've heard or seen something. Unfortunately for her, his glider easily countered her move, and Elgar slammed into her about ten meters above the treetops.

He wrapped his arms tightly around her squirming body and grabbed the fur at the back of her neck in his fist. She screamed in rage and pain, but he had her now.

All he had to do was avoid letting go when they crashed.

He blessed whoever had designed the glider's safety features when it selected one of the nearby treetops as its new destination and flared its wings to bleed off as much speed as it could before they hit.

The crown of the tree absorbed the impact of the glider, though not easily. The treetop swayed back and forth wildly as the limbs tore at him, scratching and gouging his tough hide and threatening to rip Pitaw from his grasp.

He crushed her to his chest and held on for all he was worth. He wouldn't go through all this just to fail at the last moment.

When the motion finally ceased, the wings kept them from falling from their perch. Pitaw growled and attempted to bite his hand, but he only gripped her tighter.

Even if she did get to him, his hide was tough. He'd trade her gnawing on him for seeing her pay for what she'd done to his friend.

"It's over now," he said, almost gently. "Why don't the two of us just spend some quiet time together while we wait for my backup. We could both use the time to reflect on the choices that brought us here, don't you think?"

* * *

Two days later, Elgar was ready to leave Jukus. Former Clan Leader Pitaw was firmly under lock and key in the Peacemaker facility while the details of what had happened were being sorted out by the local office.

As expected, they'd found explosives in his luggage and matched them to traces on her hands. Fur was amazingly good at picking up all kinds of incriminating evidence, it seemed.

With that evidence in hand, he and the local Peacemaker team had searched her residence and found where she'd made the bombs. She'd never expected to have anyone come after her so quickly and had neither cleaned up nor disposed of the plans.

Elgar had no idea what was going to eventually happen with the leadership of Clan Ress now that she was deposed, particularly since her son had overcome the horrendous body blow of what she'd done and been selected to attend the Peacemaker Academy.

He felt badly for the boy. What his mother had done would haunt him for the rest of his days. He only hoped he could use that pain to drive him to succeed in bringing others like her to justice.

Hak-Chet and the boy were just arriving at the shuttle pad when Elgar caught up with them. The selector sent the haunted young Juk into the shuttle and turned to face him.

"I'm pleased you'll be accompanying us back to the Academy," Hak-Chet said. "Your insight and compassion have already helped the boy, and I anticipate that now that the competition is done, he's going to break down. Your presence will be a source of strength for him."

Elgar nodded. "While our stories are not the same, I believe they're similar enough for me to support and advise him. In fact, it would be my honor to do so. I owe Hetok no less than my very best effort."

As his friend nodded, Elgar pulled Hetok's Peacemaker badge from his pocket and handed it to him. "If he does make it through the Academy, you might want to offer him his uncle's badge. I suspect it would mean a great deal to him."

"I will do exactly that," Hak-Chet said as he tucked the badge away. "I feel the boy has a very good chance of thriving, if we can keep him from coming apart in the next few weeks. Without the pressure of the competition, he's going to have far too much time to think."

"We'll help with that," Elgar assured him.

"Indeed, we will. Now, in the spirit of giving credit where credit is due, I'm both impressed and appalled at the lengths you went to capture Pitaw. I'd thought this weakness might cripple you when you were eventually forced to confront it, but I was wrong. You're a credit to the guild, my young friend."

Elgar shook his head, smiling wanly. "I thank you for the kind words, but as always, you were correct. I overcame my weakness this time. In the future, I'm going to have to address it more thoroughly."

Hak-Chet clapped a hand on Elgar's shoulder and turned him toward the shuttle. "I'd be happy to develop a remedial training plan with you on the way up to orbit."

Elgar laughed and walked with his friend into the shuttle.

* * * * *

Terry Mixon Bio

#1 Bestselling Military Science Fiction author Terry Mixon served as a non-commissioned officer in the United States Army 101st Airborne Division. He later worked alongside the flight controllers in the Mission Control Center at the NASA Johnson Space Center supporting the Space Shuttle, the International Space Station, and other human spaceflight projects.

He now writes full time while living in Texas with his lovely wife and a pounce of cats.

# # # # #

Recovery by
Casey Moores

"**B**race yourself. I do not think they want us to leave." The small yacht's SleSha pilot, Zrr'tk, made the statement rather calmly, all things considered.

"I should think not," murmured a gray haired Zuul, the only other occupant of the craft.

"Shall I presume we are now to be victims of your success?" asked Zrr'tk as the ship, the *B'tweny Wun*, yawed hard left, rolled, and accelerated on a sustained nine-G burn. Zelko was unable to respond as he progressively tightened his muscles from legs to abdomen, arms, and chest, and, finally, gulped his glottis closed to withstand the forces. From there, he focused on his Peacemaker breathing techniques. *One…two…three…*He pushed the air from his lungs forcefully, breathed in rapidly, and gulped again. After several iterations, the acceleration eased, and the craft maneuvered spasmodically. As disorienting as this was, he was able to speak again.

"Yes. Is it possible to send a transmission?" The craft yawed hard, slamming Zelko's head to the side, almost causing him to bite his tongue, and cueing him to strain again.

During the hard yaw, Zrr'tk placidly stated, "Negative, our communications are quite comprehensively jammed. If we can get clear of the atmosphere, we should be able to communicate with the stargate. At that point, your status as a Peacemaker should allow us to continue uncontested, as we will have witnesses to their violation of Galactic Law. Until then, we are at their mercy."

After a few more seconds, the yaw let up, and the craft accelerated again, jamming Zelko back into his seat once more. Unsure when he would be capable of speaking again, the Zuul glanced down at the slate in front of his right hand. He struggled to activate it to vocalize his messages.

"Are we going to make it?" the slate asked. The craft rolled rapidly, and Zelko heard the *pa-pumf* of countermeasures deploying. It was the first time Zrr'tk had dispensed them. Despite all the maneuvering, the weapons systems had actively engaged them. Though the *B'tweny Wun* had an impressive array of defenses for a small yacht, in the end, it was still just a small yacht.

"Our odds are diminishing rapidly. Despite my efforts, we are barely gaining altitude and we are certainly not escaping the range of that jammer." The sustained G-forces took their toll on the Zuul Peacemaker. Darkness coalesced along the edges of his vision. His fingers forced their way across the slate.

"Take us back to the surface. Find thick vegetation. We will evade." The *B'tweny Wun* rolled and pitched down sharply, lifting Zelko out of his seat and pushing him against his restraints. Another *pa-pumf* sounded.

"As ordered, sir. Not to doubt you, but no one knows to come looking for us."

"Leave that to me." Zelko entered a code into an application he had never used. No Peacemaker ever had.

A port opened on the side of the aircraft. A small missile, barely more than a rocket, fired and immediately made a hard burn straight up and out of the atmosphere. The *B'tweny Wun* continued its steep dive with an occasional, random yaw or roll. A *pa-pumf* followed by a sharp *klick-klunk* indicated they were out of countermeasures. They had no way to defeat further missiles other than maneuvering. Zrr'tk rolled, pulled, and leveled them out *very* close to the surface for a hard burn toward an area that fit the Peacemaker's request.

The Zuul's awareness hung by a thread as he succumbed to the sustained G-forces. Vaguely, he registered something flashing on his pilot's panel and heard a warning klaxon.

"Well, this is not good," he heard the SleSha say. Then the Peacemaker lost consciousness.

* * *

The rocket found its way clear of the atmosphere and clear of the range of the jammer. Their attackers were slow to register the purpose of the device, and, by the time they did, the signal had already been sent. The signal found its way into the outgoing information database and connected to the standardized Peacemaker update report. As Zelko had made no such report, it simply reported his last known position and health status. However, this signal flipped a single binary digit in the file from a zero to a one. The report, with its single altered digit, was on the outgoing information update onboard the freighter *Kin G'tutu* when it made its jump through the stargate.

* * *

Zelko was unable to move when he opened his eyes. In a flash, he realized his mind had blocked out the pain, which rushed back as soon as he attempted to move. As his senses slowly returned, he realized he was hanging upside down in his restraints, suspended a few inches from his seat. Craning his head back, he observed the ship had stopped upside down at an angle against the ground. Hot, bent, and twisted metal was a foot "down" from his head. What had been the floor of the flight deck intersected before him with a line of crushed metal and composites. Zrr'tk's chair was flat against it, with pieces of carapace and congealed, multicolored fluid oozing from the sides.

From his right leg, he felt for and retrieved a V-bladed knife from a zipper pocket. After bracing himself, he cut away the restraints and slowly lowered himself onto the wreckage. Zelko laid a hand on the crushed chair.

"I honor your sacrifice, my friend." He fought the urge to release a mournful howl. There was no telling how long he'd been unconscious, so he could only assume his antagonists would be coming soon.

He reflected on his survival and evasion training. *Immediate actions: Assess your situation. Alone. Medically very sore and a little scratched up, but well enough for now. Collect what equipment you can.*

He decided to add *as quickly as possible.* The crash had crushed the emergency equipment pack, but he was able to maneuver it out. After a brief glance around the wreckage of the ship, he grabbed more rations and stuffed them into the bag. As he did, he heard the unmistakable clinking sound of broken equipment. He decided to sort it out later and threw the pack over his shoulders.

Move away from the area. Go as fast as terrain allows while remaining concealed. Alter course as able so trackers do not have a straight line to follow. Camouflage as able.

Starting out at a run through the vegetation, he smiled mournfully. His pilot had, as requested, put him down in one of the few forested areas of the planet. It would give him a chance. He moved quickly through the forest, randomly turning sharply, changing direction often, but still maintaining awareness of the wreckage's location. It was important to move away from it. The roar of an aircraft echoed overhead and behind him. There was no need to worry until he could hear the much softer whir of seeker drones. Every time he turned, he reached out, snapped off a piece of local vegetation, and found a place to secure it to his pack or coveralls. Every little thing would help.

Once he moved far enough away that he could no longer hear the noise of the enemy engines, he began surveying the area.

Find a hole-up site concealed from air and ground, away from lines of travel or communications, access to water, environmental protection, multiple avenues of escape, possible areas for communication.

Zelko could only chuckle every time his training told him to attempt communication. It would be weeks before that was possible. In the meantime, he would only be giving away his position.

Not too close to water, where they're sure to look. Not too far from water, which I need to survive. Not too low in the valley, impossible to escape down there. Not too high on the ridgeline, too easy to spot. Not too overgrown, I'll get bogged down in that vegetation.

Eventually, he identified a pair of collapsed trees crossing over each other. The open area underneath them would be good enough for immediate concerns. In the long term, they would be an obvious hiding spot.

In the hole-up site, re-assess injuries, take inventory, improve camouflage, determine your location, communicate if able. That would be minimum two weeks from now, probably closer to three.

Once concealed, he took a deep breath and thought things through for the long term. Zelko knew he would have to evade for quite some time. He had to survive, avoid capture, and still be able to signal his position when it was time. He dug into his pack to take an inventory, but stopped and chuckled wryly. He pulled out the pieces of his cracked communicator and shook his head.

With horror, he realized he'd forgotten the "sanitization" step, which meant the secure communications equipment on the *B'tweny Wun* remained intact. His enemy would have an abundance of time to access it and retrieve the codes. If help arrived, his failure could put them in grave danger.

* * *

"Entropy," Dani'po muttered to herself as she stormed down the low-ceilinged corridor. "Corridor" was a stretch; it was more like a narrow access tunnel. The Veetanho ducked and proceeded as quickly as she could.

The Peacemaker lieutenant's assignment to Blue Flight was only a few weeks old. In fact, she'd barely filed her final report on her previous mission. After learning Blue Flight had never gone anywhere or done anything since its inception, though, she'd spent the remainder of that time lobbying to be re-assigned. She had taken just enough time to review the roster and information packets.

Her final assessment of the entire alert process for the Blue Flight Recovery Team was that it was a total disaster. No Peacemaker had ever used the emergency beacon in recorded history, and, by the response, it showed. After they received notification from the guild master about a potential downed Peacemaker and received orders to execute the Blue Flight Recovery Protocol, she encountered only failure. The orders required a uniquely high number of Peacemakers for the mission. However, no one had updated the Blue Flight contact roster since its inception decades earlier. When she obtained the roster of available individuals, she found many of the prospective team members did not have accurate or useful contact information. What should have been a simple process of alerting the team turned into a slowly worsening exercise in futility.

She quickly surrendered her attempts to make quiet, subtle notifications to the chosen Peacemakers and resorted to using the emergency recall channel all Peacemakers were required to have. Even so, she could not account for several of her twelve members. Since she was prepared beforehand, she left immediately available members to scramble around, collect their gear, and prepare for the mission.

Meanwhile, she tracked down the remaining members she could locate.

Their inability to respond to the call would normally be a serious offense resulting in their immediate suspension, but, considering the current circumstances, she couldn't. Blue Flight needed them.

She located and pushed the call button next to the tiny oval portal that Goka called doors. After an eternity of silence, the portal opened, revealing two identical, shiny black Goka crowded next to each other. For the life of her, she could not tell them apart.

"Ch'rli. Shi'in. You two are being alerted." She paused to register any sort of excited or apologetic response. There was none, they simply stared back at her with those void-black orbs. "Did you not receive the emergency callback?" As she said so, she noted the loud pinging sound echoing around the small room. The two skittered around in place nervously.

"Apologies, Lieutenant…" started one.

"…we were copulating," the other finished.

"You were, uh…how do you even…no, never mind. Grab your things and come with me at once, I've already wasted enough time tracking you down."

The left one chose that moment to pop his head into the air and said, "Oh hey, do you hear that sound?"

The other responded, "Oh yeah, how long has that been on? That's the Blue—"

Dani'po shushed him and looked around suspiciously.

"Do not finish that sentence. I can see you have company. We do not refer to that around civilians."

"Oh, don't worry about them," said the left one.

"They're unconscious," said the right one.

"Uh…" Rarely was she at a loss for words, but she was now. She swallowed, adjusted her goggles to better peer behind them at the immobile forms. Unbeknownst to the pair, she blinked twice.

"Nothing sinister, we assure you," chirped the right one.

"This is perfectly normal. They will recover soon," said the left. There was a moment of uncomfortable silence. The two eyed each other awkwardly and then focused on the Veetanho. "Well, Lieutenant, are we going?"

"Yes, of course." Dani'po was insulted by the statement. She waited on them, of course, not the reverse. Frustrated, she blurted, "Don't you need to grab your gear?"

In a flash, they each produced a pair of knives. "We already have. So *where* are we going?"

* * *

The team, as many as they could collect before jumping, gathered in the briefing room. It was a lecture-style arc, with the floor descending toward the speaker in four tiers and modular seating to accommodate different races. Each seat had a restraining belt to hold the occupants down in the microgravity environment. Though they used magnetic boots while moving about the ship, the seats and restraints worked to organize the group and contain them in a neat orderly manner for the briefing.

Dani'po stood at the front and surveyed the occupants. It did not take long to discern that most everyone was entirely clueless as to their purpose and to the importance of the situation. Rajeur, an opSha, distractedly tapped away at some mindless game on his slate. He would be her "natural" ears in the field, to augment the auditory hardware. Hezel, the XenSha, exhibited the telltale thousand-yard stare of one lost in her pinplants. She would be the natural "eyes" of the group, considering her ability to see in an unusually wide range of spectrums. *Protect those two,* she noted.

An Avaka named Bromli sat front row center. She knew Avaka were the sketchiest of the smaller creatures. The file noted it had previous covert operations training. This likely meant either piracy or thievery. *What had the Selector been thinking? Uncultivated creatures…use it as fodder on point or the flanks.*

Ch'rli and Shi'in were hunkered down in the front right corner, skittering and chattering away to each other dejectedly. From the body language she could make out, it seemed they were regaling each other with tales of their recent conquests. *Such a strange, disgusting pair. But damn near indestructible to less intelligent races. They have their uses.*

Olben, a recently graduated Enforcer, stood in the far back, an unmoving wall of giant purple fur. She could count on him. Same with Gormanlu, the K'kng who stood next to the Oogar. The pair looked like they would be well-suited for security at a rowdy merc pit. Gormanlu, however, was the most refined looking of the entire group with neatly trimmed silver hair and a fine black suit framing his enormous muscular frame. The pair also had the distinction of being the only ones, apart from her, of course, to launch with their entire programmed inventory. Enforcers were always prepared. Both were powerful, intelligent, well-trained, and well-equipped. The Oogar and the K'kng would be the core of her ground team. She dismissed thoughts that maybe they should lead it.

Ka'Ri, a Pushtal and the most recently graduated Peacemaker, sat in the front row nervously sharpening her claws. *They actually sharpen their claws? I thought that was an expression. In any event, I can forge a clean slate into a useful tool.*

Rubri and Indri, the two Maki pilots, were relaxed and talked quietly to each other off to the left side of the middle row. The Krin, named Wix, calmly waited on the far-right end on the same row, with a serious and professional demeanor. *There's a pilot you call on when things get bad.*

The HecSha was an entirely different matter. Its flat, wide lizard head glanced curiously, almost suspiciously, around the room. She was still unclear how the HecSha wound up on the ship. He certainly was not on the roster and was definitely not a Peacemaker. Disturbingly, his presence meant he was now privy to the existence and capabilities of Blue Flight. *That one is certainly not to be trusted. I need to keep a sharp eye on him.*

The brown and gray-feathered Buma who ran the ship pushed his way through the lower entry portal and floated to a podium before the crowd. He maneuvered his boots to the floor and connected them.

Finally, my introduction. Time to take charge and set the standards for the operation.

The Buma rolled his shoulders back and grabbed the podium, allowing him to assume a tall, noble posture.

These things are always so diplomatic and formal. It's annoying.

"Welcome all. I am Lieutenant Su Doens, your Blue Flight Leader." He turned his head, and his giant eyes regarded Dani'po. "Lieutenant Dani'po, can you confirm this is all your ground team that made it aboard?"

If the Veetanho had not been in such perfect control of her emotions, she might have blanched. There were two significant problems with the question. For one thing, his phrasing implied failure on her part to better locate and organize her team. For another, his tone was a little too dignified, perhaps a bit superior. *Does he think he's assuming leadership of the operation?* "Yes," she said very curtly.

He nodded, ignored her obvious disdain, and addressed the crowd. In his eyes she could see both cluelessness and an attempt to exude confidence.

"Before I begin, I would like to introduce our newest member, Lerux." He motioned to the HecSha pilot, who nodded slightly. "In our race to launch, I noticed we were short one pilot, located him, and deputized him to fill the gap. I would ask everyone to welcome him and offer as much assistance as you would desire for yourself were you to find yourself in his position."

Seriously? You found a random pilot off the station for a mission of this importance?

"Members of Blue Flight, welcome aboard the *Stryx Wunfyf*." He paused as if he had just made some grand announcement. "Decades ago, the need was recognized for a rapid response unit within the Peacemakers for a variety of eventualities, not the least of which was the unlikely event that a Peacemaker came into danger. This was the genesis of Blue Flight, of which you are now a part. As all of you are, at least as of right now, aware, such an event has occurred. Peacemaker Zelko, who was on a mission investigating reports of biological weapons development, sent out a distress signal." There were murmurs throughout the auditorium, which the fine feathered figure did nothing to disperse. Ignoring the low rumble, he continued.

"This signal is a last-ditch means of communication. Under usual circumstances a Peacemaker would have time to send a report, whether it included a threat, a warning, or evidence of wrongdoing." The various species used their individual forms of body language to convey agreement, except for the HecSha. "The type of signal we received is only used when there is no time to send a report, when the danger is so immediate that the only available action is to launch the distress signal. This is the way to guarantee Blue Flight is activated when time is of the essence. In these circumstances, we have unrestricted access to the Cartography Guild's best kept secret: the ability to transit hyperspace in a mere 120 hours." There were a few confused gasps at this statement.

Dani'po clearly heard one Goka ask the other, "Really? We can do that?"

The other, also caught off guard, jerked his head over to reply, "Um, sure, yeah, of course we can. Everyone knows that. Science and stuff."

Honestly, does anyone ever read their information packets? I thought all but one of these individuals was a Peacemaker.

Dani'po glanced at the HecSha, hoping to catch it in an expression of astonishment. Unfortunately, the thing was unmoved and expressionless. *Does it even understand the Buma is speaking?*

Su Doens continued, "Unfortunately, that is all we know. We do not know whether this was an act of aggression, a severe equipment failure, an environmental disaster, or something which we could not even guess at. We must assume the worst, of course." Dani'po allowed a slight sigh to escape her lips in impatience. Again, some of the crowd indicated agreement.

"That is only the first item in the list of what we do not know. Even if we were to guess at the nature of the Peacemaker's distress, it would not help us determine where the Peacemaker is now. By the time we arrive, fifteen days will have passed from the time the call went out. Peacemaker Zelko may have been evading, fleeing a natural disaster, or trekking across terrain to reach a population center for that entire period.

"We do not know what his status will be. We will assume he is badly injured, regardless of the reason, and be prepared to provide field care to transport him to this ship, where we have excellent medical facilities.

"Even if we determine that Peacemaker Zelko is deceased—" there was some low conversation at this statement, "—we will investigate to locate the remains and determine the cause, both of the distress signal and of his demise."

The Oogar rapped a knuckle on a nearby table, and Su Doens nodded to him.

"Can I ask why there are so many of us?" Olben asked. "Enforcers *always* work alone, and Peacemakers never deploy as more than a pair."

"As I said," Su Doens replied, "this has never happened in recorded history. Our numbers are to show how seriously we are taking the situation. We must prevent word from getting out that we let one of our own fall, if that is, indeed, what happened. Further, we must deter others from thinking they can obstruct Peacemakers, much less openly attack them. Finally, we are completely blind. It will take quite a bit to make up our complete lack of intelligence in the system and of the situation."

The Buma went on like this for quite some time, listing things they did not know. Eventually, he finished, and he motioned for Dani'po to brief her team. First, however, he directed Gormanlu and the Avaka, to follow him for a separate tasking.

"Am I to understand that you are reducing my team?" she asked as the K'kng and Avaka floated out.

The tall avian gestured to the ground team. "Please remain here for a moment." He motioned for Dani'po to follow the other two. He released his boots and propelled himself out the door. Seething, she did the same.

In a separate, smaller conference room, Su Doens collected the trio.

"My apologies, Lieutenant Dani'po, I should have discussed this with you first." *Not if you've assumed authority over the whole operation, as you obviously have. This is what happens when two lieutenants are assigned with no clear chain of command.*

"I would have preferred it, Lieutenant Su Doens. What is your task for these two?" Safe behind her goggles and her Veetanho stone-faced expression, she regarded the two more closely than before. *I would have liked to have the K'kng with me. The Avaka, not so much.*

"I am sending them to the closest major settlement, where Peacemaker Zelko's investigation took place. As you are aware, it is a Zuul city. Gormanlu has a particular aptitude for diplomacy. I hope to utilize this to ensure they are cognizant of our presence. Also, to encourage them to provide us with assistance and whatever information they have." *A simple communications transmission cannot accomplish this?*

"I had imagined you would take that role," she replied, and turned to face the Avaka. The Buma followed suit.

"Naturally, Gormanlu's job *could* have been accomplished with a simple transmission. But his real role will be twofold. One, to provide physical presence to enforce our wishes. They will be much less likely to interfere with our communications or perform any overt aggression while he is among them. Two, he will distract from the real mission, which will be Bromli's clandestine attempt to accomplish Peacemaker Zelko's investigation." He took a theatrical pause, as if waiting for the words to sink in. "Peacemaker Zelko found something there. In the event we cannot recover him, we must recover the information."

"It will mean the difference between one search team and two search teams, Lieutenant," Dani'po stated behind an emotionless wall.

"Understood, Lieutenant Dani'po. I believe it is well worth the cost. To compensate, I will give you tactical control of the shuttles for the search. You will also find Peacemaker Hezel has an impressive array of search drones." Lieutenant Su Doens nodded as if the matter was settled.

Don't do me any favors, Lieutenant.

* * *

The Buma seemed to be doing everything it could to guarantee failure. The entire time in hyperspace, it emphasized the importance of haste in the operation. Now, all of the sudden, it preached caution and slow, ponderous prudence. Every hour Zelko and Zrr'tk weren't located was an hour in which they could be captured, killed, or just simply dead from dehydration, malnourishment, etc. Then, not only would their message never get out, but the nature of their situation would never be known.

For the sake of cohesion, Dani'po had graciously deferred leadership of the overall operation to Su Doens since he had held the rank of lieutenant longer. She also presumed he'd been with Blue Flight for some time and, thus, any shortcomings were his responsibility. She decided that, rather than jump into a major power struggle, it was best to let him take the lead and make whatever mistakes he was certain to make. When the time was right, she could simply take command and resolve any adversity he could not overcome.

The planetary government had proved cooperative, yet unaware of the cause of the Peacemaker's disappearance. Gormanlu's diplomatic mission had produced a map of the likely crash sites as well as where the local Zuul forces had already searched. There were specific details of where they had found some remains as well as evidence of the Peacemaker's passage.

Naturally, Dani'po was not predisposed to trust such information, but it provided a starting point. She set her team to search the untouched areas to give the appearance of confidence in the information. Meanwhile, she focused the shuttles on searching for the wreckage.

Peacemaker Hezel confirmed via drones that they were following signs of the Zuul Peacemaker's passage. They'd briefly picked up a beacon from the *B'tweny Wun*, Zelko's ship, but it disappeared as soon as they got a fix. The trail was somewhat obvious—a little *too* obvious.

"Blue Ground Lead, this is Overwatch Two. I have what I believe is the wreckage of Peacemaker Zelko's ship. I'm coming about to observe more closely."

The ground team leader raised her hand to stop the team's progress while she processed the data. She knelt, crushing some leaves as she put a hand down to brace herself. The statement itself was simple enough, but the Veetanho felt there was still a disturbing lack of data.

Too easy.

"Overwatch Two, please clarify. Is there doubt as to whether or not it is *B'tweny Wun*? Are you seeing debris and are merely unsure whether or not it is the correct wreckage?"

If it were the latter, that would be more troubling. How many aircraft had crashed here? Was there some planetary effect that could cause ships to crash, or was there a more nefarious reason? Experience argued for the latter.

Some native insect buzzed in front of her face, and her hand shot up and snatched it out of the air. Certainly, nanites would kill most maladies these creatures might carry, but one never knew.

"Blue Ground Lead, Overwatch Two. I am yet uncertain whether or not it *is* wreckage. Approaching now to clarify." There was an uncomfortable pause. "Yes, it is indeed the wreckage of an aircraft. It looks slightly swallowed by the jungle, which is why it was hard to discern. A beacon activated which lead me to it."

A beacon spontaneously activated?

It also occurred to her that a crashed vessel which had been there long enough to be overgrown was definitely *not* the vessel in question. Dani'po scratched her temple where another insect landed, adjusted her goggles, and blinked. *Unless someone staged the vessel to look that way...*

"Lieutenant Dani'po, I've found our Peacemaker!" This was from Shi'in. Dani'po, the exemplar of emotional restraint, visibly recoiled.

Too easy, indeed...

"Covering positions, team. Move to enclose. Shi'in, maintain a healthy distance until we've authenticated. Eyes out, everyone." Dani'po rose to a crouch and scanned the area. The rest of the team was still up, standing tall, and spreading slowly toward the forward right flank where Shi'in was located. Rajeur, her opSha, was squinting as if focused on a specific sound, or possibly *sounds*. Something caught Hezel's attention, and she crouched, peering intently into the forest, tightening the grip on her rifle.

"I do not understand, Lieutenant, we found Peacemaker Zelko. He seems weak and injured, he needs some water, I'm going to—"

She was cut off when the unmistakable report of a muffled laser pistol echoed through the forest. A laser pistol normally posed no threat to a Goka. Unless, of course, someone jammed it down their throat.

The rest of the team, in unison, jerked their heads in the direction of the shot, where Shi'in and the presumed survivor were. Their training *should* have saved them.

"DOWN! AMBUSH!" Leaves and dirt kicked up from her boots as she dove for the cover of a nearby tree as the forest erupted in a wave of gun and laser fire.

Flashes and slugs poured into Olben, the most obvious and heavily armed target. As his body shuddered unceasingly from the withering fire, his right arm dropped uselessly to his side and released his giant rifle with a heavy *thud*. He began to roar, but a scorching flash to the throat interrupted him. Stumbling back half a step, his head lolled drunkenly to the side with empty eyes. His knees buckled, and the Oogar Enforcer crumpled into the forest floor.

The Veetanho gave him only a fraction of a thought as she searched for targets to return fire. Smoke and splinters flew from the tree next to her as it absorbed slugs and burns in its thick wood. Dani'po allowed herself a brief calming breath before returning fire wherever she saw any hint of her opponents. There were seven, maybe eight, in an arc around their position. Recognizing her exposure to one on her left flank, she flattened, took quick aim, and fired three rapid shots. The Zuul attacker was either hit or keeping its head down.

"Overwatch Two, contacts from the ground. Looks like smoke plumes. I'm marking the positions."

Well that sounds like missiles. Wouldn't they know if there were missiles in the air? Unless, of course, they were not expecting it. The air assets were just as complacent as the ground team had been.

Maintain vigilance, the Buma had said. Dani'po had taken the advice somewhat superciliously. Of course, a Veetanho would maintain vigilance. What she had not done was convey that advice to her team. They were paying the price. They had operated under the belief that no one would attack a large group of Peacemakers, especially with a command ship at the stargate and representatives at the nearest settlement. She assumed they would hold the appropriate vigilance, as they should have. That had been a false assumption. It was a failure of leadership.

Refocusing, she alternated her attention between picking targets and sorting out where her team was. Somewhere, off in the far distance, was a deep popping noise.

"Blue Ground Lead, Overwatch Three. Overwatch Two is down." He sounded surprisingly calm. "I'm defending against multiple launches. Looks like—Entropy! Ah, uh, no launch sites. I think they're all trooper portable launches. Not sure if I can—ahh, I'm hit! There's another—" The transmission ended. A sharp *crack!* echoed around her.

Rajeur crawled on all fours, dragged his rifle by the sling along the dirt, and scrambled for cover behind a dried-up old bush. His forked tail was up in the air, twitching nervously. The enormous ears were upright, as hard as steel. His head frantically jerked about as he attempted to visually acquire his echolocation contacts.

The leaves on the bushes wavered as if caught by a gust of wind. Something unseen impacted him through the foliage. He gasped and lowered himself weakly to the ground as if lying down to sleep. A moment later, a grenade exploded in the bush he'd used for cover. He would not be waking up.

Her XenSha had also arranged herself behind a tree for cover, but instead of returning fire, she clung to her rifle for dear life, practically hyperventilating, tentacles spasming. Without looking or even turning her body, she flipped her rifle, gulped, and fired a few useless shots around either side of the tree.

"Calm yourself, Hezel! Get low, roll over, look for targets. Remember who you are and what you've been trained to do." It was difficult to know whether the tentacled Peacemaker even heard her over the fire, but Hezel took a calming breath, closed her eyes, scooted down, and rolled over to face the enemy. Another grenade exploded off to their right.

"Ground Lead, Flight Lead, sitrep."

Fighting for our lives with no time to make a progress report, you smug little feather brain.

That was not fair. The Buma was simply trying to determine how bad things had turned. He had given all the right guidance. Their situation was entirely her responsibility.

"Flight, Ground. Taking fire, multiple casualties. Request air cover but be advised, there are trooper portable anti-air missiles. Will update as able." Her tree was still thumping away as it absorbed slugs and scorches, though fewer than before.

From on her left flank, there was a *hiss* and a *crunch*. Sparing a glance, she caught sight through the branches of Ka'Ri's muscular, tan fur. The Zuul that Dani'po had shot rose into the air, run through by a blade. It choked and spasmed as Ka'Ri kicked it and drew out the blade with a loud sucking sound. After another low growl, the Pushtal lithely sank back down out of sight without a sound.

Hezel focused, clearly picking out the heat signatures of the enemy Zuul through the foliage and took aim. Her tentacles lay flat against her back. She frequently flinched from return fire, but she was in the fight. She fired and something downrange gave a growl of pain. Hezel grinned, turned her head, and nodded to Dani'po. Then, a laser flashed from behind her and burned a neat hole through her head. Her entire body slackened, and her eyes, still fixed on her lieutenant, glazed over.

Frantically, Dani'po searched for the attacker and found several Zuul moving through the trees. She fired a few covering shots in their direction and dodged to the side. Another growl meant another dead Zuul to her front. Taking a risk, she moved around to the chewed up, burnt side of the tree, and scanned for targets. One brazenly stood and took aim at her. She fired first. As the tall, brown furred canine fell backwards, she spotted Ka'Ri in a paw-to-paw fight with a Zuul. The large, tan, feline favored her left arm and looked ragged. In some places, her hair was singed and her skin charred, in other places, the hair was matted with blood that may or may not have been hers. Likely some of both.

Scanning right, she picked out a few more enemy corpses leading in the other direction, with no clear indication as to the method of their demise. The enemy Zuul raked Dani'po's tree with fire from the other side, effectively evening out the damage. She poked out the side, took aim, fired, and quickly ducked back before the enemy riddled the spot with return fire.

Sensing movement immediately behind her, she found Ka'Ri had dragged herself up behind Dani'po, coming to rest on her right elbow. The Pushtal's right eye was swollen shut and the entire side of her face was wet with blood. Her left paw clutched her side to hold her insides together.

"Cleared…that quadrant." She coughed and took a heavy breath. "Saw Ch'rli skitter away, one of them is…out there." She grimaced and scrunched her eyes closed. Dani'po found an uninjured spot on the Pushtal's shoulder and gently touched her.

"You've done very well. Rest a moment while we finish them off." Ka'Ri nodded and settled back. Dani'po pulled a nanite injector from her belt and jabbed it into the Pushtal. To stay put would be death for both her and Ka'Ri. She tightened her grip on her rifle and pushed herself into a crouch. Naturally, the next best piece of cover was the tree Hezel had used, albeit on the other side. Dani'po leaned right, fired twice, leaned left, fired twice, and sprinted for her new tree. Barely staying ahead of the fire, she landed behind the tree, spun, and found two targets from her new angle. She put them both down.

A series of explosions echoed in the far distance. They were definitely on the ground, not the air.

Only the Goka and she remained in the fight, so she had no fear of fratricide. She unclipped a grenade from her combat harness and tossed it. When it went off, she moved toward different cover. She found one more target crouching low and took it out. Almost subconsciously, she released the drained power cell and slapped in another one.

Boots crunched into leaves nearby, and a large gray canine peered around the tree, gun muzzle raised and aimed. The Zuul took half a step forward before either could fire, and convulsed. Dani'po shot it squarely in the chest. The muzzle of its weapon dropped and fired harmlessly into the ground. Its jaws hung open, blood and drool dripping out, and it fell forward, flat on its face. A giant black insect clung to its back, and he jerked out two knives he'd buried deeply into the assailant's sides. The insect's black orbs darted about hungrily, looking for more prey. Without a word, Ch'rli skittered away.

The sounds of destructive chaos ceased, replaced with the simple sound of her own blood beating loudly in her head. While she calmed, she crouched warily, and ran from cover to cover back to her original tree. Ka'Ri had ceased breathing. Another expended nanite cartridge lay at her side, dropped from her hand. It had not been enough.

Dani'po stalked carefully from one team member to the next and checked for signs of life. There was none. After confirming each loss, she removed and collected their identification, comms, translators, and any personal effects they carried. She occasionally caught a glimpse of the Goka skittering in the distance.

She returned to the clearing where the engagement had started. The poor black-shelled Peacemaker lay alone and unmoving on a patch of grass in front of a fallen old log. There was no sign of any fighting or resistance, just boot impressions trailing out, heading toward where the rest of her team had been. She crouched in front of her dead teammate and lifted his head. Externally, there was no sign of damage, but the smell of burnt insect permeated the area. Shi'in had innocently marched in, attempted to help what he thought was their downed Peacemaker, and swallowed a laser before he knew what was happening. Dani'po had not commanded the vigilance he had needed to survive.

The Veetanho Peacemaker sat softly on the log, which was where the imposter Zuul had sat.

"Blue Flight Lead, Blue Ground Lead. Engagement is over. Only Ch'rli and I remain. The rest of the team is confirmed deceased. Still no sign of Peacemaker Zelko."

There was an infuriatingly long delay in the response. In the distance, she heard a series of explosions reverberate through the forest.

"Ground Lead, Flight Lead. Copy all. I'm calling the operation off. I'm sending Overwatch Four to extract you while we still can, Overwatch One will provide cover. Break, break. Overwatch One and Four, find a secure landing zone near the team and relay position."

"Copy all, Flight Lead."

Dani'po numbly looked around. Her collection of the lost team members was complete. She reached down and grabbed Shi'in's knives, comm piece, and translator pendant. He and Ch'rli, unlike the others, had not carried any forms of identification. These were the only effects she could collect.

Though she had heard nothing, she found Ch'rli had settled next to her, calmly watching her take the equipment from his partner. She bagged the comm and pendant and offered the knives to him. Ch'rli turned and, without breaking eye contact, slowly accepted them.

"Ground, Overwatch Four. There is a clearing eight hundred meters, bearing zero one five from your position, on the other side of a ridge. Circling to track down ground threats. Notify when five minutes from the clearing. Overwatch Four, out."

She and Ch'rli were still staring at each other. "Are you ready?" she asked.

Her last surviving team member nodded. Panning the map on her slate, she located the identified extraction site. She stood and slowly moved in that direction. Ch'rli, eyes darting left and right, disappeared into the undergrowth and shadowed her.

* * *

They were nearly to the extraction site when a twig snapped. Dani'po leapt and tumbled behind the nearest tree for cover. She jerked her rifle back up to a ready position and she leaned out. Squinting through the trees, she saw a gray furred Zuul trudging toward her. She aimed but held her fire.

This Zuul was not armed. He was scrawny, weak, and wore the tattered remains of coveralls. A black streak scuttled behind him.

"Ch'rli, *STOP!*" Breaking cover and dropping her rifle, she sprinted toward the new arrival. She and the Goka arrived simultaneously. She grabbed a handful of fur on each side of his waist and wrenched him around to block him from Ch'rli. The three collapsed into a heap. "It's Zelko! This is our Peacemaker. Ch'rli, stop! We found him!"

The Goka took two cautious steps away, knives at the ready, still poised to strike. "Prove it."

The Zuul, unmoving, stared at her with weary bloodshot eyes.

"Peacemaker Zelko?" she asked.

He nodded, swallowed dryly, and croaked, "Heard fighting, had faith you would win."

Just barely. Dani'po reached into her memory of his file. "What was your graduating class?"

He gulped, and she could see him working his tongue around, fighting to gather the saliva with which to speak.

"8-2-0-8-0-6," he croaked out. She nodded and motioned for Ch'rli to lower his knives. He did not.

"Where was your commissioning mission?" she asked.

With a pained expression, he swallowed again and took another long moment to speak. "Vega Three One."

A *boom* sounded in the distance, followed by a string of scorching laser fire and a few loud *cracks*.

Dani'po repeated her motion to Ch'rli. "It's him."

"Excellent," Ch'rli stated. "It might have been useful to discuss those questions with the rest of the team."

She silently agreed. After handing a water bulb to the recovered Peacemaker, she asked, "Peacemaker, do you have any injuries?" He shrugged. Nonetheless, she quickly stabbed him with her last nanite injector before he could protest. He tensed, snarled through clenched jaws, and kneeled on the ground. "Can you walk a little further?" He nodded.

A blinding light lit up the forest. Squinting and peering through the trees, the light dimmed, and in its place they could see a telltale mushroom cloud rising into the sky. A nuclear device had been set off. Soon, a great roar permeated the forest, followed quickly by a strong rumble through the ground.

"Ground, Flight! A nuclear device has just gone off in the city. Overwatch Four is approaching the extraction site. Get there *now*! We have multiple missiles tracking on your position inbound from orbit. I assume they're planning to nuke the entire area. *Move!*"

"Climb on," Ch'rli said calmly. The Zuul complied, and the Goka began crawling quickly toward the extraction site. Dani'po raced to keep up.

The deafening roar of engines overpowered her senses, and there was a blast of wind as they approached the clearing. The HecSha pilot brought the ship in quickly, killed the velocity, and dropped into the grass. The trio charged up the ramp, found seats, and strapped in. Before they could buckle in, the shuttle lurched back into the air.

"Secure?" the pilot queried.

Dani'po checked the other two and shouted, "Secure!"

Acceleration kicked in and jammed them into their seats, making it difficult to breathe. A rattle on the ship's skin indicated ground fire from small arms, but no missiles. The acceleration forces intensified, and, with no warning, the shuttle shook violently. Dani'po's muscles tensed as she fought to maintain consciousness. She forced a glimpse at the recovered Peacemaker. His eyes were closed, but he had a look of rage on his face, and he gave a low growl.

She was certain the shuttle would shake itself apart when it suddenly stopped. "We're clear," the HecSha said.

"What about Overwatch One?" she asked.

"They went down just before I landed to pick you up," he replied.

"And our diplomats?"

"They have not responded."

"Peacemaker Zelko, what's your status?" Dani'po queried.

There was no answer. The G-forces prevented her from turning her head to check. It was nearly impossible to speak.

"Lieutenant, Peacemaker Zelko appears unconscious," Ch'rli chimed in. Unable to do anything whatsoever to help him, Dani'po closed her eyes and focused on maintaining her own consciousness.

* * *

The Veetanho Peacemaker relaxed and held her breath as they escaped the atmosphere. She immediately contacted Flight Lead, who confirmed four nuclear detonations. One obliterated the city and three destroyed the entire area they had searched. Peacemakers Gormanlu and Bromli were presumed lost. All that remained of Blue Flight were the two lieutenants, Ch'rli, the HecSha pilot, and the crew of the *Stryx Wunfyf*. Most of Dani'po's previous missions had been solo. She had never led this many. She had never *lost* this many.

An unidentified vessel had hidden in the shadow of one of the system's moons. It had launched the missiles, immediately run for the stargate, and transitioned before the *Stryx Wunfyf* could intercept. Though Lieutenant Su Doens had ordered the stargate chief not to allow them to do so, the chief claimed the vessel threatened them with destruction. One could only assume the departing vessel had paid them handsomely, but the Peacemakers would start a war with the Cartography Guild if they tried to prove it.

Dani'po spent the remaining time before rendezvous attempting to revive their survivor. Frantically, she had given him another shot of nanites, followed by a dose of stimulants. Zelko gave no response whatsoever. He was alive, but she could not wake him up.

She buckled herself in as they approached the Blue Flight yacht. With a *clang* and a *hiss*, their shuttle docked. Five had gone out, but theirs was the only one to return.

As the airlock opened, the Buma and the Blue Flight medical chief, a Jeha, entered quickly. The large, segmented insect scuttled up and assessed the unconscious Peacemaker.

"I believe he is in a coma. I will do what I can," the Jeha stated.

With the assistance of Ch'rli and the HecSha pilot, the pair prepared Peacemaker Zelko for transport to the infirmary. They strapped the patient to a litter and floated him into the yacht.

"Lerux," Dani'po said. The HecSha stopped and looked at her. "Good job getting us out of there. You are a credit to your race."

The HecSha nodded respectfully.

The Blue Flight Leader drew in a breath and gazed at Lieutenant Dani'po, who had not yet vacated her seat. The Veetanho Peacemaker found herself drained mentally, emotionally, and physically. She could not find the will to move. Su Doens pulled himself into the shuttle and pushed himself into a seat next to her, staring sympathetically with his enormous, saucer eyes.

"I imagine you did not plan for things to go this way." Apparently, Buma were capable of understating things. She nodded and he continued, "This was certainly a mess, across the board. Preparation was almost non-existent—"

"Why was that?" she interjected. "You were assigned to this unit a year ago. Why was it not better prepared?"

"I was assigned *administratively* a year ago, but they awaited completion of my previous mission to inform me," he clarified. "I was informed of the assignment the day before we left."

Dani'po shook her head and took a small cloth out of her coveralls to clean her goggles. "This entire endeavor was a failure before we were even alerted. I thought I could compensate for the poor preparation, for the—please forgive me—what I had perceived as poor leadership. I understand now the leadership failure was mine. Even despite all that, we were almost accidentally successful. But with the area radioactive and the Peacemaker in a coma, we must assume that we will never know what was happening here."

"That is…not entirely true," Su Doens corrected.

She perked up, turned to regard him, and froze. "What do you mean?"

"I mean my backup plan succeeded. At great cost, but it succeeded. In fact, it may have triggered those missiles."

"What are you talking about? The Avaka?"

"Bromli, yes. He was a truly gifted infiltrator. The guild lost an excellent Peacemaker there. And an Enforcer, as Gormanlu fought his way through to destroy a jammer so they could transmit the information to us. Bromli discovered their secret, despite their best efforts, and relayed the information to me. I believe they detected the transmission and realized they had failed to contain what they were doing here. So, they nuked the whole area and ran. *My* failure was in not stopping them."

"Why did they not just nuke the place before we arrived?"

He shrugged. "I believe they were trying to exfiltrate the operation, but we arrived much earlier than they thought possible. I can only guess they hoped they could fool us, and the nuke-and-run plan was their contingency."

Dani'po took a moment to process the information. "Then it seems you handled the operation as well as you could. May I ask, what did Peacemakers Bromli and Zelko discover?"

Lieutenant Su Doens raised up and prepared to leave the shuttle. "That is for the guild master and the guild master alone. If Peacemaker Zelko recovers, then we will inform him together. Though I doubt he will be the guild master much longer. This was the greatest disaster in guild history.

"In the meantime...You and I have discovered both the importance of this unit and the many ways in which the guild inadequately arranged and prepared it. Will you, Lieutenant Dani'po, please request to stay on and help me make Blue Flight what it should be?"

The Veetanho broke her ingrained stoicism and chuckled cynically. "After this great disaster, after my drastic failure, I would imagine you could only report me and relegate my career to inconsequence. Why would you want me to stay on?"

The Buma reached out a feathered arm and put a hand on her shoulder. "As I said, no one else in the guild truly understands what happened here. As you said, the guild, through neglect and insufficient planning, ensured failure long before they chose you or I for this assignment. I believe—I mean to say, *I know* you are the best possible choice in the entire guild to help me make Blue Flight what it should be. Do you think you can do that?"

She took an eternity to build up the courage to answer.

"I think I have no choice. Yes."

* * * * *

Casey Moores Bio

Casey Moores was a USAF officer, as well as a rescue and special ops C-130 pilot for over 17 years, airdropping, air refueling, and flying in and out of tiny little blacked-out dirt airstrips in bad places using night vision goggles. He's been to "those" places and done "those" things with "those" people. Now he is looking forward to a somewhat quieter life where he can translate those experiences to fiction.

He is a Colorado native and Air Force Academy graduate, but has also become a naturalized Burqueño, planning to live in New Mexico forever.

# # # # #

Unforced Errors by
Marisa Wolf

Balin woke as he ever did, with a ripple of scales and an internal check on his dwindling life. His cells hadn't tipped the balance into the long slide of molecular death, so he sat up and reached for his sharpening sheet. In the security of planet-side gravity, he didn't have to worry about flakes from his claws winding up in any critical systems.

The long, smooth strokes of claw against sheet completed his waking up process, though he shifted each scale twice to ensure everything had survived the night. The genetic countdown of the Phidae ensured that each of his species had a general idea of when their life would wind to a close, but sense dictated they monitor other signs, nonetheless. How mitochondria measured time did not entirely align with the rest of the galaxy.

Scratching carefully under a few scales, he stood and padded across his small quarters to the cubby enclosing the sandblast, taking time to flare each thick plate for a thorough cleaning while he scrolled through his messages.

Nothing flagged immediate action, but Civix had sent a text instead of his usual video. *It's time. See me at 29:12.*

Perhaps his Coordinator had finally reconsidered. Balin ran the tip of his longest claw through the smaller scales sweeping back over his head and bared his teeth to a final flurry of fine, fast sand.

Properly scoured, he closed off the sandblast closet and squatted comfortably to open the storage area under the alcove of his nested bedding. Balin lifted his favorite harness, securing it across his broad chest before buckling on belt and holsters. He unlocked and holstered his Peacemaker pistols and cupped his claws carefully around his badge before fastening it to the harness. Last, before leaving the safely dimmed light of his room, he scooped up his goggles and adjusted them carefully around the slightly flared scales of his audial conduits, tightening the strap under the base of his skull.

He took a cursory look in the mirror behind his desk, ensuring the metal-dipped tracings patterning his scales remained pristine. Tall, despite the curve to his spine that allowed him to curl defensively, broad shoulders, impeccable claws—he did not look like a being ready for death.

Ultimately, the inevitable winding down of his body's systems didn't mean he was *ready* for death, and he'd never believed in wandering around the arboreal walks or deep tunnels of his home planet waiting for that quiet end.

He stretched and sent a request to Civix, then considered giving his Coordinator time to reply before heading to his office. But if he gave Civix time to prepare, the Caroon might hide all his good snacks. Couldn't have that.

Balin maneuvered through the halls, his size, long tail, and gleaming badge ensuring he had the space he needed. Safer that way— there were few enough of his kind off Adghalu or its moons, and he rarely spent any length of time here on Core. While strangers tended to give him space, it took only one raised scale and a being with soft skin, and it all turned to blood.

Sometimes he put protective clothing over his razor-edged scales, but that led to so many needed repairs, so he kept his scales tucked flat and figured anyone with sense would stay out of his way. Not his fault if someone wanted to shove through a Peacemaker and ended up unexpectedly bleeding through the hall.

His walk remained uneventful, and he made it to Civix's office while the smell of the Caroon's meal was still fresh.

"You have orders for me?" he asked as soon as the door opened, lifting his long nose to smell out the food.

"You mean do I have snacks for you, Balin?"

"You know I mean both."

"Yes. Come in and stop sniffing. I got you your own tray."

Balin made a low noise in his throat, somewhere between approval and amusement. He squatted comfortably in front of Civix's desk, leaning on his thick tail rather than attempting to make the stool any kind of comfortable.

Civix turned from the display on the side wall and gestured with his own long snout to the far corner of the desk. Delighted, Balin shifted to better examine the arrangement of bowls, each filled with a different delicacy. Their species shared a love of small, crunchy insectoid treats, and had similar enough physiologies that they could eat many of the same creatures. Though the Caroon was furred and the Phidae armored, they shared a similar build and range of sizes, and their digestion proved equally able to handle scuttling creatures from an impressive spread of worlds. The wonders of the universe, demonstrated in many-legged snacks.

He carefully closed his claws around the spiciest-smelling assortment and busied himself by scooping out one at a time with his tongue as though he had come here for no reason except food.

Civix grumbled, as he always did, and sighed, also usual, then shuffled behind his desk and settled in with another sigh. A few clicks of his claws—similar to Balin's own, though shorter and thicker—brought up the holographic screen between them. The Caroon remained outlined behind the pictures and reports that collected on the holo screen between them.

"We've lost three bounty hunters and run up a hell of a credit expenditure, and we're still no closer to bringing this shit-digger in." Civix grunted and snagged a bowl of his own, eyes fixed on the scrolling information. He enlarged a headshot of the Cochkala "shit-digger" in question, a former member of the Wathayat Trading Consortium now wanted by both the Trade and Cartography Guilds.

"So, it's time to send a Peacemaker," Balin said, knowing his co-ordinator's mind. He'd asked for the contract the first time it had come around, but there had been more pressing work than one contract breaker, regardless of the size of the contracts and the complaints of two guilds.

"Sisseron was mostly a problem of the Wathayat Trading Consortium and not nearly at the level of a Peacemaker's attention."

"Not critiquing you, Civix. You've been trying to keep me on Core for rounds, and this runner ruined some paperwork. But now…"

"Now he's blown up half a station and killed or somehow thoroughly waylaid three reliable guild bounty hunters. Including, I'm sorry to tell you, Cleric."

Balin's gaze jerked back to the holo screen, and he dialed his goggles in for better focus. Sisseron the Cochkala had killed a good alien—Cleric couldn't be kept comms-silent while he lived. The Human had been the first of his kind Balin had ever met. Maybe all Humans were so, but Balin had been impressed with the being's resourcefulness. The Cochkala had killed him and had decided to break far too many of the few laws of their Galaxy. Therefore, the threat would be honored, definitively. Balin was good at definitive.

"What are the orders?" he asked, after eating a few more insectoids one crunch at a time.

"Dead with proof of body to soothe the Trade Guild, alive for full value." Civix sat with a thump. "I'll warn you though, at least two of the bounty hunters got him tagged and secured, and he still managed to escape. I want you to go because I trust your judgement."

"I don't lose what I put claws on," Balin replied, Cleric's rounded Human face in his head. "Send me the last reports and any information we have about the bounty hunters' ships, trajectories, contacts, in case there are any patterns that might help."

"One more thing," Civix added, without reacting to the request. They both knew granting it was a given. "I'm sending someone with you."

Balin placed his bowl on the desk, tail tensing. "That's not how I do things, Civix. I've had, what, two deputies in the eighty rounds I've been doing this?"

"Not a deputy."

"Civix." Balin straightened off his tail and leaned forward, claws carefully placed on the edge of his coordinator's desk. "Don't."

"He's been out of training for a year, Balin. He's not a—"

"He's a soft-clawed tree-rat in a bunker for the first time. I don't want a—"

"—rookie. He isn't. New, but not still shaking the earth off." Civix relaxed his furred shoulders, his body the direct opposite of Balin's tension. "And you're taking him."

"I don't need backup."

"Sisseron might take additional resources—"

"I'm not—"

"He'll lay false trails and you might need to split—"

"—taking a—"

"Teyhi is Phidae."

Balin sat back against his tail with a grunt, jaw snapping shut.

"How much time do you have left on your countdown?" Civix's tone had changed—not softened, as the Caroon never did soft of any kind—but less giving orders and more conversational.

"Time enough for closing out Sisseron."

"That wasn't why I asked, Balin. Teyhi is only the third Phidae I've met interested in the Peacemaker Guild, and only the second to complete training. There's been a small handful through the guild in the last thousand years."

"More than a handful." Balin dialed his goggles to throw Civix into relief.

"Relatively speaking, a handful. He didn't mention a countdown in his training, but I've never known a Phidae to come to the guild without a half-life to begin with."

"There hasn't been." The words were easier when he couldn't see the Caroon's expression. "Phidae aren't a warring race. Why leave the comfort of burrow or hollow when you have three-hundred rounds to enjoy the planet you were made for?" They'd had this conversation before, and Balin didn't especially want to have it again. But now Teyhi existed, which changed things. Balin tried to silence himself by extending his tongue to grab a mouthful of crunch without taking the bowl back from the desk.

"But when you have a half-life?" Civix wouldn't let it go. That's what Balin got for not immediately agreeing to take on some dew-clawed infant.

"Why not spend it doing something exciting? Go out and explore. Fire a few weapons. Roll through some merc pits. I had an ancestor who went off planet to go through the Science Guild." Balin flicked the edge of his goggles, silently explaining the existence of machinery so perfectly suited for an off-world Phidae.

"You and Teyhi had the same idea. So, take him along, show him the ropes. It'll help me not to miss you when you're gone."

"I hope your cave collapses on your progeny."

Civix snorted and shoved the rest of the bowls in Balin's direction.

* * *

B alin, still occasionally digging his tongue into the last bowl of crunchy snacks, waited in his ship and read. He skimmed through everything Civix had sent for a first pass, then settled in to pour over each while he waited. Flight logs, Cartography Guild records, notes from the bounty hunters, last locations recorded by the various ships that had gone in search of Sisseron. He wasn't looking to connect tunnels yet, simply map out the burrow. He didn't want to dip his brain too deeply, knowing an interruption would be coming before long.

The younger Peacemaker demonstrated surprisingly good manners by sending a message with several options on timing to meet rather than attempting to catch Balin in his ship.

"Not surprising," Balin corrected himself, closing out all the open files and securing his slate. He had long become accustomed to the myriad odd habits of countless other species, many of whom thought nothing of appearing at one's den and assuming a warm welcome. Even if Teyhi were arboreal rather than burrower stock, he'd know better.

With a grunt, Balin pushed off with his tail and straightened, not bothering to think on how long it had been since he'd spent any time with one of his own species. Instead he spent time carefully locking down each of the three compartments of his ancient ship. It was unlikely that anyone would be left unattended to prowl the docking arm of the Peacemaker quarters, but Balin had been around long enough to know how little "unlikely" had in common with "impossible."

It had taken half his career to find a ship that worked for him, and entropy swallow them all if he let inattention take it from him. The Phidae had stopped making their own ships within a generation of encountering the Galactic Union, and a distressing number of ship-building beings preferred harsh angles, or over-wide spaces. This ship, its creation too far back to know for sure who had built it, suited him perfectly. Three curved sections connected by narrow doors reinforced enough to seal off breach damage, each space with room to clear his tall, powerful frame, and allow him maneuverability in zero-G, but close enough that he never felt like he would float free, forever apart from a solid surface. Two of the sections had bunks that folded out of the walls, and with trial, error, and a healthy application of credits, he had modified each of them to close around him like the cozy burrows of his youth.

He had spent far more credits on modifying the weapons systems, because comfort came from security as much as a proper place to sleep.

Balin checked through his security measures once more before stepping through the airlock and sealed his ship behind him. He considered returning to the small quarters he kept off-ship, then shrugged it off and sent a note ahead that he'd accepted now as the preferred time to meet Teyhi.

His goggles, dialed to acceptable dimness, flashed the directions from his pinplants to take him from the docking arm to the other Phidae's location. He held his tail rigid as he moved through the narrower and more crowded halls of the station and arrived at the blank-walled meeting room without incident.

The light inside had been shifted to an appropriate level, and the wall screens were dim with inactivity. Two tables with a variety of seating options took up most of the space, and another Phidae squatted behind the further one, moving something around on his slate.

"Balin Antre'Phidae, we meet flat on the earth." Teyhi stood and ducked his long head in respect to the older Phidae, holding his long-clawed hands close to his armored sides.

Balin let the moment hold and studied the younger being. He was of arboreal stock, with thinner claws, a slightly longer and thinner set of limbs. Climbing Phidae tended to be taller and more flexible, the burrowing descendants stockier and more solid. But both stood at solid heights, broad shouldered, and covered in interlocking, semi-movable scales. Teyhi's scales were more sharply angled, almost diamond shaped, with duller edges. Balin's, more of a rounded cube, lay flatter, and down the middle of arms, legs, and tail ran the razor-sharp edges that cut through rock and some bone when flared. The descendants of tree-Phidae tended to land squarely in the average of life lengths, where burrowers more often swung to the longer and dramatically shorter outlying limits.

Balin had rarely wondered if he'd see another Phidae in the Peacemaker ranks; he certainly had never considered having to deal with some flighty tree-climber.

But they were the same species, when it came to it, and subject to the same vagaries of interbreeding and genetics as any other. Old stories, rumors, and beliefs had little use off Adghalu, and he shrugged them away.

"Are you a Dimindiem?" he asked instead of completing the overly formal traditional greeting.

Teyhi's claws spread and retracted, showing his surprise at the blunt question. He shifted back, tail drooping, then straightened again and reached for his slate.

"Uh. Yes. My family's line throws one every few generations, and my mother said we were overdue." He put his slate down again and touched the edge of his goggles. "I considered off world university, but I suppose the holos of *PM and the Merc Squad* were too tempting."

Balin made a noise deep in his chest and held a hand up toward the younger Phidae, spreading his claws wide to show the lack of threat. "Don't tell me that pile of entropy is still running?"

"On its fourth reboot, and they were planning a new offshoot when I left for training. I hear in that one, some of the half-lifers were going to meet a company of Humans and get their own armored fighting suits."

"Are they going to cast actual Humans?" He was amused enough by the picture of a CASPer built for a Human also fitting a Phidae that he didn't bother to stop himself from asking the question. They had work to do, but this felt too ridiculously perfect to ignore.

"Of course not—last I heard they were going to render some retired celebrities to look Human and make the most of their recognizable voices." Teyhi relaxed, his tail curling slightly around the nearest table leg.

"The more credits they can make from the idea of those of us doomed to shortened lives, the less they have to worry about us." Balin grunted a laugh and tapped his claws together casually. "You've been around long enough to know it's nothing like the holos?"

"Yes, sir. I found out as much about your record as I could before I got here, and more since training. I'm not a newling."

"Civix wouldn't recommend you come along with me on this contract if you were." Balin snorted. "Probably. Always better to check."

Teyhi cocked his head, tail uncurling, and for a moment Balin thought the younger Phidae would manage to restrain the question crowding his throat. But Teyhi *was* young, and for all Dimindiems had far less of a lifespan to take the luxury of growing up slow, youth remained...youth.

"You are cautious, still? Even with…" Teyhi stretched his hand to ripple his claws uncertainly. "Your cells must be close to—"

"Added me up with my record, did you? Yes, my end is near. I told you it isn't like the holos—there is no need to conserve a half-life, given how much less time we get than the rest of our kind. But also, there is no need to spend it for nothing. The Peacemaker Guild invested time in our training—the least we can do is get as much done as possible before our time winds down."

"But the missions—"

"Those I prefer to be as dangerous as possible." Balin wished he had brought more snacks. Teyhi was young indeed, to not have the constant hunger chewing at his gut. "Better me than a Peacemaker with a long run ahead. It's simple enough. I won't lose time that could be spent honoring threats to an entirely unenforced error."

"And this one?"

"As Civix might have told you, this mission is properly danger-ous. What files did he send you?"

"Just the reports from the last bounty hunter who—"

"Order us some food, and I'll pull up what we have. We're going to be here a while."

* * *

Report Begins: Filed to Chrander, Zuul Bounty Hunter

Excerpt: *Tracked target Sisseron to moon base in Cresht arm, off trade routes. Believe it has been a storehouse for the goods he's been hijacking. Found discrepancies in the Cartography logs. Theory is he's not just tweaking his transponder he's swapping out codes with a virus. I know Cartography listed a general complaint, but we also know they wouldn't want something that works on their records out in the public stream. He's somewhere in this system unless he's better than I think—I went through every departing ship and everything else is accounted for. Left a few contacts prepped at the gate, and no ships of size for him to lock on to, so I'll keep monitoring the traffic until something pings.*

Excerpt: *Ran him to ground. Sending location information for tracking in case this goes waste-shaped.*

Excerpt: *Criminal contained. ETA to Core, 170 hours.*

Report begins: Filed to Jibbo, Veetch Bounty Hunter

Excerpt: *No sign of Chrander or his ship. Tracked Sisseron to this location, no one saw anything. Security complained that I roughed up too many inhabitants, but they know something they aren't saying. I will work with the gate master to parse out where the Cochkala might have gone. No evidence of the virus or changed records Chrander mentioned. The gate master swears it's impossible, but he won't look me in either eye.*

Excerpt: *Tracked to edge of Tolo arm. Target has a network to be sure, it's been a flaming nebula's gas ball to hunt even this much of a trail. These are my old flying grounds though, so I'm rustling up old bribes and older favors.*

Excerpt: *Found him and a fairly sophisticated re-sell group. False walls, double knocks, the whole deal. It's like a fencing operation out of an old holo. Rounded up a few, unfortunately shot two dead, but it was all re-sellers, no civilians caught in the crossfire. Target secured, ETA 170 hours.*

Emergency code: ship structure breached. No life signs detected.

Report begins: Filed to Cleric, Human Bounty Hunter

Excerpt: *Think he's burned through his resources and contacts, it's been much easier to track than Bounty Hunters Chrander and Jibbo reported. Commendations to them for bleeding this flaming asshole empty. I've narrowed Sisseron to three locations and will be dark until I tag him. I'm going to move under an old cover from the old days. He's clearly seen "bounty hunter" coming, but he won't see me.*

Excerpt: *Target had an ambush set up in Herunimine Station. I triggered it remotely, took out three of his shooters. For a Cochkala out of the Consortium, he works with quite a lot of other non-Wathayat beings. It actually makes him easier to track—in this corner, seems like most keep to their own species. I've got him penned on Herunimine, sending location as I'm still unclear how he escaped from both Zuul and Veetch—neither of them were idiots.*

* * *

There was no question of which ship to take. Teyhi had his first missions under his claws, but still operated with Guild-standard transport. Balin didn't have enough time left in a functioning body to lecture the rookie on proper investments, and so told Teyhi where and when to arrive.

The younger Phidae had been prompt and genuinely admiring of the small ship. It was more suited for a burrower than a climber, but Balin made a note to tell Civix how to dispose of the *Eletine*—if Teyhi didn't prove himself an utter waste.

The mission had barely gotten started but being forced to work with another Phidae made his dwindling countdown loom more pressingly. The *Eletine* had served him too well not to go to someone who would love her.

As Balin showed him the second sleeping area, Teyhi studied the burrow-like cubby and the tip of his tail curved close to his body. Balin made an effort not to grunt and though not entirely successful, he didn't make a production of it. Though the branches of Phidae had re-interbred and had long had more similarities than differences, some old instincts remained. For the climbers, the weirder instincts had bred true.

Grounder Phidae slept curled into armored balls, in tight spaces that echoed their burrows of old. Arboreal Phidae anchored their flexible tails around a projection and rolled against gravity, their bodies folding neatly into a near-perfect circle against a wall or tree, arms wrapped around their heads, appearing as a tidy sphere of scales.

"We can take the bedding out of the top bunk's frame," Balin said, another grunt working its way from his gut. "That should be enough of an anchor if we fold the bottom bunk into the compartment and out of your way."

Teyhi twitched his claws in gratitude, and Balin grunted a third time before the younger Phidae could express the emotion out loud. No one needed a sleep-deprived rookie blundering through the mission and meeting this weird drive of the arboreal stock would prevent that. Teyhi would be better suited to watching his back. No unforced errors.

Balin's tail curled contentedly behind him as he walked to the next compartment and the pilot's chair.

* * *

The station appeared normal. It was busy enough that Balin had used his Peacemaker code to jump the docking queue. He didn't love locking into the station, given they were fairly sure Sisseron had blown Herunimine as part of a quick escape. The Cochkala didn't give half a rotten meal for lives beyond his own, if saving his own hide had been worth turning his engines on the station to get out fast.

There was no reason to believe Sisseron wouldn't use the same trick twice, and risking *Eletine* gave him pause. Not enough to keep from docking but pause all the same. Alas, no other options presented themselves, and once locked into a bay and on board the station, they'd observed a normal mix of beings for this corner of the galaxy, all going about their business.

Balin didn't like it. He said nothing to Teyhi, not trusting the rookie's composure, and dialed his goggles through every range it had as they walked through the spiraling tunnels. No one looked twice at them, the crowd flowing easily enough he didn't have to mind his scales.

Nobody looked once at them. The universe was a wide place, with beings of all kinds long jaded to the uniqueness of other races. Still, Phidae were not common outside of their system, the vast majority choosing to spend their long lives enjoying the restful, perfectly adapted environs which they'd grown from. Only the half-lives reliably left, burning their lives out in glorious fashion. And even those left bare echoes of ripples in the wider fabric of the galaxy.

Beings in the universe could certainly be blasé about the variety of aliens they might see on a daily basis, but for not a single one of the living creatures on this station to even look at two, widely built, dangerously scaled, armed and unfamiliar creatures with Peacemaker badges?

It roiled his gut, and alongside the gnawing hunger of old age, that left him cranky. They'd used Cleric's report to trace the most likely ships and paths Sisseron took after the explosion at Herunimine Station. Two false leads didn't help his mood, so it remained possible this station wasn't "off" at all, but he was.

Nevertheless, every hiss of a door opening, every shadow in a corner, ensured he triple-checked at the least. The Cochkala's trail, if they had it, had revealed nothing except more disinterested shopkeepers, record-takers, and semi-legitimate traders working with the Wathayat in one way or another.

The last bored smuggler who paid no attention whatsoever to them triggered Teyhi's instincts. The other Phidae tensed and relaxed his claws but remained otherwise steady. Balin doubted anyone not of their species would notice the slight movement, never mind ascribe the correct emotion to it. A warm hint of pride curled the tip of his tail, and he flared the scales down his arms to maximize the sharpest edges.

Both Peacemakers slowed their pace as they approached a two-story intersection crossing levels and corridors. Beings moved about their business, orderly in the way of a careful station's routine.

So orderly, in fact, Balin's hand had already wrapped around his pistol when three of the figures above dropped to their knees at the same, coordinated moment.

Teyhi reacted with admirable speed, curling forward and rolling behind a directory console that chirped monotonous welcomes in various languages.

Balin had identified cover with every new bend in visibility and swept his tail to add momentum to his own fold-and-roll back to the plinth behind him. Nothing in the area made for actual safety, which meant that whoever had planned the attack had some sense.

Not much, to leave enough clues for Balin to be on his guard, but some. He could appreciate an opponent who put up a worthwhile fight.

Then, picturing the faces of the bounty hunters who'd chased this quarry ahead of him, Balin quashed the professional admiration in favor of something much colder.

He focused his goggles to compensate for his poor eyesight and shot six times. Between his and Teyhi's efforts, two shooters fell. Unfortunately, they took long enough that reinforcements fell into line. Balin lifted his pistol and fired again, taking a moment to scan the now-empty corridor. No one remained but the Peacemakers and their ambushers.

Either the station inhabitants had known this was coming or violence erupted often enough here that regulars had escape plans. Either way, he didn't need to worry overmuch about collateral damage.

"Two more down!" Teyhi called, leaving his head up longer than strictly necessarily. Laser-resistant scales were all well and good, but neither Peacemaker knew what sort of weapons their ambush party had in wait for them. Always better to take caution over dying.

Their attackers had tried to set up a kill box but acted too soon. That was the sort of unforced error Balin liked—the enemy's. He bared his teeth, locked his pinplants' targeting through his goggles, and threw the ever-digging entropy out of a handful of grenades. He never stepped onto a station without appropriately calibrated explosives, strong enough to knock down a few enemies but not enough to blow a hole in a critical, atmosphere-retaining wall.

They didn't work on everyone, but on this batch of beings that looked like nothing so much as overgrown snacks, they did the job.

* * *

"Secure it, Teyhi."

The halls, unsurprisingly, had remained clear. They were too in the open for Balin's taste, but he'd keep watch while Teyhi confirmed their kills or locked in their suspects. Retreat did them little good if they learned nothing and, so far, it seemed the rest of the station's populace had chosen avoidance. He sent his Peacemaker code to the station's security to encourage them to keep the halls locked down until he cleared them. If security weren't in on it. All the more reason to keep goggles and gun sweeping the area until Teyhi determined what was left of their trail.

He didn't spare any effort to ensure Teyhi had the matter in hand—youth or no, the other Phidae had shown admirable reactions in their brief firefight. Only to be expected of one who's completed Peacemaker training and a few resultant missions, but Balin had been around long enough to know there were few certainties. He preferred using data as a path to confirmation, not the confirmation itself, and now Teyhi had proven himself. Maybe the rookie would be worthy of *Eletine* at the end of this mission.

"They're all dead. Chitinous skin but it didn't seem to protect against the concussive wave." Teyhi called down. "No identifying markers, but one has pinplants. I'm scanning it."

"Take their guns, too."

"You think we can trace them?"

"I like taking an enemy's weapon and using it against them." Balin reached into a pouch for a handful of protein but came up empty. He must have eaten it all while on high alert through the station.

"That sounds like a line from *PM and the Merc Squad*," Teyhi responded, a hint of a laugh under his professional tone.

"Never said I *never* watched it," Balin muttered, too low to carry to the rookie.

"Nothing up here. Want to get the station logs and see if we can trace where they came from? Possible they just had a grudge against Peacemakers."

"Sending the security office a message now." Could be they were pirates looking for clout by taking out a pair of Peacemakers. Could be Sisseron's crew or someone else they'd stirred up poking into the system's happenings. Could be a waste of time he didn't have, or another critical step in this last hunt.

He grunted and hoped the security beings had edible food.

* * *

I t took too long to pick up the trail. The smattering of small ships that fled for the gate upon the *Eletine*'s entry could have been a clue, or someone else not wanting to be wherever a Peacemaker's attention was, or a complete coincidence.

Ship life fell into an unproductive pattern. Balin woke, checked his internal clock, dug dissatisfiedly through his files, and ate. He listened to Teyhi's newest idea, grunted, wished he had his ship to himself, and ate. He ate, returned to his files, and eventually took himself back to fitful sleep.

On the seventh repetition of this routine, his countdown slowed.

That wasn't exactly true. The knowledge of his body as a set of systems unwinding into entropy had its own set speed, like the throb of his blood through his joints. It neither slowed nor increased. He'd tried to explain it to Civix once, many rounds ago, but despite the similarities in their species, this distance had remained unfathomable.

Since Balin had been aware of the warmth and safety of the traditional burrow his mother had birthed him in, he'd been aware of the length of his own life. A steady pressure, a spinning away, like falling off a planet and out of gravity. The stretch of time he encompassed before his cells stopped replicating. When he'd been young, it had been vast. Shortly after he left the burrow, described the heft of it, his mother flared every scale, nearly doubling her size and scaring him for the first time in his early life.

A life that would always be small compared to his mother's, those of his relatives, and those of everyone he ever met on his planet. Were he to go home now, his childhood friends would be nearing the middle of their long, quiet lives.

And this day, for him, the pressure of the countdown echoed into the emptiness behind it. His time unspooled, its limit within reach. The nothingness behind the countdown gave each beat a new weight, almost like a slowing. Deep breaths before the end.

Entropy take every star if he'd let that happen before he had the star-blasted Cochkala in hand and the rookie safely on his way back to Core.

"Where aren't we looking?" he demanded, charging into the middle compartment and startling Teyhi out of his hanging sleep.

Teyhi's abrupt motion out of his tightly curled ball sent him floating, only the strength of his tail keeping him hooked to the wall as he worked to reorient back toward Balin.

"Where...?" he asked, reaching slowly for his goggles to keep from flipping around again. Squinting at the older Phidae, he flared his scales as he tried to wake up and catch up at the same time. "For Sisseron?"

"We've looked where he's denned in the past. We've looked into the associates the bounty hunters turned up. We've looked into the contracts he broke that registered the first complaints and the stations he's hit along the way." Balin ticked each point off on a claw, then clenched his hand together.

"We haven't spent much time looking into where he's from? And..." Teyhi succeeded in righting himself and paused before putting on his goggles. "Anywhere near where he attacked that he might have been selling the goods."

"He doesn't strike me as the sentimental sort, and the Wathayat Consortium would have scorched anyone he knew once he burned them. Let's see what patterns we can pull on the latter."

"If he does have a virus he's been using on the Cartography records like Chrander thought, he could be trying to muddle where he's selling even more than his actual location." Teyhi's hand tightened around the strap of his goggles as enthusiasm kicked in.

Balin nodded, ignoring the echoing countdown inside, and pushed off toward the main cabin.

He steadied himself on the doorway before passing through to say, "Not bad, Peacemaker."

He didn't have to look back to know Teyhi's tail would be re-curling around his anchor in pleased embarrassment. He felt a similar warmth, himself.

* * *

"It's as likely this is a ghost trail like the rest," Balin grunted, as much to quiet the surge of hope in himself as in the rookie. He glanced without interest at the covered bowl of sliphe-bites Teyhi repeatedly nudged toward him and turned back to the screen. Half the scales on his chest itched, and he knew if he started scratching, he'd never stop.

His half-life neared its end, and Sisseron remained maddeningly out of reach.

"Civix confirmed it twice. Whoever made Sisseron's virus is good, but the Cartography Guild has better. They said the virus remains active for a set time, and in eating itself leaves a faint trace they can follow to reconcile the records. I agree with Civix that that's probably not how it's all actually working, but at least we should have cleaner data and that points us here."

They'd had this conversation several times in the long fall from the gate into the main planetary system, and Balin knew Civix wouldn't mislead them.

Their coordinator had gone from hinting that they come home to offering to send reinforcements, but Sisseron didn't need Enforcers. Two Peacemakers were more than enough for one rogue Cochkala, and Balin would finish this threat. He had made it this far in his career without leaving any job undone, and he intended to keep that record intact until the end of his life.

Which could be any day now. Or a few rounds from now. His measure of time and his body's weren't entirely the same, but it was close enough that he took nothing for granted.

"Station or planet?" Teyhi asked, pushing the bowl a little closer and rustling the snacks temptingly.

"The station's easier to blast off from if things get hot." Balin tried to muster up the energy to flick his tongue into the bowl, if just to make Teyhi happy, but the idea of eating turned his stomach. "We know that's what happened to Herunimine."

"Given we've tracked him through stations before, it's not his usual move to blow the place. Odds are in our favor."

"Odds are no way to make decisions," Balin said with a grunt. "Take us in to the station, get through whatever their rigmarole is, and wake me before we dock." He made an effort not to react to Teyhi's poorly hidden look of concern and pushed out of the pilot's cabin.

He wasn't dead yet, entropy take it.

* * *

"*Eletine, this is the dock master, you read?*" The incoming message pinged his pinplants, and it took Balin a moment to orient.

In his alcove, had been sleeping, had…left Teyhi the pilot's chair. He stretched his jaw as he rolled out of his ball and focused. He'd left Teyhi in charge, but he hadn't switched off the automatic relay of comms to his pinplants.

"*We've moved you three levels over,* Eletine."

Balin, only registering one part of the conversation, cleared his mind with an effort and pushed out of his bunk, moving rapidly through the compartments of the ship. Distantly, the edges of hunger curled through his gut like an old friend.

Not dead yet, indeed.

"—going on over there, dock master?"

"*Firefight,* Eletine, *what else? Not everyone's happy to see a Peacemaker code come through.*"

"It's about *us?*" Teyhi asked, surprise in his voice.

So young.

Balin tapped the other Phidae on the shoulder, above the raised ridge of scales, to signal his presence. Teyhi nodded as the dock master replied.

"Station actual tipped off someone, all right. Don't know who's firing back, but I can't promise if it's friendly or just someone jumping the queue to get you. I've scrambled the codes so they can't track who's going where, but I hope you can pressurize fast and roll in hot."

"That we can do, dock master. You have our thanks."

"Peacemakers did right by some of mine once. Can't say I hate returning the favor. Cutting out before they notice the scramble and try to trace anything."

"Acknowledged." Teyhi spun the chair to face Balin. "Probably not a ghost trail."

"Probably not. No activity in this sector to justify that strong a reaction to a Peacemaker arriving." Balin considered, holding onto the pilot's chair as he floated. "Sisseron hasn't been one to reveal himself so obviously."

"No," Teyhi said, drawing the words out as he stared into the distance. "He's been one to get captured, three times at that, when we've seen how effective he is at going to ground. Then he's one to improbably escape."

"You think he's setting us up?" Something had felt off. Balin had assumed it was the lingering taste of death in the back of his throat. Maybe it hadn't been entirely that.

"I think he might be. Or he wanted Peacemakers specifically, to make an entirely different point."

"Sisseron already has two guilds out for his blood, you think he wants a third?" Balin's curiosity was piqued, and he circled around the chair to snatch up the unopened packet of protein Teyhi had left unattended. He punctured the bag with his tongue and grunted as he turned over the young Peacemaker's idea.

"I'm unclear what Sisseron wants, to be truthful. He would have taken in more profit, over time, if he remained with the Wathayat. If he wanted to be the head of an operation, he could have chartered out or taken a contract." Teyhi pretended not to watch him eat, and Balin appreciated the effort.

"You stay in the middle compartment when we lock into the station." Balin pushed away, floating toward the door. "If the dock master was a ruse and everything blows, get a message back to Civix to drop as many Peacemakers on Sisseron's head as he likes. The seal should hold long enough for you to get clear, and the pilot's cabin should do for you to run like entropy itself."

"And if it doesn't blow?" Teyhi didn't argue. Good newling.

"Give me a count of five to clear the hall and come out ready to shoot. We take nothing for granted on this one."

"No unforced errors," Teyhi agreed, and Balin hoped the young Peacemaker, at least, got out alive.

* * *

The walkway outside their airlock remained eerily quiet, and since they hadn't blown up, Teyhi followed as they made their way into the station. Security and comms were locked down, and they forced two sets of doors open before they saw their first living being.

Mostly living.

The Human slumped against the wall, bright red blood splashed behind and around and over it. It startled awake, lifted a large gun unsteadily, then the gun sank again.

"Balin," he said, voice strangled with what could have been shock but likely was blood in places it didn't belong.

"Entropy and waste, Cleric." Balin knew Teyhi would cover them and hurried closer to see if anything could be done.

"Sisseron blew Herunimine, and he thought he got me, so I let him. Went back to an older cover...he hadn't figured that one out." Cleric gurgled an awful sound that became, terribly, a laugh. "Tracked him here. Got here before you."

"You had an advance start on the action," Balin said, scanning the bounty hunter's smaller body and finding nothing of good news.

"And you're careful. Good." A cough, this time, worse than the laugh. Cleric didn't have long left. Outside of their merc armor, they were fragile at best. "I got a crew of boys I ran with before I linked up with the guild. They've done some things, but nothing you're compromised working with." The words were taking a toll—Cleric's chest heaved with the effort as he attempted to gesture through the doors ahead. "Sent them on and told 'em to lay down fire for the Peacemakers and that you wouldn't bring them in if they did."

"Done," Balin said, dismissing all the questions he had. Cleric's time was even closer than his own, and the Peacemaker knew better than to clutter it.

"It's bad, Balin. I don't think he's working against the Trade Guild. Couldn't get under the deals, but it doesn't add up."

"We agree—" Teyhi started, cutting himself off at Balin's abrupt gesture.

"I'll...transfer you my files. My boys wouldn't know what to do...with...but the...Peacemakers..." His eyes started to glaze, but he jerked himself forward, shoving his gun at Balin. "Get one on that entropy-ridden shitbrain for me."

Balin dropped his head for the handful of seconds he could spare to honor a bounty hunter who'd gone well beyond his scope of duty.

* * *

Six of Cleric's boys held the corridor behind them while they stalked a Cochkala—hopefully *the* Cochkala—through a storage hangar.

Plenty of cover for them, but equally as much for him, and no telling if others of his criminal enterprise had made it in ahead of them. Cleric's crew hadn't gone far from their boss, locking down the next hall over and limiting the Cochkala's possible escapes.

They'd been grateful to hear Cleric hadn't died alone and that Balin would honor the deal.

Now Balin had to honor the threat.

"Heard you're still working for the Trade Guild," Teyhi called, aiming to distract the Cochkala and cover any noise while Balin moved ahead.

"The Trade and Cartography Guilds can climb on top of each other and rut until entropy for all I care." Sisseron's voice dripped with disgust, even through their translators. "Cartography's good for taking ships in, but then the Trade Guild swallows everyone's credits and goods. So I'll let them decide amongst themselves in what order who climbs into who. Mostly, they want to twist the profit out of everyone else. I'd rather they turn on each other. Why Peacemakers put up with their entropy…"

He trailed off, appearing atop a pile of boxes and tilting his head at an unnecessary angle before dropping back down. Balin silently cursed the missed shot—relying on the googles meant a slight delay, but now he had this particular Cochkala's image locked into the display as a target. His pinplants confirmed this Cochkala was, in fact, their Cochkala.

A deep thrumming noise emerged from where Sisseron had disappeared, then a loud snuffling that became snorting, and with a wave of displeasure, Balin realized the hole-riddled Cochkala was laughing at him.

"Is that why it took so long for your Guild to send an actual Peacemaker? They like having Trade and Cartography run their routes? No wonder they weren't that worried about me after the complaints went in. Bet I shouldn't have killed *all* the bounty hunters...embarrassing for the guild, that." He clacked his teeth together. "Lesson for next time, I wager. In my defense, they weren't...I mean, I don't want to insult you." Even the translator couldn't make that sound authentic. "They weren't bad. I've escaped from dumber guards. Just...they weren't the best your guild had to send, were they?"

Cleric's face weighed in his gut, and Balin kept his mouth shut. His guild had sent competent bounty hunters, each with an impressive number of captures, and even kills, on their logs. His guild certainly had nothing to do with whatever rotting excrement this leaf-eater spewed in an effort to deceive him.

Teyhi had remained remarkably quiet, showing great discipline for a youth. Balin filed another mark in the younger Peacemaker's favor and knew *Eletine* would be in good claws.

He continued his careful path through the stacks, scanning with every sense.

Sisseron continued insulting the Peacemaker Guild, but his voice moved around too fast. Did he have the room rigged? Balin stilled and flipped through his goggles' spectrums to the trap.

The Cochkala talked too much. There had to be a trap. Cleric had been sure something less obvious was going on, and Balin wouldn't let this last mission be a failure.

Perhaps the flat-toothed creature believed he had backup coming. Or backup was stowed in the bay already. Balin could keep being careful...

Or he could throw a grenade in a direction as far from Teyhi as possible. Half the cargo was unregistered, meaning it could be vulnerable to concussive force, but, at worst, Sisseron would die with them.

At best…

The *boom* cleared his audial conduits in time for the howl of rage to register, and Balin restrained himself from rushing forward. He might have a best case, or he might have tagged a henchman.

A spilled tower of crates blocked the way between him and finding out, so he put his claws to good use and tore through the worst of it.

His luck held—nothing exploded. Better, no answering shots or motion fired. If anyone else was hidden in the storage bay, they were incredibly disciplined—or incredibly committed to staying hidden. Those were odds Balin would take, this time.

"Go shove yourself in a Goka's endhole, Peacemaker!" The Cochkala, scrambling desperately over a large crate, didn't look like a ruthless ship-stealing menace who'd spaced hundreds and stolen enough from the Trade Guild for the guild to take notice. He looked, as all criminals did eventually, like he'd seen his end coming for him.

Teyhi popped out from behind the tumble of crates and got off two shots. Balin rolled to the side, taking a glancing blow of return fire off two of his arm scales. Heat flashed along his nerves before dissipating, and Balin shifted so the same scales wouldn't be as vulnerable to a second shot. He should have shot instead of digging his claws into rubble.

Balin wouldn't make the same mistake twice. He laid down covering fire until Teyhi could get in a shot that fried the Cochkala's helmet. Balin and Teyhi bounded across the remaining space before Sisseron could recover.

Teyhi ripped a pair off cuffs from under his jacket, keeping his pistol level at the Cochkala. The Phidae shifted slightly, tossing the cuffs onto their target.

"Put these on, you burning shitpile of entropy," Teyhi snarled. "Death's too good for you, you're gonna—"

The crack of the Human gun silenced him for a long moment. He stared, uncomprehending, first at the body, then at the Peacemaker.

"It doesn't matter to me that he suffers," Balin stated, holstering the sidearm and tapping his claws against his leg. "It matters to me that he ends. That, Teyhi, is how you honor the threat."

The young Peacemaker swallowed hard.

"Load him onto the ship. Our orders were dead or alive, but dead requires the whole of the body. Stow him in the back cabin, it stays cooler."

After a long pause, Teyhi moved. Balin checked his pistol and Cleric's gun once more, trusting the younger Peacemaker would get the job done properly.

The walk back to his ship remained uneventful. Cleric's crew had handled their business, and there would be some living captives to bring back to the guild for questioning. He'd keep them unconscious and trail them behind in pods so they couldn't pull any of their now-dead boss's tricks.

At *Eletine*'s airlock, he dialed his goggles down and closed his eyes, checking the time his body had left to him.

More than enough, for one more mission.

* * * * *

Marisa Wolf Bio

Marisa Wolf was born in New England, and raised on Boston sports teams, Star Wars, Star Trek, and the longest books in the library (usually fantasy). Over the years she majored in English in part to get credits for reading (this...only partly worked), taught middle school, was headbutted by an alligator, built a career in education, earned a black belt in Tae Kwon Do, and finally decided to finish all those half-started stories in her head.

She currently lives in Texas with three absurd rescue dogs, one deeply understanding husband, and more books than seems sensible. Learn more at www.marisawolf.net.

# # # # #

Jurisdiction by
Jon R. Osborne

L ars watched the lines of travelers crawl through the arrival gates at the Magdeburg Starport customs. A commotion arose as a huge form squeezed through the gate designed to accommodate larger aliens. An enormous spider picked its way between stanchions to the first open counter.

The customs agent appeared nonplussed by the hulking Tortantula and inspected its Yack. The universal account access card acted as everything from identification to virtual wallet. The agent leaned over the counter to argue with someone Lars couldn't see over the travelers filing by. After a few minutes of increasing agitation, the agent abruptly raised his hands and retreated behind his counter.

The spider turned toward Lars and clambered over the rows of stanchions and barriers. Humans and aliens alike gave way to the arachnid while sidestepping something below Lars' line of sight. An oversized chipmunk emerged from the maze of barriers shaking its fist and squeaking at the spider.

Lars pulled out his phone and summoned the controls for his translator. The alien-tech device synched with his phone and earpiece. Lars waited for the software to parse the language.

"—walked off and left me, you big jerk," the chipmunk-like alien chittered. The phone displayed "Language: Flatar."

"It serves you right for threatening the Human," the Tortantula replied, its own translator emitting German. An armored harness covered the spider's upper thorax. A blue Peacemaker emblem adorned the harness between the first set of legs and the neck.

"I'm too old for this shit," Lars muttered. At 51, he could have retired last year. Two things kept him at Interpol: boredom and a distrust in the so-called safety net. The recent invasion of Earth had reinforced the latter.

"You've never seen an alien before?" the Flatar squeaked at Lars.

"Excuse my partner," the spider interjected. "He's grumpy from…well, he's grumpy. I am Peacemaker Ozor, and this is my partner Peacemaker Qivek. If you prefer another language besides German, please say so."

"Lars Nilsson, Interpol Special Detective." Lars balked at offering his hand; he didn't know what the spider would use to shake, and the rodent would probably bite him. "I'm Swedish, but German is fine."

"You don't look so special," Qivek quipped, glaring up at Lars.

"Yeah, only my mother think's I'm special," Lars replied, making sure the little beast knew Lars understood him. "However, I'm shepherding your furry butt around, so we're stuck with each other."

"I apologize for my partner's rudeness, Detective Nilsson," the spider remarked. "Perhaps we can adjourn somewhere to discuss the case."

"Yeah, sure. Follow me," Lars said. Qivek scrambled atop the spider. While the Humans in the starport terminal had grown jaded to seeing aliens, when Lars led the Peacemakers from the terminal and past the taxi lane, heads turned. Traffic in the busy arrival lanes slowed as drivers gaped at the Tortantula.

The café across the parkway displayed a sign proclaiming "Aliens Welcome." The staff and patrons seemed at ease with the pair of Zuul arguing over the upcoming soccer match, but many grew visibly alarmed as Lars led his charges to a table on the patio.

Lars claimed the seat facing the sidewalk and road beyond. Ozor lifted and set aside a chair to make space at the table. Qivek hopped down and stood on one of the remaining chairs. Lars resisted the urge to suggest a booster seat or highchair.

"Hopefully they serve something you can drink," Lars said. "Input your selection on—"

"I can read," Qivek interrupted. "I don't see Tequila Sunrise on the menu."

"It's not that sort of establishment," Lars said.

The Flatar emitted a low chitter of exasperation. "Humans."

Lars waited until the aliens settled on their choices before broaching the assignment. "According to the brief, Lockerbie Insurance hired you to validate Binnig's claim regarding the loss of their CASPer manufactories during Peepo's invasion."

The Peacemakers exchanged a glance. *There must be more to the story.* "Do you know the value of the automated assembly lines Binnig lost during the war?" Ozor asked.

"Each line consisted of a billion credits worth of hardware," Qivek remarked. "Binnig had eight of them around the planet, plus another at a Human colony."

Even spit-balling a credit at 40 pounds sterling, it added up to a huge fortune. "Lockerbie doesn't want you to confirm the claim. They suspect some sort of fraud."

The server eyed Ozor as she edged toward the table bearing their drinks. She was cute enough that Lars sat up straight, conscientious of how his tie draped over his middle-age paunch. He gave her what he hoped was a disarming smile. Half of the Tortantula's ten eyes swiveled to watch the drink the trembling woman set on the table and slid toward the spider. She showed less trepidation approaching Qivek.

"Careful, the rodent bites," Lars remarked in German. Startled, the server narrowly avoided spilling the cup of hot chocolate as she placed it in front of Qivek. As an afterthought, she set down Lars' coffee and retreated.

"You aren't wrong, Special Lars," Qivek said as he sniffed the steam rising from his mug. "If one more Human picks me up, I will bite them."

"Binnig hid their factories and reported them destroyed or stolen?" Lars asked, blowing on his coffee. "Sounds hard to pull off."

"An entire assembly line will fit in a transport," Ozor said while sipping iced chai through a straw. "At least one was stolen, taken off world, and lost."

"Lockerbie confirmed three facilities destroyed, presumably by guerilla fighters to keep them from falling into Peepo's hands. Two are missing." Qivek hefted the mug in both hands. Foam dripped from his muzzle when he set his cup down. Lars stifled the temptation to make a "rabid" joke. The humor would be lost on aliens.

"So, the two were taken by Peepo's forces," Lars said, trying not to stare at Qivek. "Couldn't they be off world?"

"Intelligence indicates Peepo wanted to utilize the manufactories to equip Human mercenaries loyal to her," Ozor stated.

"Or at least loyal to her credits," Qivek added.

"So, if Peepo didn't take them, and freedom fighters didn't blow them up, where are they?" Lars asked. "How would someone 'fence' stolen alien factories?"

"That's what Lockerbie contracted us to find out," Ozor said.

Lars shook his head. "Justice for the highest bidder. Earth doesn't need alien cops-for-hire."

"Your Terran Federation gave Peacemakers authorization to operate on Earth as though it were already a full member of the Galactic Union," Ozor stated.

First the aliens invaded, and, when that failed, the new government let them waltz in. Lars hid his expression behind his coffee cup. He'd read the mission brief regarding Peacemakers. They could serve as judge, jury, and executioner with few rules to hold them in check. Lars required special permission to bear a sidearm. Most Interpol officers went unarmed unless a specific operation dictated otherwise.

"If it wasn't for the Peacemakers, Peepo would still have Earth under her paw," Qivek said, wiping his muzzle then licking his hand clean. "Think on that while your snout is bent out of shape."

"We have something called jurisdiction," Lars countered, setting his coffee down. "On this world, you—"

A white van slowed and its side doors swung open. Men wearing black bandanas and goggles aimed rifles at Lars' table.

"Guns! Get down!" Lars dove for the patio, pulling his sidearm in the process. Three shooters equipped with military battle rifles sprayed the café patio with automatic fire.

Qivek jumped under the table and scampered beneath Ozor. The Flatar hauled an oversized pistol off its back. Lars crawled forward using a concrete planter as cover. Screaming patrons and shattering glass competed with the staccato reports of the rifles.

Ozor turned side-on to the van, keeping her head low. Bullets ricocheted off her chitin as an armored panel on her harness flipped open. A weapon on a powered gimbal emerged. Lars had seen a laser before, but not one this large.

"I've got the driver," Qivek called.

Lars peeked out from around the planter. He couldn't see the driver past the passenger in the front seat.

"I'll take care of the rest," Ozor responded. The laser hummed.

Lars drew a bead on the passenger. If he could drop the man, it could expose the driver. He ducked as another spray of bullets raked the café.

Qivek hopped onto the planter and leveled his pistol.

Crack!

Lars watched the passenger spasm and slump. The driver stiffened and collapsed onto the steering wheel. The van lurched forward.

Snap!

Super-heated air created a minute thunderclap as the laser beam swept along the van. The beam left a ragged, red-hot glowing line in the metal of the van. Where the laser intersected the gunners, the path became charred meat and incinerated Kevlar. The gunfire from the van ceased as the vehicle plowed into the raised center of a roundabout.

The back doors of the van burst open and a man fled into traffic. The Tortantula leapt into the roadway, giving chase.

"Wait for me!" Qivek yelled.

Lars shoved himself upright and followed the spider. Something impacted his back, causing him to stumble a few steps. Had someone shot him from behind? A tiny hand grabbed the collar of Lars' jacket as Qivek clung to him.

"Don't lose sight of them!" the Flatar shouted over screeching brakes and honking horns.

Lars sprinted, regretting the bagels and beers he'd accumulated over the years. The Tortantula wove between and climbed over swerving vehicles. The suspect dodged cars as he angled for the far side of the road.

"You're going to lose him!" Qivek chittered.

Lars didn't waste breath replying. Pedestrian tunnels dotted the roadway around the starport, and one lay ahead. They could cross under the traffic instead of weaving through it. Lars managed to swing over the railing without falling and breaking an ankle. Pedestrians jumped out of his path as he ran pell-mell through the tunnel. A few even noticed the big chipmunk clinging to his back.

Lars spotted the runner 20 meters away as they emerged from the tunnel. Ozor jumped from a truck and landed nearby. The laser tracked the fleeing man.

"I got this," Qivek announced.

Lars saw the pistol out of the corner of his eye. "Don't you—"

Crack!

Lars stumbled, pitching the Flatar over his shoulder and onto the grass. His earpiece spared him from going permanently deaf in his right ear, but the ringing made him dizzy. However, the projectile only took 20 milliseconds to punch through the fleeing man's hip and bury itself in the engine block of a parked sports car.

Lars shook his head and righted himself. The runner screamed in pain as he sprawled on the ground. The screams rose an octave as Ozor arrived and loomed over the fallen man.

Sirens sounded in the distance. How much of an incident would it cause if the local police mistook the alien Peacemakers for aggressors? Lars pushed the thought aside. They were aliens tromping over Human jurisdiction, but they were still cops. However, maybe this fiasco would prompt someone in Earth's government to send them packing.

"Don't eat me!" the man on the ground shrieked as Ozor regarded him.

Lars approached. "The spider's appetite depends on how forthcoming you are with answers."

Ozor brushed the man's legs with her pedipalps and clicked her fangs. Lars fought not to shudder.

"Why did you shoot up the café?" Lars asked.

"To kill the aliens!" the man cried. "Earth won't be safe until they leave us alone!"

"That's not the important question," Qivek remarked as he brushed off grass.

Lars leaned forward. "Who told you about these aliens?"

German police vehicles screeched to a halt nearby. Nervous law enforcement officers emerged with weapons drawn.

"Our chapter leader," the man admitted. "He told us to be on the lookout for a Tortantula."

"Where do we find this chapter leader?" Ozor asked.

"Freeze!" the police shouted. "Raise your hands… paws…whatever!"

Lars held out his Interpol badge as he raised his hands. "Don't shoot."

* * *

Superintendent Richter glared through the window at the aliens waiting in the conference room before turning her baleful gaze to Lars. "Bad enough these aliens poke their noses in my jurisdiction, but they engaged in a firefight in the starport commercial zone!"

"To be fair, Superintendent Richter, the terrorists attacked first," Lars remarked, standing his ground. Local police commanders bristling under Interpol's presence was nothing new to Lars. However, his gut reaction to the Peacemakers' intrusion gave him a new perspective. "The sooner they conclude their investigation, the sooner they can leave."

"How quick can you get them out of my jurisdiction?" the superintendent asked, her eyes straying back to the Peacemakers.

"I have a ride on the way," Lars replied. If the transportation had been waiting when the aliens arrived, this whole mess could have been avoided. Unless the terrorists went after them on the road—a distinct possibility since someone knew of the Peacemakers' impending arrival.

Richter crossed her arms. "Good."

"Any intel from the suspect we arrested?" Lars asked. Whoever provided the anti-alien terrorists with the intel could lead him to the thieves who stole Binnig's equipment. Cracking the case would not only send the aliens away, it would prove Humans didn't need Galactics interfering in their police business.

"No. The groundhog put a hole through the suspect's hip, so he's in the hospital. There were no other survivors. A year ago, I would have said he and his buddies were part of the Remember Iran crowd, but now all sorts of people have an axe to grind with aliens." Richter shook her head. "Let us deal with the locals. These aliens are worse than gung-ho Americans. Resolve their case one way or the other and send them packing."

Lars didn't bother to point out the Galactic Union considered attacking a Peacemaker a crime. Qivek had mentioned as much. "Thank you, Superintendent Richter."

* * *

"**D**id she give you anything?" Qivek asked as soon as they left the building.

Lars checked the street. Still no sign of their ride. "No. She doesn't appreciate outsiders tromping around on her turf, much less shooting it up. The suspect is in a hospital."

"The University of Magdeburg Hospital, Room 514," Ozor stated. "The suspect's name is Torben Uller. I have his home address as well."

Lars glanced over his shoulder toward the police headquarters. "How do you know?"

"I hacked their system. Their Aethernet security protocols are…quaint," the spider replied.

A rumble from down the block drew Lars attention. A six-wheeled military vehicle rounded the corner. Dents and burns marred the armor and one of the headlights flickered.

"A Mercedes Type-59 Light Logistics Rumbler," Ozor stated. A *click-whine* heralded the emergence of her laser.

"Hold your fire. I'd hate for you to shoot our ride," Lars said.

"This hunk of junk?" Qivek scowled as the LLR ground to a halt. "It's seen more years than you, Special Lars."

The top hatch flipped open. A man Lars' age poked his head out. "You called for a ride, *ja?*"

"Not exactly subtle, Jost," Lars called.

"You want subtle, you get a little meep-meep car," Jost retorted, grinning under his sunglasses. "Your pals, they won't fit in a meep-meep car, *nein?* I'll drop the ramp; climb aboard."

"Great, another Human merc with an excess of personality," Qivek muttered.

"How did you know Jost was a merc?" Lars asked as they ascended the ramp. Ozor brought up the rear. She had to hold her legs close as she entered the cargo compartment.

"He didn't give Ozor a second glance," Qivek replied.

"Detective Nilsson! What do you think? Should we paint it blue and white?" Jost crouched in the entrance to the cab. "Maybe we could put a spinning light on top?"

"Very funny. This is Jost Schlueter, a logistics specialist for Interpol and a few other parties best not named. Jost, these are Peacemakers Qivek and Ozor."

Jost flicked two fingers from his forehead in an impromptu salute. "I never heard of Tortantula and Flatar Peacemakers, but it makes sense."

"What mercenary unit did you serve in?" Ozor asked.

"The Rhine Raiders." Jost rolled up his right sleeve to expose a pair of overlapping runic Rs. "We were a small unit and didn't have a ride off world when Peepo hit. It's a sad story to tell later over some schnapps. We should roll before the constables give us a ticket."

"The University Hospital," Qivek ordered, hopping on a bench. "We should pay Torben Uller a visit."

"Sounds fun!" Jost disappeared into the cab. Six powerful electric motors hummed, and the rumbler lurched into motion.

Lars grabbed an overhead bar. "You can't waltz into the hospital. As soon as anyone sees Ozor, they'll freak out and call the police."

"We have two hours until the sun sets," Ozor said. "We could get some food, and once it's dark go to the hospital."

"Food, huh? Fine." Lars turn toward the front of the vehicle. "Jost, can you find us a drive-through?"

"*Ja!* I'll swing through a Burger Meister. How many double Meister Burgers do you want?"

* * *

One guard played on his phone while the other dozed. Even though they flanked the hospital room door, Qivek could have slipped past them without Lars's help. However, Lars didn't trust the blood-thirsty rodent alone with the suspect.

"Hey, guys." Lars presented his badge. The sleepy guard sat up and scrutinized the identification, but the other one kept his eyes glued to his phone. "Special Detective Lars Nilsson, Interpol. I have some questions for the suspect."

"Us local yokels can't handle the investigation?" Sleepy demanded.

Lars raised his hand. "I get it. You don't want outsiders mucking around in your jurisdiction. I only need a few questions for a case I'm stuck with so I can keep my captain off my back. Can you help me out?"

"Let him ask his questions," the other guard said, tapping on his phone. "The prisoner isn't going anywhere."

"Fine." Sleepy leaned back in his chair.

Lars entered the room and closed the door behind him. Uller was asleep or unconscious. Electronic beeps sounded from the monitors wired to the terrorist.

"Took you long enough," Qivek said, climbing onto the hospital bed.

"A little professional courtesy can go a long way. You should try it some time," Lars retorted.

Qivek pulled out a syringe the size of a toothpick and fiddled with a dial wrapped around the device.

"What's that?" Lars asked.

"A nanite applicator loaded with interrogation nanites," Qivek replied. "I'm going to wake him."

"Hang on a second." Lars lightly slapped Uller on the cheek a couple times.

The man stirred and his eyes fluttered open. Recognition blossomed in his eyes once he spotted Qivek. "What...what are you doing here?" he croaked.

"It should be obvious. Someone sent you to kill the Peacemakers. They want to know who," Lars replied. He never thought he'd play good cop to an overgrown rodent.

Qivek grabbed the man's beard. "Tell us who put out the hit on us!"

When Uller balked, Lars jerked a thumb toward the window. "If you're not afraid of the chipmunk, you should worry about his partner."

Ozor tapped on the glass and waved her pedipalps. Uller paled, and one of the monitoring devices beeped faster.

"Here's the best part." Lars leaned in close and lowered his voice. "She's also a master hacker. Before she eats you, she's going to send your mother all your porn account logins."

* * *

"You primates are messed up," Qivek remarked as they climbed into the rumbler. "You're more afraid of reproduction than a Tortantula eating you one limb at a time."

"You're oversimplifying it," Lars protested.

"Is he wrong?" Ozor asked.

Lars sat and pulled out his phone. "Unfortunately, no. At least we got the info."

"You pulled the old porno ploy again? Hah!" Jost called from the cab. "Threatened to send his wife his browser history?"

"I told him we'd send his mother his porn site logins," Lars replied. "He sang like a canary."

"Where to?" Jost asked, powering on the rumbler.

"Lager Haus on Hallische Street." Lars retrieved the address on his phone and sent it to Jost.

"Got it! Not exactly an upscale establishment." Jost called. "You don't want me to park out front, *nein?*"

"No. Park a block away." Lars regarded the Peacemakers. "If I'm going to chat with an anti-alien activist, you two won't make him talkative."

"It worked with Uller," Ozor countered.

"Only because he couldn't run away or throw a bunch of goons at us," Lars said. He knew, as soon as Qivek and Ozor appeared the target would rabbit. "I need to go in…Jost how adventurous are you feeling?"

"Danger with a chance of schnapps? Count me in!" Jost declared.

"It's okay; I'm used to being left to monitor," Ozor lamented. "Qivek, give Detective Nilsson one of our comm buttons."

The Flatar climbed one of the spider's legs and opened a pouch on her harness. "Special Lars, let me see your earpiece."

"Special Lars!" Jost laughed from the cab.

Lars plucked out the earpiece and handed it to the rodent. Qivek set a slate the size of an old-fashioned business card on the bench and placed both the earpiece and a black disc on top of it. After a moment the slate's display flashed amber.

Qivek handed the disc and the earpiece to Lars. He waited for Lars to replace his earpiece. "I've synced it through your translator. Keep the button on your person, and we'll be able to hear what's going on."

"Fine." Lars tucked the button in his jacket pocket. He'd do some actual police work instead of playing zookeeper. He studied the profile Ozor downloaded to his phone. Gerold Bender—suspected cell leader of Humanity First, alleged connections in the gray market, and top dog of a statewide gang. "This guy is going to be a barrel of laughs."

The whine of the motors dropped in pitch as the rumbler slowed. "I hope this is a legal lot. I'd hate for someone to boot our ride!" Jost called.

* * *

The hulking doorman gave Lars and Jost a side-eye, but he didn't impede them. Jost gave him a friendly nod and a thumbs up. Some sort of merc recognition? With Jost, it was hard to tell. Muffled electronic music thrummed in the vestibule. Stepping into the tavern proper, the bass-heavy electronica reduced nearby conversations to indistinct murmurs.

Lars' eyes stung from the mix of smoke and vapor. The proscribed smoking would prompt an inspector to shut down the establishment, but Lars guessed the bar was on a list of businesses that received less than thorough visits.

Lars blinked his eyes clear as they wove through the crowd filling the dimly lit tables. The illumination brightened marginally over the bar. Lars gestured to a heavily tattooed bartender for two beers. He didn't care about the brand, the drinks were props as much as anything.

As the bartender set down two glasses, Jost leaned forward. "You got brennivín? You know, Icelandic schnapps?" The bartender shook her head, so Jost pointed at a bottle on the shelf and gestured for a double.

Lars grudgingly paid for the drinks and scanned the crowd. "I've got him," Lars muttered. Bender was sitting with half a dozen other people at a table near the billiards.

"Where at?" Qivek demanded. A weird reverb from the music accompanied his translated voice.

"Sitting toward the back, near the pool tables," Lars replied. He gulped half his beer and abandoned the remainder on the bar. Lars tapped Jost. "Come on."

Jost downed his shot and guzzled most of his beer. "Already? I was going to get the bartender's Aethernet ID."

Lars led the way along the bar, studying Bender's group. Two of the women and one man were hangers-on, probably hoping to exchange their companionship for drugs or some other accommodation. The other two men could pass for gang members out of any entertainment video. The women flirting with them occupied their attention. The third woman, Lars didn't discount—she'd already spotted him approaching. Her wary stance bespoke someone intimately familiar with violence. The third woman nudged Bender and pointed at Lars. Lars kept his hands clear of his jacket.

"What do you want, policeman?" Bender demanded once Lars approached within earshot.

Lars held out his phone and displayed his Interpol identity card. "I have a few questions. We can do this here, or we can step outside."

"Get lost, policeman," Bender sneered. The two gang-stereotypes stood. "I don't have anything to tell you."

"We don't have to do this the hard way," Lars stated.

"What he said!" Jost yelled over the music. "I'd rather be drinking."

Bender laughed. "You're outnumbered. Go away, policeman, while you and your friend can still walk."

Qivek leapt onto the table and jammed his pistol in Bender's face. "Please, let's do this the hard way, primate. I can shoot through your thick skull and take out one of your buddies in the bargain."

Bender froze. Whether or not he could hear the Peacemaker's translator, Qivek had made his meaning clear. The woman drew a pistol and aimed it at the Flatar. The crowd, sensing something amiss, quieted around them. The groupies disappeared into the surrounding throng.

"Screw you and your alien gopher!" Bender shouted, fear creeping into his voice as he stared down the gun.

Qivek kicked Bender's phone across the table to Lars and hopped onto a vacated chair. "You might not be afraid of me, you dumb Human, but you forgot about my partner."

With a shriek of metal and shattering glass, Ozor peeled open a skylight. The spider leaned into the opening and a triangle of glowing red dots appeared on the table. The dots tracked across the table to the pistol-wielding woman.

"Put the gun away, or she'll laze you extra-crispy," Lars ordered. The woman holstered her pistol and raised her hands. Competent and smart.

"Who told you we were coming?" Qivek demanded, glaring at Bender. "Who paid you to kill us?"

"I'd answer the Peacemaker." Lars pocketed Bender's phone. "Unlike Earth cops, they can do whatever they want to a suspect, including eating them." He jerked a thumb skyward.

"Erhardt, Konrad Erhardt. He wired the money in galactic credits and sent me a dossier." Bender scowled. "He claimed sympathy to—"

"Whatever, primate," Qivek interrupted. "I should shoot you as an example. You don't fuck with Peacemakers."

"We've got what we need," Lars said. "Leaving him alive encourages others to be more cooperative in the future."

Qivek hopped off the chair. "Fine."

Snap!

The center of the table disappeared in a flash. The glowing triangle moved in the direction of the door. The crowd parted, scrambling out of its path.

"Don't get any funny ideas about following us," Lars stated, nodding toward the smoking hole.

* * *

"No brawl, no phone number, and hardly any schnapps," Jost lamented as they climbed into the LLR. "Where to now?"

"We need to pay Mr. Erhardt a visit before they figure out how to warn him," Lars replied. He held Bender's phone toward Ozor. "I'm guessing you can hack this?"

"Its antiquity will make it more of a challenge than the encryption." the Tortantula reached out with a pedipalp. "This design dates to a millennia ago."

"Jost, head for Braunschweig. Erhardt has a house north of there," Lars called toward the cab.

"Let's see what this rumbler can do on the autobahn!"

It was just as well Jost didn't have time for more schnapps.

In a few minutes, the phone chimed. "The messages in the cache confirm his story," Ozor stated, swaying as the rumbler rounded a corner. "Konrad Erhardt used two layers of aliases and a virtual private network spoofing his location in Canada. He's not good at being a criminal and covering his tracks."

"I'll take your word for it," Lars said. "If we get a hold of him, we could find out where the leak in Lockerbie originated."

"As long as he can point us at the missing manufactories," Qivek said. "Lockerbie didn't pay us to hunt down moles. We'd offer it at a discount, since we're already on a case for them, but it could alert the spy."

"Speaking of which, if Erhardt spills the beans, we need to keep him from alerting whoever pulls his strings." Lars searched for info on Binnig's local operations. One of the missing manufactories was from Hanover. Did the conspiracy spread beyond the local branch of Binnig? Binnig numbered among the top corporations on Earth.

"We'll get there in twenty minutes!" Jost yelled from the front as the rumbler accelerated. They must have reached the autobahn.

Ozor set a slate on the floor, and a holographic image of Erhardt's property appeared over it. "I've accessed the home virtual assistant. The suspect's family is out of town on a trip, so the only people present are Konrad Erhardt and four private security guards. Interesting, Erhardt's original schedule placed him with his family, but he suddenly returned two days ago."

A truck horn sounded, and the rumbler swerved, forcing Lars to grab hold of his seat. "Jost! Try not to get us killed!"

"*Ja, ja.* Don't worry. The other guys don't have armor!"

"Four guards? Sounds easy," Qivek remarked. "As long as they aren't mercenaries in mecha armor."

"You mean CASPers? Since Binnig manufactures Combat Assault Systems, Personal, I wouldn't be surprised," Lars remarked.

"Based on security footage, I do not see any CASPers on the premises. All security personnel appear to be unaugmented," Ozor reported. Four of her eyes flicked back and forth in the manner of someone reading. "Interior footage is limited to the entry points, but the doors are not scaled to accommodate the armored suits."

"A pity. It could have been a challenge," Qivek remarked.

"The guards may balk at admitting us without a warrant," Lars said. It would take him longer to fill out the first request form than it would to arrive at Erhardt's home.

"Peacemakers don't need warrants," Qivek snapped.

"I'm not a Peacemaker," Lars replied. Technically, he didn't have arrest powers except under extraordinary circumstances.

"I'm deputizing you, Special Lars," Qivek announced. "Ozor, do the honors."

The spider swiped her pedipalp across the slate. Lars' UAAC chimed, and a logo with a blue tree blinked on it.

"Hey, can I be a deputy?" Jost yelled from the front. "It might help if we get pulled over."

Qivek shrugged. "Why not?" Ozor swiped the slate again.

The commandant would have a fit if he found out. Lars smiled. The commandant *had* ordered him to expedite the investigation and get the aliens out of Earth police affairs.

* * *

"We're almost to the gate!" Jost yelled. "Should I stop and honk the horn?"

Lars clambered forward. Pocket estates lined the road, one walled yard after another. Their destination lay at the end of the road on the left. He slipped into the safety restraint. "Go through it."

"I like how you think! Hang on!" Jost stomped on the brakes and spun the wheel. The rumbler skidded sideways, the tires squealing. Jost released the brake and accelerated. Half the tires tore up the manicured grass along the driveway as the vehicle slewed toward the gate.

The rumbler hit the closed metal gates off center. The left gate swung away while the impact ripped the right gate off its hinges and flung it into the yard. The rumbler rocketed up the fifty-meter-long drive and screeched to a halt behind an expensive sports car.

"Nice Bugatti!" Jost remarked. "I would have hated to crush it."

"I'm sure he has a car or two to spare." Lars unbuckled. "Drop the ramp."

"I'm jamming local phone service, and I've taken the estate's Aethernet node offline," Ozor remarked as she skittered down the ramp. Qivek scurried up a leg to sit on her back.

"It should buy us a few minutes at least."

Lars followed the Peacemakers. Additional lights winked on, illuminating the house and yard around it.

Barking sounded as a quartet of Dobermans dashed around the corner of the building, teeth bared. Ozor raised her front legs, reared up, and hissed. The dogs fled in panic, yelping into the darkness.

"I didn't want to have to hurt them," Ozor remarked. "Animals don't know any better."

A gunshot popped, and a bullet ricocheted off Ozor's carapace. Lars ducked behind the spider's bulk and drew his pistol.

"These primates know better," Qivek sneered. *Crack!* A man cried out.

"Try not to kill the hired security." Lars peered over Ozor's abdomen. One man lay on the ground, whimpering. Another crouched at the entrance to the house, occluded by shrubbery. He peered around the corner.

The laser whined and tracked toward the entrance. *Snap!* The pulse sheared off half the bush and left the remainder aflame. The guard retreated.

"Police! Drop your guns and come out with your hands up!" Lars shouted. He added, "The Peacemakers can and will use lethal force if you resist."

Ozor sidled up for a better view of the entrance. Lars kept the spider between himself and the entrance while watching for additional attackers from the corners of the house or upper story windows. The guard hunkered in the entrance, his eyes going wide when he saw the spider. Three red dots appeared on the steps and swept up to his chest. He had nowhere to flee. He tossed away his pistol and raised his hands.

Lars went to the injured guard and collected his sidearm. Blood soaked the man's shoulder, and a spray of blood decorated a shattered brick in the wall. "Tell your buddies this job isn't worth dying over." Hopefully they weren't suiting up in CASPers.

"I can't. Something is jamming our communications," the guard replied.

Oops. "Open the door and yell to them," Lars said.

The guard tentatively opened the door. "It's Armin. These are Peacemakers and police."

Lars stepped forward but kept to the side so Ozor could shoot past him. "If you cooperate, you will not be arrested!"

After a moment, a door on the far side of the room beyond the foyer opened. Two men in suits stepped out, holding their guns aloft by the barrel. Lars beckoned them forward.

Both eyed the Tortantula as they reached the porch. "Mr. Erhardt is waiting for you in his study," one of them said.

"Take care of your friend." Lars gestured to the wounded guard. "Don't give the Peacemakers cause to shoot you."

They both nodded and tossed aside their weapons. Lars marched through the door. Light spilled from the door the guards had emerged from and left ajar. Lars kept his pistol ready. Erhardt may have told his men not to throw their lives away, but he might be willing to resist, if nothing else than to force their hand rather than take him alive.

Konrad Erhardt sat behind a huge antique desk. The décor in the room was worth more than Lars made in the last decade. His eyes flicked to the door as Ozor squeezed through it.

"Special Detective Nilsson. I'd protest you're outside of your jurisdiction, but I don't think such niceties matter to your friends."

"You would be correct," Ozor said.

"Then I suppose I'll have to let you arrest me." Erhardt placed his arms on his desk. "I suppose you'll want to handcuff me, even if I promise not to run."

"First we need you to answer some questions," Lars said, stepping toward the desk. "Why is Binnig interfering in the investigation of their stolen manufactories?"

"I'm afraid you'll have to wait to talk to my lawyer." Erhardt smiled. "I have the right to remain silent."

Qivek jumped on the desk. "I hoped I'd get a chance to use this." He jabbed a syringe into Erhardt's neck.

"Ow! What did you do to me?" Erhardt clasped his hand over the angry red dot on his neck.

Qivek brandished the syringe. "These are interrogation nanites. The more you think about lying, the more of your brain they will disassemble neuron-by-neuron. A primate like you can't have too many neurons to spare, so you'd better tell the truth."

"You can't do this! I have rights!" Erhardt moved his fingers from his neck to his temple.

"Maybe in your Human courts. Since Lockerbie called in the Peacemakers, this is Galactic Union business and falls under our jurisdiction." Qivek squinted. "Do you feel a buzzing in your skull? I bet the nanites are ready to snip apart some brain cells."

Erhardt paled. "No! Stop them! I'll tell you what you want!"

"Let's start with the manufactories. Where are they?" Qivek waved the syringe.

"The one in Korea is in an old warehouse not far from Kaesong. There's a bunch of buildings full of relics from preunification days, so it made a convenient haystack," Erhardt said.

"What about the German one?" Lars asked.

Erhardt grimaced. "It was taken to Hamburg, but I don't know if we can get it back."

"Why not?" Qivek demanded, gesturing with the syringe.

"The people we hired claim they now belong to the Red Justice Front!" Erhardt replied. "This particular branch is Kirmizi Adalet. Not only do they demand restitution of all public welfare benefits, they blame the aliens as much as the wealthy for their woes."

"Now they have their own war machine factory," Lars muttered. "This can't be good."

"Turn off the nanites!" Erhardt cried. "I told you the truth!"

"We need the specific locations of both assembly lines." Lars pointed to a slate. "You better type fast before your nose starts bleeding."

* * *

Jost stood along the Bugatti, admiring the sports car. "I'd love to give this a spin. Can we seize it like the American police?"

"No, and we don't have time," Lars replied. "We need to get to Hamburg."

"I'll be back, darling." Jost kissed the roof of the car and trotted back to the rumbler.

"I knew the Peacemakers didn't mess around, but brain-eating interrogation nanites? People will freak out if they hear about it," Lars remarked as they boarded the LLR.

"If any remain in his system to analyze, they'll read as medical nanites designed for migraines and concussions," Qivek said.

"They're designed to read as benign? Clever." Lars didn't approve, but he admitted the results were handy. Erhardt had confessed and promised to turn himself over to the local precinct.

"No. They're brain injury nanites," Qivek said. "If you stick them in someone without an injury or malady, they'll buzz around a while looking for something to repair. The stress makes them more active."

"You tricked him?" Lars laughed. "That's more fiendish than the real thing."

"You'd rather I melt his brain? You primates are crazy," Qivek said.

* * *

"We're approaching the address," Jost announced. "Want me to drive through the gate again?"

"These guys won't surrender as quickly as Erhardt's security," Lars said. "Do you have a plan besides storm the warehouse?"

"Sure we don't need a warrant, Special Lars?" Qivek cracked. They'd studied the layout of the old logistics facility, one of dozens south of the Elbe River. A chain-link fence surrounded it, but images didn't show any formal security.

"The facility lacks an Aether Net connection," Ozor stated. "It is the only facility with power in this area without at least a basic connection."

"So much for hacking," Lars commented. "The best cyber security—unplug."

"It also keeps us from verifying the presence of the manufactories." Ozor manipulated the image of the facility, highlighting potential entrances. "We'll have to get inside, and once we have confirmation we can contact Lockerbie to send a security team to hold the facility."

"Then it's no longer your problem?" Lars ventured.

"Unless Lockerbie wants to put a bounty out on Erhardt and his accomplices," Qivek replied.

"How much is this bounty?" Jost called. "Enough to buy a Bugatti?"

"I don't know how much a Bugatti costs, but you could buy ten top-of-the-line Zuul fast luxury cars," Qivek answered. "I hear Zuul or Besquith make the best ground vehicles."

"Before Jost spends his hypothetical future bounty, we need to solve the case." Lars pointed at the image. "Notice how trailers block most of the docks? It means we go in the two docks on the end, or the personnel entrance on the other side."

"What about the skylight?" Ozor suggested.

"I forgot my wings," Lars countered. "I have no way to get up there. Can you climb the wall?"

"As long as the wall doesn't crumple under my mass," Ozor replied. "I could carry you, Detective Nilsson."

"Carry me?" Lars had grown accustomed to the Tortantula's presence, but physical contact with a giant spider sent something quivering in his mind.

"It is only ten meters. You can hang onto my harness with Qivek."

"It's easy, Special Lars," Qivek chimed in. "Once Ozor rips open the skylight, we can drop a line."

Lars looked from the Flatar to the Tortantula. "I should have joined a gym. Fine, let's do this. If we're lucky, no one is home."

The rumbler slowed. "The gate is closed," Jost yelled. "Can I deputy through it?"

"Sure. Park on the end by those empty loading docks," Lars replied. The rumbler lurched forward. A metallic clatter signaled their passage through the gate, but the vehicle didn't slow until it reached the end of the building.

Jost clambered back. "If you're going to storm the castle, you'd best take some proper gear." He opened a locker in the cargo section of the logistics rumbler. Jost handed Lars an armored vest and a bulky gun Lars took for a shotgun.

"What's this?" Lars asked. Instead of the side-by-side barrels of a double-barreled shotgun, this weapon had over-and-under barrels and two triggers.

"It's a Heckler and Glock RC-11, a recon carbine," Jost replied. "The top barrel fires standard 7mm caseless infantry rounds. The bottom is a 30mm gyroc. Not as much punch as a magnetic cannon, but it launches a rocket with an armor-piercing shaped charge. It only has the one rocket, so make it count."

Lars double-checked the safety and slung the weapon. "How many rounds in the magazine?"

"Fifty." Jost grinned. "Don't ask where I got them. Them? I meant it."

"You ready to go, Special Lars, or do you primates want to chatter more?" Qivek demanded. The Flatar had donned an armored combat vest.

"Let's do this," Lars replied, following Ozor out the back of the rumbler.

The spider lowered its body to the pavement. "Climb onto my back and hang onto the harness. Don't worry about stepping on my legs; you won't hurt me."

Grunting from the exertion, Lars hauled himself atop the spider. He found a pair of straps to use as handholds. Ozor tensed beneath him and leapt halfway up the concrete wall.

Lars' feet scrabbled for purchase on the harness as he dangled by his hands. The toe of one shoe snagged on a strap. He resisted the urge to look down.

"Don't let go, Special Lars." Qivek clambered up the harness.

The ten seconds it took Ozor to ascend to the roof stretched out. Once they were level, Lars peered ahead. A skylight glowed from interior illumination. The roof creaked with each of Ozor's steps. Would her feet punch through the metal?

Qivek hopped down and scurried ahead. "To quote you primates, jackpot. I can see the manufactory. A wall of crates separates the back of the warehouse from the loading docks, but there's a gap at the other end."

Ozor leaned forward, forcing Lars to hang on so he didn't slide over her head and onto the skylight. "I see guards. They must have heard us."

"Us? I'm light-footed as a cloud," Qivek countered. "Get ready. I'm going to draw their attention away from the skylight." The Flatar scampered off into the darkness.

"Should I get down?" Lars asked. "If you have a line, I could secure it to something."

The rear pair of eyes ringing Ozor's head focused on Lars. "I'm going to jump to the top of the crates, then to the floor. Hang on tight."

Lars sought something to hook his other foot into. Red sparks popped from the roof, illuminating Qivek using a cutting tool. Voices cried out below and men ran beneath the skylight. Qivek dropped something through the hole he had made and rolled aside. Lars instinctively ducked his head.

Bang!

Lars saw the flash through his eyelids. Men yelled in the building. With one of her sharp fighting legs, Ozor ripped open the skylight. Air rushed past as she dropped through the opening. Lars bounced against her back, knocking the wind out of him.

Lars caught a glimpse of four men covering their eyes and waving rifles. The crates under Ozor's feet shifted, and the world tilted as the spider scrambled for purchase. She slammed into an industrial storage rack on the way down, twisting to keep from crushing Lars between her bulk and the metal frame.

Lars' teeth clacked together from the jarring impact. Thank God he didn't bite his tongue in half or break any teeth. "Was that part of the plan?"

"No. Ow." Ozor's translator conveyed pain. "I sprained a couple of legs. Where's Qivek?"

Men shouted in an Arabic-sounding language, accompanied by gunfire.

"Parsing. Language detected: Turkish," Lars translator announced.

"Where is it? I can't see! Something fell through the roof!"

Lars slid off the Tortantula's back. A jumble of crates blocked his view of the front of the building. "I can't see him, but I suspect he's toward the loading docks."

Crack! A man's voice suddenly cut short. Lars looked toward the end of the crates, where a gap opened. A man with a battle rifle tumbled through and caught site of Ozor.

"Another alien! One of the spiders!" The man sprayed automatic fire.

Lars rolled aside as bullets glanced off Ozor's carapace, struck crates, and sparked off the metal racking. The laser popped halfway out of Ozor's harness, but a crate was blocking it.

Lars peeked over a crate and drew a bead on the shooter. He squeezed the trigger and fired a three-round burst. He'd forgot to check the selector. Two of the bullets sent the gunman slumping against the wall.

"Police! Throw down your guns and surrender!" Lars shouted, creeping toward the gap. Ozor shifted behind him, working to extricate herself from the crates without bring more down. From the sound, the containers were empty.

Crack!

Qivek yelled something unintelligible over the return fire.

Another man poked his head around the end of the crates but ducked back. Had he spotted Lars or had Ozor drawn his attention? The man dove through the gap, his gun blazing. Bullets struck pallets and crates in the racking above Lars.

Lars flipped his selector to single shot. Had the shooter hoped to flush him out by puncturing a container above him? Nothing spilled down, so Lars waited. The gunman leaned out, and Lars put a shot through his shoulder.

Crack!

Something hissed through the air above Lars. It spanged off metal out of sight toward the back of the building.

"Any time you two want to quit taking a nap and help me out!" Qivek sounded in his ear.

Lars remembered the button. "Ozor is hurt. I'm working my way along the crates."

"Get your ass away from the crates, Special Lars!"

Lars dashed down an aisle between the racks as a forklift erupted through the crates. A loud *clang* reverberated through the warehouse as the machine collided with one of the racks. The metal framework wobbled, and Lars feared they'd collapse like dominos.

The driver shook his head and spotted Lars. With an evil grin, he ducked and reversed the forklift, aiming it down Lars' aisle. Lars sought somewhere to squeeze between pallets in the racks on either side of the aisle.

Snap!

A smoking corpse tumbled off the seat of the lift. "Qivek, how many more are on your side?" Ozor asked over the comms.

"Three more hunkered behind some crates ten meters past where the forklift drove through," Qivek replied.

Lars watched the spider climb the pile of crates. Two of her legs on the right side dragged. Once at the top, she swept a crate from the wall. Voices cried out as the crate thudded on the other side. Even empty, the industrial container would weigh a hundred kilograms.

"One left." Gunfire rattled. "Make it two," Qivek said.

Lars jumped on the lift truck. The stench of burnt meat hung in the air. Lars grabbed the joystick and pulled back. The lift whirred backward through the gap, pushing a crate across the concrete floor. It took the gunmen a moment to realize Lars had replaced their compatriot. He spun the wheel and the lift pivoted.

Lars ducked as bullets peppered the forklift.

Crack! Snap!

The gunfire ceased.

"Is that all of them?" Lars asked.

"I think so," Qivek replied, switching the barrel on his pistol.

Ozor spun toward the rear of the warehouse, crates wobbling under her feet. "What's that noise?"

Lars listened. A metal *thud* reverberated on the concrete, as though someone hit the floor with a massive sledgehammer. *Thud. Thud. Thud.*

"Entropy!" Ozor cried before the crates exploded under her.

Shards of plastic filled the air.

Whoosh! A rocket streaked through the smoke and detonated against a loading dock door. The metal door fell in flaming tatters. The trailer parked on the other side flipped into the parking lot. A CASPer emerged from the smoking ruins of the crates.

"Shit!" Lars dove behind the forklift as the mech swept its arm in an arc and the chain gun spat fire. Bullets fanned through the air, tracing a line three meters up across the wall and dock doors.

"Ozor? Where are you?" Qivek yelled.

As the CASPer strode into the open, another followed it. How many had they produced? The second CASPer mounted a heavy laser where the first had a rocket pod. The shoulder-mounted laser tracked across the warehouse before settling on the forklift.

Lars fell flat as the laser whined. *Snap!* The pulse sheared off one of the fork tines, leaving red-hot metal in its wake. The laser whined again as it cycled. Lars popped up and centered his carbine on the clamshell canopy of the war machine. He stroked the other trigger. The rocket streaked across the intervening space and punched through the armored canopy. The CASPer spasmed and pitched face forward. Its limbs clattered on the floor as it flailed, then it fell still.

The other mech turned toward Lars. Bullets sparked off the fork-lift and the concrete floor. Something tore through his right calf; he clenched his teeth from the searing pain.

Thud. Thud. Thud. The CASPer angled for a better shot.

Crack!

The CASPer jerked and staggered back. The chain gun traced a line across the concrete floor in Qivek's direction. Lars poked his head and shoulder around the back of the forklift and fired a three-round burst. The CASPer twisted unsteadily in his direction.

Crack!

Lars couldn't see the machine crash to the floor, but the impact reverberated through the concrete.

Thud. Thud. Thud.

Two more CASPers burst through the wall of crates. Both sprayed their chain guns across the warehouse. Lars peered over the seat of the forklift. One had a rocket launcher, and the other a shoulder-mounted magnetic accelerator cannon. One of the rockets streaked across the warehouse, blowing a hole in the wall.

CRACK!

A flash lit up the loading dock. A hypersonic chunk of metal tore through the hip of the lead CASPer. Its remaining rocket launched as it spun and fell, detonating against the ceiling and taking out half the lights.

The other CASPer lurched toward the forklift. Lars scrambled back as the machine shoved the forklift aside. Three red dots swept across the floor and up the side of the CASPer.

Snap!

The machine jerked.

Crack!

A spark flew from high on the canopy, leaving a tiny hole. The CASPer crumbled, forcing Lars to roll aside to keep from getting crushed.

The warehouse fell silent.

* * *

Senior officers from three different law enforcement agencies tried to lambast Lars over the battle in their jurisdiction. They all froze as Ozor limped up behind him to loom over them. Qivek leaned forward from her back.

"Special Investigator Nilsson acted as a deputized agent of the Peacemaker Guild. Any concerns should be directed to myself or the guild," Ozor stated.

"You primates give Special Lars flak, you'll have a Peacemaker show up in your office," Qivek added. "Meanwhile, you can do your job and investigate who in Binnig cooked up the scheme to defraud Lockerbie Insurance. That's your problem, not ours."

"It falls in your jurisdiction," Lars remarked to the Human officers. "If you want to read my report, it will be available through Interpol."

Lars hobbled toward the rumbler, leaning on Ozor for support. The generic medical nanites had stopped the bleeding, but his leg still burned.

"That was fun, *ja*?" Jost called from the cab. "I hoped I'd get to try the 'surprise!'"

"You could have mentioned this heap had a pop-up magnetic cannon," Lars remarked as he slumped into a seat. "Are you good to drive back to the Magdeburg Starport?"

"A cup of coffee and a bite to eat, and I'll be good!" Jost set the vehicle in motion.

Qivek hopped onto the next seat. "Too bad you're too old to be a Peacemaker."

"Yes, too bad. I could get shot up more." Lars knew he was three decades too old. Only prime specimens qualified for the academy, and Lars was well past his prime.

"People besides Peacemakers work for the guild," Ozor stated. "Once the guild rebuilds the consulate, they will need liaisons and investigators."

"Think about it, Special Lars," Qivek said. "The whole planet would be your jurisdiction."

* * * * *

Jon R. Osborne Bio

Jon R. Osborne is a veteran gamemaster and journalism major turned science fiction and fantasy author. The second book in the Jon's the Milesian Accords modern fantasy trilogy, A Tempered Warrior, was a 2018 Dragon Awards finalist for Best Fantasy Novel. Jon is also a core author in the military science fiction Four Horseman Universe, where he was first published in 2017.

Jon resides in Indianapolis, where he plays role-playing games, writes science fiction and fantasy, and lives the nerd life. You can find out more at jonrosborne.com and at https://www.facebook.com/jonrosborne.

# # # # #

Stars or Bars by Jamie Ibson

"Entropy damn them! Where did that frigate come from?" Captain Grymalkynn of Clan Ihlosi snarled. "We don't have the guns to fight something like that!"

From her sensors console, new crewmember Xandra's hands danced on the screens. "Reverse tracking suggests they lit off in the asteroid belt and cruised in on low or no thrust, Captain. Recommend we jettison the cargo and burn for the gate. We still have a window where we can outrun them."

"That might have worked for a clan as large as Hapthon, girl, but it won't do here. We can't afford to lose this cargo. Make the run for the gate."

"Aye Captain. The additional mass will reduce our window to less than a minute. *All hands, brace for hard G acceleration in five, four, three...*"

As her timer hit zero, the Pushtal pirate ship *Herald of Blades'* thrusters ignited, and Xandra steadily increased the throttle until her clawed fingers felt like they weighed three times as much as they normally did. She sank back into her cushioned crew seat and gritted her teeth, each breath labored, inhaling and lifting a ribcage that felt like she had an Oogar sitting on it.

Vanneck, the *Herald's* combat systems engineer, grunted with the effort and stabbed a blinking indicator.

"They've launched—drones? No, assault pods," he corrected. "They're overtaking us!"

The Pushtal captain reviewed the plot on the data, with the intercepting tracks, and confirmed the timing of the MinSha assault. Then Grymalkynn activated the shipwide PA.

"All hands, in two hundred seconds, the gravity will return to standard—make ready to repel boarders!"

Three minutes later, Xandra dialed the acceleration down to just one G so the packs of corsairs aboard could armor up and make ready. She slammed her own helmet on, sealed it to her shipsuit, and unclipped her carbine from the rack attached to her station. She looped the single-point sling over her shoulders—and saw stars when a thunderous crash bounced her off the ceiling of the bridge.

Then she was floating.

She hadn't activated her magboots because she'd *had* gravity, or at least the thrust-induced imitation of the same. Her suit grew tight against her black-and-white-striped fur, indicating vacuum, and she wondered how bad the damage was that they'd already lost cabin pressure. Clan Ihlosi spent a *lot* of time in space and had adopted a simple expedient to the problem of being trapped in micro-G without enough inertia to reach a bulkhead. She aimed up at the ceiling and launched a short-range magnetic grapnel. It caught, energized, and reeled her in until her magboots could lock down on the "floor."

Vanneck, on the other hand, was gaping like a fish as his helmet drifted lazily across the bridge. *He'd* been strapped in place, but his helmet had flown free, and without it he'd be dead in seconds. He was a decent sort, despite the company he kept, so Xandra tracked his helmet, and after rolling onto her toes to break the maglock, she launched herself across the cabin. She caught the helmet mid-flight, bent at the waist in a gymnastic pike tuck, and twisted to throw the helmet back to the weapons officer. She extended her legs beneath her just in time to absorb the impact, and her boots clamped onto the rear wall of the bridge. Vanneck caught the helmet and locked it in place, and gratefully began breathing atmo again.

It took a few moments for him to catch his breath, and his ragged voice breathed a sigh of thanks over her communicator. "What *was* that?" she replied. "That was a helluva bang for assault pods."

"They hit us with some kind of spinal laser," Vanneck read off his sensors. "Engines offline. Shields, offline. Power is intermittent, and the assault pods will hit us in"—he checked his board again—"thirty seconds."

"Damn them," Grymalkynn snarled from his own station. "They've vented all the fresh out into space, too. The laser slashed through all six pods of protein, and now it's all ruined. Not to mention we just lost anyone not already suited up."

Xandra felt more shudders through the soles of her boots, and launched herself back to her workstation, reading the displays while upside down hanging off the ceiling of the bridge. "MinSha naval infantry ingressing mid-hull, frame six; frame nine; frame ten…"

The power to the bridge died a moment later, plunging them into absolute black. One by one, the three bridge crew ignited their helmet lamps, and the entire room was bathed in a dead, icy gleam as sublimated frost reflected on every surface. Captain Grymalkynn cursed yet again. "I can't reach Karrl in the engine room; we have to assume he's dead. Everyone, with me to the barracks. Vanneck and I will partner with Donnell and Eetria to lead the counterattack. If we can take the MinSha troops alive, we use them as barter to escape with our lives."

"I notice my name is conspicuously absent from the thrilling heroics?" Xandra asked with a raised eyebrow.

"You're plan B." Grymalkynn slipped a card, somewhat like a UAAC, on a chain off his wrist and passed it to her. "Make your way aft with Karin and her pack. If we fail—this chip is the captain's override. Overload the power plant, scuttle the ship, and take us all to Vorrha."

She stared at the small card he offered and took it gingerly.

"If you fail to repel the boarders, kill us all," she translated dubiously. "Aye, sir."

At that moment, Ruxandra of Roxtador began to worry that perhaps this particular op had gotten a bit out of hand.

* * *

"Oh, I'm sure she has everything well in hand," Drake said with a touch of snark. "I'm not worried. Why would I be worried? A frigate full of MinSha versus an all-too-small, entirely Pushtal crew? Punch it, Meekos. We're not abandoning her."

The *Dannyn Blythe III*'s Cochkala pilot, Meekos Klo'Rook, poured on the thrust. The bounty hunters had been creeping up on the *Herald* as it flew to the Antaro system's hyperspace gate, but the MinSha frigate *Kryvayla* had been lying in wait as well and had gotten the jump on the *Herald*.

"I still don't see why you're risking your hide for some Pushtal pirate. She played her game, she rolled the dice, and she lost," their newest crewmember commented. Klovelo was a newly deputized Veetanho, and thus far, her attitude was not ingratiating herself with the *Dannyn Blythe III*'s crew. "Cut your losses and run. There'll be more targets."

"She's a deputized bounty hunter," the massive Besquith replied evenly, "with ten times the experience and vastly more contacts than you."

"She's a Pushtal—"

"And she's a member of *my* crew. Right now, you sound more and more like one of my *ex*-crew members—"

"She's a spy and a pirate!"

"—and if you keep that shit up, you're going to find yourself on the wrong side of the airlock." Drake lifted the smaller, rat-like being out of her gunner's chair and held her aloft, muzzle to whiskered muzzle. "No one would ever know."

"You...you wouldn't dare!"

Rylak laughed from his intel station. "We dare, all right. Strap your Veetanho butt down in your gunner's seat and shut your yap. Your job is to run the weapons board, not have opinions. Do you know the story of Godonii Two?"

"Of course, *everyone* knows that one. That Oogar Enforcer who fought off an army of GenSha for days." Klovelo replied, but was confused by the seemingly random question. "That was nine or ten years ago, wasn't it?"

"Yes. *That Oogar Enforcer* deputized Ruxandra personally. Since she joined the crew, we've become the guild's number one pirate-hunter team. *You*, little rat, are our gunner, and no one would blink an eye if you were killed in action. In five or six or nine years, *if* you survive that long, you might have an opinion worth sharing. Now shut up, strap in, and fire up your point defense systems, because it's about to get interesting."

* * *

"Maybe on our next ship, we should invest in some kind of point defense," Vanneck grunted. "Something that could pick off the occasional incoming assault pod? I'd much prefer the interior *not* be a target-rich environment."

Most of the MinSha assault pods had struck the *Herald* amidships, delivering their forces in a fairly concentrated area. The Pushtal, however, were on home turf and knew how to best move from compartment to compartment. Vanneck, Xandra, Packmaster Karin, and a dozen more packmates had flown down one such access conduit in zero-G and emerged aft of the intruders. Captain Grymalkynn, Packmaster Donnell, and another dozen of the crew blocked their access to the bridge. The engineering defense team hadn't exposed themselves yet, but it was time.

"Donnell, Xandra. On three, two…"

The bridge defense team tucked back behind cover simultaneously. Xandra, Vanneck, and six more Pushtal leaned out from two sides of the aft corridor. They took advantage of the micro-G with four on the ceiling and the others on the floor. All eight opened fire at the same time. With the MinSha mostly looking the wrong direction, several of their shots hit and punctured O2 tanks, which began venting their pressurized contents. The corridor became a mass of confused alien limbs and laser bolts as the *Herald*'s crew poured fire into the intruders, then retreated back behind the corners. Captain Grymalkynn's team resumed *their* attack and kept the MinSha off balance.

Tricks like that only worked once, and after they were behind cover, Vanneck gestured to the rear of the ship.

"You've got orders, Xandra, get moving. See you in Vorrha, if not before."

She waved the weapons officer farewell, and Packmaster Karin rounded up her pack and sent them bounding ahead, soaring down the corridor in a leapfrog pattern that always left at least two covering their advance. Karin and Xandra stayed in the middle, moving steadily as Karin's troops moved in a dizzying pattern, always leaving someone to watch their rear, never staying static. Xandra was impressed yet again—Skipistal had never been one for such foolish things as "tactics;" he'd trusted drugs and savagery to carry the battle, which was one of *many* reasons she'd been happy to see a change in leadership for Roxtador.

Klaar, a young male and Karin's lead packmate, reached the hatch that would let them access the living quarters spread over the next six levels. When he threw it open, laser fire from below met him, and he sailed away, bonelessly twitching. Xandra caught a glimpse through his visor as he drifted past, and swallowed hard against nausea, given the chunky mess contained within. Karin and two more of her packmates pulled flashbangs off their harnesses. On cue, they pitched all three through the open hatch. The concussive bang didn't propagate, but blinding light lit the compartment through the hatch, and then the Pushtal pack was swimming through.

* * *

"Does Assault Commander Ricktt have an update?" Commander Dyrkayl, XO of the MinSha ship *Kryvayla*, asked. She was visibly nervous, and that made the rest of her bridge crew nervous. Selected more for her accounting acumen than warrior know-how, Dyrkayl was there to ensure the interdiction contract remained profitable. Their captain had a tendency to apply violence first and verify intel second. Dyrkayl was there to gain combat experience as well, but the captain was down with a rather disruptive digestive system imbalance, made worse by days in micro-G stalking the pirates. Rather than watching and learning, circumstances had forced their XO to step into the breach.

"They've encountered...resistance," Communications Lieutenant Wyrne admitted. "It seems the ship was half-full of the damnable pirate scum, who are fighting tooth and claw. Two squads are pinned down and being squeezed between enemy forces, and we've lost communications entirely with the squad they sent to secure their flank."

"Signal their captain again. If they won't stand down, and they killed the away team, we will have no choice but to destroy them utterly," the XO said.

"No response," Wyrne replied after a moment. "No acknowledgment of receipt whatsoever. Much of the ship is without power, our second shot pierced the hull and severed a major power conduit."

"Can we...can we get Lieutenant Klerne to parlay with them? Relay our instructions through the away team?"

"Yes," Wyrne said, then paused with her finger over the comms button. Klerne was her sister, and her status indicator had just gone grey. She sent the away team's status up on the board, already show-ing 30% casualties, including Klerne, and two more went grey before their compound eyes. "Correction. No, we cannot."

Commander Dyrkayl scowled and drummed her fingertips on her console. "Close for boarding; send everyone."

Lieutenant Klirr, their weapons officer, cocked her head curious-ly. "Everyone?"

"*Everyone.*" Dyrkayl hissed.

* * *

"Well, *that* escalated quickly," Rylak said. "The *Kryvayla* just closed the remaining distance between it and the *Herald of Blades* and the MinSha are punching out electromagnetic grapples. I suspect the boarding goes poorly."

"And no indication they've picked us up; excellent. Give them another ten minutes to get fully involved, Meekos, and then pull us alongside the *Kryvayla*. On your toes, Klovelo. If they show any signs of launching, don't wait for instructions, just deal with it."

The little Veetanho turned her gaze back to her displays, ready to pounce if the MinSha launched missiles.

"Can you expand on 'pull us alongside'?" Rylak asked.

"That's *our* prey they've stolen and *our* crewmember onboard." Drake scowled a broad, toothy frown. "We're going to see how much they like it when it happens to *them*."

* * *

"**A**ll packmasters from Grym, sitrep!"

Donnell, Vanneck, and Eetria updated their status, but Ruxandra ignored them; she was busy. She squeezed Bran's shoulder, hard, so he could feel it through his shipsuit, and the first in their stack lobbed a frag grenade through the hatch. The grenade detonated and hot fragments zinged back out the hatch at them. Bran had the good sense to wait a second longer, in case of ricochets, then pushed off, planting on the open doorway itself and diving into the room at full speed. Ruxandra did likewise but launched perpendicular to Bran so they covered both corners of the compartment. Yet another MinSha was just emerging from behind the workbench, where it had ridden out the grenade, and blue globules of alien blood drifted lazily through the vacuum from her injured partner.

Ruxandra opened fire while still soaring through the open compartment, but lacking gravity and a stable platform she only got three rounds on target before the recoil spun her around. The MinSha, however, was anchored to the floor and shrugged off the slow, heavy, ship-safe slugs. It raised its chemical laser and concentrated on the doorway where Packmaster Karin was just emerging. The packmaster shrieked soundlessly and recoiled, clutching her arm. The reaction sent her spinning crazily through the compartment, splashing the bulkheads with red blood of her own, but the longer the MinSha was distracted by her, the more rounds the rest of the pack could put on target. Xandra reached the corner and planted her magboots securely. She leaned into her carbine and dumped a burst into the warrior's head. From the opposite corner, Bran did likewise, and the MinSha's helmet shattered. More blood sprayed, and Xandra fired the last of her magazine into the wounded survivor.

Bran released his carbine on its sling and jumped for Karin. He caught her gently, and their momentum carried them to the ceiling, where he locked his boots in place. The laser carbine had ruined her right forearm just above the wrist, and partially cauterized meat was all that remained. Bran immediately grabbed the shipsuit's built-in tourniquet below her elbow and reefed on it, hard.

"This is going to suck," he said over the pack's open comm channel.

Karin's face was twisted in agony, but she ground out, "I know." She scrunched her eyes shut, and Bran pulled on the tie fitted just below the tourniquet; it sliced through fur, meat, and bone to cleanly amputate the remnants of the limb. He pulled the wreckage of her arm away, and sealed the shipsuit against the stump to preserve oxygen and keep her from freezing in the icy cold of space.

Xandra became aware that Captain Grymalkynn was requesting a status update again, and she activated her comm. "Karin is combat ineffective, but not out. We're at frame thirteen, but the damn bugs keep bumping us, slowing us down."

"Keep...gah, keep moving." Grymalkynn sounded out of breath. "They've practically emptied their ship to keep the pressure on. Maintain regular check-ins. If no one answers—you know what to do."

"Aye, Captain."

An indicator light on her pinplants' visual display illuminated. Very, very few Pushtal could afford pinplants, which was why everyone was using suit communicators, but when that light caught her attention, she had to pause for just a moment to be sure it was real.

"Tell me you have good news," she said over her internal system. "Tell me you're on board."

"This is a good-news, bad-news kinda thing," Drake responded. "The bad news is, you guys are going to have to fight the MinSha for a little while yet. The good news is, if our plan works, they'll be out of your fur and gone really soon."

"If?"

"Well, yeah. We're going to hijack the MinSha ship and demand they retreat, or they all die when you blow the *Herald* to hell." He didn't sound terribly thrilled with the plan and knew how it must have sounded to her.

"*That's your plan?*" she shouted. Bran looked at her strangely—her angry face was clearly visible through her helmet, but who she was shouting at, or what she was saying, he didn't know. She clamped down hard and regained her composure. "Pardon. *That*'s your plan? The *Kryvayla* out-masses us five to one!"

"You're going to have to find a way to hold out," Drake replied. "The *Kryvayla* jumping you blew plans A through G out the airlock. Do you remember back when Hr'ent got Meerawn in that sleeper hold and threatened to knock him out, over and over, until he'd listen to sense?"

"I do," Xandra replied cautiously. Bran pointed impatiently at the door, but she shook her head and gestured for him to wait.

"Rylak's cooked up something that'll act like that sleeper hold; we just have to get onboard. Meekos will have us there in another two minutes."

"I'm not sure we've got two minutes," Ruxandra spat.

"Do what you must; we're on our way," Drake replied and cut the link.

"Who was that?" Bran demanded. "It wasn't on any of our internal channels."

"Help," Xandra replied. "I hope. Let's keep moving. Either it'll matter, or it won't."

* * *

Hard Gs slammed the crew of the *Blythe* against their restraint harnesses, but the armor they wore spread some of the pressure from the straps, reducing the pain. Meekos deftly eased up on the retros at the very last second, allowing them to settle back comfortably into their seats. They threw their restraints free and Drake, Rylak, and Klovelo bounded for the airlock in the belly of their heavily stealthed cutter, while Meekos activated their electromagnetic locks.

The *Blythe III* was several generations newer than the ship they'd used to get around a decade earlier. The new ship had foregone the interface gunbird shuttle and instead packed in electronic counter-measures, passive and active stealth systems, and a more robust power plant to run it all. It wasn't much larger than the *Herald* and was positively dwarfed by the *Kryvayla*. As Humans said, it wasn't the size of the dog in the fight that mattered; it was the size of the fight in the dog. At least, that's what Meekos claimed, and when their Cochkala pilot showed them an image of what a Terran dog looked like, Rylak immediately had that quote etched onto a brass plaque and mounted above his work station.

The trio, armored up and ready for vacuum operations, opened the hatch and climbed down onto the outer hull of the MinSha ship. Klovelo placed a tether, touched an electric charge pack to the cold-weld glue to secure it, and laid out a wedge of chromium thermite bulkhead cutting tape. It was slightly less spectacular than regular thermite, but it was also less likely to shower them with suit-melting sparks. He ignited the tape, which glowed brightly and began melting its way through the hull plating. Drake hauled on the tether cable, prying the wedge free along the molten edges, like cracking a massive tin can. Air from the compartment flashed out under pressure, and then Rylak was down through the hastily cut access, leading with his laser carbine.

Drake followed, and Klovelo entered last. The MinSha lighting onboard was set to a slightly different spectrum, and it left Drake unsettled on the alien craft. The compartment within appeared to be some kind of barracks for the much-larger MinSha, their beds a strange contraption that didn't look the slightest bit comfortable. Airtight hatches prevented the entire ship from decompressing, and Drake had to shoulder the hatch hard to force it open, given the pressure differentials. Once they were through and the hatch slammed shut again, they were back in atmo, but they kept their helmets on nonetheless.

Unlike the *Blythe*, the frigate's command center was deep in the center of the ship, and it was going to take some time to find their way there.

* * *

"**D**yrkayl! By entropy, where are you, you fool?" Captain Blirr roared from her too-empty bridge. She was about to repeat her demand when her XO replied.

"We are pressing the fight against the pirates, Captain! We are gaining ground, but slowly."

"You're on their ship? Where are my crew?"

"Most are here, supplementing our warriors. The Pushtal are tenacious and will not surrender. Their numbers have made—*there! Push, now!*" the XO interrupted herself, and Captain Blirr cursed inwardly.

"Of course they are, what would you do if given a choice between fighting or execution? Get back here! We have intruders on the ship!"

"What? That's impossible. We have the Pushtal contained!"

Blirr's attention was drawn away from the comms console to the hatch to her right. The access irised open, and a trio of armored forms glided in, guns up. Blirr slowly raised her hands and the shortest of the trio swam closer as the larger two covered her. The smallest form, likely a Veetanho judging from the shape of the helmet and her height, handed Blirr a translation pendant and relieved her of her sidearm.

"Can you understand me?" the tallest, asked. He was either an enormous Zuul, or a Besquith, but his face was hidden behind the armored shell of his helmet.

"I understand you," Blirr replied. *Dyrkayl will pay for this.*

"Good." The Veetanho returned to the bridge's primary access and covered the approach while the third, also likely a Zuul, swam to a console, plugged in a small handheld device, and began punching in commands. The tallest lowered his carbine—slightly—and swam closer. "Judging from the rank etched onto your chitin, would you be the captain of this fine vessel?"

"I am, *Pirate*," Blirr spat, and the Besquith laughed.

"Nothing of the sort, but right now you're fucking with plans above your paygrade, so if you could go ahead and recall them, we'll deal with your pirate problem ourselves and be on our way."

Blirr was astounded by the Besquith's audacity and took a moment to gather her composure.

"And if we do not?"

"Then I kill you and see if your next-in-command is more cooperative. Violence speaks louder than words, after all. If that fails, the Pushtal will overload their power plant and detonate their ship. You and your crew and your ship and the pirates all die. We don't, because we have our own ride and will be out of the danger zone before the *Herald* goes critical."

"They wouldn't," Blirr retorted, and the Besquith laughed again.

"Of course they would! They believe in that whole 'Vorrha' afterlife thing, where all the warriors gather to swap war stories while they're waited upon by those they killed in battle. For a small crew of captured pirates to take out an entire MinSha frigate? *Absolutely, they would.* Under other circumstances, I'd be surprised they haven't blown the ship already. Now quit stalling and recall your troops. Get everyone back on board, but no one comes onto the bridge until we're away and gone."

Blirr cursed Dyrkayl and her entire family line. If she hadn't been so rash, there would have been a security element aboard the ship. She cursed the illness that had kept herself confined to quarters while her digestive tract sorted itself out. She cursed the Pushtal, and she cursed the Besquith, who stood in front of her. But Captain Blirr had no death wish, and given the state her idiot XO had left the ship in, she had zero chance of defeating this trio hand-to-hand, unarmed.

* * *

"Commander Dyrkayl, from Blirr. Are you there, Dyrkayl?"

"Yes, Captain. You said something about pirates aboard the *Kryvayla?*"

"Listen to me very carefully, Commander. I am on the bridge of the *Kryvayla,* and I have been captured. My captors demand you and *my* crew return to the ship, at which point I will be released; the pirates' lives for ours. Make it happen, XO. I'm not keen to die this day."

Dyrkayl stared at her communicator and turned to Klirr, who'd taken over for Assault Commander Ricktt when she'd developed a terminal case of decapitation.

"Fall back," Dyrkayl ordered. "Everyone, back to the *Kryvayla,* now."

"But we almost have them!" Klirr protested, and Dyrkayl cuffed the weapons officer on the back of her helmet. "Do not tell the troops, but Captain Blirr has been captured! The pirates somehow snuck their own people on board!"

"What?" Klirr was stunned. *"Captured?"*

"Yes, now do as I've ordered and fall back."

Klirr turned away and began issuing orders to the assault team leaders. They had advanced deep into the Pushtal ship and rounding up everyone in the zero-atmo, zero-G maze of an alien ship was going to be a non-trivial exercise.

* * *

"They're falling back!" Eetria cried over her communicator. "Press them! No mercy!"

Xandra activated her pinplants and pinged

Drake. Bran was looking at her curiously again, but she waved him away.

"The MinSha are retreating. I suppose this is your doing?"

"Good to know. Apparently, capturing their ship's captain got their attention. Let them flee," Drake instructed her. "We'll be along shortly, but we won't leave the captain until you guys are secure."

"You recall, I'm the 'communications officer,' and not their packmaster?" Xandra complained. "I'm going to have trouble convincing the crew to let these murderous scumbags go."

"Pretend your life depends on it," Drake replied with an edge to his voice. "You can be persuasive."

* * *

"**G**rymalkynn, from Xandra."

"Go for Grym," Vanneck replied.

"No screwing around with me, Vanneck, get the Captain on the line, do it now."

"Yeah, we're a bit busy up here, Xandra, we have the MinSha on the run and we're pressing them back."

"No, you don't. They're pulling back because friendlies captured *their* captain. Put Grym on the line so I can explain."

Vanneck frowned. That didn't make sense at all; they didn't have any friendlies in-system, and he would have heard any comms traffic if another Pushtal ship happened to come by, and the odds of that happening were virtually nil. He tapped Captain Grymalkynn on the shoulder and warned him he'd have incoming comms, then Vanneck cut himself out of the channel intercept.

"This is Grym, go."

"Let the MinSha fall back, Captain. It's complicated, but friends have captured *their* captain, still on the ship. They're exchanging her life for ours."

"You'd best start explaining yourself right now, Xandra."

There was a pause, and Grymalkynn brought Vanneck, Eetria, and the other Pack commanders in on the same comms loop. Then Ruxandra's voice returned.

"No time, sir, but I will after. If you kill all the MinSha on board, they will cast off and just blast us out of the stars. You have to let them go because the friendlies have a way to ensure they don't just stand off and blast us. It will only work if you let them retreat."

"And who, *exactly*, are these friendlies who somehow managed to sneak aboard a MinSha frigate and capture their commanding officer?"

"They're a team of bounty hunters from the Peacemaker Guild. *My* bounty hunter team."

Vanneck, Eetria, and the others all began talking over each other, but Grym's command suit had priority override, and he stomped on the conflicting messages and muted them all. Grym looked at his casualty tracker and was furious to see nearly two-thirds of his troops were greyed out or blinking to indicate wounded status. He felt his fur bristle, despite the vacuum suit, and he reopened his channel to his "communications officer."

"Very well, Xandra. But I'll kill you myself if this is some elaborate scam."

"I understand, sir, and no, not a scam. Let the MinSha go. I, and my team, will explain all."

* * *

"**L**ooks like that's all of 'em," Rylak said. His systems worm allowed him to access most of the ship's internal systems. Like most shipboard systems, they were hardened against outside intrusion, but having physical access meant hacking in was far easier. He pulled up a holo of the crew status, and it showed everyone not dead was back on board.

"Good. Activate—what the hell did Meekos call it? *Bucking bronco?*"

"Some ridiculous Human thing, as usual," Rylak turned back to his console, and Drake turned back to the captain.

"All right, here's how this is going to work. My associate is releasing your EM-grapnels and retracting the boarding tube. We'll be leaving the way we came. You've got a barracks compartment open to vacuum, by the way—and you'll want to repair that—and then you're going to lose control of your ship for a bit. Nothing outrageous, but you're going to be locked out of your system for as long as it takes to burn to the emergence point and then loop around back toward Antaro Five. It's all set in your autopilot and there's nothing you can do about it."

"You bastard," Blirr cursed. "You didn't say anything about hijacking the *ship!*"

"You didn't ask. And don't give me that righteous indignation; it would have been a piece of cake to program your precious ship to go for a sun dive instead. Are we ready?"

"Bucking bronco is go," Rylak said and unplugged his interface. "Ten minutes, starting *now.*"

"Best of luck, Captain," Drake said. Klovelo led the way out the bridge—and then every interface terminal on the bridge powered down, leaving Blirr alone in the dark.

* * *

With Drake, Klovelo, and Rylak back aboard the *Blythe*, Meekos detached from where it was riding piggyback and blasted clear. Ten minutes after Rylak activated the program, the thrusters on the *Kryvayla* ignited, and the frigate pulled away in a long, slow arc that would take it all the way back to the emergence point on the far side of Antaro Five, a distance of more than five hundred light seconds that would take three full days to traverse before it returned to the planet itself. There was always a chance, of course, that the MinSha had a savvy engineer on board who could completely cut out the piloting and navigation systems and rewire a new one in its place, but Kreezasch assured him that would still likely take a day and a half to repair.

"Well, that bought us some time. Let's go meet Captain Grymalkynn," Drake ordered, and Meekos guided the *Blythe* over to the still-crippled *Herald of Blades*. With a light touch on the controls, their pilot brought the *Blythe* almost to the same spot where the *Kryvayla* had been just minutes before. They extended their umbilicus, pressurized it, and Drake reached Xandra on her pinplants.

"Can you put us in contact with the captain?"

"He's here," Xandra said. She sounded nervous—and Xandra *never* sounded nervous.

"Permission to come aboard, Captain?" Drake asked. He hated to ask, to be honest, the *Herald of Blades* was crippled, and the *Blythe* had her at her mercy. But considering Xandra had been outed as an infiltrator, it was probably best to be polite...ish.

"Permission granted, *bounty hunter.*" He sounded *miffed.*

"Meekos, Kreezasch, with me. They're probably going to need some flight and engineering expertise."

* * *

On the far end of the tube, Drake swam aboard. The interior bulkheads were scorched by laser fire, and fragments of slugs and divots of steel carved from the walls drifted lazily across the open space. Blue MinSha blood and other, less identifiable parts, had been liberally sprayed across the interior surfaces, and in some places the blue mixed with red. In the center of the carnage and blood, half a dozen Pushtal in armored shipsuits waited for them. The largest of them wore glossy black armor, although it was currently stippled with blue *and* red blood. One of the Pushtal was missing her arm below the elbow, and the seventh Pushtal, who could only be Ruxandra, knelt in front of them, her hands bound behind her. Drake offered them a communicator and they quickly linked their nets together.

"Funny way to show your gratitude," Drake remarked. "She saves your lives and you tie her up?"

"This...*traitor* lied to us from the beginning. She's been our crewmate for *months!*"

"Well...yeah," Drake replied. "Her reports to us are essential in sussing out whether a clan...fits. Some—maybe even *most*—of the minor clans are beyond recruitment and are savage, murderous scum. But you run a tight ship, First Claw. You're picky about your targets; you use tactics and strategies that minimize casualties for *everyone.*

That's *important*; we know how fucked up some clans can be. Roxta-dor was an utter disaster under Ruxandra's old First. Regardless, if she'd come out and said, 'hey, I'm a bounty hunter, and we'd like to recruit you and your clan,' you'd have told us to fuck right off."

"I think we're at that point already, Besquith," Grymalkynn snarled. "Give me one good reason not to blast you and her and your crew right now?"

"Aside from signing your own death warrants? Don't you typical-ly prefer to go out in combat? How's that going to work for you if my ship just *left*? Do you have enough atmo in those suits to get your engines functional again?"

The captain exchanged a glance with the Pushtal to his right, and the second shook his head. Drake barked a laugh, and the captain came back on.

"You said, 'recruit you and your clan.' Tell me more."

"Not until my crewmate is on her feet standing next to me, Cap-tain Grymalkynn. I already got the MinSha off your back, and I'm a little insulted that Ruxandra is on your shit list for saving your lives. Let her up so she can come back with me to my ship, and we can speak to each other face to face. My associates will remain here to help your crew assess the damage and see if they can get the *Herald* spaceworthy again. Consider them hostages to guarantee your own safety if it makes you feel any better."

The Pushtal captain seemed to consider the suggestion and nod-ded to the same subordinate to his right. That Pushtal helped Ruxandra back to her feet and untied her hands. Without further delay, Drake, Ruxandra, Grymalkynn, and another Pushtal swam back down the tube to the *Blythe*'s airlock.

* * *

The *Blythe* had a decent operations planning room. Drake led the other three into the ops room and offered them chairs. The fourth Pushtal, whom Ruxandra identified as Vanneck, the combat systems engineer, preferred to stand. Drake didn't beat around the bush.

"First, you should know the MinSha frigate was a surprise to us as well, one of those random, unlucky things. We had planned to meet you by the gate and have this conversation under far better circumstances. Having said that, we can't do anything about that now. I assume you two are aware the Pushtal have a Fangmaster establishing a government for all Pushtal on Draxis?"

Vanneck laughed, a sharp, derisive sneer, and Grymalkynn's eyes narrowed.

"Yes, the child. Magnus, whose bloodline was so weak his father renounced the title not an hour after receiving it. I know of them."

"I hardly think Meerawn *weak*," Drake replied easily. "It takes cold courage to acknowledge one isn't suited for the task at hand. Especially after one has just had their ass kicked by an Oogar in hand-to-hand combat."

"What do you know of such things," Vanneck snarled.

"I was *there*," Drake replied and nodded to Ruxandra. "As was she. She was slated to be Regent of Roxtador until Magnus received the title. This isn't my first pitch, and you're not the first Claw who didn't believe me right off the bat."

Grymalkynn's eyes narrowed tightly, a snarl of disbelief crinkling his nose. Drake shrugged and pulled up a 2D video recorded, apparently, from someone's helmet camera. On-screen, a young white-and-black striped Pushtal argued with an enormous purple Oogar in combat armor. Although he hadn't been there in eighty-five years,

Grymalkynn recognized the House of Claws, the Pushtal ceremonial seat of power since the fall of Vorrhurna. The Oogar and Meerawn of Arwoon argued and then fought in vicious hand-to-hand combat until the Oogar caught Meerawn in a rear-naked choke hold. The Fangmaster lost consciousness. He came to a few seconds later, and Grymalkynn shook his head.

"See? He lost. His first challenge as a Fangmaster and he lost. He's weak."

"Keep watching."

A few short minutes later, Grymalkynn watched Meerawn resign, and the remaining major clans back young Magnus. It was not at all how it had been described to him. It was a matter of honor and courage, not weakness and cowardice. Farnon, of Clan Grotha, had been at the Moot, too; he had been Grymalkynn's source on how the whole mess went down. Farnon had *not* been in favor of Meerawn or Magnus as Fangmaster. The old bastard had gone to his grave believing it should have been his. The *new* First Claw of Grotha was rather more in favor of the Fangmaster cub.

"Interesting," was all he could say.

"So here's the pitch," Drake said. "Magnus, the Fangmaster, believes the Pushtal are stronger when they work together. Roxtador and Arwoon, two of the largest Pushtal clans, are practically one and the same, now. With Magnus' mother as Hr'ent's Regent for Roxtador and Magnus' father as First Claw of Arwoon, it was inevitable. Oronhaia and Azrigaez back them, and those four Clans together represent seventy percent of the Pushtal living on Draxis."

"I have yet to hear 'the pitch,' bounty hunter."

Ruxandra spoke now. "So long as you and yours keep up the piracy, you're going to wind up in prison or dead. The Fangmaster and the Council want the smaller Clans to come to Draxis, to come *home*. Are we going to be mercenaries again? Certainly not, the MinSha and the Veetanho will see to that. But there are other trades, other skills, other needs. We have a need for skilled pilots, skilled crews, and skilled marines to guard our ships as Draxis expands its industry off-world. Come in from the cold, Grym, and make Draxis home again."

Grymalkynn pondered for a moment, and the massive Besquith changed the viewscreen from the helmet-cam to a still of the *Herald* as the *Blythe* had seen it. The scars on her hull were terrible, and whole chunks of the drives were gone.

Ruxandra spoke again.

"That's the pitch, First Claw of Ihlosi. Stop killing innocents who don't deserve it and keep flying, or rot in jail. The *Herald of Blades* is almost certainly ruined scrap. If we *hadn't* been here, if I *hadn't* infiltrated your crew, you'd be dead right now. Your cargotainers of food were destroyed when the MinSha attacked; your people will go hungry. *Again*. The Fangmaster may be a child, but he's of my Clan—we understand what it is to be hungry. Skipistal believed in three things: combat drugs, opiates, and sex. We were hungry, *constantly*. There was always enough Venom to go around, but never enough *meat*. Say the word, and we'll have an entire wing from Draxis meet us at whatever rock Ihlosi has been hiding on with enough food to tide everyone over. We will lift the whole clan and transport them to their new home. Draxis has vast wilds that need taming, and you can make it your own. The Fangmaster will provide food, skilled trainers, and dirt to call your own. No one will be hunting you. No more dead packmates and crippled veterans."

"What'll it be, First Claw? Stars? Or bars?" asked Drake.

Grymalkynn looked at the red and blue blood splattered on his armor and thought of his packmaster, Karin, now missing an arm. He looked a question at Vanneck, who was transfixed by the image of the ruined *Herald of Blades* and saw him nodding.

"We choose the stars."

* * * * *

Jamie Ibson Bio

Jamie Ibson is a new writer from the frozen wastelands of Canuckistan, where moose, bears, and geese battle for domination among the hockey rinks, igloos, and Tim Horton's. After joining the Canadian army reserves in high school, he spent half of 2001 in Bosnia as a peacekeeper and came home shortly after 9/11 with a deep sense of foreboding. After graduating college, he landed a job in law enforcement and has been posted to the left coast since 2007. He published a number of short stories in 2018 and 2019, and his first novel came out in January 2020. He's pretty much been making it up as he goes along, although he has numerous writer friends who serve as excellent role models, mentors, and, occasionally, cautionary tales. His website can be found at ibsonwrites.ca. He is married to the lovely Michelle, and they have cats.

# # # # #

A Natural Selection by Kevin Ikenberry & Peter J. Aldin

Langwarrin

Tossen's Bar resembled any other mercenary bar across the Galactic Union. The establishment of ill-repute featured cheap drinks, exotic dancers from a diverse range of species, and the quiet, dark recessed tables where mercenaries sealed the deadliest contracts. At one such table, with a clear view of both the U-shaped bar and the front and rear entrances, a Sidar hunched over a glass of whiskey and resisted the urge to check his slate for fear of missing a cue. A Tri-V above the bar displayed two teams of Oogar trying to move a ball of some sort. The game was violent and brutal. He sighed and looked toward the front entrance as a massive shadow moved from the well-lit passageway into the cavernous bar.

The Sidar watched the shadow resolve into an Oogar once the entrance closed and the dim light of the bar illuminated him better. Over his broad shoulders hung a black combat vest. There was a massive pistol strapped to each of his muscular legs. Atop his head was a set of dirty goggles that had seen better days. The volume of the few conversations around the mostly-vacant bar dipped perceptibly. Without looking around, the purple-furred Oogar moved confidently around the bar in the Sidar's direction. With uncanny grace, he slid into the opposite seat.

"Nice of you to join me," the Oogar said.

The Sidar nodded and pointed to a glass on the table that matched his own. "I ordered you a bourbon."

"As long as it's not Jack Daniels." The Oogar reached for the glass and sniffed. "Good. I won't have to hurt you this time."

The Sidar laughed and shook his head as they sipped their drinks. A party of three Besquith entered the bar, laughing at some joke one of them had told. Soon, Tossen's Bar would fill as mercenaries between jobs finished their daily labors.

"You're certain this Human will be here? This doesn't seem like the place a Human mercenary company would frequent."

"The pursuit of credits is quite persuasive, especially for commanders existing in a constant state of near bankruptcy. I have seen a great deal of this, and while it is not entirely a Human problem, their weaker commanders are exceptionally prone to frivolous expenditures at the cost of their soldiers. Given the promise I have arranged for them, they will be here."

"You've *promised* them something?" The Sidar reached for his amber-colored liquid and swirled the glass slightly. "Please tell me you haven't insinuated that our—"

"I have not," the Oogar rumbled. "Unlike you, I prefer that my duplicities happen through the machinations of others and not through what I reveal or compartmentalize. A less direct route often pays the most dividends."

The Sidar chuckled. "Point taken."

"They transitioned into the system sixteen hours ago and requested docking services. I expect the *Trigger Happy* to dock in less than an hour, at Dock 94, about two hundred meters from here. My contact will arrive soon to meet the Human company commander. From there, we'll watch and see what happens."

After a moment of silence, the Sidar shuffled in its seat. "I can surmise the Human you want me to interview is not the mercenary company commander?"

"That's correct." The Oogar grinned.

"Someone on his payroll?"

"You really can't handle not knowing all the details, Hak?" The Oogar rumbled a laugh like the echoes of a distant thunderstorm. "Your potential candidate is the company commander's wife. For at least the next few hours."

Selector Hak-Chet of the Peacemaker Guild cradled his glass of bourbon and took a deep sip. He turned to the Oogar and spoke softly. "You've piqued my curiosity, Golramm. I hope you know what you're doing."

Enforcer Hr'ent Golramm, unrecognizable in his attire and head-gear, smiled and nodded. "I learned subterfuge from one of the all-time greats."

"You're too kind." Hak-Chet laughed. "Asshole."

"I'll take that as a compliment." Hr'ent smiled. "Now, we wait. But I don't think we'll have to wait very long."

"I hope you're right. About the Human, that is."

Hr'ent said nothing in return, instead smiling at his old friend before returning his gaze to the patrons entering Tossen's Bar. There was much a Peacemaker could learn by observation. Knowledge, after all, was power.

* * *

Langwarrin Mercenary Guild Complex
Rooftop

Langwarrin Starport wasn't a place Zuul merc commander Ren Hahnu would have chosen for a meeting like this.

She stood upright and at ease to the side of the Mercenary Guild building's rooftop, away from the shuttle landing pads and close by the elevator doors. Bitter thoughts chased each other around her mind. In her opinion, Hahnu's Hellchasers was the finest Zuul merc company there was. The members had served their employer well in her father's day; they had served him and his business very well in her day. They should be off executing a new and exciting contract in a more lucrative region, not idling around some stinking backwater with their tongues hanging out.

But—she sighed and wrestled her churning emotions into submission—*we do what we must for payment.*

Hanhu kept her hind feet firmly planted. She'd crossed her front legs over her suit's belly plating, one paw lightly grasping the other. No fidgeting. With eleven of her brightest and most trusted fighters lined up behind her, it paid to fake calm, to project confidence.

Of course, there was another reason she needed calm, needed to maintain discipline with her thoughts and words and actions.

Elder Razzik is coming, and if I want him to finally pay us, then I'd better find a way to balance pride with diplomacy. Best not to bite the hand that feeds.

Elder Razzik. Hahnu had never met her company's owner personally. Razzik was a busy person, the President of DeepRetrieve Scout-and-Collect, a Zuul F11 survey-mining concern and a Wathayat subsidiary. When it came to his mercs, he preferred communicating through intermediaries and subordinates. But her father, the Zuul who'd established the Hellchasers, *had* met the Elder, and more than once. He'd described Razzik as a tough and wily alpha, a male with an appetite for profit and a disdain for the lives it might cost to gain that profit. Any such business ruthlessness was perfectly acceptable in Hahnu's opinion: Elder Razzik's track record as a pay-on-time-and-pay-in-full kind of Zuul made it acceptable.

Of course, her father's last dealing with the Elder had been a full decade ago, before he'd resigned and transitioned to life as a contract broker. Perhaps Razzik had softened in the intervening years.

Which might account for the fact we haven't been paid for the last two bone-rotted contracts!

The thought—no, the insult, the dishonor!—set Hahnu's pulse racing, her nostrils flaring, her jaw opening wider to allow her breath to come in shorter and shorter pants.

Calm. I must be calm.

She took a long slow breath. Held it. Released it. Her blades and sidearm might be holstered—this was only a business meeting with her boss, after all—but it was nevertheless a battle of sorts. Her primary objective in that battle must be kept clear: get the wages and operational expenses owed to her and her company.

There was a secondary objective, of course, and one that was equally important: find out what the problem was with cash flow…and whether or not the Hellchasers needed to resign and look for a new owner. Money, after all, was everything.

Razzik's personal shuttle had landed a full five minutes ago, twenty meters from where she and her mercs waited. The sleek bullet-shaped craft sat there *ticking* and *tocking* as its skin and engines cooled, and there'd been no sign until now of anyone coming out. Presumably, Razzik was attending to personal business, and he would come out when he was good and ready.

Well, I'm *hell-damned good and ready,* she thought. *I was good and ready a week ago.*

As she thought it, something chimed from above the shuttle's hatch. A loud hiss signaled the seal releasing. The hatch came away, unfolding into a ramp.

Time for the main event, Hahnu thought, straightening.

Another chime announced the ramp was secure. A moment later, Elder Razzik exited down the ramp toward her.

Hahnu's jaw snapped shut in surprise. She had expected a stately male, a Zuul with height and powerful jaws and lively eyes. She had expected him to have an armed escort in keeping with his prestige. Her expectations couldn't have been more wrong.

Razzik had no bodyguard.

And he was far from stately and lively.

The President of DeepRetrieve Scout-and-Collect was about as infirm an individual as she had ever seen. He crossed the rooftop via motorized chair, a conveyance of the disabled. He had hind legs, but they were folded and angled aside, as if no longer serving any purpose or importance. Razzik's official images depicted the Elder's fur as a lively brown, streaked with patches of space-black. Well, it may have been a decade ago, but now his coloring had faded—no, she corrected herself, it was *depleted*. It was not so much gray as it was colorless. Her troopers stirred again at her back, evidence they were as unsettled by the sight as she was.

"Commander Hahnu," Razzik said, his voice a raspy echo of the one she'd heard in recordings.

"An honor to finally meet you," Hahnu replied with a grace she didn't feel.

"Where are the rest of your company?"

You're lucky they haven't already left us weeks ago, old Zuul, she thought.

She said, "Two are in the bar across the street." *Spending credits they don't have.* "The rest are in orbit." *On a ship that currently has barely enough fuel to make it from here to anywhere else worth flying.* She gestured behind her. "These are my most trusted mercs." *The ones who'll follow me anywhere, trust me always. The ones who'll tear you to pieces if you don't pay them today.*

Razzik coughed weakly. One of his forepaws dabbed at the spittle below his jaw. "I've always heard great things about you, Ren Hahnu. I've enjoyed reading your reports. I wish we were meeting under better circumstances. And I wish I had better news. You and your troops—your fine, fine troops," he added with a prolonged look of admiration directed at them, "you came here expecting payment. And payment you deserve. You certainly do. But I have three pieces of news for you, the first two unpleasant, and the last perhaps reassuring…in its way."

Hahnu's composure began to slip at Razzik's blunt manner. "Tell me," she said, then gestured to her mercs. "Tell *us*."

"First," he told the assembled mercs in his dry, unsteady voice, "there is no money. Not enough to pay you all, at least. DeepRetrieve Scout-and-Collect finds itself in deep, deep trouble financially. And so, therefore, do I."

Disgust rippled through the Zuul ranks. One of them—her best warrant officer—muttered a string of expletives in different languages. Under the circumstances, Hahnu let the lapse in discipline slide.

"Second," Razzik continued as if he hadn't noticed the rise in tensions, "the cause of our sudden financial devastation is, sadly, my other merc company."

Hahnu knew about the Hellchasers' counterparts. She had always understood DeepRetrieve's need for two companies. They had even cooperated once on a contract on Degardo. The Maulers were limptails and idiots—that was for sure—but...thieves?

When Razzik took a shuddering breath, Hahnu interrupted. "The Maulers? The Maulers stole DeepRetrieve's assets?"

Razzik's ears folded back in a gesture of despair. "Sadly, yes. They hacked the server containing 71% of our liquid assets. Then split them with their owner."

"Their...?" Hahnu put a paw to her muzzle, felt her breath coming out hot and hard. "But you are their owner."

Razzik met her gaze fully for the first time. "Not their only owner, apparently. They betrayed me, Hahnu. They betrayed all of us."

Something more dangerous than mere disgust now rippled through the Zuul ranks. The positions of each of her people were clearly marked in her mind and Hahnu took a step sideways, out of all the possible firing lines.

"You mentioned a piece of 'reassuring' news, Elder Razzik?"

It had better be very reassuring.

"This is a travesty!" Razzik barked, and for a moment his voice showed an inkling of the command it must have carried in his prime. "Shameful! But here is 'the good news,' as the Humans like to say. The Maulers are close by. Those fiend-hounds are here. On Langwarrin."

There had been the beginnings of murmurs and growls from the other Zuul, but all sound ceased now, except for the hum of an air taxi passing overhead and the sighing of the wind through rooftop fixtures. As one, the group held their breath at this new information.

Razzik's lips peeled back from his yellowed teeth as he hissed, "I summoned the Maulers here on a pretense, but in reality to confront them. And to get back the money that will finally pay you Hellchasers your due wages."

Hahnu had worked hard to keep calm, to keep her blue blood cool. But she could feel it boiling now.

Calm be damned, she thought.

"Where are they?" she growled.

* * *

Trigger Happy

Approaching Langwarrin Starport

"Langwarrin, *Trigger Happy* on final approach for Pad 94. Thanks for the great transfer clearance. As smooth as ever." Marc Lemieux released the radio transmit button and rolled his eyes at his wife, Jessica. "Gods, I hate buttering up the natives."

His wife of almost three years frowned. Sitting at the executive officer's station, the redhead tapped her slate and looked up. "Buttering up the natives, as you say, gets us a reduced transfer rate and docking fee. The last time I checked, we don't have that much liquid credit to operate with and saving whatever we can on fees and stupid charges is critical, Marc."

"Lighten up, Jess." He smiled and raked a hand through his thick, dark hair. "Once I negotiate a nice fee for us on this next mission, how about we rent a suite for a couple of days while we rest and refit? I know the team needs a break, and you're always bitching at me about needing quality time in the sack."

Her frown deepened. "Whatever fee you negotiate won't hit our accounts until after the next mission is over. See my earlier comment. The last thing we need is a couple of nights in an exorbitant suite, Hammer."

His callsign, earned from an old movie and his occasional ineptitude, erased the smile from his face. Jessica never used it unless she was trying to make a point. The Marauders were a reasonably capable mercenary company—one of only a few dozen Human companies that could make such a claim. While much of the longtime success of the company, and the reputation the present leadership traded upon, had been built by Lemieux's father, a substantial portion of the operating funds came from Jessica's trust. Her father, James Francis, had disappeared when Jessica was a child, yet his company, Intergalactic Haulers, remained one of the most reliable and profitable long-distance freight companies in the Union. As such, he'd built up a tremendous amount of wealth that Jessica was reluctant to spend on company matters.

"We could use your yack for it." He grinned at her and tried to waggle his eyebrows.

Jessica didn't respond for a moment and when she did, her words were not for him. "Lucille? Disengage autopilot. I have the spacecraft."

<<You have the spacecraft, Jessica,>> the onboard computer replied.

Lucille was equals parts navigator, communicator, and engineer. She'd belonged to Jessica's father a long time ago and whoever had programmed her had done Marc Lemieux many favors. She was worth five or six crew members alone, and that capability also saved them a tremendous amount of credits.

"*Trigger Happy*, this is *Victory Twelve*," a female voice called over the unit's private frequency. "On final for Pad Bravo at the Mercenary Guild headquarters. They had an open slot and a lower-than-normal fee."

"Copy, *Twelve*, nice work," Jessica replied without taking her eyes from the controls. "Put her down and rendezvous with me at Pad 94. *Trigger Happy*, out."

Lemieux didn't bother watching the final approach and docking sequence. Since he trusted Jessica's piloting skills, his thoughts turned to the meeting scheduled for Tossen's Bar in an hour's time. The proposed mission was almost a "milk run" —an unchallenging walk around the galaxy in pursuit of a missing socialite. If successful, the payment would place the Marauders' main accounts firmly in the black and allow them to pay off the creditors for the most recent upgrades to his company of tanks. He knew they would succeed.

There was a quick tap of maneuvering thrusters and the soft but distinct *thump* of the ship against the main and secondary docking collars. The *Trigger Happy* was the largest of the Marauders' vessels, capable of carrying a full complement, a company of CASPers supported by six armored tanks. Along with two drop ships, there was a third hard point designed to ferry smaller ships for additional credits. On this mission, they'd taken along the ship left to Jessica by her father, the *Victory Twelve*.

"Contact. Pressurizing docking collars," Jessica said. As gravity returned, she paused for a moment. Lemieux felt his own equilibrium adjusting. He closed his eyes and let the sensation pass as Jessica resumed speaking. "Lucille, notify the crew. Fueling and rearming are the priority, and no one gets paid or authorized for liberty until they're complete."

<<Acknowledged.>>

Lemieux snorted. "They're good people, Jess. You don't have to remind them how to do their jobs every time we reach port."

"Even good people require good leadership, Marc. While I trust them implicitly, our job is to make sure they understand expectations and standards."

She pulled her auburn hair out of the ponytail it had been in and let it drape over her shoulders. Lemieux caught himself staring.

"You really are beautiful, Jess."

"Don't change the subject, okay?" She smiled, but it seemed to stop short of her eyes. Where there had been mirth and joy only a few years before, there was now a resigned sadness. "Good luck with the proposal. I'll meet you at the bar after I've released the crew for liberty. I'm allowing thirty-six hours. That should be enough time to have the *Victory Twelve*'s shunts inspected."

Lemieux nodded, his mind already drifting. The promise of a brisk walk, a real bathroom, and a long-needed drink propelled him. He unbuckled from the commander's console, grabbed his slate and a khaki shoulder bag, and pulled himself up to stand. "How long do we have in port?"

He'd taken two steps toward the hatch before realizing Jessica hadn't responded. He turned and saw her staring at him. She'd been talking, and he hadn't heard her. Again.

"I said I'm authorizing thirty-six hours," Jessica repeated in a clipped monotone. "I'm planning on meeting you in the bar, or did you not hear that either?"

Lemieux's face flushed in embarrassment. He took a deep breath and let it out as a sigh. "I didn't hear that, either. Look, this meeting is a huge payday for us. All I have to do is sell our ability to make it happen. We've got good intelligence and a damned fine team. We just need better-paying missions and this is a great step in that direction. I'm sorry, Jessica. My mind's on that, right now."

"Then go take care of it, Marc."

He squinted at her. "What is it? What aren't you saying?"

She shook her head. "I'm not as confident as you are in our ability to pull this prospective mission off. We're a combat unit. A missing person? Really? I don't give a damn how many media followers she has or anything like that. Finding her isn't something we should waste our time doing, no matter what the pay is. We need a win, Marc. Badly."

"And I'm trying to get us one!" His temper flared, and he pointed at her with one finger. "This whole setup is to get us a win and get us back on our feet. Not completing the mission at the Riff damned near bankrupted us, but we've been able to claw back to this point. One mission. One easy fucking mission gets us back over the top and into the better pools for contracts, Jessica. Let me do my job as the commander of this company. Secure the ship, see to our stores, and release the crew for liberty."

"That's my plan," she deadpanned.

"You never said yes to the suite." He smiled at her. "Interested?"

Jessica rolled her eyes. "I'll meet you at Tossen's in a couple of hours. Don't do anything stupid."

"Who me?" Lemieux laughed and pushed through the bridge hatch. Once through the open docking collars he could smell the fresher air of the station, and it called to him with the promise of easy credits, cold drinks, and the thrill of the hunt.

* * *

Langwarrin Mercenary Guild Building

Ground Level

Each one of the guild building's five floors held a small lounge area. The company commander of Razzik's Maulers, Marrek Rooss, had waited in the ground level lounge for many reasons. It was closest to street access in case he needed the extra squad he'd hidden in a mobile supply container outside. There were several windows here he could use in case of emergency. And its carpet was the most recently replaced, and the least mildewy. But the room stank like a urinal.

Not a great place to be doing this, he thought. *I'd rather be out in the open, with snipers in the hills covering me.*

A glass wall streaked with dust-smears and finger marks separated the lounge from the corridor outside. The room held fifteen hard-plastic chairs, half of them big enough to seat an Oogar, half small enough for Veetanho. Rooss's seven mercs squirmed in the larger ones.

"Langwarrin Starport," grumbled Araagah, Rooss's senior lieutenant, as he oiled his knife. "This whole place is a stinking shithole."

"You said that ten minutes ago," Rooss told him.

"And ten minutes before that," another Mauler added with a chuckle.

"Still true," Araagah muttered.

"For the last time," Rooss said, "Elder Razzik's secretary told us this was the Hellchasers' destination, so this is where we need to be. If you want to get paid, that is."

Araagah's grumble was quieter this time as he bent his head over his blade. "'Course I do."

Rooss leaned in closer, lowering his voice so the others wouldn't hear. "Put your knife away, Ara. I understand your need to keep busy—we're all on the edge of our nerves. But we can't afford blood-letting. Not here in a guild building. Not over this."

Araagah slid the blade into a vest sheath. His reply came back just as low. "You'd like to, though. Wouldn't you, sir? Start shedding some blood? Some Hellchaser blood?"

"Oh, I'd love to paint these walls a bright Zuul blue. Absolutely, I would. But dead Chasers can't give that money back, can they? And the whole point is to get paid."

Rooss stood then and arched his back. Where was the usual multiple-species adjustable seating?

These shit-stinking seats. They're all made for giants or small fry, not for Zuul. Not for us! The administrators of this bowel-stank building deserve a shot in the face. Even better, they should have their guts pulled out through their asses and strung up on…

A sound from the foyer drove the murderous fantasy from Rooss's mind. An elevator chimed. He squinted, crossing the floor to the glass wall. The others rose, too. Yes, he could see the indicator counting down.

"Finally," muttered his best close-quarters fighter from behind him. Rooss flashed her a sharp-toothed grin of agreement.

"Think it's them?" Araagah asked.

A sideways glance at his lieutenant showed that the idiot had one paw on his sidearm. Rooss gestured impatiently for him to leave it alone.

Besides, if anyone gets to shoot one of these shitcrusts, it'll be me.

Another gesture sent the close-quarters fighter to station herself at the front entrance—from there she could suggest to any would-be visitors they should came back later.

Rooss followed her to the lounge door, then hooked left toward the foyer. Reaching it, he planted himself directly in front of the elevator doors and put his forepaws to his hips.

With his lips curling in barely restrained fury, he thought, *Those bone-rotten Hellchasers better be ready to give that money back. Or guild building or not, there'll be hell to pay.*

* * *

Docking Pad 94

Langwarrin Starport

An hour after landing, Jessica signed the starport contract and disclaimers officially placing the *Trigger Happy* into the care and maintenance of the port authority for refit and refueling for 36 standard hours. Sliding two fingers across the slate, she terminated the program and leaned back in the seat.

"Lucille? Port authority has ground command. Maintain security protocols. Emergency procedures are authorized if you deem them necessary."

<<Are you certain, Jessica? Commander Lemieux does not recognize that course of action as standard operating procedure.>>

Jessica smiled. "It's standard operating procedure for me."

<<That is very true.>>

Dad always said you were the best friend I'd ever have.

She stood up from the console and walked for the first time in a couple of weeks. Despite having been on the ground for a while, she'd not left her post. Filing the mission reports and ensuring payment requests were transmitted and copied to the Mercenary Guild took time. While she worked on the *administrivia* of command functions, the company had inventoried stores, seen about refueling and rearmament requests, and prepared the ship for their short, but well-earned, shore leave. Before leaving the otherwise unoccupied bridge, she withdrew the master key and tucked it into the leg pocket of her green pilot's coveralls. Langwarrin wasn't known for violence or crime in any significant measure, but a careless mercenary company never made simple mistakes.

Trusting the wrong folks is always the first, and most costly, mistake.

Jessica bit her lower lip and sighed. Her father's bits of wisdom floated up from her memories of him before he'd disappeared after her seventh birthday. His whereabouts were one thing she traced at every port of call, often to dead and cold endings. On those planets or outposts where an office of his company, Intergalactic Haulers, remained, she would always check in for messages or status updates. Her father was always on mission and unable to communicate. In the last few months, she'd stopped frequenting the offices. There was no change. If he was alive, he either wanted nothing to do with her, or his missions were too important. As much as she tried to believe the latter, she couldn't help wondering what she'd done to push him away.

She stepped through the bridge hatch and heard the excited voices of Hex Alison and Maya Inoue. The young CASPer pilots were among her friends in the Marauders and they earnestly believed that no one knew the two of them were sleeping together and had been for months. Jessica had known and kept it from Marc as the Marauders' first rule was no fraternization. Marc Lemieux, though, toed that line several times in various ports of call with women other than Jessica. His behavior away from her, especially in the last several ports of call, was dangerously close to infidelity. When she'd brought it to his attention, he'd glossed over the events saying that he was having fun and nothing serious had happened. She'd almost believed him.

His stress, however, was nearly constant. When not on missions, he gambled and drank, trying to be the life of whatever party he could find. In those environs, surrounded by people who didn't know or depend upon him, he was free. That he owed more money than he had in his accounts didn't matter for those brief bits of dopamine-laced freedom. People loved him and followed his irrational decisions in the pursuit of a good time. He reveled in the short bits of attention he could gain before falling back into the uncomfortable role of a mercenary company commander. Despite his father's grooming attempts, it was a suit that Marc Lemieux could not wear.

"Hey, Jess!" Hex Alison called from the passageway. "*Victory Twelve* is in good hands. They seem to enjoy having a Haulers ship on their pad. Are we released for liberty?"

She nodded and smiled. With a tap on her wrist-mounted slate, she activated the speakers throughout the ship. "Marauders, this is liberty call. Departure in thirty-six hours. Miss movement and your contracts are cancelled. I will leave forfeited gear on the pad. Liberty call. Have a good time."

Maya Inoue smiled over Hex's shoulder. The Japanese-Hawaiian woman was Jessica's wingman in the CASPer section. "Are you going to go find Hammer, or do you want to come with us?"

She would have loved to spend time with her friends. An hour's head start meant bad things if she didn't get to Marc before he negotiated another mission fee. Having the money and assets to command a company did not make one a commander. "Let me know where you are later. I'm going to join Marc and see about this mission and make sure, if we take it, we get the credits we deserve for a change."

"Damn right," Hex drawled in his Australian accent. He looked the part of a surfer, but was one of the best tactical minds in the company, if not most of the Human mercenary units Jessica had ever worked alongside. "We're gonna go have some fun. Catch up with ya later, Bulldog."

Jessica smiled at the two of them. "I'm sure you will. Dinner for sure."

"It's a date," Maya said and waved as the two young lovers darted for the nearest outer hatch.

Instead of watching them, Jessica made her way to the quarters she shared with Marc and quickly brushed her hair and let it fall over her shoulders. Her wrist slate buzzed with a new GalNet message and she tapped the screen to open the message and scanned it quickly. Her mouth opened and closed with an audible pop before she spun on her heel and ran for Tossen's Bar.

It's happening! An interview for the Peacemaker Academy!

Sonuvabitch!

* * *

Langwarrin Mercenary Guild Building

The elevator was just large enough to accommodate Hahnu's eleven-strong escort along with Razzik's chair. As it left the rooftop, the airless box quickly filled with the scents of angry Zuul.

Gazing up at Hahnu, Razzik asked, "Are you sure it's best for you to do the talking? Wouldn't I…" The rest of his question vanished into a fit of weak coughing.

Hahnu maneuvered herself between the chair and the door, facing forward. As the elevator passed Level 3, she told him firmly, "I will definitely do the talking." Her troops mumbled support for her decision.

She glanced back at Razzik's slate. Either he or his shuttle pilot had jammed the device between his useless legs and the side of his chair.

"Perhaps, while I talk," she said, "you could use that to write up a new contract for us. One in which we get the rest of the money from the Maulers. A contract with a big fat fee and an even fatter bonus."

More mumbles of agreement. Razzik did not respond.

The elevator pinged. Hahnu tensed as the doors opened. She stepped onto the carpeted foyer.

Marrek Rooss stood six paces away, six of his mercs arranged behind him. She stepped closer, watching the reflection in the glass wall to her right as her own mercs fanned out around her. Razzik's chair trundled to the side of the room. Hahnu opened her mouth to speak. Rooss did the same. And both of them said the same thing.

"Where's the money?"

Hahnu blinked, snapped her jaw shut in surprise. *What did he say!*

"What did you say?" Rooss demanded. "Do you seriously expect me—?"

"Stop!" Hahnu barked. Something was wrong here. Very wrong. She leaned closer, lowering her voice. "You and me. In the lounge. *Now.*"

Rooss hesitated, eyes narrowing as he calculated. Her forces outnumbered his squad—and *outclassed them*, though he'd never admit it—so perhaps it was common sense that made him agree. "Very well. After you."

"I'd prefer to walk together, Marrek."

A huff of agreement, then he accompanied her to the lounge door. His men parted to let them through. Hahnu avoided eye contact with them, partly from disdain, partly so as not to inflame tensions further.

Without looking back, Hahnu called out to her senior lieutenant, "Keep things on ice, Bur."

Bur replied, "Nothing to worry about here, sir."

"I completely agree," muttered a Mauler, Rooss's own second, perhaps.

Rooss and Hahnu came to a stop in the middle of the lounge, far enough from the door that their voices wouldn't carry. Rooss spoke again before she could.

"What's he doing here?"

"The boss?" she replied, then snorted a wry laugh. "I'd say he wants his money back as much I do."

"So you're going to maintain the charade, uh?" His gaze returned to the glass, thoughts stuck on the Elder's presence. "Is he sick or something?"

"He's old. And," she added, bringing things back on topic, "he's angry. What did you mean *charade*?"

"Come on, Ren. I know you're surprised we're here, but is playing dumb the best you can come up with on the spur of the moment?"

"I don't think I'm the dumb one. You can't smell something rotten here? We come here asking you for the money. You're waiting outside the elevator, asking us the same thing. It stinks. It stinks bad."

"The only thing that stinks is your treachery!" Rooss's voice rose.

She made a suppressing motion with her forepaws. "Marrek. Listen to me. Who told you to expect us here?"

Hahnu heard growling and rising voices out in the foyer. Mostly Mauler ones. She kept her focus forward, watching Rooss's face, watching his paws as they swung past his weapons while he gesticulated.

"Razzik's secretary," he replied. "Now I'm wondering if you didn't just steal the old Zuul's money, but kidnapped him, too!"

"Kidnapped? Razzik asked us to meet him here. He told us you took the money."

"You're the worst liar I've ever met. Now, come clean and tell me how we get it back or you won't live long enough to regret it."

Some of the growling had moved from the foyer and along the hallway. One of her people had shoved one of theirs into the corridor. Someone barked, "Thief!"

"Marrek!" she snapped. "This makes little sense. We need to sort this out before…"

The harsh clack of armor hitting the glass turned both their heads. A Hellchaser—Daran—was sliding down it, unbalanced. A Mauler loomed above him, forelegs outstretched after shoving him, teeth bared in challenge. Daran's paw was pulling at his knife even as he slid down. Two other mercs were grappling in the foyer, others maneuvered for position. This was turning to shit and fast.

She started to say something, but caught Marrek's movement from the corner of her eye. Her reflexes kicked in. She lashed out with a boot and drove his forepaw away from his pistol before he could get a grip. She swiped claws at his face, but he dodged, pedaling backwards.

They faced each other.

"This is how it ends, huh?" Marrek snarled.

"If that's the way you want it," Hahnu said.

Teeth bared and claws raised, they lunged at each other, for blood and pride. The growing chaos outside the room receded from their minds.

* * *

Tossen's Bar

Langwarrin

"Message has been received and read." Hr'ent tapped his slate and sent it into sleep mode. "I imagine she'll make her way here quickly. To tell her husband the good news, that is."

Hak-Chet shook his head and chuckled. He nodded toward the scene at a table in the center of the room. In plain sight of everyone in the bar, a Human male and female tossed back another shot of some clear liquid and pressed their faces together in a grotesque display of attraction. "You arranged all of this?"

"I merely set the conditions." Hr'ent smiled with one corner of his maw. "She is the contact he's been in touch with regarding a bogus operation to find a missing socialite. The one you've seen on the GalNet broadcasts?"

"I paid them no attention. I have no sympathy for anything celebrity." Hak-Chet grinned. "But you've done that, too, haven't you? Hid the socialite?"

"She's enjoying Uuwato in the summer and hanging out with my mother and her friends. She finds the whole thing fascinating. She was more than willing to help. Turns out even celebrities need to ditch their entourage and unplug now and then."

"Entourage? Is that French?" Hak-Chet laughed. "You're getting soft, Hr'ent."

"I prefer to think of it as cultured, Hak. You really should come to Earth and see Paris. It is beyond description." Hr'ent waved a massive paw dismissively. "Anyway, I set up the missing socialite, and I maneuvered my chosen contact into being in charge of her recovery effort. Once our socialite's team hired my contact, I instructed her to reach out to the Marauders foremost, which she did. From there, I let history and tendencies take over, exactly as I learned at the Academy. Given that both of those Humans like alcohol and the opposite sex? Well, I was hoping for some combustion, at the very least."

Hak-Chet snorted and struggled to control his laughter. "They're close to sexual intercourse right now. You're certain this will push our prospective candidate to leave the glorious life of a mercenary behind?"

Hr'ent nodded solemnly, and the smile faded from his face. "I'm only accelerating something that has, by all accounts, already started. Hak, listen, selecting a Peacemaker is serious business. You look for what? Five or six primary criteria?"

"Six. Leadership, diplomacy, personal values and discipline, mental agility, personal fitness, and commitment to a higher ideal—be that citizenship or duty, it doesn't matter."

"My prospect has all of those traits," Hr'ent said. "But you're not going to interview her."

Hak-Chet blinked several times. "What do you mean?"

"Well, not in the traditional way you interview a candidate." Hr'ent leaned forward and smiled. He enjoyed the diminutive Sidar's discomfort. "When you brought me into the Enforcers and enhanced me, you said you felt like you were losing control while you had to see just how far I would go. Do you remember that?"

"I do," Hak-Chet replied. He nodded slowly as recognition dawned. "You sonuvabitch. You've set this little scene up to fire her up, but that's not the only thing you've done, is it?"

Hr'ent tossed back his bourbon and caught the eye of the Veetanho bartender. He waved for a replacement beverage for each of them. "As a matter of fact, the shit should hit the fan any second now."

"You really are enamored with Human culture, aren't you?"

Hr'ent grinned and nodded at the door. A redheaded female in a green flight suit was approaching the outer doors. "Hell hath no fury like a woman scorned, Hak. Watch and learn."

* * *

There were only two Humans in the bar and they sat at a table on the open floor sucking face with one another. Eight empty shot glasses adorned the tabletop in front of them. Slates for deal-making weren't present and there wasn't anything uploaded to the Mercenary Guild's system to identify that Marc had bothered to actually sign a contract. He and his contact were too busy fondling each other between giddy bursts of laughter to notice her watching them from a few meters away.

The calmness of her mind surprised her. She'd melodramatically played out similar situations in her head long before, even during her days at the University of Georgia. There was also a monologue, and an argument. Maybe even a pleading request for another chance that she might demur against. Yet, in that moment, there was nothing in her mind but a dead calm. From that calm, a single plan of action emerged, and it was solid enough that she grasped it by the neck and brought it forth. There wasn't any anger as she stepped forward toward the table. Nor was there remorse for what the last several years had brought her. In their place was a laundry list of items to do. She would leave Marc Lemieux, the Marauders, and mercenary life forever. Langwarrin was one of the few places she could do all of them, except for a full Human divorce. That could come quickly, though.

She stepped forward slowly, her hands clasped in front of her and gently wrenched the engagement ring and wedding band combination off her finger and palmed them. He'd proposed to her on a Hawaiian beach at sunset with some of their friends in attendance. The platinum band and one-carat diamond had sparkled like nothing she'd ever seen. In that moment, there had been nothing but joy and hope for the future. Clutched in her hand, the damned things seemed to burn with an unholy fire she wanted rid of, and fast. It took her only a minute to make her way through the crowded establishment and stand over the table. Marc and the blonde woman stopped laughing and stared up at her. His sleepy, drunken eyes searched her face and recognized her with a combination of shock and happiness which ripped apart her last strands of hope for the relationship.

"Hey, Jess! This is Monica, and she's our—"

"She not our anything, Marc," Jessica said. She slammed the rings to the table in front of him. Not taking her eyes from him, she activated her slate and set it to record her words. "This is my resignation from the Marauders effective immediately. I'll clear my belongings from the *Trigger Happy* and remove the *Victory Twelve* from her moorings ASAP. I am divesting my holdings from the Marauder's Trust immediately and will file an injunction against any withdrawals placed upon my accounts through the Mercenary Guild at the nearest office."

Marc Lemieux's smiling face transitioned to full-fledged shock. "You…you can't just quit on me, Jessica."

"Like hell, Hammer. I can handle your incompetence. I can handle your inability to command troops in the field. And before today, I thought your little distractions—" she glared at Monica, whoever she was, "—were harmless. That ends now. As does my employment with the Marauders."

Lemieux tried to summon anger. "You've put my company in horrible straits, Jessica. You've nearly bankrupted me."

"No, Marc. You've spent your money chasing attention and the wrong kinds of friends. I just let go of the wheel. Where you end up on the rocks is your choice. Not mine." Jessica turned. "You probably want to pawn my rings, too. If they're real, you might get something out of them. Whatever you do, they mean nothing to me. Neither do you."

Jessica turned and walked away from the table, her interview with the Peacemaker Guild forgotten. The muted conversations around her returned to their normal volume as she stalked to the door and out into the passageway. Her priority now was divesting herself from the Marauders, which meant the local Mercenary Guild's office would be her next destination. She only hoped it would still be open so she could withdraw her holdings.

When they'd developed it into a starport, Jessica knew, space had been tight in this moon crater's original township. Because of that, the port's various berths and pads sat atop existing buildings. Maya's berthing of the *Victory Twelve* hadn't just saved money; it was about to save Jessica a long walk, since the guild office was right across the street.

As she neared Tossen's front exit, she heard a loud commotion of some type and paused while security personnel jogged past the windows, heading toward the guild offices.

"Now what?" she asked and stepped into the street.

The *whump* of an explosion rippled through the ground, causing her to stumble. Instantly, she recognized the detonation as a grenade. Jessica started running toward the guild building and toward *Victory Twelve* berthed on its roof. She had to ensure she met with guild officers to leave behind the mercenary life, and she had to protect that ship! As white and gray smoke billowed into the street, she tapped her slate and ordered the Marauders to recall and secure their ship. Whatever the trouble was, Jessica meant to keep her family and her ship safe. Drawing her pistol, Jessica shouldered through the hesitating security officers on her way to the front door.

* * *

"So," Hak said. "They fought. She left. Now what?"

"Well," Hr'ent started, but his attention snapped to his slate as it beeped with a message notification. "If I've timed this right—and I think I have—I will have an answer for you in about five minutes."

He swallowed the rest of his drink and rose to his feet. Hak said nothing, but his question was clear from his expression.

Hr'ent told him, "Stay here, my friend. Order another drink. I'll be back soon with a very good story, trust me."

* * *

Smoke streamed from the guild building entrance as Jessica approached. The doors looked like partly severed limbs, bent out of shape, each hanging from a hinge. A merc, a Zuul, lay sprawled across the stoop, its green and yellow armor flayed open, its exposed paws and head shredded and burned. Six Veetanho fled through the opening, trampling the corpse and squealing shrilly in their panic. By their raiment and demeanor, they were office workers there; they couldn't have caused this.

So, who…?

No security personnel seemed willing to go inside yet, but some of them had holed up four Zuul near a mobile supply container down the street. All the mercs there wore identical armor to the dead one.

Keeping low, Jessica moved through the entrance, careful to avoid slipping on gore or debris. The smoke was fast dissipating, though it still tinged the air inside. Hugging the corridor's right-side wall, Jessica crouched low, her M1911XR sweeping ahead and beside her. The corridor's left wall had been glass, and it had shattered across the lounge beyond it. The floor was strewn with bodies. Five weren't moving, two of them were piled together against the wrecks of chairs in the lounge. But those she could see in the elevator foyer were alive and conscious, some grappling on the floor, some writhing and holding their heads or else gushing blue blood from neck and paw wounds. All of them were Zuul. All of their armor was the green-yellow she'd seen outside, although the two distinct design patterns among them indicated there were two companies present.

What the hell happened here?

She was thinking of alternative routes to the *Victory Twelve* and backing toward the street again, when she saw something strange. Another Zuul was in the foyer, pressed up against the back wall. But this one appeared old and frail. And he was using a motorized chair.

The old Zuul regarded the surrounding fray with wide eyes, with no way of getting by the wrestling bodies. If some idiot pulled the pin on another grenade...

Jessica snarled, charged forward, and vaulted bodies. This might not be her fight but letting an aging cripple die wasn't in her nature either.

The mercs who recovered enough to skirmish again seemed content to use teeth and claws, although two were drawing knives as they climbed to their feet. At the edge of the foyer, one peered up at her from the floor. He had madness in his eyes, murder in his expression, and he was fumbling for his pistol as his other paw reached for her. Jessica shot him point blank, spreading the back of his head across the carpet.

She was a few meters from the older male now. To her right lay the elevator, blocked by recovering mercs, already swinging at their opponents. To her left was an emergency exit, the green light above it indicating an active, unlocked door. But there was another Zuul between the chair and the door, getting groggily to her feet and looking around for her next opponent. Her gaze settled on Jessica. She took a step forward and bared her teeth in challenge.

That was all the excuse Jessica needed, and she charged. At the last second, as the Zuul stepped forward to swing a lethal set of claws, Jessica dove, tucking herself into a tight ball, and rolled into the merc's legs, bowling her over. She came to her feet behind her felled opponent who'd fallen onto all fours. Stunned, the Zuul's head came around to seek Jessica...and met the butt of Jessica's pistol coming the other way. Gun met skull with a dull *thwack*. It was lights out for the merc, and time for Jessica to get the old male out of here.

Holstering the pistol, she kicked the unconscious merc's legs out of the way then grabbed the back of the chair.

"Wh-what?"

"Getting you out of here, sir," Jessica replied and hauled the chair backwards. She used her ass to bang through the exit and found that she'd brought them out into a service alley. She pivoted the chair around and gave it a push so it rolled a few meters further. Kicking the door shut, she strode after the chair, scanning her new surroundings. Apart from the guild offices, the alleyway backed on restaurants, tattoo parlors, and a brothel. It had an exit at either end leading to broader thoroughfares. Five stories above her, shuttle pads stretched between buildings, blocking the sky and forming a false ceiling.

The Zuul regained control of his chair and turned it to face her. One paw rubbed his ears.

"I should thank you!" he said, much louder than necessary. Was he deaf? Or were his ears ringing from the earlier concussion wave? His free paw patted her hand, then he pointed upward. "My shuttle's up there! If you could take me there, I'd be even more grateful!"

That's where I wanna go too, gramps, she thought wryly. *Now if I could just find a way up there.* She'd have to find another building out on the main thoroughfare with access. But which way? Left or right?

Before she could decide, the emergency exit banged open again. She whirled, dropping to one knee, her M1911XR drawn. A female Zuul had burst through. She too dropped to her knees, one paw held out in supplication, the other braced to stop her face-planting. She didn't look so good; her mouth was hanging open in distress, blood stained her teeth, and her face was riddled with small cuts. Were they claw-marks, or lacerations from flying glass splinters? Her scratched and pitted armor indicated close proximity to the blast.

"Wait," she croaked. "Don't take him anywhere."

"You're not in a position to give me orders," Jessica snapped back.

"You don't understand. He's the one responsible for this."

Jessica frowned. "*What?*"

The merc's attention wavered, chin dropping for a moment before she rallied her strength. "My name is Commander...Ren Hahnu. That male owns my company. And...and the other company. He set us against each other. Fed us lies. He...he is the one ... the one who—"

She collapsed, her legs spasming to kick against the door, to block the door. Blocking the door was good. Jessica holstered her weapon, darted over, and rolled the Zuul over to check the slate fixed to her left forearm. While the data displayed was in standard Zuul, the layout of the personal diagnostics were the same, despite the species. Her pulse was strong, but erratic. That might mean internal bleeding as the heart worked harder to do more with less.

Without rising, Jessica turned her head. "What in the hell did she mean?"

She froze.

The elderly Zuul no longer looked frail and infirm. He was out of his chair approaching her on steady legs. He also had a pistol of his own, aimed at her chest. "It's unfortunate you heard that," he said in a strong, level voice. "Most unfortunate, Human. Throw away your weapon."

Scowling, Jessica lowered her pistol to the ground and, with a shove, sent it sliding and spinning away.

The Zuul sneered down at her. "See where your dull-witted sympathy has gotten you?"

Jessica allowed her shoulders to droop as she knelt there, as if defeated and despondent, her hands dropping to her sides. Her left hand—hidden by the angle of her body—went to her boot where she kept her knife. Her fingers curled around its handle.

"You may have the drop on me," she told him, "but I'm not as dull-witted as you think I am. And neither was she?"

"You know nothing."

Jessica jerked her chin at his chair and the slate poking out of it. Both appeared state-of-the-art and expensive. "I know you were up to something. I know you have money. If this merc's right, and you started an altercation between them, then maybe..." Her voice trailed off as she joined a few dots in her head. She smiled. "Maybe you'd decided it was time to disband them, but you didn't want to pay their severance fees. Easier to report them dead in combat, right? I'm sure it's something like that. When my friend here comes around, I'll know the rest of it."

Sudden anger wiped the haughtiness from the rich Zuul's face. He stepped closer, the paw holding his weapon shaking in fury. Jessica's hand tightened around her knife, easing it from its sheath. "Neither of you will—"

"*Razzik!*" boomed a voice.

The Zuul flinched and jerked around. Seizing her opportunity, Jessica drew the knife and flung it. The blade struck true, slicing his wrist. He staggered toward his chair with a cry, pressing the wound to his side. Jessica sought the source of the voice and saw the hulking form of an Oogar who had come out of the dead space alongside the guild building. In one massive hand was the unmistakable badge of a Peacemaker. He carried no other weapon. She rose carefully to her feet and sidled toward where her pistol lay.

But the Oogar's focus was entirely on Razzik, who kept backpedaling toward his chair. "Elder Razzik, I could drag you to your guild for multiple financial crimes, the most serious of which is embezzlement. But I think I'll add murder to your charges after today's little fracas."

"I…I have done nothing. I am a sick, old Zuul." He dropped heavily into his chair and his slate clattered to the alleyway, his paws going to his chest as if to massage his heart.

Jessica bent to retrieve her pistol, but she wouldn't need it. The Oogar had this under control. She was a witness to a story she'd recount for years ahead.

"Razzik, Razzik, Razzik," scolded the Oogar. "Your crimes came to our attention through our Luna-based consulate. You foolishly attempted to launder credits through a series of Human companies. While generally good people, Humans don't launder credits well, and we saw your intent months ago. We intercepted messages between your secretary and you, so we knew all about your plan for setting your mercs against each other in hopes of a little skirmish that would see them suspended, then you would be able to divest yourself of them without paying their salaries, and would also create some sympathy for you. Bet you didn't expect them to toss a grenade, though!" The Oogar looked to Jessica and shook his head ruefully. "Can you believe this arrogant, greedy bastard?"

"Well, can you believe *this*?" Razzik snarled and, from the folds of his tunic, produced a small ballistic pistol. He brought it up to aim at the Oogar, but Jessica put a round through his chest. She checked the Oogar who was standing with an expression of mild shock but no damage. She stepped over to check the Zuul in the chair.

Panting hard, Razzik hissed something before the light went out of his eyes, and he folded over, dead.

"What did he say?" the Oogar asked.

Jessica put her pistol away and stooped to pick up Razzik's slate. "Sounded like 'I hate Peacemakers.'"

The Oogar laughed at that and nodded solemnly to her. "Enforcer Hr'ent Golramm. Well met."

"Jessica Francis." She blinked. The giant Oogar was a legend in the Peacemaker Guild. "Well met."

"Thank you," he said and winked. "I appreciate you helping me apprehend this fellow."

Jessica wanted to ask how he knew her name. Instead she asked, "How did you know we were back here?"

"Feeds from the guild's security cameras. There is always information lying around if you're willing to look for and use it."

She wanted to ask more, but she turned toward the merc lying near the door. "We should help her." Listening, she realized she couldn't hear any clamor coming from inside.

"Security officers are in there now," Hr'ent told her, checking his slate. "I have requested paramedic support. They are en route also."

Another figure appeared around the corner of the guild building and for a moment, both Human and Oogar tensed.

"Golramm!" the stranger gasped. The shadow resolved as a Sidar with its hands clasped in front of its wings.

Hr'ent groaned. "Hak! I told you to stay put." He pointed up to where Jessica noticed a camera mounted. "I would have shown you recordings of the whole thing."

"I was curious," replied the Sidar. He pointed to Razzik's slumped corpse. "Dead?"

"Very," Jessica and Hr'ent said together.

"Oh, this is bad, Golramm," the Sidar fussed. "Is this a game to you? Setting up all these overlapping little plots? All you'll accomplish is calling unnecessary attention to the amount of intelligence we're collecting on other guilds."

"Now, now," Hr'ent said. "It'll all work out, trust me. Here, watch this." He tapped something onto his slate and passed it over.

Remembering she held the Zuul's slate, Jessica silently passed it to Hr'ent who cradled it in one paw like a tiny toy.

"I don't want to watch something," the Sidar continued. "You brought me here ostensibly to interview a Human. Not to get caught up in a breach of conflict and embezzlement scandal."

Jessica gasped, remembering her interview. And realized...

Hr'ent grinned at her as he reached over and tapped his slate's playback for Hak. Jessica couldn't see it, but the sounds of earlier conflict were familiar. And then her own voice said, "Getting you out of here, sir."

A few seconds later, Hak looked up, calmer, quieter. He said, "She charged right in there to protect him."

Hr'ent nodded. "This Human stood for someone in need. Her instinct was just and honorable. No hesitation. She only used extreme force when threatened and to defend an ally." He gestured to Jessica. "Selector Hak-Chet, this is Jessica Francis. I have five hundred credits that says she'll be the first Human to complete the Peacemaker Academy."

You have gotta be shitting me. Somehow Jessica kept her face straight.

"No bet. She's a natural." Hak-Chet smiled and shook his head as he turned to Jessica and extended a bony claw. "Well met, Miss Francis. I look forward to your enrollment in the academy with great anticipation."

* * * * *

Peter J. Aldin Bio

Peter J. Aldin is a nerd. An Australian nerd, but a nerd nonetheless. He is author of the space opera crime novel *Eventide* (and has written paranormal thrillers under the name Pete Aldin). His working life is split between empowering people with disabilities to start and succeed at new jobs, and designing courses and courseware for training companies. Find him at petealdin.com

* * *

Kevin Ikenberry Bio

Kevin Ikenberry is a life-long space geek and retired Army officer. As an adult, he managed the U.S. Space Camp program and served as a space operations officer before Space Force was a thing. He's an international bestselling author, award finalist, and a core author in the wildly successful Four Horsemen Universe. His eleven novels include *Sleeper Protocol, Vendetta Protocol, Runs in The Family, Peacemaker, Honor the Threat, Stand or Fall,* and *Deathangel.* He's co-written several novels with amazing authors. He is an Active Member of SFWA, International Thriller Writers, and SIGMA—the science fiction think tank.

\# \# \# \# \#

Gumbo by
Matt Novotny

"What was that?"

Jackson Rains entered the bridge just in time to see a large metal panel blow past the forward screen as the Peacemaker Guild corvette screamed toward the planet's surface.

"Incoming fire!" said the tactical officer.

"Evade! Deploy countermeasures! Activate PDLs and heat up the missiles," ordered Captain Lorm. The Cochkala spoke in calm, measured tones while gesturing angrily with her tail.

"Aye, Captain."

"Comms, broadcast the ceasefire orders again."

"Aye, Captain." The comms officer turned to his board. "Avbo combatants, Avbo combatants, this is the Peacemaker Guild corvette *Turunmaa* inbound to conduct negotiations at the request of the Mercenary Guild. A ceasefire is now in effect. You are ordered to—"

Rains braced against a nearby console as the helmsman put the ship through a series of abrupt maneuvers.

The captain gestured at Rains with her tail. "Peacemaker Rains, I suggest you make yourself useful and find out who's shooting at my ship. Let them know if they are still firing when we hit the ten-mile

255

limit that this will be a short mission for all of us. To answer your question, we seem to have lost one of our in-atmosphere braking panels."

Rains scrambled for the comm station and grabbed one of the handrails just as the ship shook from another near miss.

It's never easy, he thought.

He nodded to the comms officer, who tied in his headset and nodded to let Rains know his comm was live.

"Peacemaker Rains to Xiq'tal and Tortantula forces. Cease fire! I say again, cease fire! Under the Articles of War you are required to stand down from all hostile action and prepare for negotiation. Report your Unit, combat strength, and commanding officer for the record. Failure to comply will result in fines and censure." Having got the officialese out of the way Rains looked directly at Captain Lorm before adding, "Further action against this vessel will result in an immediate and lethal response."

Not exactly by the book, but close enough, he thought. *But if they wanted this by the book they should have sent someone else.*

Rains listened for a moment hoping Captain Lorm wouldn't get the chance to exercise her more aggressive instincts. The responses came on separate channels.

"CrRkkt of the Xiq'tal. Our force is three hundred." The voice was low and sounded like rocks being ground together, but to Rains' surprise, it also sounded...*cheerful?* "We will comply as soon as the Tortantula withdraw. Sending coordinates to our location. Your arrival works in their favor. We were about to crush them and give them to the sea."

By contrast the voice on the other channel was almost painfully high-pitched and angry.

"You can't pronounce my name. Call me Rikki. Calling in for the joint *Flatar*-Tortantula forces. We're standing down. Our force size is 500. Tell crab-cakes he got saved by the bell! Welcome to Avbo."

Jackson smiled despite himself. Obviously "Rikki" had spent enough time around Humans to pick up some of the slang. He remembered one of his DIs telling him that the best way to shut up a Flatar was to pump the room full of helium because it raised the pitch of their voices higher than the translators could pick up.

"Rains to combatants. I will hold formal negotiations within 96 hours as required by the Articles. You will be notified of time and place in advance. Acknowledge for the record."

"The Xiq'tal acknowledge," replied CrRkkt.

"Yeah, we're in, too," said Rikki.

"Rains out."

Rains turned. "Captain Lorm, will you do a flyover of the coordinates the Xiq'tal sent and see if there is a good place to land? My brief said one of the beaches was the main area of engagement."

"You wouldn't prefer to land at the starport at Durst?" asked Lorm, referring to the main Flatar-Tortantula settlement about 100 klicks inland.

Rains shook his head. "No. The fighting is here. I'm not convinced the ceasefire will last without the *Turunmaa* on station to enforce it. We'll set up a base camp here. After we meet with the Xiq'tal we can move the ship to Durst."

The helmsman interjected, "Captain, coming up on the Xiq'tal coordinates."

The *Turunmaa* flew over the coast. The coordinates were a low, rocky plateau bordered with trees that looked like the confused child of a palm tree and an evergreen. On one side were several kilometers of gently-sloping land covered with high, deep green grass that rippled in the offshore wind. The sunset left a path of gold that glittered over the sea and turned the few high clouds into streamers of light.

The effect was lovely until one noticed that at least a half klick of white sandy beach had been churned into a morass of blood, ichor, and the shattered bodies of the Tortantula and Xiq'tal. At the edge of the water the corpses of several Flatar rolled in and out with the tide.

Rains took in the scene. Even for someone used to carnage, it was hard to take; there wasn't a single body on the beach that hadn't been dismembered to some extent. He could see Xiq'tal sentries sitting farther out in the water.

Rains shook his head. "Armageddon in paradise with too many legs." He turned to the Cochkala who gave him the equivalent of a shrug.

"The Xiq'tal and Tortantula both love to fight. I'd say most of what happened here was claw to claw."

"That plateau looks like a good place to land. Setting up a base camp there gives us a good vantage point and would be easier to defend in case of an attack. I don't like being this close to the water. It's too easy for the Xiq'tal to hide."

Rains nodded. "I agree, but I think this is our best bet. We can deploy drones to keep an eye on both fronts. We need information. Right now, nothing about this situation adds up."

Captain Lorm's tail lashed from side to side. "Explain."

Rains began counting off points on his fingers.

"One. We haven't been given a clear answer on how this conflict started or why it seems to be growing so fast. Both species have troopships on the way, so the dispute has gone beyond a squabble between merc companies, which is probably why we were fired on despite the ceasefire broadcast.

"Two. Avbo is a larder world administrated by Consolidated Agricultural. They subcontract to the Tortantula and Xiq'tal for space and the planet's recreational opportunities. It has no strategic value, no unusual mineral deposits, and the soil won't grow much without extensive bio-farming; food production is limited to native species and those that easily adapt. The place is a protein factory. My brief said the Tortantula ranch something called a gresh, and the Xiq'tal export large quantities of seafood. According to ConAg, there is nothing here worth fighting over.

"Three. The request for Peacemaker intervention came from the *Mercenary Guild*, not from the Xiq'tal, the Flatar and Tortantulas, or from ConAg. The Mercenary Guild's reasoning that the groups will probably fight to the last being seems valid enough, but no one is getting paid here. That means it's personal.

"Four. In spite of the fact that the Mercenary Guild filed the request, there hasn't been any contact from the local guild representative in Durst, and we know there is a Veetanho administrative office there. So, why the silence?"

"And five. The Veetanho specifically requested a *Human* Peacemaker. Even if one through four made sense, that alone would make me question why we're here."

Lorm looked at Rains, considering. "So you're convinced this is a trap? What are you going to do about it?"

Rains smiled. "Spring it, of course."

* * *

*A*mos *Lacroix doesn't look like a merc captain,* thought Rains as he watched the man work. At 5' 8" and 160-pounds Amos could best be described as wiry. He was an older man with thinning brown hair, a crooked nose, and watery blue eyes. He was the kind of man nobody looked at twice, until he spoke.

Rains had met Amos in a dive bar on Luna playing cards and the first thing he heard was something like, "I call 'em, you betcha. You be showin' dem cards. I gar-on-tee!"

The fight that started after had cleared the bar, and he and Rains had landed in another dive close by nursing their bruises. Amos explained that his mother was Creole and his father French-Canadian and laughed that his accent made him an embarrassment to both sides of his family. His outfit, the Rajin Cajuns, was a tight-knit unit of eleven men specializing in security. They mostly kept to themselves, which was good, because when they were speaking in their native dialect no one understood them anyway. They had a mix of Mk 7 and Mk 8 CASPers. When Rains had received the mission he'd contacted Amos. The Cajuns were between gigs and the Peacemaker Guild had approved a stipend for a security force.

Amos loved his job, but more than anything, he loved to cook. He'd told Rains when he retired he planned to open a restaurant. Naturally, the first thing he had done after the *Turunmaa* had settled in was to get his crew working on the perimeter defenses and setting up his kitchen.

After unloading an enormous cast iron cauldron, Amos had poured in a five-gallon bucket of "starter" and set to work filling the rest of the pot with "flavor." Rains could see him cursing into a headset.

"Goddam, Louie, get dat auto-MAC onlin'! Dat no on in five minit I gon' kick your ass. I gar-on-tee! I no wan' excuse an' Jack-son no wan' excuse from me no way neither. You wan' make dem P-maker grouch?"

Rains gave a last look over the preparations, gave Amos a thumbs up, and then headed back into the ship. The defenses were solid but even added to the *Turunmaa*'s point defense if either group attacked, they were a delaying tactic at best.

He entered the bridge and nodded to Captain Lorm. "We're ready. The Cajuns are finishing up the perimeter defenses now. We have four CASPers on a six-on, six-off rotation. I'm going to grab a shower and a few hours' sleep."

Rains turned to the comms officer. "Please notify the Xiq'tal I'll meet with them on the beach in eight hours."

* * *

The sun was making its way into the sky as Rains headed to the beach to meet with the Xiq'tal. He took Amos and one of his men as backup, and Captain Lorm had insisted on sending a drone to monitor. For most of his life Rains had found that the right application of force would fix most problems. One of his foster parents had been fond of saying, "When you're a hammer, every problem looks like a nail." She had been trying to tell him something important but he hadn't understood until years later after spending too much time learning to be an efficient hammer. But here everybody had a bigger hammer than he did.

Three Xiq'tal walked from the water onto the beach. The lead Xiq'tal was almost twice the size and a deeper blue than the other two. One had a piece of armor plate strapped to its shell. On the plate rested two-meter-wide balls of spikes similar to a giant sea urchin. Rains could see the spines flexing. The other had a rack of missiles and a pair of MACs wired onto its shell. The weapons tracked as the Xiq'tal moved its eyestalks.

At 6'2" with a heavy build, Rains had grown up with the advantage of having a commanding physical presence, something that was both a help and a hindrance being passed from foster home to foster home. It was an advantage that evaporated during his Peacemaker training as many of the races he'd trained beside were bigger and faster than Humans, but it hadn't done much to prepare him for this. Face to face talks with the Xiq'tal was like facing an angry APC. The BAMF armor he wore was good general protection, but it wasn't up to the kind of firepower the troops on Avbo were throwing around. Rains stepped forward.

"I am Peacemaker Jackson Rains, here to conduct negotiations to end the hostilities between the Xiq'tal and the Flatar-Tortantula forces. Are you CrRkkt?"

The King Xiq'tal made a gesture with both enormous fighting claws. Rains tried not to flinch.

"I am CrRkkt," it said.

Rains waited for it to continue.

Silence.

Rains tried again. "With me are Amos Delacroix of the Rajin Cajuns and two of his troopers, Hebert and Landry." Rains gestured at the CASPers. "You'll get to meet them more personally after we have an opportunity to talk."

More silence.

So much for working on script, he thought.

"Look, CrRkkt, work with me here. I'll level with you. No one has seen fit to tell me what the problem is on Avbo. Care to tell me what's going on so we can stop the fighting?"

The Xiq'tal made the same gesture. "I will tell you, but it will change nothing."

"Why not?" asked Rains.

"We enjoy the fighting. Before, we hunted. This world has worthy prey, but they have been made weak, so the Tortantula take their place."

"How did the Tortantula do that CrRkkt?"

"Not the Tortantula. The Veetanho. But the Veetanho will not fight Xiq'tal, they send the Tortantula and Flatar, so we accept them as surrogates, because Avbo is boring."

"I still don't understand what they are doing."

"Shit."

"Come again?"

"The problem on Avbo is shit, Peacemaker. Everything flows to the sea, but not everything should. I suspected this would be difficult for you, so I have brought you echin to help you comprehend."

"What are echin?" asked Rains.

The Xiq'tal pointed with a fighting claw at the urchins. "Those are echin. They are native to Avbo. Echin breed in the brine waters of the river deltas and migrate to the deep on reaching maturity. They are a sensitive species and all efforts to breed them in captivity have failed. Observe."

As CrRkkt moved toward the Xiq'tal with the echin strapped to its back, the other Xiq'tal lowered itself onto the sand. CrRkkt reached for the nearest with a claw. The echin responded by flexing its spines. Several extended nearly another meter to strike CrRkkt's claw with enough force to chip the Xiq'tal's tough shell. CrRkkt pinned one of the extended spines with its other claw and tugged. Orange ichor filled the wound where the spine was removed. On the base of the severed spine were a series of muscular nodules.

CrRkkt passed the spine to Rains.

"Don't touch the sharp end of the spine. Echin secrete a neuro-toxin, but the meat is safe. Eat one of the nodules."

Rains looked at CrRkkt dubiously. *What the hell,* he thought, and pulled the smallest nodule he could find off the severed spine and gingerly put it in his mouth.

Rains' mouth was filled with a sweet, buttery flavor. As he chewed, the rich taste became deeper. His mouth filled with a tingling sensation, not unlike the fugu fish he had once eaten. As he swallowed his bite, it burned all the way down like a fine whiskey, resting in his stomach and warming him from the center out.

"That is echin, Peacemaker Rains. The effect is mildly narcotic but fades in a few minutes. This echin is tiny. There are echin in the deeps many times my size. In the water, they can move quickly by expelling water through the hollow spines. The large ones are very difficult to hunt, and they must be captured alive, as these were, for the meat to be at its best. The one you tasted is from down the coast. A prime echin can sell for tens of thousands of credits per kilo.

"Now try this one."

CrRkkt repeated his harvest with the other echin. The second creature's attack was slow and far less forceful. CrRkkt held out the spine and Rains took another small nodule and popped it into his mouth. His stomach heaved. Rains bent over and violently lost everything he had eaten and dry heaved until his stomach cramped.

CrRkkt waited for Rains to recover. "The Veetanho allow their waste treatment plant for Durst to empty into the river instead of using recycling technology. It carries the waste of Durst and the by-products from their harvest of gresh into the sea. The echin absorb the flavor through their spines. The second echin is what they taste like after. We petitioned the Veetanho to change the plant, but they refused. Do you understand now why we kill them?"

Rains wiped his mouth with the back of his hand. "You could have just told me."

CrRkkt replied, "Sometimes words lack proper impact."

"I see your point, CrRkkt, but there must be a way to resolve the issue. Financial compensation, help in reclamation. Who did you petition to have the plant modified?"

"Consolidated Agricultural Administrator Gathis. We already cull the effected echin and move those we can to areas free of taint, but the echin of the delta may never recover. We require worthy prey. The insult can only be paid with blood."

Amos chose that moment to chime in. "So, what I hear is you mad 'cause Vee-tan-oh mak' your fish taste bad, but you madder 'cause dey takes da fight out o' you fish?"

CrRkkt considered the voice coming from the CASPer. "If what my translator said is correct. Yes."

"Den Jack-son and ol' Amos gonna look for you a madder fish. I gar-on-tee!"

* * *

Back at base, Rains watched Amos climb out of his CASPer and then rounded on him. He had been seething all the way back from the beach and had worked up a good head of steam.

"A madder fish? Amos, what the fuck were you thinking? This whole thing is impossible already and you're making it harder."

Amos stepped into his kitchen, checked on his cauldron, then reached into a cooler and held out a bottle of Abt to Rains. "Jackson, you a city boy, no?"

"Yeah, city kid. The closest thing to country I got was songs on the radio, and those weren't exactly my style." Rains took a swig of the rich, dark ale.

Amos nodded and gestured at the beach with his own bottle "What you got down there is a hunter. He mad an' he bored an' dem Vee-tan-oo mess up his hunt, and dey pick his pocket, too. Sound like all dem crabs like t' hunt. I bet he no admit it but dey sent fish home 'for dey know it taste bad."

Rains shook his head "Maybe, but you shouldn't have—"

Amos interrupted. "Course I should. You say an' no do, that be a problem. I say an' no do, you tell 'im I not know what I speak 'bout and you in the clear to try something else. Sometime dem dice, dey gotta roll. Ol' Amos and his boys been all over. We find you something. If we don't, we buy you time, or you jus' mad it no your idea, eh?"

Rains thought about that for a minute. He could hear Vannix in the back of his head telling him not to let his temper get in his way.

Just then one of Amos's men clomped past the kitchen.

I don't want to know, thought Rains.

Amos yelled at him. "Hey, Louie! You no see I talkin' with the P-maker?"

Louie shouted back, "Sorry, boss, just coming off patrol. Why you call 'im P-maker and not Peace-maker?"

Amos gave Rains a sidelong glance "Because, Louie, I seen 'im drink!'"

Rains choked on his beer.

* * *

Jackson headed back to the *Turunmaa*. He updated his report then went to the bridge to fill in Captain Lorm. The duty officer pointed to a small room off the bridge that served as the captain's office. He knocked.

"Come."

Rains found Lorm working on her own reports. She sat back from her terminal and waved Rains to a guest seat.

"Well, Peacemaker Rains, were you able to make any headway with the Xiq'tal?"

"If you mean did I get them to stop wanting to kill every Tortantula on the planet, then no," said Rains. "But I did get some useful information. I've updated my report, and you have access in case something happens to me, but in a nutshell, the Xiq'tal are invested in hunting one of the native creatures. The settlement at Durst has a plant dumping waste into the river which taints the meat and ruins the value. It also makes the creatures sick, which ruins the hunt for the Xiq'tal."

Captain Lorm looked at Rains skeptically. "And that's a reason for a war?"

Rains nodded. "Apparently to the Xiq'tal it is, though I think they're enjoying it."

Lorm's tail lashed. "What are you going to do?"

"Go to Durst and talk to a ConAg administrator named Gathis to find out why they aren't using recycling technology for their waste instead of dumping it into the river. Amos has an idea we can placate the Xiq'tal by getting them something meaner to hunt. I think it's a longshot, but I've agreed to let him run down that angle. If they come up with something I'll need the *Turunmaa* to make a pickup."

Lorm shook her head. "The *Turunmaa* is not a transport for livestock, Peacemaker."

Rains didn't give an inch. "If it accomplishes the mission, Captain, this ship will be whatever I need it to be."

Lorm looked at him for a moment. "You misunderstand, Peacemaker. The *Turunmaa* lacks the equipment necessary to do what you ask."

Rains thought about that. "The Xiq'tal have been shipping live echin. I assume that means they have cargo containers that are suitable for the purpose. Would that work?"

Lorm nodded. "We will need the specifications, but it should. I still protest. It would leave you here with no support."

"I'll keep a few of Amos's men. One more thing. I could use an engineer to take a look at the plant. Do you have someone who can give me a qualified opinion?"

"I'll ask the chief. If anyone is qualified, it would be him."

"We have a plan then," said Rains. "Let's hope Amos comes up with something we can use. I'll comm ConAg, and the Flatar and Tortantulas, and let them know we'll be at the Durst port tomorrow."

Administrator Gathis was unavailable but would be notified. Rikki had answered with a curt, "Good. We'll see you there," and cut the connection. Rains went to see how Amos was doing. To his surprise, there was a Xiq'tal squatting to one side of the kitchen. Amos looked up from sorting through an enormous basket filled with fish and other sea creatures.

"Ah! Jack-son! Come over an' meet Se-bast-ion! Louie talk to him on patrol an invite him up! He bring us a basket of local treasure dat gonna be so good, I gar-on-tee!"

The Xiq'tal lowered itself in what came off as a bow. "Well met, Peacemaker Rains."

Rains responded in kind, "Well met, uh…"

"Sebastian is acceptable. Humans lack the mouth parts to pronounce my name. Louie explained that his daughter has a fondness for a media facsimile with a Xiq'tal character. Amos has been teaching me about 'gumbo' and 'Cajun sauce.'"

"What did you think?" asked Rains.

"I think the gumbo has acceptable flavor but lacks texture. None of the creatures in it are still alive, which was disappointing, and Amos takes the shells out. The Cajun sauce was interesting. Amos tells me it is 'hot,' but I don't understand what that means. It does seem to increase circulation."

Amos took a fish out of the basket and Rains could see it was still alive.

The basket must be full of water. Thought Rains.

"Here, Se-bast-ion, you show 'em!"

Sebastian took the fish from Amos and rubbed it in a bowl of Amos's sauce then ate it in a single bite. Rains watched the shell of the Xiq'tal begin to slowly redden until it had turned from its usual blue to a deeper purplish hue.

Sebastian lined up his eyestalks on the two men. "Amos said you would be talking to the Tortantula and Flatar. Does that mean we can fight again? It's the most fun we've had since the echin began to sicken."

"We are hoping to give you a different alternative, Sebastian. I'll contact CrRkkt afterwards."

"I see," said Sebastian, obviously disappointed. "I should go back now. Maybe I will see you again. What was the phrase? So long?"

"So long, Sebastian, and thanks for all the fish!"

* * *

The next morning arrived in a gray haze of cloud and rain. Fog reached for the beach in streamers, rolling in with and obscuring the breakers that crashed onto the beach and cleared the last of the gore left from the battle, leaving clean sand behind. The Cajuns had raised shelters over the base area and secured them against the weather.

Rains stared out to sea, watching the flashes of lightning and listening for the thunder that added a sharp counterpoint to the breaking waves. He stood for a moment feeling the rain on his face.

He wiped the rain away from his face with his hands and ran them over his short black hair. *I'd better grab a shave.*

With a last look, Rains took a deep breath, smelling the clean air and the faint odor of whatever passed for seaweed on Avbo being churned up by the waves, then he turned and went into the ship.

Three of the Cajuns would stay at the base to keep watch. Three plus Louie would go to Durst with Rains, and the last three plus Amos would go with Captain Lorm and the *Turunmaa.*

Amos caught up to Rains with a slate in hand. "Jack-son! I think we find you a mean-fish for de Xiq'tal!" He showed Rains the slate.

"It's ugly enough, I'll give you that," said Rains looking at the creature. "A nopf'h? How'd you find this?"

Amos nodded. "Din' I gar-on-tee? Ri-shard, his sister is with a small colony dat sea mine. Dey call it a nope-fish because it so mean. Dere crew see 'em comin' and says nope, nope, nope! But here the best part! Ri-shard, he remembers dis nopf'h because his sister tell him dey have a leak in one of dey reclamation units and the nopf'h, dey swarm it cause dey like the taste!"

Rains handed the slate back to Amos. "It's worth the try. I'll get in touch with CrRkkt about using some of their shipping equipment and fill in Captain Lorm. You can coordinate with her."

Amos left to get his crews ready while Rains headed for the bridge. Soon, the *Turunmaa* lifted for the short trip to Durst.

* * *

The *Turunmaa* settled onto the tarmac at the Durst starport, and Rains walked down the ramp with the Cajuns following him in their CASPers. Waiting for them was a squad of Tortantulas and a silver-furred Veetanho. The lead Tortantula was a massive creature with black fur and a startling white stripe along its back and had a saddle that carried not one, but two Flatar.

The Flatar in the front seat jumped out of the saddle and walked up to Rains, extending a paw.

"Peacemaker Rains, I'm Rikki. With me is Colonel Valk of the Mercenary Guild. Welcome to Durst." Rains was surprised but shook the offered paw.

"Well met. Allow me to introduce Chief Achatina of the *Turun-maa*, Louis LeBlanc of the Rajin Cajuns, and his troopers Guidry, Fontenot, and Breaux."

The Bakulu engineer made a gesture with several tentacles while his three eyestalks looked about. "Greetings Colonel, Commander," he said.

"Greetings," replied Rikki. "We'll get to know each other later over chow. You didn't need the tin cans."

Louie responded over his speakers. "You don't need fur either, but you'd look pretty funny without it."

Rikki pointed at Louie's CASPer. "I like him. And it's true enough, Humans do look funny without the hardware."

Rikki gestured behind her. "The FIB is Tikki. Call the Tort, Tavvi."

"FIB?" asked Rains.

Rikki smiled. "Flatar-in-Back. Think of him as a tail gunner." Tikki stood on the saddle and turned to wiggle his short tail in their direction, then mimed shooting with a gun in each paw. An odd noise came from Tavvi's translator. The Tortantula vibrated slightly as it laughed.

Valk stepped forward. "A word, Peacemaker Rains." Rains started to reply, but the Veetanho cut him off. "I wanted to explain the Mercenary Guild's position in case it wasn't obvious. Although the Mercenary Guild is the petitioner…" Valk paused as if the word petitioner was painful to say, then continued, "Our sole interest here is the cessation of hostilities between the Flatar-Tortantula and the Xiq'tal. I'm here as an observer. Nothing more."

That's interesting, thought Rains. "Colonel Valk, it's still unclear *why* the Mercenary Guild is involved at all."

Valk replied, "Peacemaker, the Mercenary Guild has a contract with ConAg to use larder planets for R&R and training purposes. In this case, two mercenary races have separate contracts for provisioning, and we brokered the contract for security for Durst, which is held by the Tortantula."

"I see. Where can I reach you if I need additional information?" asked Rains.

"The Mercenary Guild maintains an office here. Commander Rikki can show you, if need be. As to additional information, I assume if your superiors thought you needed it then it would have been provided." Valk stalked off into the rain.

Rikki watched Valk go. "Always a REMF around to bring joy to the grunts. This way. I'll show you where to park the hardware. We set aside barracks with a garage so your machines don't get lonely."

Rikki climbed into her saddle, dismissed her squad and led them toward one of the buildings at the edge of the landing field.

"I'm surprised Administrator Gathis wasn't on hand to greet us," said Rains.

Rikki snorted. "You shouldn't be. Gathis opposed Peacemaker involvement from the beginning. ConAg is a Veetanho company, and she and Valk don't get along. She thinks you're here to be Valk's enforcer. I wouldn't expect any help from that direction if I were you."

"Great."

"Here we are." Rikki led them through a large garage door. The building had plenty of room for the CASPers. She pointed to a door. "Barracks through there, sleeping quarters on the right, common room and an office for you, on the left. C Company shares this building; step over or pound on the wall if you need anything. Chow is in an hour. Why don't you get settled in?"

* * *

An hour later, Rikki collected them and took them to the mess hall. The hall had the traditional serving line, but instead of benches, the place was filled with café tables high enough for the Tortantula to use and the Flatar sat on high stools. Rikki pointed at a group of tables that had been pushed together. Several teams were already eating, including Tikki and Tavvi. There were Human-sized stools down one side of the tables and a sort of ramp set up for Chief Achatina.

Rikki turned to the chief. "We have a pretty good selection of vegetable dishes if that suits you. It's all fresh."

The Bakulu nodded his eyestalks. "That will be fine, Commander. Thank you. I've been looking forward to trying the local produce."

Rikki nodded at Rains and the Cajuns. "Same goes for you, and if you like protein you can try the gresh. Make sure you tell them you want it cooked. The Tortantula eat it raw. I'm told it doesn't have much flavor of its own cooked. Gresh is usually dehydrated and powdered to use as a protein supplement. We used to get shipments of seafood, but given the current issues the Xiq'tal stopped sending it."

"What's a gresh?" asked Louie.

Rikki replied, "A gresh is a six-meter-long slug. They can eat just about any vegetable matter and secrete a caustic slime. We process them for the meat and the slime is a high-quality lubricant after the caustic elements are neutralized."

Louie and the Cajuns stood. "I never eat slug before." Louie caught Rains' eye and glanced in Chief Achatina's direction.

To Rains surprise, the Bakulu caught the exchange. "Have no concern Trooper LeBlanc. I think I'll get my own meal, as well."

"Peacemaker, I was hoping we could ask your men for a demonstration of their machines. Many of the troops here have never worked with Humans, and they are curious about their capabilities," said Rikki.

"I'm sure we can work something out. I'm curious about something, too. I've never seen a Tortantula with *two* Flatar before," said Rains.

Rikki leaned over the table. "You probably won't see it again either. *Nobody* paints my toe claws like Tikki."

Rains stared blankly, at a complete loss for words as all the Flatar and Tortantula within earshot burst into laughter.

Rikki held up a paw. "Sorry Peacemaker, I couldn't resist. The reason you've never seen it before is that Tikki and I are twins. Flatar twins are very, very rare. Once the pair bonding with Tavvi took place well, there we were. It just worked itself out. A bond with one is a bond with both."

"Rikki, why do the Flatar and Tortantula keep fighting?"

"We have a contract. We always thought security for Durst was a freebie, but when the Xiq'tal attacked the plant we had to fight them off. It was fun."

"The Xiq'tal attacked the processing plant?"

"They didn't tell you?"

"Must have slipped their minds. Do you know why they attacked the plant?"

"It was after administrator Gathis started dumping waste into the river."

"Started—you mean, the plant wasn't designed to do that?"

"Of course not. It's a recycler like all the ones ConAg uses. Something about a contract dispute with the Xiq'tal."

In Rains' mind, every dressing down he'd received from his DIs about not being fully prepared went into instant replay. *Contracts. Everything that has happened here is about the contracts!* he thought.

"Rikki, can we delay my meeting with Administrator Gathis? I have something I need to do first."

"Sure, she isn't going anywhere."

"Great. In the meantime, could someone take Chief Achatina to the waste plant?"

"I'll see to it."

Rains called over Louie and the chief. "Chief, change of plans. I'd like you to go to the plant as soon as you finish your meal. Take…" Rains looked at Louie. "Guidry and Fontenot. I expect you'll find the recyclers have been turned off. If that's the case, restore them if you can, on my authority. In the meantime, I have some homework to do."

"I'm ready now," said the chief and headed off with the guide Rikki provided.

Rains headed back to their quarters, grabbed a chair, and pulled up his brief on his slate. Sure enough, one of the appendices was Contracts and included the contracts for the Mercenary Guild, Xiq'tal, Tortantula, and ConAg.

Rains opened the first contract and began to read.

* * *

Two hours later, with his head crammed full of terms and clauses and his eyes blurry from reading, Rains finally felt like he had a handle on the situation on Avbo. The entire thing was a cluster, and it had *everything* to do with the price of fish. Rains silently thanked Professor Flint's course on contracts that he understood most of what he read.

Chief Achatina had commed in that he had been able to restart the recyclers. There was nothing wrong with them, they had simply been turned off. There had been a token protest by the plant manager, but the presence of the Cajuns had quickly put an end to it along with a reminder that the Humans would be back if the recyclers were deactivated again.

Rains contacted CrRkkt to let him know that issue had been resolved.

Now for the fun part, he thought.

"Louie, I'd like you to pay a visit to Administrator Gathis and Colonel Valk. Tell them I'd like them to join me here in two hours, and let them know that if they don't show you'll be back to personally escort them. Also, if you would ask Rikki, Tikki, and Tavvi to join us, I'd appreciate it."

Louie grinned. "Now we talkin'!"

Two hours later both Veetanho arrived to join Rains. The Flatar and Tortantula had arrived ten minutes earlier.

"Thank you all for joining me. Administrator Gathis, good to finally meet you. If you will both take a seat—"

Gathis began angrily, "What's this I hear about you sending troops to the plant? I'll have your badge!"

Valk also jumped in, "Peacemaker Rains, I already explained that the Mercenary Guild—"

Rains interrupted. "Is trying to take over administration of Avbo from ConAg."

Valk stopped. "Wait, no! That isn't what we—"

Rains interrupted again. "Of course you are. Your contract states that in the case of an irreconcilable dispute between contracted parties, the administrative contract can be revoked. Administration then reverts to the original charter holder for Avbo. In this case, the Mercenary Guild. ConAg has a perpetual contract for administration unless revoked."

Valk crossed her arms. "We had nothing to do with creating the problems on Avbo."

"I agree," said Rains. "The conflict here was about to bleed the guild of some of its best shock troops with no gain. Regaining administrative control was a bonus opportunity."

Valk replied, "So you will be revoking the civilian administrative contract?"

Rains nodded. "More or less."

Gathis started. "What? You can't do that. ConAg operated in good faith!"

"By unnecessarily dumping industrial waste into the environment," Rains replied.

"We can do what we want with it," Gathis said.

"No, you can't," said Rains. "Your contract specifies ConAg 'must maintain appropriate conditions for agriculture and husbandry.' What you did violates that clause. The waste not only affects the echin but also the other marine life and the Xiq'tal themselves."

"I still don't understand why she did that," said Rikki.

"Administrator Gathis had a contractual dispute with the Xiq'tal. The ConAg contract states that the company, and the administrator, receive a percentage of the profits from agricultural or commercial harvests on Avbo. The most profitable species on the planet is the echin, but they are not a commercial harvest. The Xiq'tal hunt them individually and that makes them a sport animal and not subject to the contract."

"Are the echin worth that much?" asked Rikki.

"Millions," replied Rains. He turned to Gathis. "Administrator Gathis, I find Consolidated Agricultural in violation of its contract due to failure to fulfill the terms for maintaining appropriate conditions for agriculture and husbandry and will impose additional penalties after a detailed review. You are suspended pending your removal from Avbo by ConAg. You will deliver or otherwise provide access to all materials pertinent to the administration of Avbo and Durst to this office within twenty-four hours."

Valk stood. "Well, if that's it, I might as well get started."

"Not quite," interjected Rains.

"Peacemaker Rains—"

"Colonel Valk. I suspended the administrator but haven't revoked the ConAg contract. According to that contract, in the event the civilian administrator is suspended, administration cedes to the senior military representative who is also a contracted party. You have made it clear that your presence on Avbo is that of an observer only. The only military contract in effect for Avbo currently is the Durst defense contract. Specifically, that contract names the Tortantula."

Tikki looked startled. "That would mean…"

"Yes," said Rains. "Congratulations, Administrator Tavvi."

"Shit!" said Tavvi.

* * *

R ains looked up from yet another report and sighed. Tavvi looked down at him. "Don't start, Peacemaker. You stuck me with this job then offered to help until your ship shows up, so help and quit complaining."

Rikki and Tikki came in pushing a cart piled with boxes. "Gathis' staff found another load of records. Where do you want them?"

Tavvi pointed to a corner. "Over there."

Rains stood and looked out the window. It shattered in a hail of gunfire.

Pop! Pop! Pop!

"Cover!" shouted Rikki.

"That's an XT-12!" said Tikki, referring to the Flatars' preferred hypervelocity pistol.

Tavvi peeked through the door. "It's Gathis, I can see her across the way."

"Sit tight," said Rains. He could hear the CASPers powering up in the next room.

Rains spoke into his comm. "Louie, we're taking fire."

"On it, Peacemaker!" said Louie.

"I got this!" said Tavvi as she scrambled out the door. Rains watched the Tortantula charge across the intervening distance. Gathis tried to run, firing wildly. Tavvi weaved from side to side as she ran. She reached the opposite building, ran halfway up the wall, and used it as a springboard for a spectacular leap. The terrified former administrator stopped abruptly to find herself the landing zone for an avalanche of angry Tortantula. Tavvi crushed the Veetanho with a wet *splat!*

Louie yelled over his speakers, "Get out! Sniffers are picking up explosives!"

As Rains, Rikki, and Tikki scrambled through the door into the courtyard, Louie entered the room by simply walking through the wall. The security suite on his CASPer identified the package as one of the document boxes on the cart. Louie grabbed the box, then crashed through the wall where the shattered window was. He got a running start toward the least populated area of the base then triggered his jump jets on full. He hurled it away from him at the top of his arc just as the bomb exploded sending Louie tumbling from the sky.

Louie's CASPer fell in a crumpled ruin on the tarmac. The concussion crushed the tough armor like an old beer can. The hatch was sprung and Rains could see Louie struggling against the haptic system. Rains called up Louie's vitals on his slate as he ran toward the wreckage. *Not good. The base has a med facility if we can get him there,* he thought.

"Rains to Rikki. Louie's alive! We need a medic here *NOW!*"

"On the way, Peacemaker. Standby."

Rains reached Louie and pried the hatch the rest of the way open.

"Peacemaker. Ev'rybody all rig—"

Rains could see Louie fading in and out as the medsuite in his CASPer tried to stabilize him.

"We're all fine, Louie. You saved us. Just rest, the medics are on the way."

Louie had managed to free one arm. He reached out and grabbed the front of Rains' uniform.

"You tell my little girl I done good. That Daddy loves her!" His gaze fixed on Rains' badge.

"Trees. My Sabine love dem trees. You ever see dem white cypress in the bayou? Dey call 'em bald 'cause they lose their leaves in winter. It's a conifer but wit' leaves like lace that turn copper in fall. Oh, Jackson, dey shine in the sun like Sabine's hair…"

Rains looked at Louie's vitals again. There was nothing he could do. They were going to have to cut Louie out as it was. *Where the hell are those medics?*

"Dem wide ol' bases standin' in the water, Jackson, but the core o' them trees go on forever. Dey stand in the wind an' rain and sun an' don' nothin' topple 'em down. Dey reach straight out o' the bayou an' grab dem stars. I grab 'em, too, Jackson. For my girl an' my friends. You be like dat, too, Jackson! Don' you let nothin' topple you down!"

Jackson heard the med teams arrive, but he'd felt the tension leave Louie's grip. He stepped back to let them work, but Louie Le-Blanc was gone.

* * *

R ains comm chimed. "*Turunmaa* to Peacemaker Rains."

"Rains here. Good to hear from you, *Turunmaa.*"

Captain Lorm took over the channel. "Peacemaker Rains, we are inbound and should arrive within four standard hours. Please confirm your status."

"Captain Lorm, status is operational. We had some problems here. I'm uploading the details now. What's your mission status?" asked Rains.

"Mission successful, we have two stasis containers of nopf'h for delivery. Mr. Delacroix can give you the details."

"Thank you, Captain. Please take the *Turunmaa* to the plateau base. We'll take the Durst shuttle and meet you. I'd like to wrap this up."

"Acknowledged," said Lorm.

Amos' voice came across the comm. "Jack-son! We fill those container with nopf'h! Dey little ones are mean an' dem big ones are more mean! If dem Xiq'tal are lookin' for a fight, we got this righ', I gar-on-tee! Is Louie there? I can' get him on comms."

Rains swallowed hard. "Amos."

Rains heard Amos pause. "Aw, Jack-son. No, what you tellin' me?"

"There was a bomb. Louie grabbed it and ran. He was too close when it detonated. He saved our asses, but he didn't make it. I'm sorry."

"Damn it, Jack-son! You was s'posed to take care of my men!"

"I know, Amos. I tried. Louie took care of all of us."

"Ah, Jack-son. I always tell 'im no be a hero. You tell me you got the bastard who done 'im!"

"I didn't; Tavvi did. Gathis didn't go easy."

"Good!" said Amos. "I'll see you Jack-son. I have to figure out what to tell Louie's family."

* * *

The *Turunmaa* landed at the plateau base, and Amos and his crew unloaded the stasis containers. Rains arrived from Durst with the Cajuns and Rikki, Tikki, and Tavvi. Rains figured they had a right to see if Amos' idea would be enough to patch things between the two groups. The Cajuns caught up over the comms as the groups reunited but stayed back to cover the perimeter just in case there were any surprises.

Amos joined Rains and the Flatar. Tavvi, as usual, didn't have much to say.

CrRkkt walked across the beach with Sebastian and another Xiq'tal Rains didn't remember seeing before.

Rains began, "Hello, CrRkkt, Sebastian. Did you receive the information about the nopf'h we sent over?"

CrRkkt replied, "Yes Peacemaker, the statistics are promising. We are concerned that they may eat the echin, but if they prefer the tainted ones, they are an acceptable compromise. Your file also did not include the reproductive information."

Rains pulled up another file on his slate and transferred it.

"My apologies, CrRkkt. Until recently we didn't have all of the information to send to you. What we have is in the additional file I just sent. What we know is the nopf'h's aggression is linked to territory and they defend it once established. They are aquatic but able to spend short periods out of the water. Otherwise they're scavengers and ambush predators. They should have no problem adapting to the conditions here; they prefer salt conditions and should leave the echin breeding grounds alone. They show hive or pack behavior when small but become solitary as they grow.

"Nopf'h are asexual. They reproduce by explosive fissiparity—basically when they get to a certain size the chemical processes in the nopf'h's metabolism build up hydrogen in its body and it explodes. The pieces then grow into new nopf'h, but they have to hit that stage of their lifecycle to reproduce. If they are killed earlier, they are just dead, so you have a way to control how many are in a given area."

CrRkkt held up a claw. "Enough, we are satisfied you've provided what information you have. Your message said you have brought twenty of the small creatures and two of the large ones. Release several of the smaller specimens and let us judge for ourselves."

Rains entered a command on his slate, and the doors of the nearest container opened. Three of the smaller nopf'h left their tanks with wet *plops* and began crawling sluggishly out of the container to lie on the wet sand.

Nopf'h had round, rubbery bodies about a meter in diameter covered with armored plates. Thick, meter-long tentacles grew from the joins in the plates, more or less randomly, but each creature had twenty or more. Each tentacle was tipped with a large claw, and as the nopf'h flexed them they could see rows of suckers concealing feeding mouths. Each had a central maw filled with teeth and a row of purplish eyes evenly spaced in columns on either side of the mouth. The disoriented nopf'h sat for a moment drooling and burbling to each other.

CrRkkt moved toward the beasts. The nopf'h sensed the movement and sprang into motion as whirling, flailing masses of tentacles, rolling madly down the beach toward CrRkkt and hurling sand in all directions. The Xiq'tal braced and raised his claws to protect his eyestalks but otherwise made no motion to check the nopf'h's attack.

Two of the nopf'h reached CrRkkt. The first wrapped its tentacles around a leg and tried to climb the Xiq'tal's body, while the other used its tentacles to bounce into the air, and it wrapped itself around one of CrRkkt's fighting claws and fastened onto it with its central maw. Its claws scratched the Xiq'tal, but the sucker mouths were unable to penetrate the tough shell.

The third nopf'h rolled under Sebastian, then thrust itself up to his shell, trying to devour him from below. CrRkkt peeled the nopf'h from his leg with difficulty and passed it to the third Xiq'tal. His shell showed scratches and sucker marks where it had been attached. At one of the joints was a thin trickle of blue blood where a tentacle claw had scored a hit.

CrRkkt held up the nopf'h on his claw and looked at it closely, holding it just out of tentacle range. It burbled and reached for CrRkkt's eyestalks while continuing to gnaw at his claw. Still holding the nopf'h, CrRkkt walked up to the group waiting by the container.

"Peacemaker Rains, I do not think the nopf'h will be an acceptable replacement for the echin in the hunt."

Rains felt his blood begin to boil. "Can you explain why? They are certainly aggressive, and I can see that the small ones are able to do damage. The larger nopf'h should present a challenge and—"

CrRkkt interrupted, "I did not say we would not accept them, merely that they are not suitable for the Hunt. You did not tell us the creatures were so adorable. Do you know if anyone has tried to domesticate them?"

Rains felt a wave of relief. "No. CrRkkt. No one I am aware of has attempted to tame the nopf'h."

The nopf'h gnawed harder at CrRkkt's claw. CrRkkt rapped it on top of its body with his other claw. "No," he said. The nopf'h stopped for a moment, then redoubled its efforts.

CrRkkt swiveled his eyestalks to Rikki, Tikki, and Tavvi. "I will miss our battles. You were worthy opponents."

Rikki leaned forward. "We feel the same way, CrRkkt. Who knows though, it's a merc's life. Maybe we will fight on the same side next time."

"The Xiq'tal would enjoy that as well. Until next time then. I will send troops for the containers."

As the Xiq'tal turned to go, Amos stepped forward. "Hey, Se-bast-ion, I don' know if you hear that Louie was killed in Durst. We gonna have a do tonight to say goodbye. You should come, if you want."

Sebastian and CrRkkt looked at each other and something passed between them, then Sebastian turned to Amos. "I will come. Louie was the first Human I met and he gifted me with a place-name in honor of his child. I will join you in honoring him."

Then the three Xiq'tal turned and walked into the water.

Tavvi was vibrating under Rikki and Tikki. "Are we done here?" the Tortantula asked.

"Yeah," said Rikki. "Until tonight. Louie saved our asses, too," she said.

"Good," said Tavvi, vibrating harder. "It's been a long day, and I've had a-nopf'h for a while."

* * *

The "do" for Louie started quietly. Someone had set up a vox for music and played some very old songs, including "When the Saints Come Marching In." Amos hand-ed out bottles of Abt. "When we named the company, Louie wanted to call us the Saints but I thought that was temptin' fate," he said.

Later, the music changed, and the jazz flowed along with the Abt. Rikki and Tikki arrived back from Durst with several other Flatar and Tortantula from C Company that had become friendly with the Cajuns. Amos handed out bowls of gumbo to anyone who was hun-gry, and Cajun sauce was available for anyone who wanted a fire in their belly, including Sebastian, who had arrived with a container of echin nodules. "GalNet said it was traditional to bring food to Human remembrances," he said.

The Cajuns told stories about missions with Louie that grew more outrageous with every telling. As the evening wound down, Sebastian said, "It is time for me to return. I would like to honor Louie in the way of the Xiq'tal."

Sebastian moved down to the edge of the sea, followed by the group. He raised his claws to the sun setting above the sea.

Then he sang.

The sound was complex, high and sweet, and the sounds soared over a deep thrumming produced by the Xiq'tal's shell that blended with the sound of the waves. After a few moments. Sebastian dipped a bow to the group and, still singing, walked into the waves.

* * *

The sun was setting over the bayou, the red-gold light silhouetting the trees draped in Spanish moss and turning the feathery needles into halos. Rains sat on the mossy bank, watching the slow drift of water flow past the knees of the cypresses. He laughed as he spotted one of the bayou's blue crabs climbing over the base of one of the trees. He inhaled deeply, smelling the water and what was left of the afternoon rain. The scent of Amos' cooking lingered on the still air, and the sounds of laughter and instruments tuning up signaled the beginnings of another evening. This was his last night here, and he wanted to burn the details into his memory.

Jackson looked at his slate and called up the image of a blank peacemaker badge. He took yet another picture of one of the stately cypresses, applied the style that converted the image into an engraving, placed the overlay, then moved image after image over the badge's blank surface. Nothing seemed right.

Rains had never given much thought to trees, though he'd known someday if he was confirmed, he would need to choose one that made the emblem of the Peacemakers uniquely his. He remembered what Louie had said about the cypresses, and so when Amos had invited him back to the Cajuns' complex, he'd agreed, both to talk to Louie's family and to see the trees for himself.

They arrived in the middle of a party. An animated woman with iron grey hair and eyes red from tears had greeted them with a smile, the lines of her face showing her years. She swept Rains into a hug, then handed him a bottle of Abt.

"You must be Jack-son," she said. "Welcome home. I'm Louie's Mama Bes. Amos tol' me all about you, but I like to judge for myself. Come an' talk with me."

She looked at Amos. "I think dey need you in the kitchen."

"Welcome to the Bayou, Jack-son!" Amos gave Rains a wink then headed off in the direction Bes had pointed him.

Bes took Rains' arm and led him toward a group of chairs, calling over her shoulder, "Sabine! You come meet Jack-son and have a set with us."

A red-haired girl of about eight ran to Bes, holding a battered stuffed animal in one hand, and climbed into her lap, looking at Rains with wide eyes. The stuffed crab had seen better days.

Bes hugged the girl tight.

"Now, tell us about what happened with my Louie."

* * *

The complex was home to around a hundred people. The Cajuns had an extended family that ran into all aspects of what they did. From the moment Rains was greeted by Bes, every person he met had tried to make him feel like family. He had talked to Amos about it. Amos simply shrugged.

"It's what we do."

Bes had found Rains standing to the side of one of the paths in the compound looking at a cypress.

"Louie like dem cypress, too."

"They're beautiful. It was one of the last things your son spoke about. That and Sabine. When I look I want to see with his eyes," Rains said.

"The eternal tree," said Bes.

"Yes. I read the heartwood is so strong it was used for building instead of steel. The wood is beautiful. They found trees buried over fifty thousand years ago that still smelled of fresh sap when they were cut. Louie said that nothing could topple them down because of the base."

"He was right. They strong; stronger than you would believe. The base helps, but a single tree won't stand alone. The thing that makes 'em so strong is those bases, deep down under the water where no one sees, dey support each other. The knees protect the fish, and the birds come, and the moss grow. Dey shelter everything around them. Dey grow every day and the more dey grow the more shelter dey give. Dem trees strong because dey love. Even when it look all alone, it held up by what no one see." Bes looked off into the bayou. "When they finally fall, the shelter let other things grow, but you read all that. You put your hands on this tree, an' I tell you the rest. I can't give you Louie's eyes, but I show you his heart."

Jackson moved to place his hands on the cypress, feeling the texture of the bark.

"Close your eyes," Bes said.

Rains did, feeling self-conscious.

Bes continued, "Now you feel dat tree. You know what it look like and what it feel like, and if you lean in a little you know what it smell like. You think about everything you read and everything you think you know, and I tell you exactly why it is the way it is. You ready?"

"Yes."

Bes paused; the silence stretched.

"Because it can't be anything else; it true."

Bes put her hand over Rains' heart. "Be true, Peacemaker."

* * *

Rains thought about that again as he went through image after image, still not finding what he was looking for. But Bes's lesson had hit home. Rains was a Peacemaker because it was what he was.

"Uncle Jackson?"

Rains turned to see Sabine and smiled. She ran up and hugged him, her stuffed crab bouncing along behind her. He wasn't sure when he had become "Uncle Jackson," but it seemed to have stuck.

Sabine held up a piece of paper to him.

"I made you something!" she said proudly.

Rains held up the paper in the evening light. It was a picture of a cypress, drawn in crayon. Rains snapped a picture with his slate. The image settled onto the badge. As the style applied, the rough edges faded, but the heart shone from the image's surface. The truth remained. Rains leaned in to hug his niece.

"Thank you, Sabine. This is perfect."

* * * * *

Matt Novotny Bio

Matt Novotny is a writer of short fantasy, horror, and military science fiction, and he abuses the world of songwriting with Filks. He works professionally in the ARM industry where he has worn a variety of hats including Systems Administrator, IT Project Manager, and Corporate Trainer. He spends any spare time playing RPG's, backpacking, or antiquing. Matt and his girlfriend make their home in Littleton, Colorado, surrounded by ever-increasing piles of books, creepy collectables, and unfinished home and garden projects.

\# \# \# \# \#

How to Train Your Canavar
by Marie Whittaker

S omething large smacked against the pier outside, rattling the old, metal walls. Ceili stopped her staff kata and held her breath for a second. Even the softest thump against a mostly empty warehouse made an obnoxious amount of noise. Dismissing it as a side effect of an afternoon storm, she got back to her workout.

It happened again. Something hard bumped against the side of the beams supporting the time-battered warehouse, the sound radiating through the salt-crusted walls.

She sighed and kicked her equipment together on the mat. The unused warehouse she had claimed for her own purposes wasn't trusted to house anything of value because the structure was aged and nearly worn through in a few places where it was regularly splashed with sea water. Salty air was another enemy of the thin walls. The iron frame of the structure managed to maintain its integrity, but she couldn't have some hunk of gods-only-knew-what beating up the pier. It was likely the neighbor kid's water bike broke loose from its tether again, but she prepped a kayak to go out and check.

Moments later, Ceili paddled through low chop and humidity so thick that she couldn't tell what was sweat and what was water. Cloud cover blotted out both suns and darkened the surface, which

295

made it tough to see much in the waves lapping against the uprights. She stopped paddling and listened. *Thunk.* She pulled back on the paddle to turn the kayak and followed the sound until she spied a smooth, black object, the rounded top of the capsule barely breaking the surface amid broken pieces of wood. That meant whatever the debris was, it was going to be heavy. But it was oddly buoyant.

After fiddling at the side of the thing to try to find an edge to hang onto in order to tow it into the interior slip, she gave up and positioned the nose of the kayak against it and began bumping it through the waves. It wasn't easy. A flat piece of wood floated nearby and drifted against the kayak. Words and symbols were stamped into the soaked wood. Sea lice squirmed all over the thing, so she brushed them off into the water and tossed the plank onto the flat nose of the boat so she could keep control.

Soft rain intensified, coming down in a thick sheet. She dug hard with the paddle to put the object in motion. Sometimes it sank and she had to wait for it to come back to the surface. At least she'd get an ab and arm workout because of it.

One final nudge put the capsule firmly against the corner of the slip, where it rocked gently in the thrust of the waves. After the arduous job, her arms felt like overboiled noodles. She balanced to step out of the kayak and secured it with a strap so it wouldn't drift off. She tossed the plank with the odd markings onto the deck.

Ambient lighting inside the warehouse made the object seem blacker than black, as if it was absorbing the light. The only reason it had appeared shiny outside was the water coating the top of it. The surface was a sort of matte. Finally, curiosity won out. She put a hand on the exposed surface, feeling arcs and ridges along the exterior. She'd never seen anything like it.

She grabbed a thick net from a pile that was last used years ago when the warehouse was a station for offloading crates. With one side of the net in hand, she dropped into the water, knowing she'd have to dive a little to wrap it up and tether it to the hoist. Dragging the rope under, she pushed through the water next to the thing, feeling for the bottom, but she couldn't reach it. *What the hell?*

After several more tries she managed to spread the net below the entire capsule, small buoys tugging the edges upward. Once that was done, she was able to bring the edges of the net together and secure it to a central loop, which she threaded with a large hook rigged to a cable.

She heaved herself out of the water and flopped onto her back on the cool surface of the dock, breathing hard. Dangling from the iron hook above was a pully system once used to offload shipments. It hadn't been used since she was a kid, but she hoped the mechanics would come to life one last time. She rolled to her feet and retrieved a remote to bring the hoist to life.

The winch groaned into motion, chugging and pulling the cable tight. Once the weight of the object was out of the water, the pully system easily hoisted what was clearly a gleaming black egg from the water.

Excitement and awe tore through Ceili. Being Human and seeing mostly those of her own race growing up, she had studied new species and learned about other races as often as she could. She stilled the crane and stared while water sluiced off the egg. Carefully, she directed the arm to the side and began to lower the capsule onto a pallet. When it had only a few inches to go, the side of the aged net snapped and the object tumbled free, smashing to the floor with a *crack*. Ceili let go of the control and rushed to catch it, certain it would roll back toward the slip, and she'd be forced to start over. She got a hand on the side and slid to a crouch, only to find the object wasn't going to roll anywhere. The entire bottom of the thing was spiderwebbed with cracks.

Dammit.

She couldn't say the smell coming from the inside made life any more enjoyable. No wonder, if it floated with that much air inside. No substance leaked out, but there was a blue-gray membrane showing between the wide cracks.

Ceili stepped back, assessing the situation. She'd apparently rescued a giant rotten egg from the ocean. How would she dispose of such a thing? It smelled worse than the scrap buckets from her family's fish paste plant. At least it had crashed onto the pallet where she'd intended to set it down. A couple of the wooden slats were busted, but if she brought a motorized skid over from the main warehouse, she could easily pick it up and dump it outside in the plant's industrial-sized refuse bin to be tossed out.

It was a plan.

She turned to go, sliding her bare feet into more suitable work shoes and was about to leave when a strange sound erupted from behind her. Ceili stopped in her tracks and spun around just in time to see a large part of the eggshell tip onto the floor.

"Whoa, damn," she breathed, backing away a few tentative steps. Something that looked like a large insect was curled up on the pallet, the bottom of it still encased in the black shell. One…arm, she guessed, stretched upward, a pincer on the end testing the air. It withdrew and curled up again, snapping back to where many other arms, or legs—appendages—were curled around the thing's thorax.

The head was shaped a bit like a frying pan, with two bulbous, segmented eyes on each side.

She didn't realize she'd moved toward it until she peered down into the many-lensed gaze of the baby…whatever. It twisted its head inquisitively, the little "hands" moving around, with one of them creeping up where the mouth opened. A soft coo rose from the alien baby as it gazed around the warehouse and put its little pincer in its mouth.

"You are so ugly that you're kind of cute." Ceili stared. It was truly amazing something could stay alive, bobbing around in saltwater for an undetermined amount of time. She stepped back as the legs expanded and the segmented body twisted free of the shell.

* * *

Three Days Later.

"Must be nice," commented Gra'dn. Meln, his best friend, sat in front of a map of Krifay's resorts, planning out a short stay after he made his drop.

"Not my fault you joined the wrong guild," Meln said with a half-smile. Gra'dn knew his friend merely joked. The two Oogars had decided on different careers in their teens. They still managed to get together whenever it was possible, and that it helped with his current guise as an "undercover" merc was a stroke of genius by his friend.

"And at least you get to check out the sights this time." Meln circled the coast of the island of Tayah, the destination of his drop, which also happened to be one of the premier travel destinations in the galaxy. "I'm glad to see you taking better care of yourself."

The mandatory respite imposed on Gra'dn was recommended by his boss. No, not recommended, ordered. Routine physical examination had twice revealed Gra'dn's stress level was off the chart. He was on strict orders to relax. That was something entirely new for someone who suffered from hypervigilance after some of the more…colorful situations his job put him in. He'd seen things, and worse, to him anyway, done things that didn't go away. Faces stayed in the back of his mind and appeared when he least expected them. Voices of the dead chimed into conversations where they were not wanted. After arguments and several of his inquiries, checking to see if he was merely being singled out in a company that might play favorites, he finally accepted the assurances that, no, he'd done nothing wrong. Rather, he'd done everything right and now his mind was letting his body know that it needed to reset.

And so, Gra'dn, the hardened Peacemaker, was going fishing.

And not just any old kind of fishing. He was going to learn Earth fishing. Humans had, at one point, been the best in the Union at relaxing. Especially the ones from the old United States. Fishing with a rod that had a string line tied to it seemed to do the trick. Sometimes really bad beer was involved, but that's where Gra'dn drew the line. He would have good beer while he learned the ancient art of relaxing by fishing.

"Here's your place, just blocks down the coast from this bar." Meln pointed a claw at the map. "Happy days, my friend." He patted Gra'dn on a thick shoulder. "I'll make my drop and check in after the business is settled."

"I'm going to catch dinner," Gra'dn proclaimed. He rubbed his paws together. "I read that Humans populated the ocean with food species from Earth when they immigrated. The tour company is the one that sells Murphey's Fish Paste." His mouth watered at the thought.

"That stuff's almost as tasty as those square meat cans."

"You mean Spam?"

"That's the stuff. Smells horrible. Likely dumped into those cans before we were born. Probably isn't even meat, but man, that's some tasty vittles."

Meln began the process of bringing the small carrier ship in, preparing to make contact with the dock.

"I'm going to read for a while," said Gra'dn. "Physician's orders."

"Good idea," said Meln.

* * *

For as long as Ceili remembered, everything around her smelled like fish.

Her family immigrated the week after her parents married back on Earth. They'd set up a good life for themselves on the water planet of Krifay, settling on the island of Tayah. They were hard working people on Earth and that had paid off during the move. Now, the Murphey's owned an island resort which was also home base and the manufacturing plant for Murphey's Fish Paste. Highly sought after, they'd played it smart when creating the delicacy. Only two million jars were created during any one year, making their fish paste highly sought after and very expensive.

Ceili wiped down a display, marveling at the way smashed fish amounted to her claim to fame. At least she got to meet new people of different alien races when she did fishing and diving tours, which was the secondary business venture she'd set up just for herself to break up the monotony of quiet resort island life.

She couldn't complain. She had it good. Her parents had refused to fall into the same rut as other Humans after First Contact and become mercenaries. Most Humans found that to be their only option. But the Murpheys gathered their resources and struck out. Now Ceili found herself manning the resort desk and guiding fishing tours, a service that was also expensive and highly sought after throughout the Union. She couldn't believe the amount of credits people paid to go old-style fishing. When not working, if she could call it that, she read and researched about other worlds and their native species. She read about the triumphs of the Peacemakers and dreamed of traveling to new planets to research. She also kayaked a lot and dove almost daily, exploring Tayah's waters. This had been her life for nearly two years, since the day her parents left her in charge of the business.

Not a bad life at all.

But Ceili was bored with it all. She watched the skies as ships traveled past, wondering if the beings on board even bothered to glance at the little blue gem she lived on. Her parents traveled the Union, bringing in the wealthy as resort clients. Ceili managed the place. Not single-handedly, but she did it with deft precision. From her post in her extremely small world, Ceili dreamed of all the other things she could be doing while she took care of her responsibilities like she'd promised.

The door swung open, bringing her back to the moment. It had to be her morning tour. "One moment," she called over her shoulder. She quickly finished straightening the display and hustled to the reception counter.

A huge Oogar beamed at her. All fangs and purple fur, he just couldn't seem to quit grinning. A short-sleeved floral print shirt was buttoned to his chin, gawdy red, orange, yellow, and chartreuse hibiscus flowers screaming random colors. She didn't know what was more fun, his giddy expression or the way the shirt clashed with his fur.

Yep. Definitely my morning tour. Ceili smiled back. She loved to meet people of different races. "You must be Mr. Gra'dn?" she asked, checking a screen on the counter.

"It's just Gra'dn. I have a fishing lesson this morning." He glanced at a name tag on her shoulder. "It's nice to meet you, See-eye-lee."

Ceili laughed, wondering if his translator was killing it with autocorrect. "It's pronounced 'Kay-lee.' Nice try though. Some people really slaughter it. You didn't do so bad at all."

"Got it. Sorry about that. Are you my fishing teacher?"

"I am," she said, still grinning. "I guess this means you've never been fishing?"

"Not once. I'm on strict orders to relax, and since I was in the area with a friend, I signed up." Gra'dn clapped his paws together, rubbing them in excitement.

Ceili stared at his very Human gesture. And those were quite the mitts. Teaching him to fish might be a trick if he wasn't dexterous with the line.

"Well, you look like you're ready to go. I need to confirm your ID and lock our destination into the system."

Gra'dn pulled two credential cards from a pocket. Ceili's eyes went wide. "You're a merc!"

He laughed. "Is that a problem?" He guessed she would have freaked twice as hard if she learned he was really a Peacemaker.

"No, not at all. I mean…" Her eyes betrayed her by looking straight at the screaming shirt he wore. "I just never would have suspected—"

"Doctor's orders," he said. He gestured up and down the shirt with a purple paw. "Relaxing." He winked and clicked his tongue at the same time.

Ceili nodded. "Okay then. Let me grab my daypack and we'll get started." She confirmed the trip, led him out of the office, secured the entrance, and they were off.

* * *

"Anyway, the stress gets to a guy, you know?" Gra'dn looked anxiously to the spot he'd cast his bait. He'd spent most of the morning blabbing about work and his health, and how life as a merc contributed to his current state and location, carefully interchanging the word "merc" for "Peacemaker." He'd been careful not to get too into the gory details, but even a seemingly soft Human like Ceili certainly suspected he'd seen some nasty shit go down. Figuring it was past time to shut up, he took a deep breath and feigned interest in two birdlike animals passing overhead.

"Pull in your slack," Ceili prompted. "You have to keep the line lively." She readied her own rig, baiting another hook.

"Sorry for the blather. I guess I haven't been getting out much. I mean, I get out a lot but not around normal people. I mean, not normal. Or…" He grimaced.

"I get it," she said. "I don't get out at all." She laughed lightly. "Trade me." She held out the freshly prepped pole, which he accepted with a grin. Ceili wasn't very big for a Human. Her eyes glinted with the same blue as the ocean where sunlight shone. She constantly tucked hair behind her right ear and dimples creased her cheeks even when she wasn't smiling, which wasn't often. She was likeable, he decided.

"Fishing's great so far," he said.

"It can be very therapeutic." Ceili reeled in the line, inspecting what was left of his bait. Sure enough, something had carefully munched the bait while Gra'dn digressed into his story.

"Put this one out there," she pointed to an area in the bay that was hidden from direct sunlight. "Let it sink for a quick minute then slowly bring it back in. Lift it, then let it fall, then lift it again."

Gra'dn eagerly obeyed, casting, then reeling in the line, just like she said.

"Great, now watch closely and keep going," she said, coaching him softly. Humans had populated the waters on Krifay for decades with species of fish from Earth, which had adapted to the differing environments below the surface. She hoped just one would play nice. *Please make it a whopper, too.*

A second later a massive hit took his line low into the water. The reel screamed as line ripped past the bail.

"Wahoo!" Gra'dn yelled, gripping the pole with both paws but doing nothing with the reel.

Ceili burst out laughing so hard it was impossible to talk. The big Oogar became frantic, trying to wrap his paws around the base of the pole while whatever he'd hooked fought like hell, yanking the fishing boat forward. She nearly lost her footing as the boat jerked against the anchor. Finally, Gra'dn remembered what she'd taught him and started reeling like an insane person, still hooting.

Ceili grabbed a net as he brought the fish closer. He'd managed to hook a decent-sized bonefish. "Nicely done," she said.

Gra'dn's cheeks burned from grinning so hard. "Dinner's on me!" he announced, excited to get his first catch in the boat. The fish leapt from the water, glinting in the sun, twisting and flexing in the air. More fishing line tore from the reel. He held fast as his catch smacked flat into the water, tugging hard, trying to dive deep and away, but it was right at the boat and in plain view. Ceili positioned the net, and Graydon pulled it up.

And the fish slipped the hook, the line going slack and his pole losing its arch. His excitement fizzled like an untied balloon.

Gra'dn fell silent, his hopes dashed like a child who'd dropped his ice cream. Ceili put a hand on his forearm as he stared at the water with an expression of shock.

"We have an old saying from way back on Earth that my parents told me. There are more fish in the sea." She smiled.

"I can't believe that just happened," he said.

"Happens to the best of us." She patted his arm again. "Reel this one in for me?" She took the spent pole from his grasp and gestured to the rod she'd braced on a mount so she could grab the net.

With a sigh, Gra'dn took the other pole and began to reel it in, but the line went taught and another fish broke the surface. "Look, look!" he yelped.

Ceili laughed. "Set the hook this time." But she knew that fish was good and hooked even as he gave the line a quick pop and began dragging the doomed bonefish toward the boat.

"You're really good at your job." Gra'dn couldn't quit grinning.

"Thanks. It's good fun, but it gets a little old, you know? There's a whole expanse of universe out there. I've always longed to go to that Peacemaker Academy. I envy you, getting to travel from planet to planet, meeting new races and seeing new worlds. Mine is really small."

"Actually, I've been staying pretty close; same sector for a few years now, tracking an illegal shipment. You should travel."

"I don't see that happening. This might just be my lot in life. I promised my parents."

"They must be very proud of you, running the whole show here on Krifay."

"I think they are. They're great people from a great family. I was named after my great, great grandmother."

The bonefish barely moved as she scooped it up with the net, resigned to its fate and spent from fighting. She handed Gra'dn the net and took the pole in exchange, then worked the hook free from the fish's mouth with a pair of needle-nosed pliers with practiced skill.

"Your name has an unusual spelling," he said, poking at the fish.

"So, the story goes that my great-great-grandmother was conceived during a ceili back in Ireland, on Earth, where that side of my family hails from." She gave him a half-smile. "Charming, right? Being named after rowdy dance party sex. Ha, ha, joke's on me."

He smiled wide. "Actually, I do think it's charming." He lugged the fish toward the hatch she held open and watched as it darted to the bottom of the live-tank.

"Keeps them fresh until we get back to process them," she explained. "Ready for the next lesson?"

"Yeah!" He clapped his paws together. "There's more? This is great."

"You're going to love it. We're going spear fishing in the shallows."

* * *

Gra'dn imagined Ceili was the type of Human who would never starve, no matter what planet she found herself on. She handled a spear like she'd had extensive training with one, and not just for the purpose of fishing. She hurled one so fast and with such precision he couldn't help but be impressed. The top of her head barely came to his chest, but she was lithe and quick. He made a mental note not to piss her off while she had a spear in her hand.

She glanced about into the trees as they passed on their way to what she called "shallows" to fish with spears, almost like she was looking for something moving in the brush. The island of Tayah was covered in canopies of trees of various types. He could only imagine the creatures living there.

"Lots of wildlife around?" he asked, trying to get the feel of the light fishing spear she handed him.

She laughed as she tugged on a line securing the anchor. "Well…yes. More than I expected, anyway. I grew up here and this place keeps it interesting lately."

Without warning, Ceili stepped right off the side of the low boat deck and stood thigh-deep in the water. She grinned at him. "Ready?"

"Yeah," Gra'dn said, pulling in a deep breath. He tipped his legs over the edge and let himself slide into the water, then retrieved his spear from the deck.

Ceili waded toward a raised bit of sand a few meters out. He followed, looking into the crystal water for anything she might be planning to stab with her stick.

"This is the most basic way people used to fish on Earth," she explained. "Spearfishing advanced and so did the equipment used, and it can be viewed as more of a sport these days." She slicked water from her bare legs and waited for him to trudge onto the sand with her.

Once Gra'dn stood beside her, his attention was immediately drawn by glinting scales beneath the surface on the other side of the sand bar they'd come to.

He followed Ceili's lead as she walked into the pool, carefully so he didn't disturb the fish around them. Quietly, she raised her spear and sunk it into the water and withdrew it quickly with a thrashing fish on the end. She deposited it into a bag strapped to her waist and nodded to him, signaling that it was his turn.

He concentrated on trying to stab the fish by his feet while Ceili hurled her spear farther into the shallow pool, then retrieved the fish from where it had been hit.

"It takes some practice," she said when she returned.

Gra'dn managed to miss for quite a long time until her coaching finally paid off.

The afternoon flew by as they filled their hip packs with the small fish. A bank of clouds roiled in from the horizon line of the sea beyond. It was time to get back before the storm hit.

Soon enough, he found himself back at the tour office with a big package of freshly fileted fish, battling sadness that the day was done. Ceili busied herself with finalizing his payment at the counter while he glanced around.

"Your receipt has been sent." She smiled at him, handing over his Yack.

He slid a handful of chits across the counter as a tip. "Today was good fun."

The words poured from his translator and Ceili had to wonder what the sentence would sound like in his native tongue.

"I have to meet Meln. Would it be okay if I came back for another trip, and maybe a tour of the fish paste facility? Meln and I both love the stuff."

"Certainly. I also have diving tours, and we could kayak—" She stopped talking and considered his bulky form. Either he wouldn't fit on the kayak or he'd be a full-time swimmer. He didn't look like he was one for good balance.

"I'm not much for swimming."

"I can't believe you're one for fishing, either, but you're getting really good at it." She had to wonder why he'd enjoyed it so much. He was a merc. Now, *that* was excitement. Why would he want to hang out on her uneventful little island rather than engage in the adventure his job provided? But whatever.

"Let me touch bases with Meln. I'll be in touch about setting up another tour, if that's okay."

"Sounds great, Gra'dn. It was good to meet you. I had a great day."

"Me, too. Earth fishing is everything I read it would be."

* * *

"Just a few days old and look at how big you are," exclaimed Ceili, rubbing the flat spot above the hatchling's mouth. It made a soft cooing sound, as it chewed a fish head she handed it from a bucket of production scraps. Owning a fish paste company had more than the obvious perks.

"I think I'll call you Steve." She didn't like thinking of him as the thing that grew monstrously in her auxiliary warehouse. Or the beast that loved to suck down buckets of fish guts. But Steve was who he was, she guessed. *What* he was, was the real question.

She squatted down to rub his head some more as he tipped the bucket of goo over and went to work gulping down the mess. Steve changed each time she came to see him. His body grew long. He held the legs attached to his middle thorax folded tightly but he used his forelegs like arms, using the pincers at the ends to grasp food. Yesterday she'd noticed a bulbous stinger on the end of his tail, which had wagged furiously when he first saw her.

She sighed, scratching at the plates over his compound eyes. Maybe one of these times she'd come in after work and he'd be gone, having left through the interior slip, swimming off to find his way to one of Krifay's jungle islands or misty rain forests. He seemed the type of being to belong there.

She stood up and slid the last bucket toward him, which he intercepted with a rather dexterous one-armed grab while finishing up the rest of the last bucket.

"Have a good night, Steve." He didn't look up but kept cooing and gorfing slime. Ceili walked to the old front office area to hit the mat for a few staff katas before bed.

During the next week, Ceili and Gra'dn sent messages to one another to set up Gra'dn's next tour. The first message was odd and random, and she wasn't sure if it was Gra'dn or not. She answered tentatively in a professional tone in case it wasn't him. The only way she knew it was him was the reply he sent after she'd confirmed his booking: "Can't wait to try the fish paste."

* * *

Fishing was nearly a bust due to heavy cloud cover and a choppy breeze that grew into gusts strong enough to cast a thick spray into their faces. They caught one pan-sized fish that was the Krifay equivalent of a small halibut, which seemed to make Gra'dn extremely happy. "I'll pack that one up for free and get you a refund for the crappy tour," she said, holding out a basket. He set the freshly cleaned fish inside with extra care and took the basket from her hands with a dopey smile showing fangs through his hairy face. Ceili shook her head with a chuckle.

"What?" he said, laughing. "This is dinner. And who knows when I'll get to come back and fish again. Earth fishing is the best." He helped her gather the fishing rigs and bait bucket while she attempted to keep her salt-soaked hair out of her face. "No deal on the refund, either. If you must, let's consider it a credit toward my next tour, whenever that might happen."

"Deal," she said. She set the gear down, giving in to the wind and sea spray. She pulled a length of cord from her jacket pocket, scraped her soaked hair out of her eyes, and bound it in a tail on top of her head. Gra'dn was already on the dock with most of the gear.

"Looks like you'll get your fish paste tour after all," she said. "It's a good day to check out the facility."

At the plant, Gra'dn marveled at the process which took loads of freshly caught seafood through different phases, ending up in fist-sized jars moving on a conveyer belt to be labeled and sealed into cartons. He ate his fill, sampling as they stopped at different process stations. Usually bored out of her mind by that time, Ceili enjoyed watching him. He really was a big goof. She had to wonder what sort of a switch it took to make someone like Gra'dn pivot to his business side, to step into his role as a merc.

He placed two wrapped jars in a satchel that rested above his left hip as they exited the last of the long string of warehouses. The squall had let up a bit, but the wind still created a fine mist that doused them.

A tone sounded from one of the many pieces of handheld technology he had strapped to him. As he reached for a pocket on his belt, Ceili said, "Hey, I need to go inside here for a couple. Wait here?"

He nodded, keying a handheld slate. Since they were at the warehouse anyway, she might as well feed Steve. Ceili walked to the door right in front of them and keyed the first lock, then the other two.

* * *

Moments later, Gra'dn's call ended. He gawked around for a short while, but it was getting late and he needed to get going. The door was unlocked so he peeked his head in.

"Ceili?" he called.

She didn't answer so he entered the warehouse. Just inside was a partitioned area that had the look of an old office. A door hung open on the far side of the room so he kept calling and looking for her.

"Ceili? I have to meet Meln. I don't want to just take off..." He passed a thick mat and a rack with dumbbells of various sizes and a jump rope hanging over a towel rack.

Finally, a light laugh echoed toward him from farther in. He smiled and walked into the open expanse of an empty, old shipping warehouse and stopped dead. A small Canavar—and "small" was completely relative because they grew to be much larger than the warehouse it stood in—obviously recently hatched by its size, caught a fish head Ceili tossed to it. The top of the thing's back was taller than Ceili and it was at least ten meters long. Ceili laughed and patted the deadly beast's head, sliding a bucket toward it with a foot.

It appeared calm. Gra'dn didn't want to change that, for her sake.

He needed his weapons. Backing away quietly, he stepped right into a wooden staff that fell through his paws when he tried to catch it and bounced around on the concrete floor with a horrid clatter. He stilled the noise by stomping on it.

Ceili turned to see Gra'dn in the doorway, "Um, so 'wait here' doesn't mean 'stay put' where you're from?" she teased.

Gra'dn lost his composure. "That's a Canavar!

"A what?"

"They're illegal!"

"He's not illegal," she said with a snort. "He's...he's a baby!"

* * *

Steve began twisting his head in a bobbing figure eight, obviously growing fearful and defensive. To Ceili, at least. Gra'dn looked as if he wanted to smash Steve with a giant boot heel. Ceili patted one of the Canavar's forelegs in an attempt to calm the creature.

"Ah, it's getting agitated, Ceili. Come away now, please." He waved her toward him with both hands.

"He's not agitated, he's scared."

Gra'dn changed his stance but continued to gesture for her to move away.

"You're scaring him!"

Gra'dn spoke rapidly but tried to stop shouting. "Ceili, there's a reason they're illegal. That thing eats people. And everything else. I don't know, maybe it's not there yet, but you are its favorite food! It will lay this cute little seaside town of yours bare in under an hour. Please come out here with me?"

Ceili looked from Steve, who had reared up onto his rearmost sets of legs and was weaving his head far above them at a fast rate, his compound eyes on Gra'dn, who waved even more furiously. She didn't move. Gra'dn pulled a mean looking handgun from the pack he always wore on his hip.

"Hey!" she yelled. "There's no need—"

"Ceili, step over here with me. *Now*," Gra'dn said, though gritted teeth.

Ceili squinted. *So, that's what it looks like. Pivot achieved.*

Suddenly Steve dropped his forelegs onto the concrete in front of her, shielding her from Gra'dn, who was clearly the one who was agitated. It was a scary move. Ceili glanced up at the creature's underbelly, which reminded her of the bottom of a crab. Each time Steve moved, chitinous plates expanded and contracted. The creature let out a piercing scream that crescendoed into a screeching roar. Her hands shot up to cover her ears. For the first time since she'd rescued the egg from the ocean, she felt a pang of fear.

Gra'dn backed to the open door. "I don't know how it got here, but I have no choice but to report this to the guild. I don't want to leave you here like this, but if I shoot at that thing and only wound it, that will be the end of you, Ceili Murphey."

"I've never seen him act this way," she said. "He's just upset. He's never seen another person—being, I mean. He'll calm down."

But Gra'dn shook his head and stepped back.

"Gra'dn, please. Don't call anyone." She stepped from behind the massive legs and pincers, running to retrieve the wooden plank with the odd symbols. "Here, look! This debris was floating around him when I found him, still in his shell, in the bay. There's a logo right here but I don't know what it means."

Gra'dn apparently recognized the markings on the broken piece of shipping crate in Ceili's hands. "The Science Guild." He huffed. His hackles shot up. "You have limited time with that thing, Ceili. I hope you understand that. One way or another this ends bloody." He left.

Ceili's emotions chased in circles as she considered his warning. Everything had happened so quickly since the day the egg cracked. It had been what, five days? How could she have known? She walked over and closed the door after Gra'dn, then turned to look at the huge insect with new eyes. It certainly was growing fast. It dropped its head, eyes locked on her, as if it sensed the fear that was a new element between them.

She picked up the fallen staff and leaned it against the rack where it belonged, mind whirling. What if Gra'dn was right? She'd made mistakes before, but nothing like this.

Ceili turned back to the creature—the "Canavar"—that was taking up more and more space in the old warehouse. She slid the last bucket of fish scraps toward him—it. The Canavar jammed a sharp pincer into the bucket, compound eyes burning into her as fish heads and entrails blew out of the top of the bucket, splattering stickily onto the floor and its chest plates. It leaned over the bucket, an ominous clicking pouring from its segmented maw.

Ceili backed a few steps away and gripped her hand around the shaft of a spear as her heart tried to pound her backbone to dust.

And he was just a baby.

* * *

"I told her I had to report it to the guild." It hadn't been a half hour since he'd seen what Ceili was keeping in her auxiliary warehouse. He was in a shit mood and couldn't stop pacing, so he forced himself into the café booth across from Meln, who was eating a plate of something Gra'dn couldn't identify. "She doesn't know the true instincts of the Canavar."

Meln nodded solemnly and took a big drink from an antique mug. Then he perked up. "Well, it hasn't eaten her yet," he said, optimistically.

"You're always such a ray of sunshine."

Meln waved to the bartender. "You need a beer, brother."

"I'm not in a great mood, in case you couldn't tell," Gra'dn protested.

The Veetch behind the bar moved its many arms, all of which seemed to be tasked with different parts of his job. Meln held up his mug and the bartender nodded its head and clucked its beak. One limb snatched a clean mug and another pulled on an ornate tap handle molded in the shape of a mermaid with a mug in her hand. Five seconds later a full mug slid down to the waxed bar and stopped right in front of Meln, who nodded a thanks.

"Skills," he said, and slid the fresh beer to Gra'dn, who stopped it with a paw. "This place really is like the town that time forgot."

Gra'dn could care less at the moment. "Ceili wouldn't knowingly do something to get others hurt. She's got a good heart."

"First, you're so falling for a Human. Second, if there's no intent, why worry? Call the thing in now so it's exterminated. Sounds like it's not in a volatile state. Should be an easy job if it's handled now, before it gets any bigger."

Gra'dn shook his head and took a long pull from his mug, despite himself. "I am not falling for her."

Meln *mm-hm'd* into his mug.

Gra'dn put his mug down a little harder than he intended. "She's never gonna talk to me again."

Meln waved at the bartender again. "Can we get another plate of those curly pink bugs?"

The Veetch smiled and nodded, then laughed and shook its head. "They're called shrimp, and they're even better if you peel them first."

"I'll try that. Thanks, man." Meln toasted the bartender.

Gra'dn rested his chin in a paw, pensively spinning his mug in the pool of condensation. "No one wins in this situation."

A plate skidded down the bar, stopping beside Meln. He grabbed one, put it between his paws and rubbed it fast, then dropped shrimp skin on the bar while he popped the peeled shrimp into his mouth. "Which guild?" he managed to ask as he chewed.

"What do you mean?" Gra'dn felt himself growing angrier by the moment. He checked himself, making sure not to take it out on his friend.

"Well, you said the Canavar isn't quite to murderous rampaging killer stage. To me, it sounds like there's time to make a sound decision on what's best for this adorable, tasty island and your friend," said Meln, munching away. He grabbed another shrimp, looked at the bartender, shrugged, and popped it in his mouth, shell and all.

"So, which guild?" Meln stopped crunching, smiled, and tapped his mug against Gra'dn's. "Life's about choices, man. Find 'em."

* * *

Ceili backed through the old office and out the warehouse door, grasping a fishing spear like it was a lifeline. She locked every lock, her thoughts surging around the question of what the hell to do next.

It was late in the afternoon and most of the employees had surely gone. No tours were due to show up. These were the good things. She turned to run to the tour office, intent on finding Gra'dn. He had been so very correct.

A screeching peal rent the surrounding shipyard and plant. Ceili stopped dead. Two men, still in their protective work suits from processing, ran toward her.

"Run!" one of the men yelled. He grabbed her arm, barely slowing down. "Ms. Murphey, it isn't safe. There's a-a—something big's in the empty warehouse!"

"Okay!" Ceili ran with the man as he exited the employee gate, slowing as he cleared the property. Convinced he was long gone, she locked the gate and then walked to the front office, turning the locks and setting the alarm on the storefront.

The thought that the thing she'd been feeding, fostering to grow, would hurt others, weighed heavily. She wouldn't call Gra'dn. She liked the guy, and what if the Canavar hurt him? What about everyone else, including her employees?

She would deal with the Canavar herself.

She walked back through the office and into the plant, grabbing a few empty scrap buckets from the processing line. She filled them to the top out of the huge bin of discarded bits from that day's catch and headed to the back warehouse.

Before she could enter, she noticed immediately what had caused the horrible sound earlier, and what had drawn the employees to see what they had. The Canavar had torn through the weathered metal and latched onto a huge refuse bin outside, dragging the heavy container back through the wall. The Canavar's forelegs and head were sunk inside the bin as it rummaged for scraps.

Ceili set the buckets on the floor. Hearing the sound it related with the delivery of food, the Canavar backed out of the trash bin, all the legs on its segmented body pulling back as the body moved like a huge, plated serpent. The head swiveled toward Ceili.

"Hey there, Steve," she said, sliding one of the buckets toward him with a foot. The creature caught the bucket and started sucking down the goop.

Keeping an eye on the young Canavar, Ceili made her way around him to the corner where the pile of old nets lay, just beneath the retracted crane arm and dangling control box. Proceeding like it was any other day, she went to work spreading one of the larger nets across the floor, threading a cable through the outside edge and securing the cable to a hanging hook. She worked quickly, only stopping when the unnatural silence caught her attention.

There were no sounds of a scrap bucket being sucked dry. No happy cooing. She turned to find the Canavar had retreated into the darkness of the expansive warehouse.

"Steve?" she called softly.

Nothing.

She ran to the bucket she'd given the Canavar only to find it had not finished the meal. The other two buckets were untouched. She grabbed the handles and sprinted toward the flattened net, placing them in the middle.

"Steve, come and get it!" she yelled.

Eerie clicks resounded from the darkness. Ceili's breath hung up in her chest. The rhythm of thick insectoid legs tapped around her, slowly at first, then faster, in a continuous echo of *clicks* and *pops* that she couldn't locate.

Ceili grasped a fishing spear in one hand and a gutting knife in the other as the echo faded and the Canavar came into view.

"Hey, buddy," she said, trying to calm her racing heart so her voice didn't betray terror. "I brought you some grub. Aren't you hungry?"

The Canavar glanced at the buckets for a long moment, then it swiveled its flat face and bulbous eyes in her direction.

Though it was forty feet away, Ceili had to wonder just how screwed she was.

One of the long legs in the central thorax thumped loudly on the concrete floor, banging so hard the sound poured back at her from the metal walls and vibrated through her shoes. A second leg repeated the motion as the segmented body turned her way, growing nearer at a painfully slow rate. The front section reared up and the tail coiled upward behind it, the bulbous stinger twitching at the ready.

She knew better than to think the Canavar couldn't move any faster. It sensed fear, using sound as one of its weapons, that was the tactic.

Obviously, she'd confused the bait.

Ceili sprinted toward the net trap, dropped the small knife, and snagged the remote for the crane, snapping a toggle with the other hand while still grasping the spear. She positioned herself in the middle of the net next to the rancid bait buckets as the motor cranked to life.

Just as she hoped, the Canavar sped toward her with a centipede's choreographed stride. As much as she wanted to turn and run, she had to stand her ground until it was at least partially on the net so the legs and pincers would hang up.

The wait was horribly short lived. The creature closed the distance fast, emitting a roaring scream as it lunged at her, striking with pincers as Ceili engaged the crane. The cable pulled tight faster than she anticipated. She leapt back off the net, trying to clear the taught cable as the crane's arm continued upward, dragging the rope edges together. Her shoe caught the line and momentum caused her body to pitch forward toward the floor, where she fell flat onto her chest. Her lungs locked up from the impact. The remote flew from her grasp, but she managed to hold fast to the spear.

Pain tore through the back of her thigh, ripping a scream from her throat. The Canavar shrieked as it was lifted from the floor, limbs flailing, caught in the tangle of the net. Ceili's ankle was stuck between the cable and the rope, hooked so tightly she couldn't get it loose by kicking or yanking her foot around. Her entire leg burned as if fire seared through her veins. She managed to fold her body into a tight ball as the thing's sharp leg retracted from her thigh and plunged forward again, stabbing through the fleshy part of her calf on the same leg. Ceili let out a shrill scream, still working to free her trapped foot.

She found herself dangling upside down on the outside of the net, her body pressed close to the thrashing Canavar. Their faces were inches apart. In that moment, their eyes locked. Growing quiet, it jabbed the tip of a foreleg through the net and into her shoulder and another between her ribs on the opposite side. Her entire body lit up with white-hot pain.

Ceili Murphey saw her demise looming and knew that she had one shot at killing the murderous creature she'd mistakenly helped come to life that day. She leaned back with the spear and stabbed it into the Canavar's open mandibles as it lunged straight at her face through the net. The maw snapped down on her hand as the spear sank deeply into its mouth and was snapped in two. She could only hope the strike hit something the beast needed to keep drawing breath. It thrashed and beat at her, trying to lock its parted jaws around any part of her body. She was losing strength by the second. Blood flowed from so many places on her body, she couldn't track her own injuries.

What an odd way to die.

At least the Canavar was trapped for the time being.

* * *

It didn't take much for the company of mercs to kick through the wasted sheet metal. Oogar yelled and lasers swung around as spotlights swept over her and eventually blinded her. Blood ran from punctures and tears in her legs that grew deathly numb and colder by the second. Flashes of purple swarmed below. The Canavar's legs continued to thrash, and she couldn't feel whether her hand still grasped the spear.

Time swirled and churned with a distant memory of pain and fear. The crane's motor surged to life. Lasers shredded everything surrounding her. Something wet sprayed everywhere. The floor grew nearer as gloved paws clutched her, gently guiding her onto a gurney. The last thing Ceili saw was a visor flipping up and the purple face of Gra'dn, the stressed out Oogar peering fearfully into her eyes.

* * *

Tuesday Morning, A Week Later

Gra'dn walked through the door to Murphey's hoping he wouldn't require a medic after Ceili sank a fishing spear through his torso. She glanced up from the counter where she'd been working, a black glove covering her regenerated right hand. She was still a little pale, but the nanites were hard at work helping her heal. He held the door so his two associates could follow him in.

"An Oogar, a Buma, and a Sumatozou walk into a tour shop..." she said dryly, without a smile.

The Sumatozou's trunks twitched, and a wide grin spread over its mottled face.

The Buma's eyes widened, and it threw its head back in a mock gesture of surprised deadpan.

Ceili eyed the two aliens. They were loaded with gear of unknown capability strapped to what seemed to be every available space on their bodies. The Buma, a birdlike creature, watched her with great care. One of its wings was cocked at an angle so its hand rested with a sort of thumb hooked into one of the many belts strapped across its torso. Were they here to arrest her?

"This is Tycho," said Gra'dn, who was also geared up in his armor and weaponry. He gestured to the Sumatozou, who raised a thick, gray arm and waved a stubby hand her way, still smiling.

"And this is A'sha." Gra'dn tipped his head toward the Buma.

"Hello, Ceili Murphey," it said in a robotic monotone that sounded from the translator hanging high on its chest.

"They're from the Cartography Guild. I told them about your interest in travel and learning about new worlds," said Gra'dn. He looked at the Buma. "And she's good with new species."

Tears glistened in Ceili's eyes. She smiled. "It's nice to meet you."

* * *

Ceili cast long, the fishing line hissing from the reel until the soft, telltale *plop* sounded when the bait broke the surface of the calm bay. Gra'dn swung his feet in a slow to and fro beside her on the dock, halfheartedly watching his line as it grew slack, his bait clearly lost and his hope of something biting the line non-existent.

"Your bait's gone. Loose line," Ceili commented.

Gra'dn blinked then sighed with a smile. "Everybody's a critic." He sat up a little straighter and cranked the reel to reset his cast.

She gasped in mock exasperation. "You hired me to show you how to fish on Earth." She laughed. "I suppose you really do have it mastered, though. I think fishing is meant to be relaxing unless you're fishing for dinner and nothing else is on the menu."

Clamoring to his feet carefully so he didn't drop his rig in the water, Gra'dn twisted to cast the fresh bait to a new spot, then settled beside her, contentedly gazing at twin sunrays glinting into the silver horizon line.

"I wanted to thank you. I mean for everything you did to introduce me to your friends and all."

A smile formed, but he didn't look at her. "You're welcome, Ceili."

She sighed, chewing the inside of her cheek. "I'm sorry I didn't believe you. About Steve, I mean."

"There's no need for an apology." He continued to gaze contentedly ahead.

Ceili sat down on the dock beside him.

"I have a confession," he said.

"What it is?" She didn't let on that her stomach had dropped.

"I'm not a merc. I'm just undercover as a merc."

She snorted. "You're a Peacemaker."

"Yeah. That's why I intervened with the Cartography Guild."

"I knew it."

A half-awkward silence ensued. Unable to let it continue, Ceili picked up her pole to reset her cast for no good reason other than to break the quiet.

Ceili followed Gra'dn's line of sight and gazed out into the distance where the silver ocean met a lavender sky.

A new life of adventure awaited her.

Stars woke, speckling the darkening dome of the universe. Myriad new worlds were now within her reach.

* * * * *

Marie Whittaker Bio

Marie Whittaker is an award-winning essayist and author of horror, urban fantasy, children's books, and supernatural thrillers. Writing as Amity Green, her debut novel, *Scales*, the first in her Fate and Fire series, debuted in 2013, followed by *Phantom Limb Itch* in 2018. Her supernatural thriller, *The Witcher Chime*, was a finalist for the Indie Book Awards in 2017. She is the creator of The Adventures of Lola Hopscotch, which is a children's book series concentrating on getting sensitive childhood issues out in the open between children and adults. Many of her award-winning short stories appear in numerous anthologies and publications.

Marie enjoys teaching about publishing, writing craft, and project management for writers and is the Director of Superstars Writing Seminars, a world-class writing conference concentrating on the business of writing.

A Colorado native, Marie resides in Manitou Springs, where she writes and enjoys renovating her historic Victorian home. She spends time hiking, gardening, and indulging in her guilty pleasure of shopping for handbags. She is fond of owls, coffee, and all things Celtic. A lover of animals, Marie is an advocate against animal abuse and assists with lost pets in her community.

# # # # #

Shadows in the Key of Fear
by William Alan Webb

1

Main Prison Compound, Heinlein City, Mars

Jaypaas peered over the shoulder of one of the med-techs surrounding a Veetanho who lay still on the stainless-steel floor. Blood bubbled from a wound in her stomach and trickled down her side, leaving a red trail in the white fur. In the weak Martian gravity, it traveled slowly down the rodent's side to puddle under the small body. The basic medical training courses she'd taken at the Peacemaker Academy told her the little Veetanho's wound was fatal, but a dying convict was not Peacemaker business.

"Why was I summoned?" she asked. Jaypaas couldn't tell which of the med-techs was in charge, so she left it up to them to decide who would answer. "I wish to perform my duties well, but fail to see how this requires the presence of a Peacemaker."

A young Human female, with close-cut red hair, stood, stripped off a pair of bloody gloves and met Jaypaas' eyes.

"Thank you for coming, Peacemaker. I'm Kim Han, Deputy Director of Medical Services for the Heinlein City Prison System. I'm very sorry to have troubled you, but the prisoner asked for you, by name."

"Did she state the reason for requesting my presence?"

"No."

Jaypaas lowered the volume on her translator. "Will the Veetanho live?"

"No. At least, not without a massive infusion of nanites."

"Are nanites not available for prisoners?"

Han turned her face away before answering, which Jaypaas had learned during her time among Humans meant she disagreed with the answer she had to give.

"No, they are judged not worth the expense."

Jaypaas said nothing more. Curiosity made her want to ask who had stabbed the Veetanho, but that wasn't her concern, either. In fact, none of this required her presence that she could tell. Glancing back at the dying rodent, she saw that its eyes were open and watching her with a pleading look she had seen before.

"What is the prisoner's name?"

The red-haired med-tech checked her wrist slate. "Braka," she said.

Jaypaas nodded and knelt beside Braka's head. Getting down on all four legs would have been easier, but Zuuls considered that the same way Humans did about expelling methane in public. She put her muzzle near Braka's left ear. Blood trickled from the dying Veetanho's mouth. In another lifetime, Jaypaas might have stroked the prisoner's nose in a gesture of comfort, but she had learned to control those impulses.

Jaypaas heard it whisper something that made no sense. She increased the gain on her translator to maximum, and it picked up the softly whispered word, yet the translation was nothing more than a repeat of the word.

"Kurtz."

Braka reached out and grabbed Jaypaas's sleeve. Pulling herself up, she mouthed something too low for the translator's microphone to detect. She repeated it, then a subtle change came to Braka's eyes, a change Jaypaas had seen too many times before. Regardless of the race, there was a commonality in the eyes of every creature at the moment of its death. Jaypaas stood up, careful to show none of the sorrow she felt when someone died unnecessarily, even a criminal.

"Does this word 'Kurtz' mean anything to you?" she said, directing the question at the med-tech.

Han shook her head and asked the other med-techs. A couple said it sounded like a name. Satisfied, Jaypaas thanked Han and her crew for their help.

She moved quickly toward the barred door that led into the corridor, reveling once more in Mars' weak gravity, when one of the techs called for her to stop. A Human male waved his hands in what she had once thought was an aggressive motion, until learning it was a gesture of apology.

"I'm really sorry, Peacemaker," he said. Blood covered his blue uniform, of the type that Humans called "scrubs." "I forgot that Braka did say one other thing. It didn't make sense to us, but maybe it will to you."

"Thank you for your help. What did the deceased prisoner say?"

"Just one thing we could understand...Nepal."

* * *

Jaypaas's Quarters, Heinlein City

Jaypaas tore off a strip of the dried meat Humans called "jerky" and chewed without tasting it. She focused on a small Tri-V screen, watching replays of an attack on a mountaintop in a place called Nepal. Apparently, that country had a long tradition of providing mercenaries for armies on Earth, fierce, feared mercenaries, and with those armies now more or less obsolete, Nepal had decided to form their own Galactic Union mercenary company. Somebody had attacked them during a ceremony to announce the name of this new merc outfit, and only the presence of two old CASPer Mk 5s had prevented a massacre.

As a Peacemaker, the questions Jaypaas needed answered were who had attacked them and why? If they were Earth-grown terrorists, it did not involve her or the Peacemakers. But among the dead from the assault team was a notorious Oogar with a long, dishonorable record as a merc. A record so bad that no reputable merc company would hire him. Terrorists were almost always politically motivated, and an Oogar joining a Human terrorist group defied belief.

What changed everything was that civilians had died. Why mercs would care enough about a new company forming to attack them, she couldn't say. Jaypaas only knew that if responsibility lay with a merc company, a rogue merc outfit, or any criminal organization involving non-Humans, then that very much made it her business.

Her duty was clear. As much as she hated the idea, Jaypaas would have to go to this Nepal, starting with its capital city, Kathmandu. And that meant going to a planet she detested: Earth.

* * *

2

Pattaya City, Thailand, Earth

Eyes closed, Rohit Qabba's head weaved with the playback of his magnum opus, *Shadows in the Key of Fear*. He intended it to be the musical expression of a nightmare, but the composing itself had become a nightmare. Two years after he'd started, the piece remained unfinished.

Feeding the melody through his pinplants meant there was no signal degradation due to inferior speakers, headphones, or the limitations of his own hearing. This allowed him to feel the full effect of his latest addition, a low-frequency swell that began at fourteen hertz, well below the threshold of unaided Human hearing, and ended at thirty hertz, well above that threshold. It was tricky, and he needed to experience it in context. That meant listening to the whole thing again for at least the thousandth time.

The new section had just begun when someone called him. Irritated, he continued listening to the composition as he checked the caller's ID, admiring his own musical skill and talent as he simultaneously cursed whoever was interrupting his session.

It was Mahesh, his point man in Nepal. He answered by having an electronic voice respond with *sagen*, the German word for "say" or "speak."

"You asked me..." Mahesh's trembling voice said in Nepali, which his pinplants translated in real time. "No, wait, I'm not supposed to say that...there is...please forgive me, a Peacemaker just landed in Kathmandu. He...or she...I don't know; it looked like a big dog...*It* was met by a squad from the Nepali Police. I thought you should know."

Qabba cut the connection. Using his wrist slate, he sent orders for the informant to receive a five hundred credit reward. Routed through more than twenty financial agencies, it was nearly impossible to trace any of his financial dealings back to Qabba. Even the Peacemakers couldn't do it quickly, or so he'd been assured by those who'd set it up.

With that done, he silenced the music and thought about his options. From the balcony of his fortieth-floor penthouse overlooking Pattaya Beach, sunlight glittered off the Gulf of Thailand like shattered glass. Thin cloud streaks hurried south in an otherwise perfect blue sky. The fresh breeze so high up carried the faintest bit of a chill, which was refreshing in such a hot climate. Qabba gloried in his wealth.

He stared over the water without seeing it. At length, he called someone he'd never needed to call before. She answered with a surprised, "Is this really you?"

"Is the line encrypted?"

"Of course, using the latest quantum scramblers. Why?"

"I need to ask you something, Chaar…something dangerous."

"Dangerous to you or dangerous to me?"

"Potentially? Both of us, and your father, too, if they crack your encryptions."

"Who is 'they?'" Her voice still had a playful tone, teasing him.

"The Peacemakers."

Qabba thought he heard a gasp, except pinplants didn't work that way. Besides, Chaarumathi Yadav wasn't the sort to be easily frightened…or frightened at all, for that matter. Now she was all business.

"This involves the Peacemakers?"

"It does. We may need to have one killed."

* * *

Tribhuvan Starport, Kathmandu, Nepal, Earth

Based on their reactions, none of the Humans who gawked while Jaypaas followed the security Human through the starport had ever seen a Zuul in person. A few waved, one called out "Welcome, Peacemaker," but mostly they pointed and stared. She didn't let it bother her, being well aware of her race's resemblance to what Humans called "dogs."

Regardless, Jaypaas made sure that disdain for Earth, and for Humans in general, was not reflected on her face or body. In particular, she concentrated on relaxing the muscles that caused her hackles to rise. While the Humans present might not notice, in an era of ubiquitous cameras and recognition software, somebody, somewhere, would inevitably report her. The last thing she needed was another reprimand.

Her Human escort carried a solid-propellant rifle slung over one shoulder, which her pinplants identified as an automatic rifle called an AK-47. It was crude by galactic standards, but extremely reliable and cheap, another indicator that this Nepal place was poor, even for Earth.

News of an attempted murder in the starport reached her before she landed. It seemed unrelated to her investigation, but a Goka assassin was certainly an uncommon enough event to merit a quick look.

She followed the Human through a small room into an emergency medical facility, where the dead Goka lay on a stainless-steel examining table. The body had shrunk like a deflated balloon, while the head lay a foot from the torso. Jaypaas noted a clean separation at the neck, as if done surgically.

Then her nostrils flared. At the bottom of the Goka's carapace was a symbol burned into the chitin. Her slate identified it as a phrase in the language of Geshes, the Goka's home world. It meant "the Brotherhood of the Free."

They were on Earth? Now she had no doubt of a connection between Goka and the so-called terrorist attack. Jaypaas hadn't known the BOF had gotten into the system, and the incident under investigation was exactly the type of thing they were known for. Among the countless criminal enterprises scattered in every corner of the Galactic Union, the BOF were not a major player. Yet despite their limited potential for mayhem, and to the people killed on top of the mountain, the distinction between a large and a small organization of murderers didn't matter; dead was dead. On the spot, she fired off a message to Peacemaker Intelligence informing them of the BOF's presence.

Then she spoke to the Nepali Policeman who had brought her there. "I wish to speak with the Human who killed this Goka," she said.

* * *

3

Earth's gravity hurt Jaypaas's lower back, like she had a ten-pound brick strapped to the base of her spine. After the weak gravity on Mars, it would take several days for her body to adjust. In the interim, she repeated several of the mantras she'd learned to control pain.

In the presence of the Goka's mangled body, the Human female named Joanna Weiner confused Jaypaas. Of average height, with curly red hair cut shorter than most Human females preferred, there was nothing about her to indicate prowess with the long, sharp blade lying on the chair beside her. Yet the headless Goka testified that her looks were indeed deceiving. The fact that she still possessed her weapon told Jaypaas much about her standing with the local authorities.

"May we have privacy, please?" Jaypaas said to the security officer. Once he left, she continued. "I am Peacemaker Jaypaas. You are Joanna Weiner?"

"Yes. You may call me JoJo."

"May I ask who you are?" Jaypaas said, turning to the man rubbing his knee in a chair beside JoJo.

"I'm Larry Weiner, Peacemaker. Her husband."

Jaypaas's pinplants flashed both of their histories into her mind within a micro-second.

"You are both registered mercenaries with long histories. Mister Weiner, I see that your brother is a member of the Golden Horde. Is this correct?"

"It is."

"The government of this Earth nation—Nepal—is in the process of forming their own mercenary company, called…the High Mountain Hunters. Are you in any way associated with that process?"

"I sold them some refurbished CASPers. I was impressed with the company commander. When I saw the attack I came to offer my services."

"As an equipment broker?"

"No, Peacemaker. I want to join the company."

Jaypaas found that genuinely surprising and allowed her expression to reflect that. "May I ask why?"

Weiner's eyebrows moved together in the gesture she had come to know meant anger. "Somebody doesn't want the Gurkhas to have a mercenary company and committed murder to stop them. Killing aliens that can fight back is one thing, slaughtering unarmed civilians is quite another."

"Do you believe the attackers were Earth-born terrorists?"

"They were mercs." Weiner's tone left no room for argument.

"Why would mercs attack another merc company, one that did not yet exist?" she said.

"Why do mercs do anything, Peacemaker? Because they were paid to do so."

"Who would have paid them to do this, and for what reason?"

"That part I haven't figured out yet."

Jaypaas shifted her attention back to JoJo. "I have seen the Tri-V replays from the attempted assassination in this starport. You decapitated the assassin approximately one second before he would have killed your husband. Did you know the assassin was present?"

The small woman shook her head. "No, as a precaution, Larry and I always split up when passing through a public space where there might be danger. Today there was."

"Before you slew the Goka, did he say anything that might indicate a motive for assassinating you?"

"Not that I heard. Larry?"

He shook his head. "I was too worried about getting my pistol out to listen."

"In your opinion, was this attempted assassination in any way connected to the so-called terrorist attack?"

JoJo answered for both of them. "We think it had *everything* to do with the attack. Somebody doesn't want us helping the Gurkhas."

Jaypaas considered her next thought before voicing it. "I am alone on your planet. I would like to deputize the two of you to help me in my investigation."

JoJo raised her eyebrows and sat up straight, while her husband chuckled. "I know a lot of people who would say you're out of your mind. Why not the Nepali Police?"

"Until I have more data, there remains the possibility of a conspiracy that might involve the local authorities."

"I hadn't thought about that…a deputy, huh? What the hell, I'm in."

"I don't like seeing innocent people killed by renegade mercs," Larry Weiner said. "I'm in, too."

"I hereby deputize both of you to aid me, an authorized representative of the Peacemaker Guild, in my investigation. Do you have any verifiable evidence that mercenaries are responsible?"

"There's no other reason for an Oogar to be involved."

"The process of elimination is not considered evidence."

"It should be. Look, I have a bad knee, Peacemaker Jaypaas, but I'm damned good with computers. If you can get me access, I can get you answers."

"What type of access do you mean?"

"To financial records. Legitimate financial enterprises really don't want to attract the attention of the Peacemakers, so they'll cooperate if I have credentials."

"As my deputy you will have that. Should I assume that you would use your skills to, as you Humans say, follow the money?"

"Exactly!" Weiner pointed at Jaypaas when he said it, and she had to remind herself it wasn't an aggressive gesture.

"Then let us merge our efforts and ferret out these criminals."

* * *

4

Kaeng Krachan National Park, Thailand

Meeting Chaar Yadav on a slatted foot bridge over a muddy river certainly had the privacy Rohit Qabba had requested. Except he hated any place not air conditioned and was already eaten up with mosquito bites. What good was being rich if it couldn't buy you comfort?

"I don't like this even a little bit," he said, speaking Nepalese like a native. Along with his music, Qabba considered linguistics his greatest talent. "Meeting in person is stupidly dangerous."

Yadav was slender, with long brown hair that fell halfway down her back in a ponytail. She replied in the same language. "That is why we meet here, in the middle of nowhere."

"Where who knows how many satellites are focused on us right this minute?"

"That's a lower risk than tapping our phones, or hacking our translators."

"Let's just get this over with. Are we covered on that other deal?"

She frowned. "If by that other deal you mean Nepal, the one that could land my father in jail, not to mention us, the answer is yes. If you mean dealing with the Peacemaker, no. No one is willing to kill a Peacemaker, not at any price."

He cringed at hearing the words spoken out loud. "Because of the Goka?"

"Oh, Seessuss…that was definitely a mistake on my part, I should have used somebody better."

"No kidding! A fucking Goka! The place is overrun with giant cockroaches, but not that big. And was he really wearing gray clothes?"

"I warned Kurtz he was a bad choice, not just because he was an insectoid, but because Seessuss in particular was a *murkha*, a dumbass. But that is taken care of. None of this will blow back on us."

She didn't look or sound as confident as her words.

"You're *sure* of that?"

"I am, one hundred percent. Everything leads back to one person, and it's not you or me. I set the whole thing in motion before any of this happened, as a fail safe."

"How?"

"Suffice to say it involved a Martian prison and a convict with a family they loved too much and couldn't protect. Now we're going to leave Mister Matthew Kurtz holding the whole bag of flaming shit."

"By himself or as part of the BOF?"

"Preferably by himself; we can use the BOF for some of our later projects. But if whoever comes to investigate the murder of the Peacemaker gets through Kurtz, the trail leads to the Brotherhood, not to us. It's a dead end. They're freelance, so that makes them more expendable than our people. Besides, Kurtz is a dick. I don't mind seeing him go down for it."

Qabba grinned. "No argument there. What a waste of oxygen."

"Even so, I wouldn't burn him if I could help it. Street people have their uses."

"Better him than us, though."

"True, but he's five people removed from me, and each person in the chain only knows the one above them. Only one man in the world has dealt with me personally."

"What if they get up the chain to him?"

"That is impossible."

"Nothing's impossible, Chaar."

Hidden in the shadows under the brim of an American style baseball cap that read, in Russian, *Leningrad Polytechnic, Go Polar Bears*, her large brown eyes reduced to slits from her broad smile.

"Theoretically speaking, if they somehow got that far, they'll find the one person who knew my identity was missing, whereabouts unknown, and that he disappeared right after giving my orders to the one below him on the ladder. If they kept investigating, they'll discover that I recently changed the water in my piranha pool, which eliminated any environmental DNA, and had the red-bellies left any bones to cremate, a good place to scatter the ashes would have been the river beneath our feet."

Qabba glanced down. Was that gray powder near his foot? He tried to keep his admiration from reflecting on his face but couldn't.

"I have never before been tempted to become involved with one of my business associates..."

She rose on her tiptoes to look him in the eye.

"It's not going to happen now, either."

* * *

Nepali Trauma Center, Kathmandu, Nepal, Earth

At first Jaypaas was grateful that the man, Ganju Limbu, who three days before had personally fought the attackers, sat in one of the trauma center's chairs. With

Limbu seated, that allowed her to do the same, and take her full weight off her aching paws. Unfortunately, Earth's chairs weren't built for aliens, and pretty soon the base of her spine hurt more than her feet had. No sign of her discomfort reached her face, though.

"Let me make sure I understand what happened," Jaypaas said. "Nepal authorized the formation of a mercenary company, which is to be called High Mountain Hunters. A group of your most prominent species gathered at a religious site—"

"Religious *and* cultural," Limbu corrected. Jaypaas made a notation on her slate.

"The purpose of this gathering was to announce the name of the new company and to award the first two franchises. You, as owner of one franchise, bought two CASPers to show visitors what Human Mercenary mecha looked like."

"Correct," Limbu said. Jaypaas noted both deference and authority in his tone.

"What model CASPers were they?"

Limbu looked down. "Refurbished Mk 5s. It's all I could afford."

Jaypaas kept her face and vocal tone neutral, all the while thinking that if they could only afford rebuilt Mk 5s, the High Mountain Hunters wouldn't be around for long.

"Mk 5s…thank you. And during the ceremony, four Human atmospheric aircraft, which derive both lift and propulsion from one or more sets of horizontally revolving overhead rotors—"

"They're called helicopters."

"Yes, helicopters. These helicopters approached the mountaintop where the ceremony was taking place and opened fire without provocation. Your CASPers returned fire, after which the intruders attempted to disgorge a group of armed Humans?"

"Yes."

"And during the course of this incident seven of the Human attackers were killed, along with an Oogar who fought with them. Further casualties among the combatants involved three of the defenders killed and nine wounded, one of whom is your youngest son. Ten civilians died as a direct result of this incident with nineteen more wounded. Is this an accurate representation of the facts as you know them?"

"It is, but you should also know that one of the more severely wounded is the son of Amir Pun, who has also been awarded a franchise."

"Thank you for that information. To the best of your knowledge, was this a terrorist attack related to Earth's political struggles?"

"That seems to be the million-credit question, doesn't it?"

"I do not understand. There is no payment for either asking or answering the question."

Limbu waved his hand, another Human gesture Jaypaas had learned which meant "never mind."

"That's just an expression."

Jaypaas didn't understand that, either, but decided it wasn't important. "Tomorrow I wish to see the site of the attack. Can you arrange that, or should I speak to someone else?"

"I can do that," Limbu said. "I'll arrange for transport from your hotel in the morning."

"Excellent, thank you. I am quartered at the Galaxy Hotel, please have my transportation ready one Earth hour after sunrise."

* * *

5

The Streets of Kathmandu, Nepal, Earth

Nepal's chief industry for decades had been tourism, and while most tourists came from China, an influx of Americans and Europeans was also noticeable. Even so, at six feet two inches, with light brown hair and blue eyes, Matthew Kurtz stood out as he walked down a crowded sidewalk toward the Galaxy Hotel. Fortunately for him, with the sun not yet up it was cold enough that his long coat didn't seem out of place, since it covered up a laser rifle, a miniature sub-machine gun in a shoulder holster, and a belt with two pistols holstered one to each side. Four grenades bulged in his coat pockets.

An ear bud allowed him to coordinate with the rest of his crew, who were the eight survivors of the attack group from four days earlier. He had two pinplants but none of the others did, so while he didn't need to move his lips to communicate with them, he needed the ear bud to hear their responses. None of them had stopped complaining about targeting a Peacemaker.

"Quit yer bitchin'," he said. "This is what happens when you fuck up a mission."

That was met with more chatter.

"Slyšel jsi toho muže," said Staff Sergeant Filda Merik, cutting through the others without effect.

"Use your translator, Staff Sergeant," Kurtz said.

"I told them 'you heard the man.' In other words, shut up and focus on this job, or we won't get paid."

"We're killing a Peacemaker; we'll never get a chance to spend it," said one of the crew.

Merik cut in before Kurtz could. "You can bow out any time you want, but if you do, don't count on ever working for us or the Brotherhood again."

"Yeah, yeah," said the chief complainer. "I'm here, aren't I? But if this Peacemaker has a CASPer, like those guys the other day, could you let us know in advance this time?"

"Zuuls don't use CASPers," Kurtz said.

"But they *do* have armor, and we don't."

"There's nine of us and one of her. That's the only armor we need."

* * *

The Galaxy Hotel, Kathmandu, Nepal, Earth

To Larry Weiner, gaining access to even the low-level databases seemed like cheating. Before his days as a mercenary consultant and weapons broker, he'd made a good living as a hacker. The police never caught him, but it wasn't for lack of trying. Now, instead of spending hour after hour trying to break into the financial databases, the Peacemaker Deputy had full access.

Good thing I'm in a different business now, he thought. The names and account numbers on his screen were worth untold billions, not of dollars, but credits, and it was only the least secure of the financial databases. How much more did the *really* secure ones have?

Having access to information didn't necessarily translate to results, however, as Weiner knew all too well. He'd been at it for nearly fourteen hours straight and even coffee could only keep you alert for so long. At some point, all it did was give you a headache and make your eyes burn, and he was there. Yawning, he rolled his shoulders and felt his muscles pop, then he stood up.

He and JoJo had taken a room at the posh Galaxy Hotel in downtown Kathmandu, a few doors down the hall from Jaypaas. JoJo had already gone downstairs to meet the Peacemaker, so Weiner ordered a room service breakfast that would take an hour to deliver. In the meantime, he decided to head to the roof for some fresh air and a cigar, chuckling to himself at the inherent contradiction. As he always did when away from home, he slipped on his shoulder holster and inserted the laser pistol. He pulled his favorite oversized sweater over his head to ward off the morning chill.

When he'd checked in, the front desk clerk had noted his bad knee and gave them a room near the elevator. Two men were already inside when the doors opened. Weiner had never seen either man before, but he knew by their hard stares and scarred faces what they were; mercs.

He nodded to them, but they just glared back, so he kept his eyes on the floor and tried to look harmless. There had been no missing the tattoos on their necks, though, three stylized letters that would have been hard to decipher if he hadn't seen them before, BOF, the Brotherhood of the Free. Adrenaline washed out all traces of fatigue. In that instant, he knew who had attacked the ceremony on the mountain.

A square tower on the roof held the shaft for the elevator. The doors opened facing the rear of the hotel. Weiner stepped out without looking back at the mercs, stuck a cigar in his mouth, and lit it without first toasting the foot. That affected the taste, but he wanted the Mercs to ignore him. He exaggerated his limp and breathed heavily, as if moving took a tremendous effort. In his peripheral vision he saw it had worked, as they both headed to the edge of the roof looking down at the hotel's main entrance. He had no idea what was going on, but warning sirens screamed in his mind. The weight of the laser pistol was a comfort.

Through his pinplants Weiner called his wife. *"Jo, head's up, you're walking into a trap—"*

* * *

6

The Galaxy Hotel Restaurant, Kathmandu, Nepal, Earth

Jaypaas ate breakfast in a far corner of the hotel restaurant, trying to remain unnoticed, which didn't work. Through most of the Galactic Union the sight of a Zuul would draw as much notice as a gust of wind. On much of Earth that would also be the case, especially near starports like Houston, Texas, but not in Nepal. It was her intention to leave as little mark of her presence as possible, so instead of acknowledging the pointing customers at nearby tables, Jaypaas concentrated on her slate and pretended she didn't see them. Only when JoJo Weiner showed up and sat in the chair opposite her did Jaypaas look up.

"Did you enjoy your Earth breakfast?"

"I have eaten Earth food many times at Heinlein City. I particularly enjoy what most cultures call sausage or bacon, but chicken eggs have never appealed to me. In this particular facility, I find it very strange to say that I enjoyed these…banana pancakes. It is not typically the type of food my people eat, but I found it oddly appealing. The taste of this—" she pointed at a bowl of soggy Muesli, "—I did not find pleasing."

"You drink coffee?"

Jaypaas nodded once, then drained her coffee, wiped her muzzle, and slid back her chair. "It is very bitter. I like that."

Joanna waited until their eyes met and then she tapped the end of one of the pinplants behind her left ear. Jaypaas nodded imperceptibly and reached out to her own pinplants.

"Is there something wrong, JoJo?"

"We're about to be ambushed. Larry is on the roof, and he says there are two mercs up there with laser rifles. They're members of the Brotherhood of the Free."

Jaypaas growled deep in her throat. Oddly enough, she had learned to do it from a Human.

"If they plan to attack a Peacemaker then they are more foolish than even I believed them to be. Are you well armed, JoJo?"

"Very well armed."

The Zuul considered her options for several seconds. *"If we do not emerge as expected, our assailants may come in looking for us. That would endanger many innocent civilians inside the hotel. I have contacted the Kathmandu Police, but we cannot wait for them to arrive. That risks a fight here in the hotel."*

"What should we do?"

"Precisely what we planned."

* * *

Matthew Kurtz rubbed his eyes as Jaypaas walked past. Using his pinplants, he sent the alert that would send his team into action. Once the Peacemaker exited the restaurant and headed for the lobby, he took a last look at his surroundings. Assassinating a Peacemaker would bring the weight of that entire guild to bear finding him, so it was mandatory that he put as many stargates as possible between himself and Earth. The payday would make it worthwhile, but the reality was that might this be the last breakfast he would ever eat on his mother planet.

* * *

Weiner held the laser pistol close to his chest with his right hand and smoked the cigar with his left. He leaned against an old-style, waist-high brick wall and looked down on a courtyard parking lot framed by two other wings of the hotel. Out the corner of his eye Weiner saw one of the mercs nod to the other, who immediately turned toward him and shouldered the rifle.

But Weiner anticipated that and took two steps to his right, interposing the elevator housing between them and blocking the merc's shot. The scuff of shoes told him the merc had broken into a trot, so at most he had three seconds to get ready. He used two of those to move away from the edge and brace his feet in a shooting stance, and the third to aim where he thought the merc would show up as he rounded the corner of the elevator tower.

The man appeared exactly where Weiner anticipated, walking quickly with the rifle at his shoulder. Sighting Weiner he turned to shoot, but Weiner fired first. A shaft of ruby light sliced a six-inch gash over the man's heart. Exiting the man's back, the laser burst disappeared into the half-light of dawn.

The merc's momentum caused him to topple forward, out of sight of his partner. Weiner grabbed the dead man's rifle and limped to the side of the small tower. Peering around the corner, he saw the other merc with his rifle also shouldered, peering downward toward the hotel entrance. Weiner took two seconds to control his breathing and steady the sights, and then pressed the trigger.

As disabling shots went, it was easy. From fifty feet away, Weiner put a one second beam into the small of the merc's back, severing his spinal cord. The man collapsed in a heap. His rifle clattered to the roof.

"Mercs on the roof are neutralized," he told JoJo and Jaypaas. *"One is alive, stand by while I interrogate him."*

JoJo answered him. *"Make it fast, Larry. If these guys hear sirens, they might come in after us."*

"They also might take off."

"I cannot risk innocent lives, if it can be avoided," said Jaypaas.

The merc lay with his mouth half open, staring wide-eyed at the bright blue morning sky. Weiner leaned over the merc's face, and the man locked eyes with his, pleading.

"Unless you want this beautiful face to be the last thing you ever see, tell me right now how many men are downstairs waiting in ambush!"

The mercs mouth moved in a chomping fashion.

"How many?"

The man closed his mouth.

"Listen to me…without nanites you're a dead man, but I've got five injectors in my pocket. You tell me how many people are down there, I save your life. That's the deal. Now tell me!"

The merc blinked and his lips compressed. They moved, trying to form words. Weiner put his ear close to the man's mouth and the answer came out as a faint whisper.

"Seven."

Weiner rose. The merc's eyes widened. "Nanites?" he said, that one word containing all of the terror flooding his brain.

"Sorry. I lied."

* * *

When JoJo told her the number, Jaypaas involuntarily raised her ears. It was the one physical reaction to alarming news she hadn't yet been able to suppress.

"That is an unfortunate number," she said. "The percentage chance of imminent death is too high for me to request that you continue your service. I therefore release you from your deputization, JoJo Weiner. The Galactic Union thanks you for your service to the Peacemaker's Guild. I will wait to proceed until you are safely out of the line of fire."

"I like you, Jaypaas, but you've got one annoying habit."

"I do?"

"You talk too much." In the far distance they heard sirens.

* * *

7

"Hey Kurtz, do you hear that?"

"Yeah, I hear it. Sirens. The targets are standing in the lobby, near the doors, but not moving. We'll have to take them in here. Stand by to enter on my say-so."

Famed throughout Central Asia for its huge glass and marble lobby, filled with koi ponds and greenery, the Galaxy Hotel maintained the area to be the cleanest public place in all of Nepal. Thousands of people passed through the lobby each day to shop at the exclusive stores along the north side or eat at the restaurants to the west.

With the sun just coming up the crowds were still light. Kurtz didn't care about collateral damage, though. Having a clear field of fire was his only concern. Sliding behind one of the lobby's thirty square, marble-encased pillars, his hand closed on the butt of his pistol. Two people blocked his aim, a mother and young girl of eight or nine, so he'd have to cut them down first.

The short woman standing next to the Peacemaker didn't worry him, so once he'd hit the dog-like Zuul in the back he figured he could take her out as he ran toward the front doors. A quick glance showed nobody was watching him. Drawing the pistol, he held it in both hands and took careful aim at the mother. He would sweep the pistol sideways to take her and her child out with one shot, and with any luck it would go through her and kill the Peacemaker and the middle-aged woman helping it. This might work out better than he'd planned.

Kurtz was about to give the *go* signal when people outside the lobby doors began screaming and running. Had his team jumped the gun? He looked up to see what was going on, and for one second his gaze left the Peacemaker. When he turned back, the Zuul held its own pistol aimed right at Kurtz's head. The last image processed before a laser beam struck him neatly between the eyes, was a dot of ruby red at the tip of the Peacemaker's pistol barrel.

* * *

Much like an old Earth-style police scanner, Jaypaas possessed a small device affixed to her belt that scanned her immediate environment for pinplant signals other than her own. If one was detected, it alerted her so she could decide whether the user posed a potential threat or not. After sweeping the lobby, she only detected one other pinplant user and concluded that had to either be the Human they sought, Matthew Kurtz, or a member of Kurtz's company.

Using the most advanced decryption algorithms available to the Peacemakers, Jaypaas intercepted an outgoing signal and deciphered it. Then, applying the most recent Tri-V image of Kurtz, she activated a tiny camera on the back of her uniform shirt to scan the area behind her. Using the source of the pinplant signal to narrow down the search area, she spotted a man standing behind a wide column some thirty meters to her right rear. Even though the man exposed no more than slice of the right side of his face, recognition software gave a 98.44% chance it was Kurtz.

"Have you acquired a target, Larry Weiner?" she said.

"Roger that. I've got two on the rooftop of the nearest hotel. They have not seen me yet."

"Are you prepared, JoJo?"

"Always."

"I give you both one more opportunity to avoid what will surely be life-endangering service."

JoJo responded for both. *"You're doing it again, Jaypaas."*

"Doing what again?"

"Talking too much."

For the first time since she'd arrived on Earth, Jaypaas curled her left jowl in her version of a laugh. She could never admit her feelings to anyone else, not even her friends in the Peacemaker's Guild, but she secretly loved fighting. Not for the first time, or the last, she wondered if she should have been a merc instead of a Peacemaker.

"Larry Weiner, you may fire at the most opportune moment."

"It's about time…one of them's heading right for me."

* * *

Kuala Lumpur, Malaysia, Earth

Unknown to Qabba, Kurtz, or anyone else, upon learning where the Peacemaker would be staying while in Nepal, Chaar Yadav had anonymously overpaid a trusted technician to install a camera on the side of the hotel across the street. The lens took in the entire front side of the Galaxy Hotel except for the front doors, which were blocked by a covered drive-through. Now she leaned back in bed, propped up against six pillows, and focused on the Tri-V to watch the Peacemaker die.

The camera didn't have the best angle, but any better and it might have been spotted on the side of the hotel. Security was always uppermost in Chaar's mind. Fortunately, living in the penthouse of a 79-story condominium building had more advantages than merely being able to view the Malacca Strait twenty miles to the west. It also allowed signals to be received directly and from any direction with minimal interference. In turn, this meant the signal only needed two relays, each using state-of-the-art encryption keys, to hide its ultimate destination.

She stretched and hoped she didn't have to see Rohit Qabba for a while. The man annoyed the shit out of her with his preening and so-called music. What was that piece he'd played for her called, *Shadows in the Key of Fear*? What the fuck did that even mean, anyway? The guy was a pretentious prick, no doubt, but as long as he got her money-making jobs she'd put up with his arrogance.

Dawn in Kathmandu hadn't yet lit the valley formed by the two skyscraper hotels, when she bolted upright. The flash of a laser lit the upper left quadrant of the screen, coming from the roof of the Galaxy. It had started!

Then a laser fired from the hotel where her camera was anchored, back at the roof of the Galaxy. Then both beams crisscrossed each other in mid-air, and she realized it was a firefight between opposing sides.

What the hell?

* * *

8

As Jaypaas took out Matthew Kurtz with a perfect head shot, she heard the distinct sizzle of a laser behind her. Trusting that it was JoJo doing the shooting and not Kurtz's mercs, she fired a second time at Kurtz's falling body. The beam cut through his mid-section.

The Zuul whirled in time to cut down a small merc, possibly female, as she pushed through a set of doors far to her right. Two others already lay in a doorway on the left, propping them open with their bodies. Jaypaas saw another merc through the glass, kneeling outside on the curb and aiming. There was no time to scream a warning, so she jumped on top of JoJo just as a rocket zoomed into the lobby trailing smoke.

The rocket missed her left shoulder by inches and exploded against a column twenty feet to the rear. It was an old-style Terran RPG, with a shaped charge warhead. The explosion showered her with steel splinters from the warhead and shards of marble from the column. Pain flared along her back and legs from penetrating hits, while the blast wave knocked her off JoJo Weiner. That saved both their lives.

While Jaypaas writhed in pain, JoJo remained unhurt because the Peacemaker had shielded her. Through the smoke and dust filling the lobby, she found the merc with the RPG loading a second round into the firing tube, centered her sights on the merc's chest, and fired a one second burst.

By sheer chance, it struck the warhead and set off the charge. The explosion dwarfed the first one, as waves of flame washed over the shooter, the drive-through unloading area, and anything within one hundred feet. JoJo fell on top of Jaypaas, shielding the Peacemaker as the Peacemaker had shielded her.

The metal frames around the glass doors turned white-hot and JoJo felt intense heat, but no flames penetrated into the lobby. In three seconds, it was over, leaving only a blackened hulk still kneeling on the curb holding what had been the RPG launcher. A merc she hadn't seen staggered through puddles of fire, his blackened skin peeling away even as flames consumed what was left. The head tilted back, and it looked like the merc was screaming in agony, but she heard no sounds.

"Jo! Jo, what happened? Talk to me, are you okay? Jo!"

She raised her head and blinked. It felt like she had a sunburn.

"I'm okay. That was an RPG going off in the shooter's hands. It must have had a thermobaric warhead. Jaypaas is hurt, but I can't tell how bad."

"I am not critically wounded, as you Humans like to say; I am fine," the Peacemaker said, doing a pushup until she could get her knees under her body. Blood soaked her clothes in a dozen places. "Are you injured, JoJo?"

"Thanks to you, no. And forgive my saying so, but you look don't look fine."

"I am in a great deal of pain, yet my wounds are superficial. Have the police arrived yet?"

"It sounds like they're close."

"You stay here, JoJo Weiner. You have done the Peacemaker Guild and the Galactic Union a great service this day, but I would not have you risk further harm."

"You think I'm gonna stay here?"

"It is the wisest course."

JoJo got up and stood beside Jaypaas. She frowned up at the taller Zuul and shook her head.

"Not on your life, sister."

* * *

Pattaya City, Thailand, Earth

Athunderstorm rolling over the Gulf of Thailand formed the perfect backdrop for *Shadows in the Key of Fear*, or so thought Rohit Qabba. The towering black cloud blotted out the morning sun. He watched lightning flash and fork across the dark sky and thought they looked like bolts from an angry god.

He couldn't believe he'd finally finished the song after being stuck on it for so long. Listening through old-style headphones, his head dipped side to side in time with the music. The ominous opening stanza had given way to the frantic, discordant transition to the staccato middle when Chaar called. Qabba didn't want to answer it, but there was no choice. He didn't bother to hide his irritation, though.

"Hold while I turn down the music." Walking inside from the balcony, the heavy curtains across the wall of floor-to-ceiling glass cast the room in cool shadows. The vacuum tubes on the ancient Dynaco amplifier glowed orange, providing enough light for him to see the volume knob on the equally antique Marantz pre-amp. "What do you want?"

"The whole thing blew up. Kurtz is dead along with his crew. The Nepali Police might have prisoners."

"The Peacemaker?"

"Scratched up but otherwise fine."

"All right. Should there be another attempt?"

"I don't think so. We'll have to write off the Brotherhood here on Earth, but we should be fine. I've ordered Tegu be taken off the board."

That got Qabba's attention. "Is that necessary?"

"I think it is."

"Then we're down to three degrees of separation…is that enough?"

"We'll be fine."

His impulse was to berate her for fucking this whole thing up so bad. It was supposed to be a simple snatch and grab, and now she was targeting Peacemakers for assassination and fucking that up, too. This wasn't something his pinplants could help solve, so as Qabba thought about what to do next he lost track of time.

"Rohit? Is everything alright?"

"Yes, I was considering your suggestion. I think you're right. Despite his usefulness in the past, Tegu has become a liability."

"I'll take care of it immediately."

"Thank you." He broke the connection but didn't turn the volume back up on the music. Instead, he accessed a number he didn't call often and had never wanted to call. If building a network took a lot of time and money, destroying it was both faster and even more expensive. Protecting himself, however, came before everything else.

When the call was picked up, Qabba heard road noises in the background and knew it was a handheld device. "Who?" was all they said.

"Snow White and her dwarfs."

"That's six big reds."

"Four. Snow White herself took care of two dwarfs."

"When?"

"Soonest."

The connection went dead. Qabba shook his head. Four million credits was a lot even for him, but he made it a policy that once he'd spent money, he never thought about it again. Then he booked passage on the next luxury starship heading for Karma. It was time to hit the recruiting trail again.

* * *

9

Larry Weiner gulped beer to quell the fire in his mouth. Once that was gone, he downed a glass of water.

"That's hot," he said, nodding at the platter of chopped meat in the middle of the table. Nepali meat dishes crowded every available inch of tabletop. Jaypaas had ordered one of everything on the menu as a reward on behalf of the Peacemaker Guild for their help in determining the guilty parties in the attack on the naming ceremony. The Weiners had done their best to make a dent in the heaps of food, but the platters remained full.

"Are you not gonna eat, Jaypaas? You should be celebrating, you cleaned up the rogue mercs."

The Zuul wiggled her ears. "Larry Weiner, I have another request for you."

"Sure, anything."

"I have your records; I know what you have done in the past. If I give you higher access using a Peacemaker code, do you promise not to use it for illegal activities?"

"Jaypaas, I don't know what you've read, but—"

The Peacemaker raised her paw. "What you have done prior to our meeting is of no consequence to me. We have caught those who executed the attack, it is true, but not the one who ordered it."

Weiner leaned forward, elbows on the table, and got very close to Jaypaas so he could speak in a low tone.

"You'll give me high-level access codes, so I can track payments back to their source?"

"That is my proposal, yes, on condition that you not use them for personal gain."

"I've got more money than I could ever spend now, so that's not a worry."

"Please forgive me pursuing this question further, but for some there is never enough wealth."

"Is that why you're a Peacemaker, to get rich?"

Jaypaas paused to search for an appropriate English language response. "*Touché*, Larry Weiner. What period of time do you anticipate this endeavor may require?"

Weiner grinned. "Not long enough."

* * *

Kuala Lumpur, Malaysia, Earth

It had taken five days, longer than Weiner anticipated. The intricacy of Chaarumathi Yadav's network impressed even him, but eventually he put it all together.

The building manager initially resisted helping them, not least because he had never met a Zuul before or seen a Peacemaker badge, but after contacting his corporate offices he couldn't take them to the penthouse fast enough. Once the elevator arrived at the top, they heard deep, rhythmic vibrations that rattled its cage.

"What are those painful noises?" Jaypaas said.

"I think it's supposed to be music," answered JoJo.

The Zuul's confused tone came through the translator. "Do you find it enjoyable?"

"It sucks."

Jaypaas knew that was a negative answer and drew back her lips in her best imitation of a Human smile.

"That's a little scary," JoJo said. "You might not want to do that anymore."

"I will remember your advice." She turned to the manager. "Thank you for your cooperation. Further assistance is not required at this time."

The man smiled in relief and touched a sensor to open the doors. They had only cracked open four inches when Jaypaas drew her sidearm, alerted to danger by the smell of blood. Two heavily muscled men lay dead in the elevator's alcove.

"Stand back," she said to the manager. Dropping into a shooting crouch, Jaypaas and JoJo swept the area with their pistols. They found no targets. A quick inspection of the area showed no blood, but multiple holes in the walls from laser shots.

Crouching between them, JoJo looked up at Jaypaas and shook her head. Beyond the alcove, two highly polished teak doors stood half open. They crept inside, guns first.

* * *

Jaypaas tilted back her snout. Her nostrils flared at a familiar scent, although it took nearly two seconds for her to recognize it.

"Get out!" she shouted. "Get out now!"

Across the room, JoJo gave her a questioning look, but Jaypaas knew she might only have seconds. In three strides she was near enough to grab the back of JoJo's shirt. Lifting the woman in one paw, she ran for the door. The manager stood by the elevators, holding open the doors, but Jaypaas grabbed him, too. Carrying both Humans, she strained to run toward the red *Kelaur* sign marking the emergency stairs.

JoJo hung limp in Jaypaas's grasp, but the manager squirmed and kicked. "What are you doing?" he said. "Put me down!"

The Peacemaker ignored him. Gritting her teeth at the pain in her shoulders, she put him down long enough to open the stairwell door, pushed him through, and bolted after him.

"Down the stairs!" she yelled.

When the manager started to protest, she picked him up again and went down two steps at a time, with JoJo out in front. They'd made it down two flights before Chaarumathi Yadav's luxury condominium exploded, in a blast so powerful it blew off the entire top floor and shook the building like an earthquake.

* * *

10

Larry Weiner was in her hospital room when Jaypaas woke up. The Peacemaker gazed around the room for a few seconds, which allowed her brain to process what had happened.

"How is your wife?" she said.

Weiner nodded. "She's going to be fine. Nanites are a wonderful thing. You're fine, too, in case you care."

Jaypaas cocked her head. "Under what circumstances would I not care?"

"Never mind."

But she misunderstood that comment, too. "Zuul's have the same instinct of self-preservation as any other species."

"I know…Do you want to hear what happened?"

"I do."

The explosive device used C-4, widely available and untraceable. It was a timed device, which caused extensive destruction to the high-rise condominium building.

"It was there to kill *you*, Peacemaker."

"So, the Human female named Chaarumathi was not behind the attack, as we believed." It wasn't a question.

"No, it appears not."

"Have you ascertained who was?"

"I think so."

Her lip rose just enough to display a sharp canine. "Please send me the data."

* * *

Four Months Later, Dorka's Dump, Orbiting Dorka Planet

All things considered, Rohit Qabba decided he had nothing to complain about. Granted, he'd been forced to avoid Karma Station because that damned Zuul Peacemaker had been sniffing around, which put him way out at the ass-end of nowhere in search of new business partners. But with enough credits, life could be good even out here. Nothing distinguished Dorka's Dump from a thousand other seedy dives throughout the galaxy, which suited Qabba just fine.

He sat at a table in the darkest corner, facing away from the common room. The hooded coverall he wore couldn't hide his basic bipedal, humanoid shape, but it did make it impossible to tell *which* bipedal humanoid race he was. A few hundred well-placed credit chits guaranteed that the ones who knew weren't talking.

Assorted riffraff jammed the place, with a deafening noise level of shouted arguments, discordant music from a hundred cultures, and drunken singalongs in at least as many languages. Qabba disliked such places, despite the countless hours he'd spent in them, so he listened to his grand creation, *Shadows in the Key of Fear*, his eyes closed as he marveled at his own genius.

Only when he felt the small table tilt did he open his eyes, anticipating seeing whoever had requested the meeting. The mysterious contact came highly recommended from trusted sources, and the money involved was lucrative enough to bring Qabba to a public meeting place. Whoever it was promised a new enterprise that would bring him riches beyond his wildest dreams.

The reality was different.

"Greetings, Peacemaker," he said, trying to keep the shock out of his voice. "To what do I owe this honor?"

"Greetings to you, Rohit Qabba," Jaypaas said, leveling a laser pistol at his chest. "I wish to discuss Nepal."

* * * * *

William Alan Webb Bio

Before he became the World's Oldest Teenager, Bill had a pretty normal childhood growing up in West Tennessee. That is to say, he engaged in all kinds of high-risk behavior, such as drinking whole milk and eating eggs for breakfast, riding his bike without a helmet, and going to school when a classmate had a runny nose. An obsession with military history probably began before he was three years old; his earliest memory is of watching a TV show, *Silent Service*, that only ran for one season in the year he turned two.

At 13, the same fate befell him as so many of his generation, namely…he encountered a Besquith. The creature said it was a werewolf, but Bill knew better.

The evil monster forced him to read a Robert E. Howard "Conan" story, and from that moment on he was addicted. Unfortunately, Howard was just a gateway author that led to more and more stories and authors…Michael Moorcock, Roger Zelazny, Robert A. Heinlein…you've undoubtedly heard this sordid story before. And as with so many others before him, he hit rock bottom when someone passed him a 20-sided dice and said, "Here, roll this."

After a lifelong struggle, during which he took up the vile habit of writing genre fiction, he has made huge progress in his fight against his demons when he encountered a shady figure in a dark alley, who brought him crashing down again with just two whispered words, "Four Horsemen."

That was the end. Or the beginning, depending on your point of view.

# # # # #

Tangent Orange by
Mark Stallings

The shuttle ramp dropped into a swirl of dust. "Man, this is an arid planet." Reynor said with distaste as he tromped down the metal ramp and gazed out. All of a meter and a half tall, the Radskhat looked like a large raccoon. Dark brown fur covered his body. He had a short, pointed muzzle with light gray highlights and a short, ringed tail. Reynor was unusual for his kind; he had an ambition beyond stealing whatever he could lay his digits on.

The vista before him wasn't inspiring. In the distance was a bluff or plateau. The dust made it difficult to judge distances, so it could have been a couple kilometers away or forty. Nearer stood the decrepit bones of industry of some sort; warehouses and towers, long disused. Reynor wondered what kind of product would have gone through them. The immediate vicinity was made up of an open saloon, an inn about midway down the street, and at the far end of the main street, a building with three times the neon signage necessary to tell non-existent customers about a casino. The rest of the buildings were closed shops with metal shutters over the windows and doors. As a Radskhat, his race was used to scavenging on the wrong side of the track, but this place looked too poor for even his kind.

"For someone so small, how do you manage to sound like a being thrice your size?" Sempay asked from next to him. It continually surprised Reynor how quiet the Besquith was. Sempay pulled his faded blue dust cloak over his wolfen ears and settled polarized goggles onto his eyes. "I dislike how the dust gets into my fur."

The pair walked down the ramp and headed into the small town. Hardly any people moved around. They passed old buildings, the building materials long stained and eroded with the weather. It was obvious that upkeep hadn't been a priority.

"This is the recreation spot the captain suggested?" Reynor asked in disgust. "Did we land at the wrong spot? Is there another place on Aztec we maybe missed?" Reynor chittered in disappointment. He had hoped his first trip out of the Academy as a badged Peacemaker would be more…interesting.

Sempay shrugged massive shoulders under his cloak. "Let's go see what this place has to offer. We have three days, at least, before the transport's drive is realigned."

Reynor noticed curtains moving and blinds bending as the residents of the buildings along their path checked them out. "We are being watched," he whispered to his companion.

Sempay just grunted and kept walking. "They are no threat; but keep your eyes open. This place doesn't feel right."

Reynor looked at him. "How so?"

"There is an air; people shouldn't be this afraid of us," he replied.

The door of the closest saloon opened, and a mixed group of thugs poured out into the street. There were thirteen of them wearing mismatched clothing. They were unkempt and bore a number of improvised weapons: clubs, a chair leg, and several long knives. They were from a mix of races, too. A couple Pushtal, some Zuul, Hec-Sha—Reynor had no clue how the lizard people managed the arid climate—and wasp-like KzSha. Two Jivool pushed to the front. They wore matching harnesses from one of the mercenary companies, but the insignia had been removed. Both carried sidearms.

"What do we have here?" one Jivool asked looking at Sempay. "Looks like an old man walking his pet." The ruffians laughed.

Sempay kept walking past the crew. "We aren't looking for trouble here."

The other Jivool stepped forward to block their path. "Well, what if we are?"

Reynor bristled at that, indignation flooding through him. He figured he'd set them straight and inhaled to speak while reaching for his pouch where his badge resided. Sempay's vicelike grip grabbed his upper arm. Reynor stared up at him in astonishment.

Sempay bowed his head. "My good sir, we are simple and poor travelers and aren't worth the effort." He said it with a meek and ingratiating tone, completely unlike his Besquith kin. Reynor couldn't believe the sounds coming from the senior Peacekeeper. "We will be on our way." He guided Reynor around the bearlike alien that was more than double the Radskhat's height and matched the hunched Besquith's mass.

They continued down the street. Reynor opened his mouth to protest and Sempay whispered to him. "Not now."

The inn keeper was standing in the open doorway of his establishment, so the pair steered for it. They stopped before the Jakota. "Are you open?" Sempay asked.

He stepped through the entrance and motioned for the two to follow him. Once they were through, the Jakota closed the door, then headed for the bar on the other side of the table-filled room. They were the only ones in the place and the low-pitched *tick-tick* of the air unit struggling with the heat rattled though the ceiling.

"You may call me Silver. What can I get you?" he asked the two from behind the bar.

Unsure as to what Sempay was doing, Reynor let him take the lead.

"Two drinks and some information?" Sempay asked. He pulled the hood off his head and removed the goggles.

Silver flashed a toothy grin. "All I have is Goka piss."

Reynor jumped at the hearty laugh that erupted out of his partner. "That will be fine as long as it's chilled." Sempay sat on one of the stools at the bar and waved for Reynor to do the same.

Silver fetched a crystal bottle with a faded label and set it and three glasses on the bar top before he went into the back.

As soon as he left, Reynor turned to Sempay and hissed, "What are you doing?" They could hear Silver rattling around in the back.

Sempay shrugged. "Getting a bearing and finding out what is going on here. Relax and learn."

Silver returned with an ice bucket and set it on the counter. "We have to keep it in the freezer, or it melts too fast," he told them apologetically. Silver used some tongs to drop a cube into each of the glasses with a *clink*, then splashed some of the liquid over it. Finished, he passed each of the glasses out and raised his. "To fresh meat."

Reynor picked up his own glass, raised it, then slugged back the liquid. It burned its way across his tongue, down his throat, and roiled in his stomach. His eyes watered and he coughed. "What was *that*?" he croaked.

Silver chuckled, and Sempay slapped his companion on the back.

"We used to have a distillery here. It shut down when we lost the mineral processing contract." Silver lifted the bottle. "This is the last of it. What brings you two to the butthole of the universe?"

"Our transport's fusion drives took on a flutter in hyper. While they re-tune the magnetic bottles, we had time to kill and the captain recommended this slice of heaven," Reynor said bitterly.

Sempay nodded. "He painted a different picture than what we've found." He pointed at his empty glass for a refill.

Silver grunted, "You both should finish up and head back to the transport. Things here have changed in the last year." He poured them each another but skipped pouring one for himself this time.

Sempay took the glass and sipped a little. "Oh?"

"Yeah, two groups moved in and muscled their way into the lithium processing market. A lot of good people got pushed around, and one family disappeared." Silver wiped his glass and put it under the bar. "You met one of the gangs. They treat the people of this town like slaves to work the processing." He shook his head. "They are holding families hostage so the workers will finish and package the product without causing trouble." Silver spat into the sink. "They've torn the soul out of this place, and with the fighting between the two groups, the people are crushed in the middle."

Reynor stood up. "Well, we are—"

"We are looking to maybe help you out. Tell me about these two rivals," Sempay interrupted, shaking his head slightly at Reynor.

Silver looked at the two sitting at his bar and narrowed his eyes. "I don't know what you two are playing at but the only thing you will help is the body recycler. These gangs don't care about people, and the local constable panders to both sides."

Sempay cocked his head, his ears forward. "Which group is stronger?"

"That would be the one you ran into," Silver said. "They call themselves the Orange Circle. I'm not sure why. There are three siblings that run the group, but Oladipo is the roughest." He lifted the bottle and looked at Sempay.

Sempay shook his head. "What about the other crew?"

"Paper Hand hangs out down at the casino. The boss, a Jeha named Tivek, came here from one of the core worlds. They don't have as many people, but their muscle is an Oogar named Graga,"

Silver said. "I think Tivek's waiting for the syndicate to send him more muscle."

Sempay stood up.

"Where are you going?" Silver asked.

"I think I need to make some friends." He looked at Reynor. "Let's go see if they want to hire us."

Astonished, Reynor stood up and followed his Besquith companion to the door.

Once they got outside, the Radskhat rounded on the Besquith. "What are you doing?" Reynor hissed.

Sempay flashed a toothy grin, making Reynor take an involuntary step back. "That's twice now."

Reynor's Peacemaker training quickly asserted itself, and he straightened. "Apologies, I didn't mean to question a superior."

Sempay huffed. "You mistake my amusement for aggression, my young friend. Not everything is as it seems. At times, people see what they want to see. Look at this town. There is a cancer here. Well, two if you count the gangs separately." His eyes narrowed as the constable stepped out of his office and leaned against the wall across the street from them. "Maybe three."

Reynor followed his gaze. "Why don't we just arrest the lot of them? We are Peacemakers after all." He jumped at Sempay's barking laugh.

"All new Peacemakers think that when they strap on their shield the universe will bend to them just because they wear a piece of metal in a particular shape." Sempay chuckled. "Out here, with these thugs, flashing a badge will get you buried in a shallow grave out in the dust fields."

Reynor was shocked. "But everyone knows what happens if you mess with a Peacemaker."

"Yes, my friend. What happens exactly?" Sempay asked, eyes alight with mirth.

"Ah…" Reynor scratched his furred ear. "Well, the Enforcers are sent in to back up the Peacemakers."

Sempay leaned in, "And why did Enforcers get sent in?" he prodded the junior officer.

Reynor wasn't sure what he was after, then he started, eyes wide "Oh no!"

Sempay cackled. "Yup. They are sent in *after* we are dead and don't report. They are sent in to *avenge* us."

Reynor looked at the run-down town and pondered the implications. "So, we are on our own," he said softly.

"Exactly. Which is why we can't go at any of the problems straight-on. We need to come at it from a tangent." Sempay pulled his dust cloak up and settled his goggles in place. "Now, let's go cause some trouble."

* * *

The pair of Peacemakers traveled down the dusty road. As they went, they could see movement in the second-floor curtains along the main avenue; locals too scared to come out. Once they reached the casino, two Zuuls standing outside straightened.

"What the black hole do you want?" one of the Zuul asked gruffly.

"I want to talk to your boss, Tivek," Sempay said.

"You think you are the town princess?" the first Zuul asked.

Sempay pulled his hood back, revealing his Besquith visage and bared his fangs. "Yeah, I'm definitely your princess. Go get him before I decide to use my feminine wiles on you."

The Zuul took a step back, hands up in mock surrender. "All right, I'll get him." He went inside.

Reynor snorted quietly and tried to look meek next to Sempay.

After a few minutes, more people came out. One was a meter and a quarter tall Jeha, his deep purple exoskeleton indicating he was from the home world.

"I've been told you want to see me. What on this planet makes you think you have anything I want to hear?" Tivek said. His feet undulated, showing his agitation.

"I heard you might be interested in some muscle," Sempay said. "Maybe you'd be interested in an audition?"

The Jeha looked up and down the street then back at Sempay. "Well, I don't think you're playing a prank on me, so what d'you have in mind?"

"I have a score to settle with your rivals," Sempay told him. "If you like what you see, maybe we can come to an arrangement."

The Jeha bounced with excitement. "If I like the show, you have a deal."

Reynor watched the exchange with fascination. He had never seen his partner manipulate someone so well. It was obvious Tivek was buying everything Sempay was selling.

Sempay pulled his hood back up over his ears. "Then you might want to stay out here for a bit." He turned, motioned for Reynor to follow, and headed back up the street. As they walked, Sempay whispered to Reynor, "When we get closer, I want you to deploy a hack drone so we can eavesdrop."

Reynor whispered back, "I'm on it." He fumbled at his belt for one of the micro drones that was standard equipment for Peacemakers.

As they approached the bar at the far end of the street, their movement caught the attention of the crew that had accosted them earlier.

Several of the crew rose from the steps in front of the building and approached the pair.

"What in entropy do you two want now? I thought we had sent you packing," one of the Jivool growled.

In a flash, Sempay punched him in the snout. Few non-Jivool knew there was a nerve cluster in the nose. Hit it hard enough and it causes a brain blink—a momentary blackout preventing any reaction. The second strike was to the right side of the neck, precisely where the blood vessels fed the ear and brain, and the location of a second nerve cluster that transmitted a danger signal to the primitive part of the Jivool's brain forcing its head to turn to protect that side. The third strike was a hard knee to the inside of the right thigh. This nexus caused the leg to collapse and the thug to fall. His journey was aided by a downward blast to the now exposed left side of the jaw. The sudden ferocity from a previously docile person overwhelmed the Jivool and stunned the three other toughs. It certainly surprised Reynor, even though he knew it was coming.

"Let your boss know that this old man can still kick your ass," Sempay told them as they stared wide-eyed at the unmoving Jivool.

Sempay nodded at Reynor. "Let's get out of here." The pair walked back to the bar. Silver was standing in the doorway. He had watched the whole thing.

"Did you like the show?" Sempay asked shouldering his way through the door.

Reynor followed. "I have some questions."

Sempay sat on the stool at the bar "Silver, how about some of the good stuff?"

Once Silver had shuffled into the back room, Sempay looked at Reynor. "What questions do you have?"

Reynor took a seat on a stool next to him. "Well, what are we trying to accomplish here?"

"If we can stir up enough trouble, we can get the two groups to turn on each other." Sempay nodded at Reynor's belt. "Did you get the drone in place?" he asked.

Reynor cocked his head, his whiskers twitching. "Yeah, the listener is in place." He pulled out a slate, tapped a few keys, and the audio came up.

"What the heck happened?" said a rough voice.

"It was just a misunderstanding, boss. The old man caught me by surprise. It won't happen again."

"That must be the guy you hit," Reynor said quietly.

Sempay hushed him so they could hear the conversation.

"You want me to go take care of it?" another voice said.

"Nah, we got that shipment to take care of. We'll let Junior here take care of his own mess later," said the voice that must've been the boss. "What time is the shipment due to be here?"

"Should be here tomorrow at noon if those skaggs can keep up production," a third voice said.

"I think that's one of the Pushtal," Reynor whispered.

"Is everything in place?" the boss asked.

"Yeah everything is out in the blue warehouse. Me and the boys will head over there midmorning," the Jivool said.

Just then, Silver came out of the back room, his eyes wide at what he was hearing. He slammed the bottle on the counter. "What on orbit are you doing? You're gonna get us all killed."

Sempay looked at him. "Take it easy, we know what we're doing."

Silver's eyes narrowed. "Who are you?" he asked.

Sempay waved at him to be quiet.

"Make sure you drop the payment, so the constable isn't in the way," the boss said.

A female voice came into range. "When can I see my son?" she asked.

"Not right now," the boss said. "Let's get this into the other room." There was a shuffling noise and then voices faded out.

Reynor fiddled with the data feed. "I think I can hop it to another room if you give me a minute," he said.

"It's okay. I think we have enough," Sempay told him and looked at Silver. "Needless to say, once we get them to turn on each other, things will change quickly. Trust me. When we're done, this will be a different town." He tapped the top of the bar with a claw. "How about that drink?"

Reynor put the slate away, squared on the bar and asked, "So, what kind of shipment are we talking about?"

Silver held up a bottle and poured three glasses. "Lithium delivery. That's what was going on in this town before these two crews moved in. They have the locals extracting the isotopes and the rest gets processed out for a variety of things like electronics, weapons, circuitry, and batteries," Silver explained. He put one glass in front of each of them and picked up the third. "Here's to success."

"You two wait here," Sempay said. "I'm going to go do an information exchange with our new friends to see if we can't turn up the heat a little."

Sempay finished his drink in one swallow, set the glass back on the counter and headed out the door.

Reynor fiddled with the slate. He tried to get a better read with the eavesdrop drone. After a little bit, he put the slate away.

"Your boss is going to get us all in trouble. I feel it," Silver said morosely. He stoppered the bottle and took it into the back room.

* * *

S empay walked down the street to the casino and walked in the front doors. The two Zuul guards let him pass. He pushed the doors open and was assaulted by noise and lights. Games for several dozen species binged, bonged, blinked, and otherwise called out to the empty casino and lack of patrons to separate from their credits. When it opened, it must have been amazing. Today, it was a sad reflection of its former glory days.

Sempay looked around until he spied the entry to the back area. He headed for the door. Next to it was a very large Oogar who stood just under two-and-a-half meters tall, his purple fur dull and matted in places. Like the casino, he had seen better days.

The Oogar spoke with a gruff deep voice. "What do you want?"

"I have some information for your boss," Sempay said.

The Oogar did not look impressed. "What is it?" he asked.

"I've told you, it's information for your boss. Are you having trouble understanding?" Sempay asked.

The Oogar bristled, not liking Sempay's tone. He took a step forward just as the door to the back opened.

"What's going on here?" Tivek said.

The Oogar looked chagrined, reflexively turning toward the Jeha and shuffling back a step. "He says he has information for you, boss. I'll take care of it."

"You'll do no such thing, Graga," he told the Oogar. "This is our new friend, and he's taking care of business for us." Tivek looked at Sempay. "Why don't you come to my office where we can talk." He moved back into the room.

Sempay gave the Oogar an, "I told you so" look, walked into the office, and closed the door, leaving the Oogar on the outside. Sempay turned and studied the Jeha.

"So, what is so important?" Tivek asked.

"Well, I found some information I thought you might find especially valuable," Sempay said. "Just how valuable is up to you."

"Well, what is it?" Tivek asked, his arms rippling in agitation.

Sempay took a seat. "The other crew has a shipment coming in tomorrow. It will be at a blue-painted warehouse at noon."

Tivek's arms waved in excitement. "By all the songs, how did you come by this?"

"That doesn't really matter. What matters is if you find that information valuable." Sempay leaned forward and stared intently at the Jeha.

"Oh yeah, it's valuable all right. In fact, why don't you take what you want out of this box." He pulled open the small strongbox. Inside were credit chips of a variety of denominations, red diamonds glinting in the center of each. Tivek flowed to the door and opened it. "Hey, you idiots, get in here. I got something for you."

The first in the room was Graga. He noticed the open strongbox and the Besquith scooping credits out. He looked at Tivek and snarled in indignation. "You're just letting him help himself?"

Tivek went back around the desk and sat in his chair. "That's none of your black hole business," he said gruffly.

Several Zuul and a Lumar, a two-meter-tall brute with four arms, also came in.

Sempay stood up and moved for the door.

"Where you think you're going? You're gonna help us with this, aren't you?" the Jeha asked.

Sempay shook his head. "I think you have this well in hand. You don't need me. I'll be back when I have more information."

"You're just gonna let him go?" the Oogar whined.

"We have work to do," Tivek declared. The Zuul and Lumar moved out of Sempay's way.

Making his escape, Sempay left the casino and headed back to the bar where Reynor and Silver waited for him.

He pushed open the weather-worn door and resumed his perch at the bar. He picked up the drink Silver had poured for him while he was gone. He savored both the flavor of the beverage and the annoyed expressions painting his compatriot's faces. "Did you pick up the signal?" he asked Reynor.

Reynor stared at the senior Peacemaker uncomprehendingly until he finally grunted and picked up the slate. After a few claw taps on the pad, Tivek's voice came across. Another tap and it ceased. Reynor looked up chagrined. "I should have figured you would put a bug in their office."

"That's all right." Sempay chuckled. "You'll learn that more information is always better." He turned to Silver. "We're going to need two rooms for tonight."

Silver looked at Sempay, then at Reynor, almost as if he were weighing his options. "All right, but it's gonna be double. If any of this blows back on me, I'll need to vanish."

Sempay smiled a fanged grin at Silver, fished out two credit chips, and set them on the counter. "Will this cover it?" he asked mildly.

Silver's eyes bulged and he quickly swept the red diamond encrusted chips off the counter and into his apron pocket.

"Let me show you to your rooms."

* * *

At first light, the pair set off to the warehouse. They had scouted the area around the warehouse with a drone as the sun came up and found a spot to observe the deliv-

ery, and what they hoped were to be some antics and friction between the two crews.

Their vantage point was on top of the roof of the neighboring
building. They had grabbed some boxes and a pallet as well as a partially torn and well-used tarp from inside the building they were
perched on and pulled them up onto the roof to break up the roof-
line. This way they wouldn't be obvious, and even if they *were* spotted
they hoped they would be mistaken for homeless squatters.

The blue warehouse had clearly been selected for the quiet nature
of this part of the town. The only thing moving were a couple of
gray, half-meter-long Chiran lizards digging at the corner of the
building trying to find shade. The *skrit-skrit* of their nails on the wall
echoed eerily off the buildings.

Right at noon, a transport trundled down the street toward the
warehouse. Its tires crunched down the road, and Reynor could
make out figures in the cab of the vehicle as well as on the bed of the
transport itself.

The whine of a ground effect car from the opposite end of the
street showed that the Orange crew had arrived. The vehicle stopped
at the edge of the large door to the warehouse. One of the Pushtal
got out and rapped on the door as he watched the transport come to
a stop. Not getting a response from inside the warehouse, he hammered on the door. The driver and the two transport crew members
disembarked to talk with the Pushtal. The Pushtal driving the car got
out to see what the hold up was.

Sempay and Reynor watched intently.

The door shook then retracted upward. After it had lifted a meter, the sudden whine of needler weapons echoed off the walls, and
all five of the Orange Circle gang were on the ground. The door continued trundling upward.

"What do we do?" Reynor asked in a whisper.

"Observe," Sempay said tapping his slate to get a better angle on their drone's camera.

Four people came out once the door was up. Sempay hissed as an Oogar came into view. He barked orders at the others who began dragging the bodies into the warehouse. It was only a few minutes before the five bodies were inside.

A forklift trundled out carrying a large metallic crate. Soon enough, they had it strapped down on the transport and the door to the warehouse closed. The Oogar and two others climbed into the transport. The others jumped into the ground car and took off in the opposite direction. The transport engines revved up and it headed down the road, eventually turning toward an even rougher section of the town.

"We've seen enough." Sempay tapped on the slate to recall the drone. "Let's get out of here before Orange comes looking for their missing people."

Reynor was stunned at what he had just witnessed. "We have to do something," he sputtered. "We have to arrest them."

Sempay looked at the junior Peacemaker in sympathy. "Look," he said gently, "nothing has changed other than five of the Orange Circle are gone. We have a video of what just happened and a plan. We work the plan, and we'll get to a point where we can make an arrest without getting killed." He stuffed his slate in his jacket. "Let's go talk to the constable and see what we need to fix there for when we *are* ready to make arrests."

* * *

Sempay held out a hand for Reynor to stop just shy of the constable's office. "Follow my lead in there. Don't mention who we are. We have to see what we are dealing with and how corrupt this guy really is," he explained softly. "You good?"

"Yeah. This isn't anything like the scenarios we went through in the academy," Reynor said.

Sempay snorted. "You'll find that life outside the classroom is a lot different." He resumed walking up to the office and opened the door, gesturing for Reynor to proceed him. He followed, pulling the door closed behind him. He was surprised to see the constable wasn't alone.

Another Besquith was sitting at the desk. He was about the same size as Sempay with jet black fur. His golden eyes regarded the pair.

"Oh!" Sempay exclaimed. "I hope we aren't interrupting." Reynor noticed that Sempay had adopted the subservient tone again. "We can come back..." He turned for the door as if to leave.

"Hold right there," the constable said. "It's good that you showed up. Otherwise I'd have had to send for you." He pointed at the newcomer. "This here is Peacemaker Marrok."

Reynor started at that and shot a glance to Sempay. He was awash with emotions. *Another Peacemaker? Here?*

Sempay bowed, subtly shaking his head "no" to Reynor. That caused a bolt of momentary panic to ripple through Reynor. Involuntarily, he took a half-step backward and took a firm internal grip on his Radskhat instincts to flee.

"Oh, a Peacemaker," Sempay said ingratiatingly. "How fortunate you are here. This town could use you, and I'm sure the constable would welcome the assistance," he whined.

Marrok stood up. "I bet he would but cleaning up the insects in this town isn't worth my time. I just got back from the Peacemaker Academy on Ocono, and I have an important meeting to attend at the regional barracks. I'm going to deputize you..." He hesitated. "What's your name?"

"Rhys, Honored Peacemaker," Sempay said subserviently.

"Rhys, you are now an acting Peacemaker Deputy charged with helping the constable here clean up this shithole. The two gangs are your problem. This town can handle one; I don't care which one. Again, that's your problem." Marrok moved closer to Sempay. "Now, I'm going to transit for Peacemaker Headquarters, and when I come back here in two days I'll be bringing twenty enforcers with me. If there isn't peace, then we will kill everything and everyone regardless of who is who."

Reynor shot a quick glance at the constable, and he appeared rocked at Marrok's declaration, who towered over them. Reynor also noted that Sempay had hunched a bit to make himself appear smaller. Reynor did the same.

"Oh yes, it will be as you say," Sempay simpered.

Marrok headed for the door. He opened it and paused in the threshold. "Two days, then the Enforcers will bring peace, permanently." He didn't wait for a response and left.

Reynor stepped back so he could watch Sempay and the constable at the same time, his thoughts racing as fast as his heartbeat.

Sempay looked after Marrok thoughtfully for a moment then turned to the constable. "How long has he been extorting you?" he said softly. Reynor hadn't expected such a direct question.

The constable was shocked. "I have no idea wha—"

"Stop," Sempay said in a command voice while flexing into his full Besquith height and presence, all pretense at meekness falling away like a cloak. He stared at the constable who visibly deflated under his gaze.

Reynor was impressed. *I need to learn to do that.*

"For two years. Just after the two outfits showed up, he came along. He makes visits about every six months to collect his payment. I don't have a choice, so I get money from both groups and give the bulk of it to Marrok. He has the Enforcers. We have to do what he says," he said defeatedly.

"Well," Sempay told him, "not everything is as it seems." He turned so the constable couldn't see and winked at Reynor. "How do you get your payment money? From the two gangs?"

The constable sat back in his chair and told them everything over the next couple of hours. When he was done the constable looked at the pair. "What are we going to do? We have two days."

Sempay scratched his chin thoughtfully. "Do you know where the Paper Hand keeps their stuff? Where they process their lithium?"

"Sure. It's over by the old concrete plant," the constable said.

"This is what we are going to do. You are going to go sell information to the Orange Circle that the Paper Hand swiped their shipment," Sempay said.

"Okay. What are you going to do?" the constable asked.

"I'm going to tell my buddy Tivek that Orange knows." Sempay grinned.

"Ah, that could lead to some shooting." The constable frowned. "The townspeople might get hurt."

Both Reynor and Sempay looked at him.

The constable held up his hands. "Look, I might be taking money to look the other way and pay off the Peacemaker, but these are still my people, and I'm doing what I do to keep them from getting wiped out. They are forced to work and their families are being held hostage, but they aren't harmed otherwise. That's the deal I was able to make."

"All right, we will take care of the workers. You just sell that info to the Orange Circle and get them the location of the shipment." Sempay headed to the door. "We don't have much time to set this up."

Outside, Reynor and Sempay watched the constable head to the cantina where Orange Circle hung out.

"What about the *Peacemaker*?" Reynor asked. "We should have exposed him. There's no way he came from the Academy. *We* just came from there." Reynor's whiskers twitched in anger.

Sempay put a calming hand on Reynor's shoulder. "I'm glad you kept it under control. You did yourself credit there."

"Are you sure he's a fake?" Reynor asked. "Maybe he was appointed while you were on training rotation?"

"I've met all of the Besquith Peacemakers. We have to give up our clan and join with the Peacemaker clan. There is a ceremony where all the Besquith Peacemakers past and present come to welcome the new Besquith into the clan." He tapped his nose with one claw. "So, I've met them all."

"I'm not sure how he set himself up as a fake Peacemaker. Are there even twenty Enforcers in this sector?" Reynor asked.

Sempay snorted. "Not in a sector this small. Probably three or so back at the garrison, at most. Even three in one location is a lot."

"Where do you think he is going for two days?" Reynor asked.

Sempay shook his head, "It's a ruse. He's probably sitting up in orbit counting his money and laughing at the puppets he thinks he's forced into dancing to his tune."

Reynor felt a little better. He admired Sempay's calmness. *I have a lot to learn from him. Once again, jumping in with Peacemaker badges would have caused more problems than they solved.*

"You go get those workers out of that shop," Sempay said to Reynor. "I'm going to go set the hook. Then we can meet back at Silver's."

Reynor was excited to finally be doing something. "I can do that."

The two headed in separate directions into the evening.

* * *

Reynor's earpiece chirped from the drone, signaling it was time to go. He carefully shut the door and exited the back of the building with the last of the workers. He jogged with them for a block then cut into a side street. He pulled out his slate to get a feed from the drone.

He could see a couple of ground cars and a truck moving under low power, lights off, toward the warehouse. He tapped the slate and sent the drone in an orbit a couple of blocks out to where he saw a couple more vehicles coming at the building from the opposite direction.

"Time to go before I'm caught in the middle," he said to himself.

He tapped his earpiece, "Sempay, the bread is out of the oven and the sauce is ready." He shrugged at the lack of response, set the drone to observe, and headed off to the rendezvous point. It felt good to be making a difference. Reynor just wished that Sempay trusted him enough to tell him more of the plan. He sighed as he shuffled along. *Patience,* he could hear his instructors say.

The trip back to Silver's bar was uneventful. He checked the slate every once in a while, not wanting to get too absorbed in the two crews slugging it out. Shortly, he pushed open the door to the bar.

The place was empty of customers and Silver was sitting at one of the tables, not standing in his usual place behind the bar. He didn't look at Reynor when he came in.

Reynor pulled out a chair. "Where's Sempay?"

Silver just sat, staring morosely out the window. After a time, he said quietly, "They took him."

Reynor shot to his feet, knocking over his chair while a bolt of wild emotion washed over him: panic, shock, outrage, fear. All swirled, threatening to overwhelm him until he used his Peacemaker training and pulled in a long, slow calming breath. Once he was more in control of himself, Reynor asked, "Who and how?" His calm tone drew a glance from Silver.

"I warned you to leave," Silver said sadly. "Two of the Orange Circle toughs were in here when Sempay got back from seeing Tivek. They hit him with a neurolytic weapon." He picked up his glass and took a long pull of the dark liquid, draining it in one go. "He didn't have a chance."

"How long ago was this?" Reynor asked pulling his slate out.

"About twenty minutes."

Several minutes passed as Reynor worked. "Ah!" He set the slate in front of Silver and tapped on the screen showing the frozen image of an unconscious Sempay in a cage resting on a multicolored brick floor against a white-washed wall. "Where is this?" Reynor asked.

Silver cocked his head and looked at Reynor for a long moment. Reynor felt as if he was being evaluated. Apparently, Silver liked what he saw because he nodded then squinted at the slate. "That's the back side of their compound." He looked up at Reynor. "The bar across the street from us is the front side of it. They own the block of buildings behind it and sealed it all up so the only two ways in are the bar at the front and the garage on the far side." He got up and shuffled to the bar.

Reynor tapped on the slate a few more times, changed to the drone app, and set it to orbit the compound. Silver set a fresh glass in front of Reynor then grabbed the bottle to fill both glasses to the brim.

Reynor studied the Jakota for a moment, picked up the glass, and raised it. "Honor the threat," he said quietly and downed the entire contents of the glass, then set it upside down on the table. The intoxicant blazed its way down his throat to explode like a nova in his gut. Reynor's eyes watered and he grabbed a cloth off the table to wipe them. When he was finally able to see again, he noticed Silver was sitting rock still, his eyes wide and fixed on him, glass frozen halfway to his mouth.

Silver was finally able to croak out, "Peacemaker."

* * *

Reynor quickly looked behind him. The place was empty, and the door shut. He realized Silver was focused on him. He sighed.

Silver shuddered, then he too slammed back the drink, poured himself another, and downed that one, too. When he reached for the liquor again, Reynor grabbed the bottle holding it away from him.

"No one can know," Reynor said softly.

"You two." Silver took a deep breath. "You two came here on purpose, didn't you?" he asked accusingly.

"Nope. This vacation spot was an accident," Reynor said. He was about to say more when the slate emitted a soft *beep-beep*. He tapped on the screen, leaned in, and zoomed the picture. He held the pad out to Silver. "What is this?"

He peered at the image. "The drain?" He glanced up and shrugged. "It allows the monsoon rains to drain from inside the courtyard. Otherwise, the basements flood and undermine the foundations." Silver looked confused. "Why?"

"That's my way in," Reynor said with a smile.

"No one can fit through that," Silver said with certainty. "Maybe a small child but that won't help us."

"I can. I'm a Radskhat," he said proudly. "We don't have a fixed skeleton. I can fit through the smallest openings. It's how we are able to liberate so many things." Reynor said with a grin.

Silver snorted. "You mean steal."

Reynor waved a hand. "Labels," he said dismissively. "Okay, let me set this in motion." He tapped on his slate, switching over to the implant Sempay had dropped.

"Tivek!" Reynor said.

Silver sputtered. Reynor waved at him to be quiet.

Tivek's voice came across the slate. "Who is this?"

"That doesn't matter. What you should care about is that the Orange Circle just took out your warehouse and you're next," Reynor said matter-of-factly.

Tivek sputtered, "How do you kno—"

Reynor tapped the slate to cut off the transmission. He met Silver's eyes. "That will cause the stir I need to get Sempay out. Can you get transport over to the garage doors?" he asked.

Silver shook his head. "You're crazy. Yeah, I can get there. When?" He stood up.

"I'll need twenty minutes," Reynor said and started emptying his pockets into his bag. Once ready, he reached into the bag and pulled out his weapon. He tucked it into a reinforced thigh pocket made specifically for it. "Okay. See you in a bit."

Reynor headed out the back of the bar. Once outside, he looped down the alley to get a decent vector on the compound. The streets were deserted. In a few minutes he was across the main drag and looking at the back wall of the compound. This was similar to a couple of the training exercises he had been on, only this time they wouldn't get shot with stunners if he got caught.

He took a deep breath and pulled out his slate. A couple of taps and the drone oriented to give him a view of the main street. There was movement from the Paper Hand. The activities from the last couple of days had whittled down the size of the crew, but there was a decent group headed toward the Orange Circle bar. Another tap on the slate, and the drone hovered over the courtyard. It was still deserted.

Reynor stowed the slate and pulled out his weapon. He knelt by the opening for the drainpipe. Looking down, he saw only dust and a faint light of the courtyard on the other side. He breathed out slowly and squirmed into the small opening, weapon first.

The Radskhat physiology evolved from their ancestor's ability to get into and out of trouble. It allowed them to loosen the ligaments and tendons of their musculature, thereby enabling their cartilage to bend and flex. With practice, it became simple for them to get through spaces that normal beings couldn't possibly fit into. This unadvertised ability came in handy when a fellow Academy graduate locked Reynor's data slate in an equipment lockup as a prank.

The space under the wall was about three meters long. He stretched and relaxed and wriggled. He was about three-quarters of the way through when he heard footsteps in the courtyard. Reynor froze. His heartbeat hammered in his ears, and he kept the pistol pointed forward.

He heard a pair of voices talking about what they were going to do to the Besquith. His breath caught, and he resumed wriggling forward. The seam in the drainpipe caught on his sleeve, binding him up for a moment, but with a tug it ripped free. What would normally have been a small sound was amplified by the pipe.

"What was that?" one of the guards asked.

"I don't hear anything," the other said.

Footsteps moved closer to the opening.

Reynor readied his pistol and held his breath.

The thug stopped in front of the opening. His boots clearly visible. Reynor heard faint pops of pistol fire. The guard swore, and they both ran off. The Paper Hand hitting the front of the Orange Circle facility was perfectly timed.

Reynor frantically wriggled the rest of the way out of the pipe, shook himself, and moved toward the cage. Sempay watched him as he approached.

"I didn't know you could do that," Sempay said.

Reynor shrugged. "This has been a learning trip all around," he quipped and examined the lock on the cage. It was a simple twenty-four hexagonal-key keypad. He pulled his slate out and held it to the pad. He triggered a cypher cracker and waited the few seconds for it to brute-force the pad with combinations, the indicators flashing blue, then amber, and finally green. With a *click*, the lock disengaged.

Reynor stowed his slate and pulled the cage door open. "Can you walk?"

Sempay stood and walked out of the cage. "Other than a headache, I'm unharmed. What's the plan to get out?"

"Transport outside of the garage. Let's move." Reynor turned in the direction of the garage and led the way, his pistol at the ready.

The door to the garage was unlocked. It was empty inside except for a hover bike being worked on, a tool rack, and a desk with a terminal.

"Hang on. Let's get some intel," Reynor said and pulled a connection stick from his chest pocket. It was a small metallic object about the size of a coin only designed to be inserted into the port on a terminal. He plugged it in. A series of screens flashed on the terminal. Reynor grunted once and pulled the device out and put it away. "Okay, we have a backdoor into their mainframe."

There was a small portal door next to the large double doors of the garage. "Our ride should be outside any minute," he told Sempay.

Sempay nodded approvingly. "You've been busy, haven't you?"

Reynor grabbed his slate and oriented the drone on the street outside; it was clear. He orbited the drone to the front of the bar. There he could see several bodies in the street and in front of the bar. He showed Sempay the image. "It looks like the distraction might have played out. When the ride comes, we need to get out of here."

They could hear the whine of a vehicle outside the door and they stepped out. Reynor engaged the inside lock on the garage's door and pulled it closed gently while Sempay climbed into the taxi. Reynor joined him.

"Where to?" the mechanical voice of the driver-assist module spoke.

Sempay looked at Reynor questioningly.

"Three Two Four Jurak Centro," Reynor told the bot, and the vehicle surged forward and turned at the next intersection.

"What's that address?" Sempay asked.

"It's the dry cleaners near Silver's place. I saw it when I set the workers free." He slumped back in the seat and closed his eyes for a brief moment. His slate pinged at him, and he sat up, fishing it out of his thigh pocket. He tapped the screen and murmured thoughtfully. "This is interesting…" He showed Sempay.

Sempay smiled a big toothy grin. "Oh. That *is* interesting."

* * *

The next morning, the pair were in the constable's office.

"Are you ready for this?" Sempay asked him.

The constable didn't look happy but sighed and

nodded. "Yeah. Let's do it."

He grabbed a device with a microphone attached with a cord and headed out into the street. Once there, he raised the microphone and yelled into it. "Tivek, get out here!" He turned a dial. "Oladipo, get out here." He nodded at Sempay. "The constable override will get them out here."

There was movement at either end of the street. From the casino, Tivek and two of his guards, a Zuul and the Lumar, stepped out. "What do you want, Cancar?"

All this time, Reynor realized, he never knew the constable's name was Cancar.

From the other side of the street, the Orange Circle crew stepped out, a Jivool, a Zuul and a Pushtal. The Jivool spoke, "What is this Tivek? Haven't you had enough?"

Tivek laughed. His arms waving in amusement. "How's your brother, Oladipo?"

"Better than you're going to be." The Jivool looked at the bar and waved an arm. The Oogar who had been working for Tivek came out. He had a neuro-stun baton in his hand. He grinned.

"Graga! You traitorous scum! I'll turn you into a rug," Tivek screamed.

The Oogar huffed. "Tivek, you are welcome to try." He lumbered down the street. On Tivek's side, the Lumar shouted a challenge and lumbered forward. The constable scrambled away from between the two groups.

Sempay looked at Reynor and nodded meaningfully at the street. "The time for subtlety is over."

Reynor nodded. He stepped to the edge of the porch, pulled his weapon, took a breath, let a bit out, and as the Oogar passed in front of him, he took aim and fired.

With a loud *crack*, the side of the Oogar's head erupted with a spray of blood and brains. Both groups, who had been moving toward each other, skidded to a halt in the dusty street.

Reynor stepped into the street holding his pistol, smoking barrel skyward, in one hand and a glimmering badge in his other. "I am Peacemaker Reynor. You will submit, or you will join this sack of shit in the dirt."

"You're not a Peacemaker. Get him!" Tivek screeched.

Another *crack* came from behind Reynor, and the Zuul next to Tivek fairly exploded.

"I am Senior Peacemaker Sempay. My colleague has offered you a way out. I suggest you take it."

Reynor watched the Orange Circle crew while Sempay covered the Paper Hand. Both groups deflated. "Constable Cancar, would you please escort these groups to your holding area?" Reynor asked.

The constable, who had been staring at Reynor openmouthed, shook himself and jumped forward. "Yes, Peacemaker!" He picked up the stunner from the ground by the Oogar's corpse and pointed it at the gangsters. "All right! Get moving." He waved them toward the office.

"Not a moment too soon," Sempay said pointing at a ship descending. "Shall we go greet our colleague?"

Reynor looked at the ship and nodded. "Constable? You have this?"

Constable Cancar nodded. For the first time, he didn't look defeated. "Yeah, I got this." He poked at the crew filing into his office. "Straight back. Orange Circle in the left room; Paper Hand on the right."

Reynor holstered his pistol and started for the landing area. They got there just as the landing ramp touched down on the tarmac.

The Besquith, Marrok, strode down the ramp. He saw Sempay and Reynor and immediately headed for them.

"Well, Rhys, did you take care of business?" Marrok asked.

"Almost, we have one more thing to take care of," Sempay stated. He gestured to Reynor. "If you would do the honors?"

Marrok looked irritated. "Do I need to bring the Enforcers out here?"

Reynor looked at him. For the first time in his life, he felt calm and unafraid. "Go ahead. Call them out here."

Marrok was infuriated. He roared at Reynor. "How dare you oppose the Peacemakers?"

"How dare I?" Reynor smiled. He lifted his left hand to show Marrok his badge.

Marrok's eyes bulged, glued to the Peacemaker badge. His hand grabbed for the weapon in his holster. *Crack!*

Fixated as he was on the Peacemaker badge, he never saw that Reynor had drawn his own weapon.

Marrok glanced down at his chest, blood welling down the front, then looked up at Reynor. "Peacemaker…" He started and slumped on the ground.

Reynor sighed but kept his pistol trained on Marrok.

"You okay?" Sempay asked softly.

"I will be," Reynor said.

* * *

Silver and Constable Cancar walked the two Peacemakers to their shuttle.

"Silver," said Reynor pulling out a data stick, "this is a list of the lithium buyers I pulled from the Orange Circle's systems. With this, you can work directly with them, and the town can stand on its own." He handed it to the Jakota.

"What do you want me to do with the people in the jail?" the constable asked.

"We will send word to the real Peacemaker regional office, and they will send a transport. They'll also want to look at Marrok's activities. This kind of scam doesn't operate in a vacuum," Sempay said.

"I appreciate it, Peacemakers. I'll work with Silver here to make sure it doesn't happen again," Cancar said.

"Now that the town knows you were only trying to keep innocents from getting killed, we can work together," Silver said. He held up the data stick. "This will make it easier, and hopefully bring some life back to this place."

Reynor and Sempay made their goodbyes and boarded the shuttle. Once they strapped in, it boosted to orbit.

Reynor looked at Sempay. "That was quite the adventure."

Sempay smiled, leaned back in his seat, and closed his eyes. "Just wait until the next one."

* * * * *

Mark Stallings Bio

Mark Stallings is a member of Pikes Peak Writers, speaks at international conferences on technology topics, is a writer of Wuxia, Fantasy, Thrillers, and Military Sci Fi. He is a competitive shooter, avid martial artist, drinker of craft beer, and motorcycle enthusiast. Mark is currently working on a fantasy trilogy due out later this year. You can find him at MarkStallings dot com.

# # # # #

Curiosity Killed the Pushtal
by Chris Kennedy

Peacemaker's Office, Karma Station, Karma System

It had taken several days, but Keromnal had finally finished processing the criminals from his last case, and he sat back. The bench creaked dangerously as his 10,000-pound body shifted.

"Stupid Trade Guild," he muttered. "In all this time, they still haven't built a seat that can adequately hold a Sumatozou."

Something was bugging him, but he couldn't put a trunk on it. He forced himself to relax like he'd been taught and allowed his thoughts to flow. He knew his problem had something to do with the latest group of criminals he'd just processed. The case had been brought to him by some Humans and had involved a crew of Science Guild personnel—led by a proctor, no less—who had killed a stargate control station crew.

That would have been concerning, in and of itself, but the crew was also found to have been raising—and worse, modifying—Canavars, which put it squarely under his purview as the sector's Peacemaker. He'd deputized the Humans and honored the threat the Canavars had posed. Driving the Behemoth carrying them into a star had ensured they wouldn't cause any further problems.

His trunks twitched in annoyance, the red stripes denoting his first-born status fluttering in his peripheral vision. He closed his eyes and allowed his thoughts to flow. In a few moments, he had it. *Stopo-*

ver System. The system he had caught the Science Guild crew in was called Stopover System in the ancient Buma language as it had nothing of value, other than being in the right place to stop over on the way to the Morgoth system on the fringe of the galaxy. Morgoth held a Science Guild facility—the same one the Canavars had been headed to.

He would dearly have loved to pay a visit to the facility, but if one of its proctors thought killing a stargate control facility's crew— *including a Vergola!*—was permissible, then there was no telling what else they would do. Things had become…unstructured with the strife the Merc Guild was currently engrossed in. They had gone to war with the Humans for some reason but had almost lost it. The Peacemakers had intervened before the guild had completely imploded. The stability of the galaxy rested on having a strong Mercenary Guild, as attested by recent events while the guild sought to redefine itself in the aftermath of its ill-fated war. If rumors were to be believed, the Goltar had assumed control of the Speakership after millennia of Veetanho domination. There were also rumors of a gunfight during a guild meeting that had killed nearly all the representatives.

While he found the latter rumor somewhat difficult to believe, the Merc Guild had been acting strangely lately. It had lost its focus during the war, and now? Now it wasn't even taking new contracts. The second and third-level effects of that decision were starting to have truly heinous repercussions around the galaxy. In the absence of a strong Merc Guild, the other guilds saw it as an opportunity to redress previous inter-guild issues, as well as making wholesale changes within their own guilds that wouldn't have been possible previously. Who would the victims call for help? With no Merc Guild to supply troops for hire, organizations were on their own, and many weaker ones were simply being crushed.

It also gave some people the idea that there would be no enforcement of the laws, which was obviously what happened in this case. A Science Guild that didn't fear the consequences was one that would raise Canavars and kill stargate control station crews.

Neither could be allowed to continue.

Which put him on the horns of a dilemma. He could go to the Science Guild facility where the Canavars were heading, but he had a suspicion he wouldn't be coming back if he did so. He would have to take an absolutely overwhelming force if he intended to take down the Science Guild station...or he would never be seen again. It wasn't that great of a step from killing a gate crew to killing a Peacemaker. He was fairly certain he had enough evidence for his superiors to send in an Enforcer or ten, but if the rot there was truly as bad as he figured, they'd go in underprepared and be slaughtered, too.

Keromnal needed more information on the Science Guild facility to set the terms...but without actually going there.

Having determined what he needed, figuring out his next move was child's play. There were only two ways to get to the Science Guild facility, and one of them—Stopover System—only went to Morgoth.

He needed to talk to his sister.

* * *

Gate Master's Office, Gate Control Station, Karma System

"Greetings, Honored Brother," the gate master said with a bow as Keromnal walked into her office. A slightly smaller version of himself, Shragontal's trunks had the green stripes of a younger sibling. She had also filed her tusks a little bit, so they presented sharp points. Most non-Sumatozou wouldn't have noticed, but he did. Then again, it was his job to notice things. "How goes the peace-making business?"

"Well met, Sister," he replied. "It goes well, but after I processed the last of the Canavar smugglers, I got to thinking."

"Curiosity killed the Pushtal," she replied. "I would think a Peacemaker would know that."

Keromnal chuckled. "As a race, that is certainly true of the Pushtal, and the Peacemakers spend a lot of credits policing them. Still, thinking is a requirement of the job."

"Which is why you are suited to be one, while I carry on the family's business with the clan."

"Indeed." He had always been looked down on in his family and peer group for overthinking things, but that is what made him a good—and some would say *very good*—Peacemaker. While he could follow orders when he needed to, he wanted them to make sense. "Because I said so," didn't work well for him, and accepting those kinds of directions was a large part of being a gate master. He'd known he wouldn't last long as one, and he'd been prepared to leave his clan and join either the merchant or merc clan, but then he'd been selected for the Peacemaker Academy.

Keromnal chuckled again. "Anyway, I was thinking about the Science Guild facility on Morgoth—"

"What about it?" Shragontal asked, her ears flapping slightly.

Keromnal's gaze narrowed. "What have you done?"

She had trouble meeting his eyes. "What do you mean?" she asked. "I don't know what you're talking about."

"You may be able to fool the other races, Shragontal, but I grew up with you, and I notice things. You've done something you don't want me to know about." When she didn't immediately say anything, he asked, "Do you really want to have me figure it out on my own?"

"I haven't done anything," she muttered, still not meeting his eyes.

"Okay," Keromnal said, dropping his bulk onto a bench, "let's think about this. When last I saw you, you were mad about the stargate control station crew being killed. Although the people who did the deed were dropped into a star, that probably wouldn't have been enough for you."

"Sure it was," she said. "How much more justice can there be than being dropped into a star?"

Keromnal looked up suddenly. "I don't know—you tell me." Her eyes looked off again. "No? Hmmm. Let's think about this some more. The people who did the act were punished, but that wouldn't be good enough for you. Why not? Hmm…because you would have wanted the people who ordered the action—the Science Guild masters in Morgoth—punished, too, which is why you jumped when I mentioned that system. Also, when I last saw you, there was a group of Human mercs here that didn't leave when I did. Hmmm…" The answer was easy. "You didn't!"

"Didn't what, dear Brother?"

"Please tell me you didn't hire the Humans to go to Morgoth."

Her head swung back to him, and she met his gaze defiantly. "And what if I did?" she asked. "The Science Guild people who paid for it deserve to die, just like the mercs who actually did the deed!"

"No doubt," Keromnal agreed, "but one small group of mercs is unlikely to be able to take down that system. If they are doing one illegal thing there, they are probably doing other things, as well, and they will have a strong defensive presence. You have likely just consigned those Humans to their deaths."

"As long as they kill those Science Guild bastards, that's fine!"

"No, it is not," Keromnal said, trying to keep his temper. He counted off the points on his fingers. "One, that group of Humans didn't need to die, and you had no right to send them on what even *you* should have known would be a fool's errand. Two, you have now warned the Science Guild that we're onto them. They will now take precautions against any additional action we take against them. They will probably increase their defenses and, even worse, may hide the evidence of what they were doing there. Three, you have greatly increased the odds of guild-on-guild infighting between the Science Guild and the Cartography Guild."

"*So what?*" she raged. "I didn't start it; *they did!* Besides, what do you care? You spurned the Cartography Guild!"

Keromnal smiled. "I didn't spurn the guild; it just wasn't for me. I wasn't cut out to be a gate master. That, however, doesn't mean I don't care, or that I don't have any loyalties to the clan and guild; it only means the Peacemaker Guild comes first for me, and doing what's right."

"Doing what's right means bringing the people that paid for the death of a Vergola to justice!" she shouted.

"Yes, it does," Keromnal said, acknowledging her outburst with a small nod.

"But—" She stopped whatever she'd been about to say. "Did you just agree with me?"

"Of course I did. The people who paid for the crime—the Science Guild in Morgoth—need to be brought to justice. And you made it harder for me to do so by sending the Humans into the system."

"Well, I didn't know you would—" She paused. "I didn't think—"

"No," Keromnal said. "Like always, you *didn't* think. You used your baser instincts, and you reacted to what you perceived as a threat. I doubt your superiors will be happy about you doing it, either, once they know, as it may very well incite a war between the guilds. Even though all the guilds are making power grabs at the moment, none of them want an outright war, and you may have forced your masters into that position."

"But…but…you were the one who dumped their ship into a star!"

"Yes I did," he said, "and then I sent their crews off to a penal planet, never to be seen again. I talked with the gate master in Stopover System; he promised to say we were never there and to erase the ships' arrivals from the logs. As far as the Science Guild would ever have known, their ships had an accident in hyperspace and were never seen again. That story, however, has now been torn to pieces by your rash act."

Shragontal's trunks twisted in anguish. "I didn't mean to!" she cried. "I just wanted—"

"I know what you wanted. It was the same thing I wanted, but I was willing to work within the law and put together a case to bring them down; you just acted on a whim."

Shragontal looked up while bowing in apology. "I'm sorry?" she asked.

"Are you?"

"Yes, Brother, I am. I acted rashly."

"You should have known I wouldn't let this go without a final resolution."

"If I'd thought about it—"

"Yes, if you'd thought about it." He blew his breath out both trunks. "Alas, you didn't."

"So what do we do?" she asked.

"*We?*" Keromnal asked. "There is no 'we.' *I* build a case and *you* do nothing. You've already done more than enough, thank you very much. No, on second thought, that's not true. I need information from you—something only a gate master would be able to obtain."

Shragontal bowed in submission. "Just let me know what you need."

* * *

Keromnal sat down at Shragontal's terminal and cracked his fingers.

"Here," Shragontal said, leaning over him. "Let me show you."

Keromnal turned and raised an eyebrow at her. "I've got this. I just needed your password."

"But—"

"I was a gate control trainee for many years before I went to the Academy," he explained. "Remember?"

"Oh, yeah."

"Good, now let me do what I need to, and you just go inspect something, why don't you?"

"But—"

"But nothing. I'm not going to do anything that will get you into trouble." He smiled. "Well, not any more than letting me sit here in the first place would."

"If you're sure…"

"I'm positive. I don't need any help." He made a shooing motion. "Now go, and let me do my search."

She left, looking back over her shoulder a couple of times as she let herself out of the office.

Keromnal smiled at the screen and got to work. As he'd expected, the software had changed somewhat, but it was still close enough to what he remembered—and what he still had loaded in his pinplants—that he was able to navigate the system.

Just as Karma was the center for Peacemaker operations in the sector, it was also the sector lead for the Cartography Guild, and, as such, was the central repository for the sector logs. At the end of each month, the logs for every stargate in the sector were sent to Karma for archiving. The gate masters, and their masters over them, were nothing if not thorough. He'd had an idea about the level of information he'd be faced with, but, if anything, the amount of data was even more than he'd expected.

There were two main avenues of travel to get to Morgoth. The first—and "open to the public" one—he quickly gave up on. Not only did traffic go through the waypoint system to get to Morgoth, due to the stellar geography, travelers could also go to several other systems on the fringe, and the level of traffic made sorting through it difficult.

Stopover System traffic, though, was only headed for Morgoth, and the fact that the system's coordinates were a Science Guild secret—also known by the Cartography Guild, of course—meant that only Science Guild personnel knew of it. And usually only the high-ranking personnel...or the ones engaged in illicit activities.

He found the most recent ship to go through the gate in the Stopover system, then backtracked its travel over the preceding several systems. The search was arduous, but eventually he found where it had originated. Then he took the next most recent ship and backtracked it. This one took longer, as it had changed its name and transponder codes. He then did the next most recent ship, and continued until he'd backtracked all of the ships for the last year, stopping only twice to shoo away his sister. She'd be able to see what files he'd accessed—he wasn't going to start deleting things. If she really wanted to know what he was looking for, his trail would be easy to see.

It didn't take a big thinker to figure out what he was looking for, so he was sure even his sister could figure it out.

At the end of his session, several hours later, he had three systems that kept appearing on the itineraries of ships passing through

Stopover System. One, of course, was Karma itself. The ship with the Canavars had come through here, for example. He smiled. Right under his nose the whole time. Like most criminals, though, they didn't get caught because they'd broken the law; they got caught because they were stupid and had fucked up.

He had no idea why they'd killed the crew of the gate control station—and with all the mercs dead, he never would—but they had, and the Humans pursuing them had brought Keromnal in on the case. Had they not killed the crew, the Humans might not have involved him, and he would never have known. Funny how things worked out, sometimes.

The other two systems were both out-of-the-way systems and little traversed, outside of the traffic going from them to Morgoth. What decided it for him was the fact that the ships coming from one of them always changed their transponder codes. He chuckled. The fact they were trying to hide made them all the more obvious. While it might have distracted someone who wasn't really searching, trying to hide only highlighted them even more to someone who was actively looking for anomalies.

Criminals were so stupid sometimes.

Having determined the object of his search, all he needed was transport to get there. He dove into the local files and immediately had what he was looking for. A Sumatozou cruiser was docked at Karma Station, stranded there when the Merc Guild stopped taking contracts. He saw who owned it, and he smiled. That would do…that would do quite nicely.

* * *

The Watering Trough, Karma Station, Karma System

"So...how's business?" Keromnal asked.

Colonel Fragontic's drink stopped halfway to his mouth, and his red-lined trunks twisted in wry humor. "I only thought I was in trouble before. Now I know I'm in trouble!"

Keromnal gave him a small smile. "I don't know what you're talking about."

"Ever since we were boys, one thing was true. Lock up your candy when Keromnal starts getting coy!"

"Coy? I didn't know you even knew that word, Fragontic."

"Hey, just because I make a living charging into blazing laser beams and magnetic accelerator cannon rounds doesn't mean I'm an idiot." He chuckled. "Well, maybe it does, especially the MAC rounds, but it doesn't mean I have to be a completely uneducated one. I took most of the same classes as you growing up, and you're not the only Sumatozou who can rub two brain cells together periodically."

Keromnal joined in the chuckle. "No, I know you're not stupid, which is why I was excited to see you were on station here."

"Bah. 'On-station,' you say. I'd say we're stuck at this hell hole while the guild council tries to figure out how to remove their collective trunks from their asses. I almost went back home to Sumas for some rest and relaxation. If you're not going to do anything, might as well do it somewhere nice, eh?"

"True. But you didn't."

"Have you seen the price of F11 recently?" He slapped the table with one of his trunks in frustration. "Damn war with the Humans drove up prices, even though we weren't involved in it. Too damn expensive to travel home and back for no reason. The troops can get drunk just as easily here, and staying here will let me pay them another couple of times before I go broke."

"So you'd be available for some business?"

"The guild says we're not taking contracts, remember?"

"I am aware, however, this isn't a guild contract. It's a Peacemaker bounty contract. To the best of my knowledge, you're still able to take those."

Fragontic's trunks stilled, and he looked cautiously at Keromnal. "What's the job?"

"You wound me," the Peacemaker said. "It almost sounds like you don't trust me."

"I still remember being left to face the authorities while you got away with the candy. To this day, my ass still hurts when I sit from the paddling my father gave me. I think I'd like to know *all* the details this time."

"Why do you have to bring that up every time I see you?" Keromnal asked.

"Mostly because every time you see me, you try to talk me into doing something that is liable to get me killed, or worse."

"So your wife is still mad at me?"

Fragontic smiled. "Let's just say you shouldn't hold your breath on being invited to dinner the next time you're back on Sumas and leave it at that, shall we?"

"Fine," Keromnal said. He chuckled, reliving the memory of the last time they'd been together. After a moment, Fragontic joined him.

"Okay," the merc finally said, "so what's the deal, really? All this beating around the bush is beginning to scare me."

"Just between you and me, the Science Guild has been raising Canavars." He put up a hand to forestall Fragontic's question. "I don't know why yet; I just know they have. I caught one group with at least four of them—"

"At least four?" Fragontic asked. "How do you not know how many they had? Aren't they kind of hard to hide?"

"I didn't want to search the ship; I just had them drive it into a star."

"Huh. Must have been a big ship."

"It was. It was a Behemoth."

Fragontic whistled. "Ouch. That'll hurt the old bottom line." He nodded once. "So that's how it is. You're playing for keeps."

"Yes I am. This isn't the first time we've seen Canavars recently, either. If it's Science Guild personnel that've been behind it all—and it looks like they are—I aim to put a stop to it. Things are crazy enough in the galaxy at this time without people dropping Canavars onto populated planets."

"Just like the bad old days of the Great Galactic War," Fragontic said. He sighed. "Okay, you've got my attention. Just tell me we're not going to have to fight any Canavars on this mission of yours."

"I don't know," Keromnal replied. "I have intel on a secret Science Guild outpost, and I'd like to check it out. I don't know if they're breeding Canavars there...or something worse. All I know is that the guild is trying very hard to keep it from being noticed...which makes me really want to know what's going on there."

Fragontic cocked his head. "What's worse than Canavars?"

Keromnal shrugged his trunks. "I don't know, and that's what scares me."

"And that's also where my company comes into the picture."

"Correct. I need to take a look at that system, and I don't want to do it without some support."

"I really want to tell you no," Fragontic said, "but my accounts are so empty it's a luxury I don't have. This is a paid gig, right?"

"It is," Keromnal said. "Standard rate." He looked around to see if anyone nearby was listening. "As it turns out, I know someone here who could probably get us some shorter transitions there and back. Two less days in hyperspace each way would also help cut down on costs."

"Shragontal is the gate master here now?" Fragontic asked. "I didn't know that. Hmmm…"

"She also has a mate with a really big MAC, too."

"How big?"

"Bigger than yours."

"Well that's disappointing." Fragontic shrugged. "All right; no adding her to my herd. In that case, I guess I'll have to take your job. When do you want to leave?"

"I believe time is of the essence. As soon as you can have the ship ready to go."

"You wound me, Peacemaker!" Fragontic said in mock pain. "I run a tight ship, and it's always ready to go!"

Keromnal raised an eyebrow.

Fragontic shrugged. "Okay, the ship is ready, but I'll probably need time to recall the mercs from the bars. How about we leave in twelve hours?"

"I'll be there."

* * *

CIC, SMS *Pride of Sumas*, Hyperspace

Keromnal took his seat at the back of the Combat Information Center as the ship went to battle stations prior to exiting hyperspace. The captain of the *Pride of Sumas*, Captain Bragontic, nodded once to him in acknowledgment then went back to what she was doing. She'd been less than thrilled at his lack of intel on what to expect in the Tregoth system.

Keromnal had a sensation of falling as the ship emerged from hyperspace, then the ship—and his own system—stabilized.

"Drones out!" the captain called. "Status ASAP!"

The main Tri-V viewer was set to show the battlespace around the *Pride*, and it remained blank. Keromnal began breathing normally again after a couple of minutes. Entrance into the system was what he'd been most worried about. There was no defense for getting hit with thousands of missiles upon emergence; anything after that, he could handle. While he'd thought there wouldn't be a lot of defensive systems—the Humans had said there weren't any in the system they'd been to—that hadn't quelled the butterflies in his stomach.

"One habitable planet in the system and two gas giants," the sensor tech said after a few minutes. "I don't see any evidence of civilization on any of the planets. Oh...there you are! Contact! I've got a contact coming out from behind the habitable planet."

"What is it?" the captain asked.

"It's a transport, ma'am, and it's burning hard for the stargate."

"Any chance of stopping it or getting weapons onto it before it gets there?"

"No, ma'am, there isn't."

Bragontic looked over her shoulder at Keromnal. "What do you want me to do?"

"Set a course for the planet, please, and get me a comm channel to the gate master." After about ten minutes, they had the channel, although the transmissions lagged due to the distance.

"Yes?" asked the gate master, a Sumatozou named Dragopal. "What can I do for you?"

Keromnal bowed. "Well met, Gate Master. I am Peacemaker Keromnal, on a mission to check out this system. There is currently a ship proceeding toward the stargate. I request you do not activate the stargate. I believe that ship has contraband in it, and I would like to search it before it leaves the system."

"Certainly, Peacemaker. We will not activate the stargate until you've conducted your inspection of the vessel."

"Thank you." He turned back to the ship's captain. "Belay my last. I'd like to go search that ship first."

* * *

CIC, SMS *Pride of Sumas*, Tregoth System

"The transport is still heading for the stargate," the sensor tech said two days later. The *Pride* was passing the planet, but its quarry was almost to the stargate. It had ignored all attempts at communication, and it hadn't stopped as its crew had been ordered to.

"Any idea?" Keromnal asked.

"None," the captain said. "It's heading at the stargate as if it were going to open."

"Could you call the gate master again?"

"Certainly."

After a couple of minutes, Dragopal appeared on the Tri-V. "I don't know what that ship is doing any more than you do, Peacemaker," he said, forestalling Keromnal's question. "You have told me not to activate the stargate for them, and I will not."

"Okay, thanks," Keromnal replied. "It was just that it didn't appear like he was stopping…"

"And you thought I would let him through. Don't worry; it won't happen."

"Thirty seconds until the transport reaches the stargate," the sensor tech said.

"Thanks," Keromnal said to the gate master. "I appreciate your support."

"No problem—" The gate master interrupted himself at something offscreen. "Wait! That's not possible! Shut it down," he ordered someone offscreen.

"What's happening?" Keromnal asked.

"The stargate is activating," the gate master said. "We didn't do it, and we can't stop it."

"Stargate just came on!" the sensor tech called.

"Turn it off!" Keromnal directed. "Shut it down!"

"We can't! All of our controls have been deactivated! Nothing is working!"

"Can't you pull the power?"

"Not in what time we have!"

"The transport is gone," the sensor tech called. "The stargate deactivated after it went through."

"Where did the ship go?" Keromnal asked.

"I don't know," Dragopal replied. "After it went through, the stargate shut down and the system relinquished control again. We can now operate the controls, but the system shows it hasn't been accessed since yesterday's activation period. Whatever just happened, it wiped itself clean afterward. It also used up the power stored in the capacitors; I won't be able to use the stargate again until it recharges."

"What do you want us to do?" the captain asked.

Keromnal flipped his trunks in frustration. "Well, the ship is gone, and we can't go after it, even though I have a good idea of where it's gone. What do we have at the planet?"

"We've found one small complex, and that's it," the sensor operator said.

"How small?"

"Well, it's hard to tell," she said. She brought up the image of the planet on the main Tri-V. Tregoth, the planet, was barren, and most of it appeared brown, with a small equatorial belt of green. She zoomed in on a spot in the southern hemisphere on the main continent. "It's right here," she said, and an "X" appeared in blue.

She continued to zoom in on it, and two small buildings grew in the viewer, located next to a mountain. The buildings were small—a three-story office building and perhaps some sort of barracks.

"What's that black spot on the mountain?" Keromnal asked.

"You're not going to believe this," the sensor operator said, slewing the picture over to the mountain and zooming in further, "but those are *doors*."

"Doors?" Keromnal asked, his voice tinged with awe. "For us to see them from here, they'd have to be…"

"About sixty feet high and a little more in width," the sensor tech said with a nod. "They're huge."

"What do you need doors that big for?" the captain asked. "Even our largest combat vehicles could go through those doors three-across."

"I can only think of one thing," Keromnal replied.

"Don't say it," Colonel Fragontic said. "Please don't say it."

"Canavar."

"Damn it," Fragontic said. "Next you're going to say that you want to go down there."

"No," Keromnal replied. "I definitely do *not* want to go down there."

"That's a relief."

"Just because I don't want to, though, doesn't mean I won't. We still need to go down there and check out the facility."

Fragontic sighed. "I was afraid you were going to say that."

* * *

Dropship One, Outside the Facility, Tregoth

"Looks deserted," the pilot said, waving out the cockpit window at the Science Guild facility. "I'm not getting any indications of people out there, although it's possible they're underground or cold-blooded, like the MinSha or something."

"See anything…umm…really large, like a couple of hundred feet long?" Keromnal asked.

"Only those buildings there," the pilot said, pointing to their 2:00 position. "Aside from those buildings, this place looks dead. I haven't seen anything moving within ten miles of this place."

"Fine," Keromnal said. "Set us down here."

"You got it," the pilot said. Keromnal and Fragontic left to go to the back as the pilot coordinated the landing with the other craft. With a gentle bump, the dropship touched, the ramp came down, and the Sumatozou troopers lumbered down the ramp to take up positions around it.

The physical attribute that put the soldiers at their biggest disadvantage on the battlefield—their size—was also one of their greatest strengths. While they were far bigger targets than the other merc races, they could also carry larger and more powerful weapons, although it slowed even them down somewhat. They were also able to take more damage and still function than many of the other races, but they weren't very fleet of foot.

Being large also made them immune to the fear caused by races like the Besquith. It was hard to get too excited about something you could squash underfoot if needed. While packs of Besquith could still take down Sumatozou, the individual trooper was far less worried about going hand-to-hand with a member of the Besquith race. While slower than the Besquith, the Sumatozou soldier only had to get one solid bashing attack in to disable his or her opponent.

Once everyone had set up a perimeter, Fragontic waved Keromnal out, and the Peacemaker strode down the ramp. As soon as he was clear, the dropship lifted, along with the three other craft that had brought the company to the surface.

"Where to?" Fragontic asked. "Want to check out the buildings first or go straight to the mountain?"

"Mountain, I guess," Keromnal said, looking at the buildings. Although in decent shape, they looked deserted, and no movement could be seen around them. "Let's go make sure there aren't any of the—"

"Don't say it!" Fragontic interrupted. "It's bad luck to say it. It will only call them here."

"Okay, let's go make sure there isn't anything we don't want to see holed up in the mountain."

Fragontic nodded. "Fair enough." He gave the orders and the company lumbered forward.

"I don't get it," Fragontic said as they marched. "Why would they have their base way out here?"

"Because no one would see it. And, if things went badly, no one would notice. This follows the operational patterns the Humans noticed. One of their other divisions was raising Canavars, and they did it on uninhabited desert worlds."

"That makes sense. That way, if they escaped, they wouldn't eat all the local civilians."

Keromnal nodded. "Also, no one would know if they had to nuke a Canavar or two that escaped. Very few people—outside the Science Guild, that is—come here. They could hide the evidence for quite some time."

Keromnal pointed in the direction of their march. "Everyone is aware there may be robots in the mountain, too?"

"Yes," Fragontic replied. "We looked at the report you got from the Humans." He nodded to a soldier trudging along near them with an odd-shaped weapon.

"Is that a taser rifle?" Keromnal asked.

Fragontic nodded. "Yes, it is. The way I have it figured, if the taser round is big enough to put down a Sumatozou, it's big enough to fry a robot. Then I doubled the amperage of the rounds, just to make sure."

"Makes sense." Keromnal felt his legs growing unsteady and stopped. The motion wasn't in his legs; the ground was vibrating.

"Did you get a brief on the planet?" Keromnal asked. When Fragontic nodded, he asked, "Did you see anything about a potential for earthquakes?"

"No," Fragontic said, stopping. "I didn't see anything at all, but the ground is moving." He looked behind them. "Shit!"

Keromnal looked back and saw a dust cloud that was rapidly growing larger. "A herd of animals?" he asked.

"None here," Fragontic said. "There's only one thing it could be. *Run for the tunnels!*"

The troopers picked up their pace, but they were all heavily loaded and in combat armor; their progress was not what Keromnal would have called fast…and certainly not compared to the two creatures he saw coming up behind them.

The monsters were easily 250 feet long and at least 40 feet thick. The closest analog he could think of was a giant centipede, only 250 times bigger! He stumbled to a stop as he watched the monsters sprint toward them. They each had two sets of serrated claws and raced forward on hundreds of legs. One of them stopped and the front part of its body rose, rose, and then went still higher, until it was easily 100 feet in the air, its red eyestalks spinning to take in all the terrain in front of it. Its segmented mouthparts broke open, and it screamed a mind-numbing challenge that reverberated off the mountains. A single thought ran through his brain. *Canavar.*

Keromnal could see its claw-like pincers snapping as it dropped down.

A hand grabbed his shoulder and spun him around. "Run!" Fragontic screamed in his face.

Keromnal ran.

As fast as the monsters were rushing forward, though, he knew there was no way the troopers would win the race. The ground shook more and more as the Canavars got closer, then all shaking ceased. Terrified of what he would see, Keromnal risked a glance over his shoulder.

He was just in time to see one of the Canavars' bodies falling to the ground like a brown avalanche, coming down onto the office building with all its weight. The building exploded outward as if hit by a nuclear bomb. The second Canavar raised itself up next to the barracks building and slammed down on top of it, with similar results. The creatures both screamed again as their tails—complete with some sort of shining metallic spike—lashed through the remains of the buildings, scattering the debris far and wide.

If there'd been anything valuable in the buildings, they were going to have a *really* hard time finding it.

Keromnal's head whipped back in his direction of travel and saw they were going to get to the tunnels after all—crushing the buildings had provided enough of a diversion for the Canavars that the troopers would make it. The ground started vibrating again, though, and Keromnal knew they were almost out of time.

The first of the soldiers raced into the tunnel, and Keromnal immediately saw that any safety he'd foreseen in the tunnel from farther back was nothing but a mirage; the tunnel was big enough for the Canavars to follow; there would be no escape.

He made it into the dubious safety of the tunnel—only one of the creatures could follow them in at a time—running harder as a Canavar screamed again from just outside. He looked behind him and saw the mouth of the leading Canavar thrust forward, and the last Sumatozou in line disappeared into its maw. The monster pulled out of the tunnel to swallow the soldier.

"Here!" one of the soldiers in the lead yelled, pointing to a recessed doorway on the side of the tunnel. He lowered his shoulder and hit it at full speed. Whatever the structural rating of the door was, it was never intended to stop a combat-laden Sumatozou, and the door sprang from its hinges at impact. The soldiers followed the leader into the much-smaller tunnel behind the door and its promise of safety. The ceiling was low, causing the troopers to duck slightly, but the tunnel was Canavar-free, and they poured in.

* * *

Tunnels, Canavar Facility, Tregoth

"Okay, Mr. Peacemaker," Fragontic said after he'd organized the remaining soldiers—a total of three had been eaten by the Canavars—into exploratory parties and sent them on their way, "we're here." He closed his eyes for a moment as the Canavar in the tunnel screamed. While the noise had been terrifying outside the tunnel, there was something about the way the screams reverberated inside the tunnel system that made them petrifying to all but the most stout-hearted. "I also have to think we've found your evidence that there's a Canavar facility on this planet, even if it isn't currently in operation. What now?"

"Can you call down the dropships and have them shoot up the Canavars?"

"I did, and they appear to have killed the one that was outside when they arrived. Used up most of their ammunition in so doing, too. You're going to get a big bill for expended ordnance when we get back."

"That's fine. If you get us all back, I'll be happy to pay it."

"There is, however, at least one Canavar in the tunnels with us, and the dropships can't target it. Any other guidance for me?"

"Kill it and get us back home so I can pay you those fat stacks of credits you mentioned?"

"Your attempt at levity is appreciated. Is that all you've got?"

"No," Keromnal said. "They wouldn't have just raised these creatures and allowed them to run free; they would have had some method of controlling them. If we can find it, we can use it to control them, hopefully long enough to get onto the dropships and out of here."

"So there's nothing else you need here?"

"I have a feeling that anything that was going on here, beside the Canavar project, was housed in the buildings outside. As both of them are now destroyed, I'm happy taking what we can find in the tunnels, if anything, and getting the hell out of here. I don't think there's anything here, based on what I've seen, that's worth the lives of any more of your troopers."

"Fair enough," Fragontic replied. "Any idea where these control devices might be?"

"Probably back, deeper in the tunnels, wherever they housed the Canavar."

"You don't think they left the Canavars outside?"

"No. I think they would have kept them in some sort of den. If they left them outside, uncontrolled, I think those buildings would have been destroyed a lot sooner."

Fragontic frowned. "Looking for their dens means going out into the main tunnel with the big, ugly worm."

"Maybe, and maybe not. At the other facility, the Humans found some back tunnels. Maybe there are some here. If not, well then, I guess we'll just have to figure out a way to lead it outside where the dropships can take care of it."

"Like sending a Peacemaker running up the tunnel?"

"That would work, I guess, but it wouldn't be my first choice."

"You sure?" Fragontic asked. Keromnal nodded. "All right," Fragontic said. "I'll just keep it in my back pocket for later, then. We'll look for tunnels first."

* * *

"You're in luck," Fragontic said ten minutes later. "We found a tunnel that appears to lead deeper into the facility." He led the Peacemaker to the back of the administrative complex. An open door led off into the darkness.

"What are we waiting on?" Keromnal asked.

"Just your go-ahead, since we're here on your credits."

"Well, you have it; let's go."

"You got it." He waved several of the troopers forward, and they moved down the passage, lighting it up as they went. The troopers stalked forward with their knees bent; the way they sidled forward, the lights stayed relatively steady. The tunnel went on a long way. Additional troopers went past and into the tunnel, then Fragontic motioned to Keromnal. "Let's go."

Fragontic went into the tunnel, and Keromnal followed him. The Peacemaker hadn't spent much time underground in his life—Sumatozou generally didn't—but the tunnel seemed to run fairly straight. They walked for almost five minutes, then came to another door.

"Kill the lights," Fragontic said. Within a couple of seconds, Keromnal couldn't see his hand in front of his face. One time, a section of a space station he'd been in had lost power. It had been just as dark…for three seconds, and then the emergency lighting had kicked in. Listening to the troopers breathing in the darkness was terrifying.

"Door opening," a voice whispered.

Keromnal could feel motion but had no idea whether the door had actually been opened…and if it had, he had no way to tell what was looking at them from the other side of the doorway.

"UV goggles," Fragontic whispered.

"Put these on," a voice said from next to Keromnal. The trooper put a pair in his hand.

Keromnal put the goggles on and he could see again. Most of the troopers—not all—had some sort of emitter that illuminated the area around them. Almost the entire squad was already in the tunnel beyond the door—it was a huge passageway, like the main tunnel that entered the mountain. Fragontic waved him forward, and he followed the merc leader. Keromnal had a number of questions he wanted to ask, but when he drew a breath, Fragontic shook his head and indicated he shouldn't speak. He nodded and followed the mercs.

The group stuck to the left side of the passageway, and Keromnal spent most of his time watching for rocks and other debris on the ground so he didn't kick something and make any unnecessary noise. Because of this, he almost didn't notice when the trooper in front of him stopped suddenly.

Keromnal took an extra step, but then came to a stop just inches from the trooper. As his head swiveled up, he saw the reason for the stop—they'd come to a den. At least that's what he took the huge cavern that jutted off the main passage to be. Straw covered the floor, and a large number of gantries lined the sides of the cave. Chains also hung from the walls, all of which had been snapped off. The last link on each was sprung open and dangled precariously.

Fragontic moved close enough to whisper, "Looks like they left the Canavars chained up, and they had to break free to get out. There is another cave just past this one that looks the same."

"Any sort of equipment to control the Canavars in either of them?" Keromnal asked.

Fragontic shook his head. "None."

"Shit."

"Yeah."

"So what do you recommend?"

"We'll set something to remote detonate here and then go back to the smaller tunnels and the front of the complex. When we get there, we'll detonate it. Hopefully, it will either draw the Canavar further into the caves and we can escape, or it will flush it out and the dropships can kill it or drive it off."

"And if it doesn't?"

"I'm out of ideas, and we're back to using the Peacemaker as a diversion."

"I hope it works then."

"Me, too."

"*Canavar!*" a trooper yelled from behind them as he started firing his heavy MAC.

Keromnal spun to see the creature just outside the cavern he was in. It tried to rear, but only succeeded in smacking its head into the tunnel's roof, creating a shower of rocks. It screamed—though whether in pain or annoyance, Keromnal didn't know—then moved forward and swallowed the closest trooper.

MAC rounds and a few laser bolts deflected off the creature's chitinous armor; the thick, brown armor plates not showing any form of damage.

"Run!" Fragontic yelled, and Keromnal spun. "Not that way, dammit!" Fragontic yelled, spinning him back to face the Canavar. "There's nothing back there but cave. We have to run past it!"

A number of the troopers continued to fire at the monster, keeping its attention, and Fragontic grabbed the Peacemaker's arm and pulled him along as he ran past the beast. Troopers streamed along both sides of the monster, fleeing as fast as they could, and Keromnal raced forward as fast as his legs could carry him.

One of the troopers yelled, and Keromnal glanced over his shoulder to see a trooper hanging out of the Canavar's mouth. One of its tusks had hooked on the entrance to the creature's mouth—what would be the lip on a normal creature—and the Canavar couldn't get the steel-tipped projection unhooked. As the creature sucked the soldier in, the trooper released his MAC and pulled something off his belt. Whatever it was exploded as the mouth closed on him, then the Canavar spat the trooper out. He flew across the cavern, slammed into the wall, and lay still at the base of it.

Keromnal slowed to go to the trooper's aid, but Fragontic grabbed his arm again and pulled him forward. "We can't help him!" They ran.

The Canavar lay still for several moments, and Keromnal was able to get past most of the creature's body, but then it started moving again, going in the opposite direction of Keromnal's travel. He slowed.

"Run. Faster!" Fragontic shouted. "It's going into the cavern so it can turn around, then it will be after us!"

The merc colonel's admonishment was all Keromnal needed to run harder, and he joined the stream of troopers racing through the tunnel. With everyone running full out, the lights were no longer steady—they bounced back and forth in a weird stroboscopic effect.

The creature roared its soul-splitting scream, and Keromnal couldn't help himself; he looked over his shoulder. He immediately wished he hadn't; the creature was emerging from the cavern. It ate the trooper that had stayed to cover their escape, and the lights behind him went out. It didn't matter; he knew the monster was coming as fast as it could.

"Into the smaller tunnels!" Fragontic exclaimed as they reached the administrative spaces. His troopers happily obliged and dove into the safety of the smaller tunnel.

Keromnal kept going.

"What are you doing?" Fragontic yelled from the mouth of the little tunnel.

"It's chase the Peacemaker time!" Keromnal gasped as loud as he could. "Tell the…dropships to be ready!"

He could hear the creature scraping the sides of the tunnel as it raced after him, getting closer and closer, and he put everything he had into his flight toward the light at the end of the tunnel. A quick glance over his shoulder showed he wasn't going to make it.

Still, he knew he needed to get as close as he could. He dropped his head and put all of his concentration into keeping his arms and legs pumping as if his life depended on it.

One hundred yards to the light…ninety…eighty. He could feel the rush of the giant monster behind him now, and the Canavar's breath on his back. The intensity lessened slightly, and Keromnal knew it was pulling back to strike.

He threw himself to the side of the tunnel, and the Canavar's mouth went past, just missing him, and the plates on the side of the monster's head glanced off his armor. The force of the blow—even a glancing one—drove him into the tunnel wall with the force of a hover car crash. He slammed into it and fell to the tunnel floor. Unable to stop its momentum, the Canavar kept roaring past him, like the subway trams on Capital Planet. It slowed and finally stopped, but then it moved forward again, unable to back its way down the tunnel. It went forward to turn around outside.

As soon as it emerged, the four dropships took it under fire, and Keromnal could see the rockets and MAC rounds impacting its head. It lost its right eye stalk in the initial barrage, and it screamed in pain. Keromnal put his hands over his ears; its roar of agony was even worse than its normal scream.

The dropships continued their one-way battle, staying always just out of reach as they fired into the creature's face. It moved to the right side of the tunnel mouth, and Keromnal found himself drawn forward to watch the ongoing fight.

He had just reached the tunnel entrance when one of the dropships crashed a hundred yards outside it, and he threw himself to the ground as hot debris flew past. Apparently, the ship had gotten too close to the monster, and the creature had grabbed it and flung it down; the remaining three craft now kept a more healthy distance from the creature.

They ascended to about fifty feet, and Keromnal couldn't understand why—that put them right where the creature was best able to strike at them. They stayed far enough away from it that they were always just out of reach, though, having already learned their lesson. After a few minutes of striking and missing, the Canavar reared back and roared its frustration to the heavens. This was obviously the moment the pilots had been waiting for—they tilted their craft to fire up into its mouth and unleashed all of their remaining rockets, while firing their MACs at the fastest rate possible.

The Canavar's scream was cut off as something vital was hit, and it collapsed to the side, slamming into the ground with enough force that Keromnal was thrown from his feet. He climbed up to find the Canavar slowly sliding away. The dropships hovered close by, looking for another kill-shot, but none presented themselves. After a second, Keromnal saw where the monster was heading—the body of the other Canavar, which the dropships had killed previously.

The Canavar kept moving toward it, slower and slower, until only its front legs were dragging the rest of the body, its head held only a few feet off the ground. It finally made it to the other Canavar. It rose up slightly, then collapsed with its head on the other Canavar's body and went still.

Keromnal started to breathe a sigh of relief, then saw motion out of the corner of his eye.

"What were you thinking?" Fragontic yelled, scaring him so much that he jumped about a foot in the air—no small feat for a person who weighed over ten thousand pounds.

"I wasn't thinking, much," Keromnal said when he could talk again. The rest of the troopers were right behind Fragontic, gazing in awe at the two dead Canavars.

"You got that right," Fragontic said. "If you'd have gone and gotten yourself killed, how would we have been paid?"

Keromnal gave the merc colonel a weak smile. "I knew we needed to get it outside the tunnels, and I remembered what you said about 'chase the Peacemaker.'" He chuckled. "I don't know; it seemed like a good idea at the time?"

Fragontic shook his trunks in disbelief. "Well, it worked out in the end." He nodded toward the Canavar bodies. "Got what you needed here?"

"Yeah, I did. The Science Guild is raising Canavars." He turned and looked into Fragontic's eyes. "I'm going to have to do something about that."

* * * * *

Author Bio

A Webster Award winner and three-time Dragon Award finalist, Chris Kennedy is a Science Fiction/Fantasy/Young Adult author, speaker, and small-press publisher who has written over 25 books and published more than 100 others. Chris' stories include the Occupied Seattle military fiction duology, The Theogony and Codex Regius science fiction trilogies, stories in the Four Horsemen, Fallen World, and In Revolution Born universes and the War for Dominance fantasy trilogy. Get his free story, "Shattered Crucible," at his website, https://chriskennedypublishing.com.

Called "fantastic" and "a great speaker," he has coached hundreds of beginning authors and budding novelists on how to self-publish their stories at a variety of conferences, conventions and writing guild presentations. He is the author of the award-winning #1 bestseller, *Self-Publishing for Profit: How to Get Your Book Out of Your Head and Into the Stores*, as well as the leadership training book, *Leadership from the Darkside*.

Chris lives in Virginia Beach, Virginia, with his wife, and is the holder of a doctorate in educational leadership and master's degrees in both business and public administration. Follow Chris on Facebook at https://www.facebook.com/ckpublishing/.

# # # # #

We Are Not Heroes by Quincy J. Allen

1

Fifteen Hundred Hours

The Day After Rsach Klixtylbyt Named Valedictorian

Peacemaker Academy, Ocono

"Good morning, everyone," Master Instructor Droizhiun intoned as he entered the amphitheater-like classroom for Advanced Tactics Theory. The four dozen fresh seniors, from eleven different races, immediately went silent. Droizhiun was infamous for his intolerance of disruptions in his classes. There wasn't a soul at the Academy who didn't know or hadn't heard he was as hard as titanium, and, more importantly, that no one on Ocono was more qualified to teach Advanced Tactics Theory than the aging Sumatozou. He moved with a slow but strong stride. His face was a picture of aged wisdom, with a wrinkled, bifurcated trunk, massive skull, and thick red-striped skin faded from age.

"I have a surprise for you today." As Droizhiun reached the center of the floor, he brushed at the fabric of his star-speckled, black suit and adjusted the Peacemaker pin affixed to his collar. He met the expectant gazes of his students. "You'll be happy to know that your exam on the liquidity of battlefield operations has been postponed

439

until tomorrow." He gave them a flash of thick, yellowed teeth, and there was a collective sigh of relief from the entire class. Droizhiun eyed a dark gray Jivool in the top row of the classroom. "That should give you one more opportunity to cram, Mr. Su Banai," he added.

The young Jivool was embarrassed as a faint chuckle came from the other students.

Droizhiun motioned toward the door to his left. "How many of you paid attention during your tour of the Hall of Heroes when you first arrived at the Academy?"

A half-dozen hands, paws, and claws rose into the air.

"Not nearly enough," Droizhiun lamented, "but not at all unexpected." He narrowed his eyes and considered his audience. "As a result of your lack of attention, I am now assigning you all with a very simple task." A collective groan passed through the class. "This weekend, you must all return to the Hall of Heroes and read every history listed there. It shouldn't take you more than seven or eight hours. Yes, there will be a test. More importantly, during next week's first class period, each of you will present to the class who you feel is the most significant Peacemaker honored there and why you feel he or she is deserving of the title. Know that there is no right answer to this particular quandary. What you will be graded upon is having a thorough understanding of the Peacemaker you choose and why you feel his, her, or its deeds are noteworthy." Droizhiun drew in a slow, ponderous breath, a sound not unlike like a great bellows, and let it out even more slowly. "Those who fail to complete this exceedingly simple task will be expelled from this class and required to take the entire course during the next session. There will be no exceptions."

Gasps erupted from several of the students, but Droizhiun's quick eyes darted to each offender of his precious silence, holding the sternest of reprimands.

"The penalty is so severe because, in some respects, this may be the most important assignment I am ever likely to give you. Understanding the greatness that came before you may just instill within you an idea of what Peacemakers need to be capable of." He cleared his throat. "Additionally, you may *not* select the Peacemaker you are about to meet."

He motioned toward the door he had entered through, and all eyes turned in that direction.

"During last night's graduation ceremony—where Rsach Klixtyl-byt was named Valedictorian—I ran into an old friend whose image has been present in the Hall of Heroes for twenty-nine years. He was the oldest GenSha to graduate this Academy, doing so on his thirty-seventh birthday. It is my pleasure, and privilege, to introduce to you an old friend." He let his eyes move across the expectant faces staring down at him. "Please welcome Retired Peacemaker, the honored Voth Kobun."

As the students respectfully rapped their knuckles upon their desks, a GenSha slowly entered the room. The old bull's fur was nearly white, an indication of exceedingly advanced age, and his stripes, normally green on a GenSha, were a dusty yellow. Had there been a Human in the room, he would have described the old Peacemaker as a hornless, great white buffalo on two legs.

Voth's stride was firm and deliberate. Despite his advanced age, he carried himself with the sturdy poise and confidence of a being accustomed to respect. His countenance was calm. His dark, intelligent eyes, surrounded by deep wrinkles, took in every detail of the room and the beings therein with a glance. He paused to stare at a pair of young GenSha bulls sitting halfway up the auditorium. He gave them a brief nod and then looked over the rest of the students. For all his obvious years, he was still a formidable member of his race.

He wore a crimson Peacemaker sash of a style that had not seen active service in decades, with a "RETIRED" patch just below his Peacemaker badge. The badge was decorated with a skeletal tree adorned with GenSha skulls on every branch and a vertical string of alien letters running up the right side in two rows. The rest of the sash was covered with ribbons, citations, medals, and even two Apex Achievement Awards with the crossed daggers denoting Combat Operations. The Triple-A for Combat was the highest award a Peacemaker could receive, and very few were handed out. When they were, it was usually done posthumously. Above the awards and citations was a single, metallic disk a few centimeters across engraved with the simple depiction of an avian in flight. It was not of Peacemaker or GenSha origin, but it clearly held a place of honor for the old officer.

"Thank you, honored Droizhiun," Voth said, giving his friend a smile. "It is, indeed, an honor to be here." He raised his eyes once again to the cadets looking down at him. "And thank you all for your kind greeting." He bowed his head slightly and then straightened his sash. "When we spoke last night, Droizhiun asked if I would be willing to relate to you the details of one of my missions. He did not specify which, out of respect, I imagine. However, I believe I know the one he has in mind." A sad look flickered across Voth's grizzled features. "It is not a story I like to tell, and I've only related those events completely a handful of times in the nearly thirty years that have passed since." He drew in a long breath and let it out slowly. "Having thought the matter through, and particularly because of the nature of this course, I feel this is the right place, with the right audience, to tell this tale—perhaps for the last time." He met the eyes of every student, and he could see curiosity and enthusiasm fixed in the young faces. He pointed to the Triple-A medallion immediately below the silver disk. "Can anyone tell me what this is?"

A number of limbs rose into the air, and Voth nodded to a young female Sidar with a thick crop of stiff, midnight-blue hairs running up the middle of her elongated head.

"You," he said.

"It's the Apex Achievement Award for Combat," she said almost reverently.

"Correct," Voth replied. "This is the reason my image adorns the Hall of Heroes." He let his eyes move across the room. "And I don't deserve it," he said flatly.

The curiosity on each and every face was replaced by astonishment.

"In the Jesc arm of the galaxy, in the outer Crapti region, on a world called Sylphux, I encountered a group of Duplato that changed my life forever."

* * *

2

Twenty-Nine Years Earlier

Sylphux Emergence Area: T-Plus Sixty Seconds

Aboard Peacemaker Ship _Sarikon_

The discomfort of shifting out of hyperspace made it feel like Voth's molars were wiggling out of his skull.

After five years of service and more transitions through a gate than I can remember, you'd think I'd be accustomed to it, he thought.

Shaking his massive, furred head in a futile attempt to dislodge the buzzing, he did a quick post-transition systems check of his ship, the _Sarikon_, and found nominal readings across the board. He shifted in the acceleration couch of the cockpit and gazed at the star field outside the viewports. He'd requested a dorsal docking slot on the bow of the coreship, if for no other reason than the view. His credentials afforded him at least that one small privilege this far out from the core systems of the Jesc arm. By necessity, he was keeping a low profile. Peacemakers—especially those working solo—were often targets for less savory sorts this far out from the galactic center…and he was definitely working solo.

Centered in his view, above the curve of the massive coreship just visible at the bottom of the forward porthole, lay a tan, green, and blue world with white polar regions. He hoped this would be his last destination before heading back to the Peacemaker station on Kravuun 3. It had been two months, and he missed the comfort of his own bunk. He pulled up the automated course to Sylphux programmed into his navi-comp, and when he verified it was also nominal, he activated the comms.

"Gate control," he said, his voice a low rumble, "this is the _Sarikon_ on track for Sylphux. Disconnecting from the coreship in two minutes."

He'd named his ship after a river that flowed through his ancestral home on Amberia. As a juvenile, he'd spent most of his free time running along the Sarikon river, stumbling from one adventure to the next, and generally getting into trouble and back out again through wits, will, and a good deal of fighting with whomever or whatever he encountered. It seemed only reasonable that he give that name to his first ship.

"*Sarikon*, we're reading you and confirm detach in under two minutes," an equally deep voice responded with the serene certainty of every gate controller Voth had ever encountered. "Orbital insertion in three hours seventeen minutes at current speed and projected entry point."

"Copy that," Voth replied.

"A bull of the GenSha?" the controller asked in Voth's native tongue. The controller's tone changed to one Voth recognized as a friendly greeting amongst his people. The question took Voth by surprise. He hadn't expected to discover a GenSha working as a gate controller, especially not this far out.

"Affirmative," Voth replied.

"Your ancestors have honored us with your presence," the controller said.

The phrase made Voth smile. He hadn't heard a formal GenSha greeting in over a year. His Peacemaker duties had mostly kept him on the periphery of the Galactic Union, and there weren't any other GenSha stationed on Kravuun 3 where he'd been assigned two years earlier. His assignment had been a punishment of sorts, but not one he resented. He'd earned it for punching another Peacemaker who was about to get a lot of people killed unnecessarily. He'd been exonerated in the subsequent investigation, but the bloodied officer's mentor had seen fit to reassign Voth for a tour in the boonies.

"It is good to hear a little bit of home," Voth said with a smile. "It has been a while."

"I know the feeling," the controller replied. "I am the only one of us assigned to the gate, and I have another seven months out here before I can go home. What brings you to our dusty little corner of the galaxy?"

Voth tensed for a moment. He started to respond, but then realized he should probably remain anonymous. His target might have people monitoring the general in-system comm traffic, especially for anything coming through the gate. He quickly punched in a security code on the terminal beside him and sent a complex and highly encrypted signal to Gate Control.

"Message received," the controller said, his voice returning to the serene, laconic cadence of a controller fulfilling his duties. "Standby to receive a new, pre-plotted course for your navi-comp that will take you through the asteroids of the Strahkos Belt and give you an orbital insertion for the major starport on Sylphux.

"Understood," Voth replied as he watched his computer receive the data packet. "Disconnecting," he said, and activated the sequence that would separate him from the coreship. There were several loud *clunks* that reverberated through his hull, and *Sarikon* floated free, drifting away from the behemoth ship that had carried him through hyperspace.

He accessed the file and input the data into his navi-comp. There were a few jerks of the hull as his thrusters adjusted course and he programmed the autopilot. "Data received and input," Voth replied. "I did have two questions, Control."

"Go ahead."

"The *Botai*, a large cargo and passenger transport, passed through the system six days ago. Did it make any stops in-system before hitting Sylphux orbit, and has it passed through the gate since then?"

"Stand by." Voth knew the controller was reviewing gate records. "Negative to both, *Sarikon*. She made orbit and Captain Yobovo set her down at the primary starport on Sylphux, where she still sits, according to our records."

"Copy that," Voth said. "Thank you for the information."

"We are honored to serve. Ancestors keep you," the controller added formally.

"And grant you longevity and peace," Voth said, giving the traditional GenSha response. "*Sarikon*, out," he added with a wistful smile.

He missed his people, missed the tranquility he always found in their company. But he had a job to do, and he'd chosen his path years earlier. He cut the comms and turned back to the terminal. There was time to kill before insertion, so he punched in several more commands, pulled up the official file on his quarry, and reread it for the hundredth time.

Dulk Tomar.

The big Lumar's pale gray face glared up from the screen. The mugshot was eight months old, taken immediately after his initial arrest. Dulk's thick forehead and perma-scowl shadowed deep-set purple eyes, larger than average canines, and a mottled pattern of scar tissue running from below his left ear and down across half of his neck where it disappeared beneath the collar of a light combat vest. The fabric on the right shoulder was torn, which coincided with swollen and bruised tissue around his right eye and a gash in his left cheek. His upper arms were cuffed behind his back and the lower ones in front, with stout cables running front to back around his waist, a standard setup for the four-armed races of the galaxy who were deemed dangerous, Lumar in particular. Dulk's skin and vest were also spattered with the blue-green of MinSha blood. Apparently, he had murdered—torn apart, actually—a MinSha trader in the middle of the Pemmick starport on Odulan Prime and been sentenced to death for it. The judge, an elderly Jivool, hadn't even allowed Dulk into the courtroom for the hearing. He merely watched the security video, saw Dulk attack the MinSha without provocation, and that was it: case closed.

Two months later—three weeks before Dulk's scheduled execution—six Lumar broke him out of detention, killing three officers in the process. Six more were beaten and bound before the group made their escape into rainy Pemmick's extensive storm drain system.

Why didn't they kill the others? Voth thought. That one fact had troubled him since he had first read the file. During a breakout, criminals generally killed everyone in the area, and certainly any officers involved. It seemed peculiar to Voth, but he hadn't been able to even formulate a theory.

His orders were simple, though: capture or kill the violent Lumar and any associates who had helped him.

Three months after Dulk's escape, he and four associates were caught on surveillance robbing an armored truck full of weapons in Pemmick. The driver, as well as one security guard, were killed. Three others had been beaten, one severely, and locked in the truck for the authorities to find.

Voth, acting on intel from a local snitch provided by Pemmick law enforcement, was able to track the sale of several cases from the stolen shipment. This led to a small gang of Sidar working an extortion ring out of a warehouse at the Pemmick starport. Three days after Dulk sold the weapons, those very same Sidar made the mistake of shooting up the headquarters of a rival gang in broad daylight, losing two of their own in the process. Voth connected serial numbers of the weapons used by the Sidar back to Dulk's robbery, and with the help of the Pemmick Police, managed to track down and kill two of the Sidar while arresting a third. The surviving Sidar, after a bit of heavy-handed convincing, admitted that Dulk had said he was headed for Sylphux with the bulk of the weapons. He also claimed he didn't know what they were for.

For the next six days, Voth had done his best to identify the ship his quarry had taken. He finally confirmed Dulk had set off for Sylphux by himself, along with twenty-two unmarked crates on a transport named the *Botai*.

Voth boarded the *Sarikon* and fired up the engines, hitching a ride on the next outbound coreship headed for Sylphux. Although not hot on Dulk's trail, he was as right behind the convict as was possible in interstellar space…which had brought him to the view that filled his viewscreen now.

Voth settled into the acceleration couch and spent the next couple of hours poring over Dulk's file as he waited for the orbital entry alarm to go off.

* * *

3

Voth entered the Star Trixer and winced at the harsh music blaring from the overhead speakers.

He'd landed the *Sarikon* at the starport, disembarked, and made a few discreet inquiries regarding Dulk. The dock workers remembered the big, surly Lumar and his cargo, but none of them could, or would, say where Dulk was headed. Voth finally settled on the probable location of the transport ship's captain, a Pendal named Yobovo.

Voth pushed the oppressive music from his mind and scanned the interior of the only bar in the starport. The lighting was low, but he was still able to see clearly. Most of the illumination came from patterns of neon lighting along the walls. The décor was fairly industrial, with exposed steel and burnished aluminum used liberally for the bar, tables, and chairs. The walls were a gray metal and looked as if they'd been stripped from the interior of a salvaged starship.

A handful of Lumar sat in a tight group in the far-left corner. A dozen or so Duplato were spread throughout in twos and threes, along with a handful of other races, talking and raising glasses. Except for the Duplato, most of the patrons had sidearms strapped to their belts. In the far-right corner, Voth spotted the group of Pendals he was looking for. They were hard to miss. The hoods of their telltale cloaks were pulled low over their wide-mouthed heads as they sipped at their drinks. One cloak was dark gray, while the other two were brown.

A few of the patrons, though none of the Pendals, glanced in Voth's direction when he entered, but nobody looked twice. He'd opted to keep his Peacemaker badge inside his jacket, and his clothes were nondescript: a simple black jumpsuit with a thick hide jacket to ward off the chilly winds of a Sylphux winter. He had a GenSha-manufactured pistol holstered low on his thigh and two combat knives secured to his belt in the back, the grips down for easy access. The pistol was a 15mm semi-automatic slug thrower with a twelve-round magazine. Two spare mags were carried in front of his right hip for easy reloading.

He moved through the place as discreetly as a two-meter GenSha could and stood before the Pendal in the dark gray cloak.

"Captain Yobovo?" he asked as he stepped up to the table.

All three Pendals went still and stared up at him from within their hoods with those strange, wide-set eyes. Voth towered over them, and he probably outweighed all three combined, although they, like the Lumar, had four arms.

"You're a long way from home, honored GenSha," Yobovo said quietly. His eyes darted to Voth's pistol as he set a glass of pale green liquid in front of him. "I can't imagine what might have brought you to my table."

Voth cautiously looked to his left and right to see if anyone was staring. The other patrons seemed far more interested in their own conversations.

"May I sit?" he asked.

"Please," Yobovo replied confidently.

Voth's limited experience with Pendal expressions told him the captain was probably curious. He reached over to an empty nearby table and pulled up a much larger chair than those that held the Pendals. He took his seat, and the chair creaked under is weight.

"I'm Voth, by the way," he said as he settled in.

"So, how can we help you?" Yobovo asked. "Do you seek surreptitious passage off this chilly little world? Perhaps to avoid the local constabulary?"

"Far from it," Voth replied, trying not to smile at the irony. "Although, I am happy to hear you are so forthcoming with such arrangements. It should make this easier."

"All credits spend the same," the captain said easily, "and we are decidedly disinterested in the plots of the other races."

"Dulk Tomar," Voth said, cutting to the chase.

All three Pendals focused on him more intently.

"A recent Lumar passenger aboard the *Botai*." The captain leaned back. "I will assume you are not an old friend."

"Correct." Voth leaned forward. "You said you are not interested in the plots of others. Does that also mean you don't inhibit the plots of others?"

"You see the truth of it," Yobovo said, nodding.

"Well, what I need is a very simple thing."

Yobovo exposed a mouthful of sharp, pointed teeth, the Pendal version of a smile. "What might that be?"

"I need to know what Dulk is planning and where he was headed once he off-loaded the cargo from your ship."

"Well," Yobovo started slowly, "such information obviously has value, or you would not have come all this way to seek it."

"How about two rounds of drinks?" Voth offered. He knew he was low-balling, but something told him the Pendal wasn't really after anything and just wanted to play the game. Starship voyages, after all, had a lot of boring downtime.

The captain flashed another smile.

"Make it three, and I'll tell you what I can about my recent passenger, although I can assure you, it isn't much."

"Three it is," Voth agreed.

"I believe there are three pieces of information that you might consider valuable." The Pendal leaned in and one of his independently tracking eyes shifted toward where the Lumar were sitting.

"I…*overheard* him in *Botai*'s mess hall," Yobovo said. "He kept to himself during the entire voyage but had a strange habit of muttering during his meals. I got the impression he was headed toward a Duplato mining settlement forty klicks north of the city. They mine iridium, I believe."

"Okay, that's one," Voth said.

"Before he left the *Botai*, he booked passage with us to the Strahkos Auction House Station located within the asteroid belt that rings this system."

"Did he say why?" Voth asked.

"He did not," Yobovo said simply. "However, he *did* arrange passage for sixty-eight other Lumar males as well as fifty metric tons of cargo."

Voth's eyes went wide.

"Sixty-eight Lumar?" Voth blurted. "What on earth could he be planning?"

"I wouldn't hazard a guess," the captain said. "He did seem rather determined, however."

"When are you scheduled to take off?" Voth asked.

"Forty-eight hours," Yobovo said. "With or without the Lumar," he added. "Although, I would prefer it was with. He's paying for his passage with a metric ton of iridium ore."

Forty-eight hours isn't much time to sort this out, Voth thought. *And if he has sixty-eight Lumar with him, a firefight in the starport would be both messy and ridiculously long odds.* He doubted he'd be able to convince Dulk to simply surrender under any circumstances. Then something else occurred to him. *Only a metric ton of iridium?*

"That doesn't seem like much for sixty-nine passengers and that much cargo," Voth observed.

"It's a short hop to the belt," Yobovo replied. "And we were headed there with a mostly empty hold anyway. The bulk of our cargo will be loaded at the Strahkos Station for delivery...elsewhere."

I'll have to go to the mine. Voth didn't like the idea, but there wasn't much choice.

"I don't suppose I could convince you to delay your launch," Voth offered.

"I'm a ship captain, not a Peacemaker, friend." Yobovo tilted his head to the side slightly, both eyes fixed on Voth. "Schedules are schedules, and you don't have that kind of money. Besides, I leave policing up to the authorities," Yobovo added with a peculiar expression on his face.

Does he know? Voth thought. *Unlikely, but it doesn't matter.*

"Understood." Voth rose from his seat. "Well, I do appreciate the information. You have been most helpful. I'll let the bartender know about the three rounds."

"Most appreciated," Yobovo said. Voth turned to go. "Oh, and Voth, if Dulk isn't able to make it to the ship in time, it would only be a slight loss, and one we could easily bear if we had to."

Voth glanced back to find all three Pendals looking at him with blank expressions on their faces.

"I'll keep that in mind," Voth said, then went to the bar and arranged for the three rounds of drinks.

* * *

4

Three hours later, Voth nestled his two-seater aircar, retrieved from the small hold of *Sarikon*, into a narrow canyon about a klick outside the Botsuwa'avum Open Pit Mine. The mine was a sprawling crater in the mountainous landscape, two klicks wide and nearly a kilometer deep. It had looked like an asteroid impact from space when he'd first made his orbital insertion, and it now lay just over the next hillside.

Coming in, he'd kept his aircar about fifteen meters off the ground, using sensors and image enhancement to navigate the increasingly hilly terrain in the moonless night. He'd scanned the ridgeline with IR as he approached to see if anyone appeared at the sound of his lift fans. When nothing appeared, he cut the power plant, zipped up his black infiltration suit, and pulled the hood over his head. The suit would mask his thermal signature to about ninety-seven percent, and in the darkness, he'd be virtually undetectable to anyone without enhanced optics. As the aircar turbines came to a stop, he heard a faint, mechanical droning loud enough to penetrate the cockpit of his aircar.

The mine, he thought. *They're working non-stop.*

He pulled the optic enhancers, commonly referred to as OEs, from his belt and scanned the hillside directly ahead of him. Like the rest of the terrain, it was lightly forested with clusters of thick, reed-like plants rising four to ten meters into the air on stalks anywhere from a centimeter to fifteen centimeters in diameter.

Time to get moving.

The clock was ticking, and he needed as much intel as he could manage if he was going to apprehend Dulk in the next forty-five hours...and do so without getting killed by the equivalent of three armed platoons of Lumar.

He climbed out of the aircar, grabbing his heavily silenced carbine and three grenades from the rack built into the narrow space behind the seats. He slung the rifle, clipped the grenades to his utility belt, and checked to make sure his sidearm and knives were secure. Glancing at his chrono one more time, he secured his vehicle and set off up the hill at a medium pace.

The air was cold enough to see his breath, but the hood was designed to channel what he exhaled into his suit to help keep him warm. Every thirty meters or so, he scanned the hillside and ridgeline for any heat signatures, but aside from a few small creatures of indeterminate shape and intention, there was only the cold night air. The closer he got to the ridgeline, the louder the mine became, and he was grateful for it. With the grinding of metal treads and chewed up rock, nobody would ever hear him coming.

He was about twenty meters from the top of the hill when he checked with the OEs again. He froze and went down into a crouch. The thermal outline of a small figure, well over a meter tall, crept through a small notch in the ridgeline.

Definitely not Lumar, Voth thought. He continued to watch as the lone figure sneaked between the clusters of trees, obviously heading away from the mine and doing so surreptitiously. The being moved slowly, methodically, and did so on all four limbs. Its arms were much longer than its legs, and it seemed to be hunched over though still mostly upright.

Duplato, Voth deduced. *One of the miners? But why is he sneaking out?*

Its outline didn't give any indication that it had a firearm, but it could still have a blade or a small needler hidden somewhere. Voth considered a number of possibilities, but there was only one way to know for sure.

He changed his course and began stalking the unhurried Duplato. Voth did his best to move quietly through the trees, fairly confident the noise from the mine and his training would keep him from being detected. He stayed in the Duplato's rear quarter. The species was most comfortable underground, and their arms ended in fairly severe claws that were useful in mining operations. Voth definitely didn't want to grab the being, if he could avoid it.

His long stride brought him up behind the Duplato in short order, and he drew his pistol when he was a few meters behind it. He didn't want to shoot, but he would if left no other option.

"Halt," Voth ordered in a firm voice, "and remain quiet."

The Duplato froze in his tracks, and his long arms shot up into the air.

"Please!" he cried. "Don't kill me! I-I was just looking for some tubers to eat. We're all so hungry!"

"Turn around." Voth leveled the weapon, prepared for anything.

The Duplato slowly turned to face him, its eyes wide, and then it relaxed, at least a little.

"You're not one of them," it said in a melodic voice.

"One of who?" Voth asked.

"One of the Lumar." The Duplato cocked his head to the side. "They've taken over the mine." He got a confused look on his face. "What are you doing here?"

"No, I'm not a Lumar. And I'll ask the questions for now," Voth said, holding the pistol steady. "What are _you_ doing?"

"Trying to get us some help," came the immediate reply. "I don't want to die."

"So, you're being forced to work?"

"Yes. We all are."

"Curse their ancestors," Voth growled, gritting his teeth. He holstered his pistol and pulled a flap aside on the infiltration suit, exposing the Peacemaker badge affixed to his chest. The badge gleamed faintly in the darkness, but there was no mistaking what it was. "I am

Peacemaker Voth Kobun." The Duplato's eyes went wide, and then Voth covered it back up. "Put your arms down."

"Gladly," the Duplato said, relieved.

"What's your name?"

"Ginkhur. Are you here to save us?"

Voth blew out a frustrated breath. Things were terribly complicated. He had hoped he would be able to track Dulk to a hideaway where the big Lumar wanted to lay low for a while. This was infinitely harder. He'd been prepared to simply follow Dulk up to the asteroid belt, hoping for a better opportunity that didn't involve facing Dulk's fellow Lumar. But with the miners basically enslaved and only forty-four hours to resolve the matter, he was running out of options. Voth's mind raced. He needed more information.

"What do they want the ore for?"

"Their leader, a Lumar named Dulk, hasn't said, although we think it's to buy more weapons. The others took over the mine and locked it down six weeks ago, and Dulk just joined them a week ago. They said nobody would get hurt, so long as he and his fellow thugs could take half of whatever we mined by tomorrow morning. At first, only some of them had weapons, but now most of them do."

"Why would he need more weapons," Voth asked, "especially on Strahkos Station in the belt?"

"Strahkos Station is why we think he wants weapons."

"I don't understand," Voth said.

"When the Lumar first arrived, they brought with them a MinSha. It was badly injured, and for the next few days, they tormented it; we could hear its screams. When the Lumar threw the body into the pit, we saw what they'd done. Its eyes had been gouged out and most of its limbs ripped off. The wounds were sealed with dermaplas...so it didn't bleed to death."

"They questioned it?"

"The entire time," Ginkhur said, shaking his head. His voice was full of fear and pity. "It was all about something that happened in the asteroid belt. Apparently, a group of MinSha slaughtered over a hundred of Lumar up there. The MinSha was sorry...it said its orders were to kill the Lumar laborers once the job was done."

"And you believe it?" Voth asked. "That the MinSha wiped out a Lumar crew in the asteroid belt?"

The Duplato looked down, and he shook his head. When he raised his head, there was a mixture of both sadness and anger in his eyes. "Yes. Mates and young as well." The Duplato let out a frustrated sigh. "That's part of the reason we acquiesced at first. We felt at least some compassion for the Lumar. It seems Dulk's brother and entire family were among the dead. I overheard several Lumar say the bodies are still up there, drifting lifelessly through the core of a mined-out asteroid." Ginkhur locked eyes with Voth. "Compassion is a two-edged sword, Peacemaker, and it cut the other way when Dulk's people killed a dozen of mine because they didn't want to work." The Duplato stared at Voth. "He's mad, you know, grief-stricken beyond reason. He keeps muttering to himself about killing them all, although I can't say I really blame him."

"Doing something about the slaughter of his people is one thing," Voth said, "what he's done to get here, is another."

"Are there more Peacemakers nearby?" Ginkhur asked, looking around hopefully.

Frustration crossed Voth's face. "No," he said.

"Then, they're coming, right?"

"No. It's just me, and that's all there's going to be before the Lumar leave."

"Then my people are dead."

"Why do you say that?"

Ginkhur looked nervous. "Dulk assured us we'd be left alive, just locked up in one of the shafts until they lifted off."

"Dulk *has* left people alive when he didn't have to...on two separate occasions."

"As strange as it seems, I believe his intentions," Ginkhur acknowledged. "Like I told you, he's mad. I can't really tell you why, but I suspect he would see himself as doing exactly what the MinSha did to his kin. He sees himself as a hero—above the MinSha. But he may very well be alone in that sentiment. Several of the other Lumar drilled holes in the mine entrance where they plan to put us...holes that could only be for explosives. They tried to hide them from view, but I've been doing this a very long time. I know detonation bores when I see them."

"Blasted Lumar," Voth said. "I don't see a clear way out of this without your people paying the price." He looked at Ginkhur. "I need to see what's down there. And you're going to tell me as much as you can about the mine as you can."

"All right, Peacemaker, although I don't see how much difference you can make by yourself. Even with my people's help, we'd just be kicking off the slaughter a bit sooner."

"Maybe," Voth said. "But Lumar are easily enraged and generally aren't the brightest stars in the sky. I just need the right setup...and a catalyst."

Ginkhur shrugged. "If you say so."

"Do they have any night vision or IR equipment?" Voth asked.

"Not that I've seen." Ginkhur shrugged again. "They're mostly miners...and a dozen or so local thugs who rallied around the death of those in the asteroid belt. About fifty of them now have battle rifles, and there are two vehicle-mounted weapons on the two trucks down there."

"Show me," Voth said. A rough idea was forming in his head, but it was the longest shot he'd ever heard of.

They set off up the hill, and when they reached the crest, Voth used the OEs to get his first good look at the mining facility—*and the upcoming battlefield*, he thought.

Immediately before them, five hundred meters away and well past the base of the hill where the ground leveled out, sat a dozen buildings of varying sizes, creating a small compound of sorts. A dirt road went straight through the center of it, and in the middle of the compound were two open-bed trucks, each with a swivel-mounted machine gun welded to a rack above the cab.

If I do this, I can't let them get to those, Voth thought.

There were two large buildings on the near side of the road, elevated half a meter above the ground on wooden frameworks. Voth assumed they were barracks of some kind. The windows of the one on the left had soft light pouring out, illuminating the barren soil around the building. Four Lumar with battle rifles stepped out of the nearest door and walked to the right, disappearing from view behind the other barracks. Those windows were boarded up, and there was a pair of big Lumar guards, rifles slung, standing along the closest side.

The small structures to either side of the barracks looked like tool sheds and storage buildings, except for one twenty meters to the right that had thick power cables coming up through its roof and out the side. The cables were connected to suspended power lines that fed the buildings as well as the halogen lights that illuminated the entire facility. Across the road, close to the edge of the mining pit, was a row of five buildings that looked almost like single-family domiciles. The dirt road continued in a long spiral that looped around the open mining pit until it reached the bottom.

"Most of the Lumar sleep in that big building on the left," Gink-hur said, pointing. "My people are housed in the big one on the right, when we aren't working our shift. We do sixteen hours on and six off in rotating shifts. With a twenty-eight-hour day, it really messes with our internal clocks."

"I can imagine," Voth replied.

"A group of armed Lumar use dump trucks to take us back and forth into the active shafts to mine." He pointed to a twenty-meter square machine that was making a terrific clatter and belching dust. "We go past the big ore-processing facility a hundred meters to the right, and down to the mine shafts. They drive all the vehicles. There are only four active shafts left, and those are near the bottom of the pit. With us separated into groups, the Lumar always have hostages in case we revolt. We are stuck and pretty much helpless at this point."

Voth examined the big ore processor. A heavily shielded cable ran from the power shed all the way to the processor, and there were "High Voltage" warning signs at regular intervals. The dirt road passed in front of it, and there was a dump truck tilting its bed into the far side of the processor. Suddenly, a terrible grinding sound filled the air. Moments later, raw ore, separated from the local rock, started pouring out into an empty cargo container.

Voth scanned from the processor, across the compound, and past the Lumar barracks, to where a row of forty big cargo haulers were lined up. Thirty-six of them were fully loaded with bulky, metal cargo containers, and the suspension of the loaded haulers were compressed dramatically. About a klick past the haulers, the dirt road bent around and disappeared behind a low hill, presumably leading back to the starport.

As Voth watched, a large Lumar came out the front door of the largest house across the road and shouted something, presumably at the Lumar walking or perhaps standing on the other side of the Duplato barracks.

"I think that's him," Ginkhur said, pointing. "Dulk."

Voth hit an actuator on the OEs and zoomed in. He immediately recognized Dulk Tomar. Even without the scarring, there was no mistaking the bruiser's fearsome features. Dulk shouted something again, and the four Lumar Voth had seen before, moved into view, walking quickly toward the ore processor.

"That's a patrol," Ginkhur offered.

"How many watch the crews in the bottom of the mine?" Voth asked, lowering the OEs.

"Ten," Ginkhur said quickly.

"Leaving almost sixty mostly-armed Lumar down there." *Still long odds,* Voth thought. "And how many of your people are locked up in the barracks at any given time?"

"About thirty, with ninety or so working the mine at any given time."

"How'd you get away?" Voth asked, curious how resourceful the Duplato miner might be.

"We were told that if anyone tried to escape, the others would pay for it." Ginkhur shrugged. "I stole a single det-charge when they weren't looking, blew a side shaft about halfway up the pit two days ago, and dug myself out after the sun went down. They figured I was dead, so they didn't come looking or kill my friends. I climbed up the ridge as soon as the sun went down." He gave Voth a confident smile. "Like I said, I've been doing this a long time."

Voth's respect for the miner went up a few notches.

"What was your plan?" Voth asked.

"About eight klicks north is another mining facility...all underground. My cousin runs it, and I figured we could figure something out before everything went to Izlian shit here."

"Brave. If you had been caught..." Voth let his voice trail off.

"We may not be soldiers, Peacemaker, but none of us want to die. I don't know if you know anything about my people, but we'll protect what we have if given half a chance."

"Fair enough," Voth said. "Does your cousin have any weapons up there?"

"No," Ginkhur replied. "And it's a smaller crew."

"So, you'd still be outnumbered and outgunned."

"Yes, but we could at least reach out to somebody back in the city."

Voth shook his head. "There's no military on this planet, and only a handful of local cops, who I doubt would be willing to stand toe-to-toe with three platoons of armed Lumar. And any merc crew you might be able to reach would never get here in time." Voth took a deep breath after he rattled off the list of reasons he wasn't going to be able to get help either.

"Izlian shit," he muttered under his breath. "No choice."

"What?"

"Never mind," Voth said. "Give me a minute to think." He lifted the OEs again and examined the layout of the facility one more time. Then it hit him. He glanced at the Duplato, a hopeful look on his face. "Do you think you could get back into the barracks holding your people without being seen? Maybe from underneath?"

"Probably. The flooring is just wood." He held up his thick claws. "These will make short work of that."

"Good. And the ore processor will cover the sound."

Ginkhur nodded. "Definitely."

"When is the next shift change?"

"In about an hour. They'll swap everyone out in under thirty minutes."

"Perfect." Voth lowered the OEs and locked eyes with the Duplato. "Then I think I have an idea."

* * *

5

Voth and Ginkhur crouched behind a cluster of trees about twenty meters behind the Duplato barracks as a dump truck rolled down the road, its bed holding thirty-two Duplato miners. The miners returned from the mine were forced back into the barracks at gunpoint, some of them roughly. The truck rolled past the ore processor—which had gone quiet as it hungrily awaited another load—and continued its long spiral down to the lower mine shafts.

"You are certain you want to take the risk?" Voth whispered as he lowered the OEs and looked at the small figure beside him.

"Yes. I believe your plan can work, and we're dead anyway if it doesn't. Besides, you're taking a lot more risk than I am."

"Very well," Voth replied. He unslung his carbine, made sure the selector was set to single shot, and raised the weapon. He scanned the area one last time, sweeping back and forth with the scope to make sure there were no Lumar watching. The compound was well illuminated, but there didn't appear to be any Lumar in a position to see Ginkhur's approach. "Go now. If you are spotted, I'll cover you, and we'll adjust the plan accordingly. Fall back to this spot if that happens."

"Understood, Peacemaker," Ginkhur said with a determined look on his face. He scuttled off into the darkness using his four-legged gait, stealthily approaching the back of the barracks. He disappeared beneath building, squirming his way between the support struts, and Voth lost sight of him in the deep shadows.

Voth used the OEs and could just make out the Duplato scratching at the floorboards above him in the back corner of the building nearest the power shed. A few minutes later, he was pulled inside.

Now all Voth had to do was wait for the signal. He gave the compound one last scan with the OEs and then turned his attention to the ore processor and the curving road that led to it from the bottom of the mine. As he often did during stakeouts, he found himself reviewing his plan, factoring in variables and contingencies should things go awry at different points during the engagement. He realized a lot could go wrong, and a single, lucky shot could bring the whole plan crashing down. *Only the ancestors know what will be,* he thought. *Either I will join them this night, or I will not.*

The grumble of a large vehicle in the distance broke him from his reverie. He scanned the road and spotted a loaded dump truck making its way up the spiral. Voth checked his equipment: three grenades clipped to his belt, pistol on his thigh, knives on his back, and his trusted carbine at the ready. He took a deep breath and went through a Peacemaker breathing exercise to clear his head and heighten his focus.

No mistakes.

The dump truck finally made it to the ore processor, turned around, and dumped its load into the machine, eliciting a steady, thrumming crunch of chewed rock and earth. The driver pulled away as soon as the bed was empty, lowering the bed as he trundled down the dirt road, the engine roaring at full speed.

Voth checked his chrono: 0200. He raised the OEs one last time and scanned the compound. Everything was quiet, just as it should be at that hour. He returned the OEs to their case on his hip and grabbed his rifle. With the rock crusher covering the sound of his passage, he darted from the trees and headed straight for the power shed.

The dark silhouette of his infiltration suit was momentarily highlighted from the halogen lamp above, then he was under the shadow of the roof, pressing his back to the shed wall. He slung his rifle, pulled out one of his combat knives and quickly pried boards off the shed. It took him a few minutes, but when he had enough of them set aside, he stepped into the dark interior.

Inside sat a medium-sized, thorium-based power generator on a pair of wheels. A trailer hitch stuck out one side; it looked like it had been parked a decade earlier and the shed simply built around it to support the two breaker boxes hanging from the walls. To his left, the box had several leads running out the top, and they clearly drove the power for the compound and the lights along the road. To the right, much thicker cables ran into the box and out again through the side wall.

Those must be for the ore processor, he thought. *Perfect.*

He unclipped one of the grenades from his belt and unscrewed the bottom. The grenade was called a "sleeper" and it was used both as a standard thrown grenade and for setting traps. He pulled out a two-meter-long spool of strong, thin wire from the exposed recess and attached one end to the pin of the grenade. He set the grenade into a notch of the power generator and ran the other end of the wire to the door latch.

"Here we go," he said out loud. He pulled the OEs from the case on his belt, attached a strap to its housing, and slipped them over his head. He secured them and set the optics to variable night vision. He checked his rifle one last time and slung it over his shoulder. Turning, he tripped the main breaker feeding the compound. With a loud *click*, the light seeping into the shed went out. The OEs adjusted automatically as he stepped through the back of the shed and into the night. For the Lumar, the near darkness would make it difficult to see anything, and his infiltration suit would make him nearly invisible. With the OEs, he could see everything clearly, though the image lacked color and had a slight orange hue to it.

He moved around the shed and scanned the compound before dashing across the road. He scrambled over the edge of the road as quietly as possible, leaning into the steep incline of the mining pit. He started making his way toward the houses. A few moments later, a deep Lumar voice carried over the sound of the rock crusher.

"Kralt! Dokkit! Go see what's wrong with that Duplato-cursed generator!"

"Yeah, yeah," one of them shouted back, "we got it."

Voth poked his head up over the edge of the mining pit and saw Dulk step off the porch of his house as two Lumar moved across the street with flashlights in their hands, heading for the power shed thirty meters away. Several more Lumar appeared on the porches, but none had come out of the Lumar barracks.

"And somebody radio those slugs down in the mine and tell them to turn off anything they don't need. This is the second time this week!"

Well, that's lucky, Voth thought.

He dropped back down and moved behind the houses; it was time to get into position. Passing between the last two buildings, he crouched beside one of the porches. Peeking around the corner, he saw two Lumar standing on the porch of the first building, talking in low voices. Dulk's attention was fixed on the two Lumar approaching the shed.

Voth only had one chance. He unscrewed the bottom of the second grenade with three quick twists, pulled out the wire, and secured it to the pin. Then he waited and watched.

One of the Lumar opened the door to the shed and stepped inside, the second close behind. Suddenly, the second leapt backward with a terrified shout.

Voth closed his eyes and turned his head away.

BA-BOOM!

The grenade detonated with the sharp *crack* of military ordnance, but that was nothing compared to the massive explosion as the power generator released all the energy at its core in one, burning instant. The ore processor went dead as a shockwave blasted outward. Splinters and shrapnel clattered into the surrounding buildings. Lumar screamed. A gust of hot wind hammered into Voth, and he heard the *thud* of several bodies as they slammed against the porches and walls of the domiciles.

He opened his eyes and crouched low as he dashed to the nearest truck. He jammed the grenade into the wheel well and wrapped the other end of the wire over the tire and around the wheel mount.

He unslung his carbine just as he heard a voice behind him.

"Hey!" a Lumar shouted. "What's that?"

Voth turned to see a Lumar standing on the porch of the last building in line, pointing at Voth's shadowy form.

Voth raised his carbine, aimed, and fired twice with the muffled *thud* of sub-sonic rounds. The Lumar looked surprised and fell backward as another Lumar came out the front door, a battle rifle in his hands. The Lumar glanced in Voth's direction, but he obviously couldn't see him in the darkness. Voth fired twice—chest and head—and the Lumar tumbled back through the open door.

Shouts erupted across the street as heavy boots stomped against wood floors and bare earth.

Voth turned to his left and saw that Dulk had been slammed through the porch railing and into the building. He was still, but Voth couldn't tell if the Lumar was breathing or not. It didn't matter. In a crouch, he raced toward the other truck. As he passed between the buildings, he got a good look at the Duplato barracks. A third of the building was gone, obliterated by the explosion, and some of the timbers were on fire.

I hope they're all right, he thought.

Another Lumar stepped through the door of the last building, rifle in hand. He turned toward Voth, obviously seeing the movement, and raised his rifle just as Voth put two rounds into him—chest and shoulder. Running made it difficult to center his aim, and the Lumar spun sideways, roaring his rage as his rifle sailed into the darkness. Voth fired again, silencing the Lumar.

Shouts erupted further up the street as the Lumar in the barracks realized there was more going on than just the generator blowing up. Voth dashed up beside the door of the last truck, dropped the carbine magazine and slammed home another. Changing the selector to full auto, he yanked the last grenade from his belt, and peeked over the hood to discover two dozen Lumar spreading out into the street in search of whomever was attacking them.

Voth threw the grenade into the thickest bunch of them and immediately opened fire with his carbine.

Several Lumar fell, and the muffled *thump-thump-thump* of his rifle caught the attention of others. They zeroed in on his muzzle flashes and raised their weapons.

BOOM! The thrown grenade detonated with a flash that filled the compound.

His OEs adjusted automatically and then returned to normal as six Lumar sailed through the air, a few slamming into other Lumar. Screams and roars filled the night. A dozen Lumar dropped to the ground, clutching where shrapnel had pierced their bodies. The remaining Lumar in the street were either wounded and screaming or scrambling for cover. Some of them knew where Voth was, while others were looking in every direction for their attackers.

Voth's carbine clicked empty. He dropped the spent mag and slammed his last one home before opening the door of the truck. Throwing the carbine onto the seat, he settled in and fired up the truck. Bullets ripped into the vehicle with a clang and clatter of ricochets. Both the windshield and rear window shattered. Glass flew into Voth's face, and he felt trickles of blood flowing into his fur. He ducked, slammed the truck into reverse, and jammed his foot on the accelerator. All four wheels spun, sending up a cloud of gravel and dust.

The truck lurched as it gained purchase, squirming left and right as it went careening backward down the road. More gunfire riddled the vehicle as it rapidly backed away. The headlights shined briefly through the shattered walls of the Duplato barracks before they were shot out, and Voth saw what he was hoping for. The Duplato hostages had managed to stack the bunks, forming a thick, multi-layered barricade that had protected them from the blast.

Voth didn't get far before a half-dozen Lumar jumped into the other truck—four into the bed and two others into the cab. The driver fired up the vehicle and put it into motion.

Voth ducked down. *One…two…three…*

BA-BOOM!

A flash filled Voth's cab as the grenade exploded and cooked off the other truck's power plant. He glanced up and watched the truck flip through the air, flames and smoke spiraling after it. Lumar bodies soared in every direction. The truck slammed onto its roof, still on fire, and the ammunition for its machine gun started popping, sending hot metal everywhere. It was mostly just fragments of hot casings flying around, but it was enough to send several more Lumar to the ground, screaming.

Only one last bit, Voth thought as his truck raced backward.

He went about eighty meters, then lifted his foot off the accelerator and looked over his shoulder. Keeping his head low, he guided the truck straight into the ore processor. It slammed into the metal chassis of the twenty-meter structure with a *crash*, and the Lumar's gunfire slowly stopped.

The Lumar couldn't see him in the darkness, so they would have to approach the truck to see if he was dead. He only hoped none of them had grenades. There hadn't been any in the stolen shipment, but that didn't mean Dulk or somebody else hadn't gotten their hands on some military-grade ordnance.

Voth left the truck running as a Lumar shouted orders.

Most of the Lumar were crouched behind cover, their pale, gray scalps poking up here and there. And then Dulk rose up on the porch.

"What are you all doing?" he screamed.

The night went silent as all the Lumar froze in place and stared at him in fear.

"Spread out!" he bellowed, pointing toward the ore processor. "There's only one invader, you imbeciles, and I think you got him. Use those rifles I gave you and move up!" Dulk was clearly enraged, just as Voth had hoped for. "If he isn't dead, then kill him!"

Lumar are big. They can be brutal, and they are dangerous. But once set into motion, they react with their hearts and the momentum of a juggernaut, not with their brains.

Voth didn't wait to see what they were going to do. He knew. He grabbed the carbine, rolled as quietly as he could up and through the back window, and then stood in the bed of the truck where the machine gun waited. He checked the receiver and found it had already been chambered.

"Move it!" Dulk screamed.

Voth ducked down once again, peered through the back window, and waited for them to get closer. Slowly, they moved forward in groups of five and six.

When they had crossed about two-thirds of the distance, their weapons raised, Voth took a deep breath, stood, and opened fire.

THUDDA-THUDDA-THUDDA!

Flame spewed from the machine gun. Smoke poured from the barrel. Tracers shot into the night and pierced flesh and blood and bone. Working from the edge of the pit outward across the road, Voth cut into them. A half-dozen Lumar opened fire, while others ran for cover or dove sideways in a desperate attempt to stay alive, but it was all in vain. Voth had backed the truck up against the only cover nearby.

A round grazed Voth's right shoulder.

He swiveled the weapon and killed the Lumar who had shot him. Another round nicked his left arm. He swiveled again and kept firing, focusing on any Lumar who had the sense—or was it stupidity?—to shoot back. Several managed to make it over the edge of the pit, but they looked like they were scrambling for their lives, not coming after him.

It was all over very quickly.

When the last Lumar before him fell, he aimed at their barracks and opened up again, riddling the building from one end to the other in case any hadn't exited. When the belt feeder ran out of ammo, about three hundred rounds later, he released the thumb actuator and stared at the slaughter. There were Lumar bodies everywhere, from about twenty meters in front of the truck all the way up the road past the houses. The other truck was still on fire, as was the power generator. Thankfully, only a few small timbers inside the Duplato barracks were burning slightly.

The night went quiet as he took it all in.

His eyes drifted down to the red-hot barrel of the machine gun. He could hear the metal pinging as it cooled in the chilly night air. He pulled his pistol, winced at the gash in his arm, and dropped to the ground. As he did, he spotted movement in the Duplato barracks. They were shoving beds aside and emerging from the damaged building.

Voth peeked over the edge of the pit and saw the curving backs of three Lumar about ten meters down, hiding. He pulled off the hood of his infiltrator suit and exposed his badge. In a deep, booming voice he shouted, "By the authority of the Peacemakers, I order you to drop your weapons and come back up here. If you do not do so immediately, I will let these Duplato come down there and kill you with Dulk's own weapons."

A moment later, three rifles clattered down the steep incline. The three large, four-armed Lumar came scrambling back up the slope. Voth leveled his pistol, and their eyes went wide.

"Do not worry," Voth said. "I'm arresting you, not executing you." All three of them looked relieved and continued to scramble to the top. "Hands behind your heads and get moving." He motioned toward the compound with his pistol. They did as they were instructed, and when they reached the Duplato barracks, Voth ordered them to sit on the ground with their legs crossed.

The Lumar took their seats as Ginkhur stepped through the shattered end of the building and dropped to the ground. A handful of Duplato stood behind him, wary looks upon their faces, but the others remained hidden behind the stacked bunks.

"Holy goddess," Ginkhur said in a whisper as he scanned the compound. "It worked."

"Indeed," Voth said.

"All of you," Ginkhur said, turning toward the other Duplato, "find some functional weapons and cover those Lumar. Everyone!" he shouted into the barracks. "Come on out. We have to get to the others in the mine!" The miners pushed the stacked beds away in an avalanche and came pouring out.

"What do you intend to do?" Voth asked as the Duplato dashed past them.

"If it's all the same to you, we'd prefer to capture the remaining Lumar ourselves…assuming they're willing to surrender. There's only ten or so of them down below, and with all the rifles up here, they'll be outnumbered about three or four to one."

"What if they take hostages?" Voth asked.

"Then they won't last long down there. Lumar don't see well in the dark, and we do. It *won't* be a problem. And if they surrender, we'll take them to the constables back in the city. We're miners, not killers, and, like I said, I sort of feel for why they were doing all this."

Voth nodded. "Then be my guest," he said.

* * *

6

Fifteen-Forty-Eight Hours
1 Day After Rsach Klixtylbyt Named Valedictorian
Peacemaker Academy, Ocono

His eyes cast downward, Voth let out a long breath, as if he'd just performed an impossibly difficult task. He raised his eyes and searched the faces of the students before him, one at a time. He found himself wondering if any had identified his sin, picked up on the terrible mistake that had haunted him for twenty-nine years.

Most of them had looks of awe on their faces. He'd expected that. His tactics had been sound. He'd been lucky. He'd single-handedly defeated sixty armed Lumar, including Dulk whose lifeless eyes still frequented Voth's dreams from time to time.

On the surface, Voth's actions were a feat worthy of the Triple-A for Combat.

But that's not the whole story, Voth thought.

"The image of me you will find in the Hall of Heroes," he said slowly, "is both the absolute truth and a complete lie. It shows me standing among a bunch of dead Lumar in bright sunshine holding a belt-fed machine gun in my hands. As I explained, that engagement was at night, the gun was mounted, and most of those Lumar never even saw me when I shot them down."

"A lie?" a green HecSha student blurted. "You can't be serious?"

Voth smiled. "Do you really believe someone just happened to be standing there with a holocam?"

"You're saying it's all public relations garbage?" another student asked. "Propaganda?"

"No," Voth said simply. "I did what I said I did, just as the other Peacemakers and Enforcers installed in the Hall of Heroes did. What you will find down there is…*inspiration* based on actual events. It inspired me when I was your age. And I know it will inspire you when you go there. Every story in the Hall of Heroes is true, at its heart. The details and the holos might be a little altered, but I assure you, the lives saved, and the lives lost—all of it is perfectly true."

"So, why are you telling us this?" a pale Sidar said, her leather wings shifting uncomfortably.

"Because," Voth intoned seriously, "it is imperative that each and every one of you understands that we are not heroes. *None* of us." The room went completely silent.

"We are Peacemakers; police officers," he continued. "We serve and we protect, and we stand or fall in the doing. But before you draw the weapon they will one day issue you, before you take the life of another being, engage your head. Do *everything* you can to see the whole picture. Understand what is driving those you pursue and those you protect. Such information is critical, especially when so many lives are on the line." His eyes bored into them. "Let me say it again…" He paused as something akin to anger crossed his face. "We are *not* heroes. We exist to serve the public trust and protect the innocent, and, yes, that sometimes means protect them from evil…or even from themselves, which is, by its very nature, a slippery slope." The anger faded, and a rueful smile crossed his lips. "So, what does this all have to do with my story? Well, you see, I made a mistake that night…one that nearly cost me my badge." He saw confusion on their faces. "Can anyone tell me what my mistake was? And I must add that, in hindsight, it's arguably the most dreadful mistake I've ever made."

He heard them breathing. He watched as they poured over his story in their minds, but nobody seemed to have the slightest idea. And then, at the back of the room, the Jivool student Instructor

Droizhiun had called out for cramming for exams raised a tentative paw.

Both Voth and Droizhiun looked up to the dark-furred claws pointing toward the ceiling.

"Mr. Su Banai," Instructor Droizhiun said. "You have a theory?"

"I do, sir," the Jivool said, though he sounded doubtful.

"Then, by all means, regale us with it." There was no missing the doubt in Droizhiun's voice.

"Peacemaker Voth," Su Banai said almost apologetically, "you didn't check the Duplato's story…didn't confirm that Dulk or his lackeys actually intended to kill all the miners."

Both the Sumatozou instructor and the retired GenSha Peacemaker stared at the young Jivool with a good deal of astonishment and respect.

Voth took a deep breath, and he found himself feeling the same embarrassment he'd felt when his station chief had pointed out that fact on Pemmick a week later during his debrief.

"That is exactly correct." Voth closed his eyes for a moment, remembering the dead Lumar scattered around that dirt road, illuminated by firelight. Opening them, he explained. "I killed fifty-seven Lumar—laborers and criminals alike—including Dulk, the one I had been after. However, as young Su Banai pointed out, I never confirmed that Dulk or anyone else actually intended to kill the Duplato. Especially since Dulk had gone out of his way on Pemmick to not kill when he could avoid it." Voth paused as a wave of embarrassment washed over him. "I took the Duplato at his word, *blindly*, and he could very well have been manipulating me to kill the Lumar, just as the MinSha had killed the Lumar."

Silence filled the room.

"So, did he?" a HecSha asked, sounding almost accusatory. "Did Ginkhur lie to you?"

"No," Voth replied. "But that isn't the point. In the morning, after the Duplato miners captured seven of the remaining Lumar and killed three, I inspected where the explosives had, in fact, already been set. I even questioned the Lumar prisoners, and one of them admitted it. It seems he had a conscience and didn't agree with what several other Lumar intended. I even checked up on the rest of Ginkhur's story regarding Dulk's motivations. It took some digging—three months of it on my own time—and it turned out the MinSha *had* slaughtered a hundred and fifty Lumar miners and families in one of the asteroids of the Sylphux system. It was all a vendetta—a well-deserved one, I might add—against the MinSha trader Dulk had first killed in the starport on Pemmick. The MinSha simply didn't want to pay them. I should point out that if I or any of my own people had been in Dulk's shoes, we could just as easily have gotten caught up in something like those events." Voth paused, his eyes bored into every student before him. "Who among us would *not* do anything to avenge the death of our families, our loved ones…our comrades? But that does *not* apply to Peacemakers, regardless of race. As Peacemakers, are we not held to a higher standard? Both of intention and action?" He took a deep breath. "That's the question you need to ask yourselves, every single day. I can't tell you if things would have gone differently if I'd had more information. I honestly don't know, but my instincts tell me that what happened was the only way." He looked up at the young enthusiastic faces that would, in all likelihood, be wearing a Peacemaker badge in a year. "But that does not negate my mistake. It does not absolve me—or any of you—from the obligation we have to understand *why* we are pulling a trigger before we do so. Just imagine if Ginkhur *had* been lying to me and all those deaths could have been avoided. Yes, it was unlikely in those circumstances, but you will face even more complex situations in the years ahead." He looked at them imploringly. "Always remember: we are not heroes, and we cannot behave as if we are. We are Peacemakers. It is vital that you understand the difference before you wear the badge and carry the gun."

Voth went silent. He could see that he'd had an impact, and it was as it should be.

"Thank you for the privilege of speaking to you today," he said. Without another word, he turned and walked out the door as the students, and even Master Instructor Droizhiun, rapped knuckles on desks like thunder.

* * * * *

Quincy J. Allen Bio

National Bestselling Author Quincy J. Allen is a cross-genre author with a growing number of novels under his belt. In 2019, his media tie-in novel *Colt the Outlander: Shadow of Ruin* was a Scribe Award finalist, and his noir novel *Chemical Burn* became a Colorado Gold Award finalist in 2010. He co-authored the fantasy novel *Reclaiming Honor* with Marc Alan Edelheit, released October, 2019. In November of 2019, he and Kevin Ikenberry published the novel *Enforcer*, set in the Four Horsemen Universe. He also has a fantasy steampunk series, the Blood War Chronicles, and book four, entitled *Blood World*, is due out late 2020.

His short story publications are numerous, including an appearance in Larry Correia's *Monster Hunter: Files* from Baen. He has a growing list of novelettes appearing in Chris Kennedy Publishing's anthologies, both in and out of the Four Horsemen Universe. Additionally, he has two short story collections in his Out Through the Attic series, and he continues to add to his short-story credits with each passing year.

He works out of his home in Charlotte, North Carolina, and hopes to one day be a New York Times bestselling author.

# # # # #

Last by
Kevin Steverson

Chapter One

Peacemaker Academy
Ocono

"I disagree," argued Professor Zeemna. "He is barely passing. He does not deserve to go on a commissioning mission."

"Respectfully," Professor T'Lanon said, "I do not agree with Professor Zeemna. I am in favor of Millzak being assigned a commissioning mission like the rest of his class."

"You would be," sneered the Veetanho. "You have babied that...that substandard candidate since the day he stepped foot on Academy grounds."

"*That* candidate has a name, and it will be used when referring to him," admonished Dean Krithnaim. "All candidates will be treated with equal respect, regardless of where they stand on the order of merit. I will not tell you again, Professor Zeemna." A Maki, both tips of his tail rose over his shoulder and waved slowly behind him, letting all observing know he was truly agitated.

"Sir...I—" Professor Zeemna answered, "I apologize. You are correct, but Candidate Millzak is last in his class. Last."

The dean turned to his left and spoke to Professor T'Lanon. She was in charge of the after-hours study hall for students having trouble with their academic assignments. "Has he ever failed a course?"

"No sir, he has not," the MinSha answered, a small amount of pride showing through. "He has passed every course up to this point." She glanced over to the other side of the table to ensure Zeemna heard it. "There are nights, late nights, I leave him in the study hall assured he will lock up when he leaves."

"Ask her if the candidate has ever scored higher than a marginal rating in any course," Zeemna suggested, unimpressed at the dedication the object of her displeasure showed.

"That will be enough, Professor," the Dean said as his tail moved faster, impatience coming through in his tone. He turned to the others sitting around the conference table. "Opinions?"

Captain Mullnark volunteered, "He can fight; that cannot be denied. He has good instincts and countermoves. He doesn't always plan ahead in his sparring, but he holds his own against even myself." The large Besquith looked around daring anyone to disagree with his evaluation. A little long in the tooth, the older Peacemaker still welcomed all challengers.

"He can shoot," Lieutenant Arlichaa said. He was the weapons instructor at the Academy's range. "He is skilled with a blade, as well," the Goka added.

Professor Mul-Zinth, a Jeha spoke up. "Candidate Millzak passed his classes in my department. Several instructors took extra time with him. Granted, his scores were far from stellar, but they were passing scores. He has memorized the procedures and the required programs to disable ships, communication devices, and personal slates. He can also program rudimentary searches. What he can't do himself, he knows how to tie in the patches that all Peacemakers have access to in order to accomplish the mission. In short, as far as computers are concerned, he can get the job done."

Deputy Selector Bellgrund, the only Peacemaker in the room not assigned as faculty, stood up. "Candidate Millzak will be assigned a commissioning mission like the rest of his classmates. Period. He was selected to attend this academy and has passed the courses, assignments, weapons qualifications, and the physical training, including unarmed combat, required."

Peacemaker Bellgrund was a Buma and though she was only four feet tall and resembled an owl from the planet Earth, the birth world of Humans, she had the ability to command a room as she was doing now. The fact she held the rank of major had nothing to do with it. It was, in fact, one of the reasons she had been selected to begin training as a Peacemaker Selector on her own commissioning mission before her final year at the Academy so many years ago.

She continued, "Professor Zeemna, you are incorrect in your assumption that Candidate Millzak has never scored more than a marginal rating. Every peer evaluation Millzak has received has been of the highest rating possible. Unlike some sitting at this table when they were Peacemaker candidates, his classmates think highly of him." The Deputy Selector stared at the Veetanho, letting everyone in the room know who she was referring to.

After a few tense moments, she continued, "A small percentage of his race have the mental capacity to apply as Peacemakers. Few are accepted and attend this academy, even fewer have received their badges. He did not apply...I selected him. As a general rule, I stay out of the Academy's business after a candidate I select is enrolled. With this candidate, I am making an exception. With all due respect, Dean, you *will* send him on a commissioning mission."

Dean Krithnaim smiled at his old friend. "Rest assured, I feel no disrespect. As a matter of fact, your presence here to ensure fair treatment of one you selected is welcome. It does me good to be reminded the candidates at this academy are not numbers…grades, if you will. They are not simply names on an order of merit list. Those learning here and successfully graduating will become Peacemakers. That is no small feat. Though we now reside here at the Academy, we are all, in fact, Peacemakers. We swore an oath to uphold justice. Millzak is a candidate in good standing, regardless of how close he may be to the cut line. He will be assigned a mission. It is just."

Later, after the meeting was over and the instructors had left to perform the various tasks to prepare candidates for missions or to get ready for the upcoming graduation ceremony, Bellgrund and Krithnaim caught each other up. They were interrupted by yet another old friend.

Hak-Chet stepped into the conference room. "I thought I would catch you two here," he said.

"Where else would we be?" Bellgrund answered. "Surely not in the auditorium where they are preparing for the graduation. You can have the pomp and circumstance, my friend."

Krithnaim said, "I, for one, am glad the guild master presides over graduation ceremonies. That's one tradition that needs to stay in place as long as I am dean. Standing that long in one place is bad on these old paws."

Hak-Chet smiled and spread his wings slightly. A Sidar resembling a bat-like Pteranodon, the positioning of his wings added to his facial expressions. "You are not that old, sir."

"I am old enough to consider retirement," Krithnaim argued.

"You say that every year," observed Bellgrund. "Hak, it is good to see you again. I take it you are here for a specific graduate?"

"I am," answered Hak-Chet. "I think he is the one."

"I hope you are right," she said. "I truly do." She let the subject drop, and the three talked for a while about trivial matters.

Finally, Bellgrund said, "Well, I need to go see a young Lumar before I leave Ocono and wish him well on his upcoming commissioning mission. Be well my friends."

* * *

Chapter Two

Peacemaker Academy
Ocono

Millzak stared at his slate and reread the orders displayed on it. Once he was sure of its meaning, he slowly grinned. He had been assigned a commissioning mission. A follow-up message would be sent shortly with the name of his candidate partner. He thumbed the tab for his notes and went through the list again, comparing it to the gear on his bunk, line by line. Holding the slate in his two upper hands, his other two touched the items, his lips moving as he read the list to himself, sounding out the more difficult words.

A voice from his open doorway called his name. She had waited until he put his slate down after finishing the list. He looked over and down, grinning. "Deputy Selector Bellgrund, I am happy to see you."

"And I am happy to see you," Bellgrund said, looking up at the seven-foot-tall Lumar, unable to keep joy from her own face. "I see you are preparing for your upcoming mission."

"Yes," Millzak answered. "I have orders."

"That is very good," the Deputy Selector said. "In a year you will graduate and be a Peacemaker if you continue to work hard at it."

"I will," agreed Millzak with a serious nod. "It has not been easy, but I will not fail. Many times I have to read things again and again." He indicated his slate. "I have learned to program some things on a computer. That was the hardest to learn. And math, math is very hard."

"I know," Bellgrund agreed. "But you learned, and that is what is most important. How have you been other than your classwork?"

"Good," answered Millzak, rolling both sets of muscular shoulders like a prize fighter before a bout. "I am good. How are you?"

"I am well," answered Bellgrund.

"Can I ask a question," Millzak said with a slight tilt to his head.

"Certainly, you may," answered the Deputy Selector as she leaned against the doorway.

"Why did you pick me?" Millzak asked. He had been asking himself this question for several years. "I am not smart like some Lumar. The smart ones are business owners and in government. They learn about medicine, and others are teachers. I am not smart enough for that."

"You are smart enough, Millzak," she answered. "Never let anyone tell you different."

"I study hard to remember things," he countered. "I have learned to use reminders to help me remember. I watch some of my classmates answer questions without looking up the answers to learn them first. Some do not study at all, and they pass. I am not like them."

"Maybe you are not quite like them," answered Bellgrund, "but they are not like you. Tell me, have you made friends here?"

"Yes," answered Millzak, nodding. "I am friends with many. Sometimes I sit, and I talk with them when they are upset, or something is wrong. When they are happy, I am happy with them. If they need help, I help. If they want to talk, I listen. If they need to just sit and sip a drink and stare, I will sit with them. Talk is not always needed."

"Do they help you when you need it?" asked the elderly Peacemaker.

"Yes," answered Millzak. "If I need help, I ask them to help me. Sometimes it is to study with them. Many times, they explain things to me again after class. I think, if you need help, you should ask. There is no shame in asking for help."

"I agree," Bellgrund said. "You show wisdom beyond your years in believing that. Let me ask you, how do you know when they are happy…or sad? Do they tell you?"

Millzak stared off for a moment thinking hard. "Not in the beginning. I just knew. I could tell. It is like I can tell when one is not being truthful. We had a class in the body language of a lot of races. I did not understand many of the terms the professor was teaching. The big words can be very confusing, but I passed the exams because I knew what the subjects were feeling. I could tell if they were not being honest. I could see through them."

"And that, my young Candidate, is why I selected you," answered Bellgrund with a tilt of her own head. When he looked confused, she explained in more detail, "You gave indications of a natural empath. You have the ability to read someone and determine if they are telling the truth, to know what they are feeling." She continued. "My fellow selectors thought I was wrong in selecting you, a Lumar with no hope of passing the entrance exams. On my orders, those exam scores were waived. They laughed at the thought of someone reading minds, until I reminded them I had not said that. I did not call you telepathic. No one of any race reads minds. But an empath doesn't read minds, they read body language incredibly well and feel emotions to a small degree. Beings will tell empaths things they normally keep to themselves, opening up to one they've only known for five minutes as if they have known them for five months. Yes, there were many other Lumar who scored higher than you on the tests, but there was no one on your planet with the natural ability you possess. Are you familiar with the Human term *savant*?"

"I do not know what that means," admitted Millzak, he picked up his slate. "But I will look it up. How is it spelled?"

Bellgrund waved it off. "It is not important. What is important is you have worked hard, and you are going on a commissioning mission. I am proud of you."

"You are also afraid," observed Millzak. "I see it. What are you afraid of?"

The Deputy Selector smiled. "If you tell me how you know, I will tell you my fear."

Millzak thought hard. Finally, he spoke, "You have your wings crossed as if you are trying to hold your feelings inside. Your eyes squinted slightly when you said the word fear. Your shoulders are tight, and you stood up, away from the door jam, no longer comfortable. You feel...nervous, and I feel it. I am sorry, I do not know what else to say or how to explain,"

"Well, it is enough," admitted Bellgrund. "You called out the things I was doing without realizing it, and when pointed it out, I admit I was doing those things. I am nervous and a little frightened...for you. I want you to do well on your mission and continue on to graduate. I will be honest with you. I am looking toward retirement. Over the years I have brought many to this academy from the various races in my assigned sector. Most were follow-ups to applications. There have been very few I selected who had not applied. The other Lumar who have become Peacemakers are literally geniuses. They are above average intelligence for any race. You are above average for a Lumar, but not for most other races and you are far from a genius. Before I leave, I wanted to show my fellow selectors there is a wide pool of candidates they have been missing, that they should look beyond scores and grades. Look for other talents."

"I am your experiment," Millzak said. The word came out slowly, giving away the fact it was not one used often by him.

"Yes, in a way you are," admitted Bellgrund. "At least you were in the beginning. Now, I truly want to see you graduate because you want to be a Peacemaker so badly. You have worked hard and refuse to fail. I admire that in you. No one, at any level in the Academy, has worked as hard as you do to simply pass. I don't think anyone has...ever. There are some who worked hard to be the top of their class, but none have put in everything they had to simply retain their place here. There have been those who failed out of the academy, but they didn't have the desire and work ethic to pass as you do. Now, I want it because you do."

Millzak nodded. "I believe you. Thank you for selecting me...and for caring. I will not let you down."

"I know you won't," Bellgrund smiled. "You don't know how to fail. Sometimes it's good to not know something."

* * *

Professor Zeemna walked into the Assignments Office, moving past the two desks and the assistants working at their consoles, to the administrator's office. The Otoo sitting on his raised stool looked up from his computer and stopped what he was doing.

"Professor Zeemna," Administrator Bwagoln said. "What brings you to my office? If it is about the commissioning assignment detail message, as soon as I add this last one, I will be sending them all at once to the candidates."

"No rush, my friend," Zeemna said waiving it off. "No rush at all. I know you have been putting in long days this close to the end of the year."

"Well, yes," answered Bwagoln, relaxing. One of his small pincers swiped across an eyestalk. "I tell you, I will be glad to get into some water when this day is through. I tend to get 'crabby' the longer I am away from it." The normally somber administrator laughed at his own joke about his race's resemblance to the Earth animal.

Professor Zeemna laughed along with him. "I came to help you out with the last one. I believe you received a last-minute addition to the list I sent earlier this week."

"I did," agreed Bwagoln, "a Candidate Millzak. I haven't pulled up his file yet to see where he would be best utilized. I admit, I do not even know his race. Between commissioning assignments and the assignments of graduating Peacemakers, they tend to run together."

"I sympathize with you. Send him with Candidate Zerze," suggested Zeemna. "He is number one in the class and will be the valedictorian. There is no one close enough to catch him. I understand he is going to the Trindlark System where there is a labor problem along with other issues."

"Why, yes,' Bwagoln admitted. "It seems like a financial issue, having to do with profit sharing and wages in that dual-planet system. How do you know Zerze is assigned there?" Both eyes on the end of their small stalks narrowed.

"You mentioned it last week," said Zeemna dismissively. "Since there are two problems, I suggest Millzak handle the financial issue with the profits and pay while our future valedictorian handles the labor issue on the sister planet. Two planets, two assignments. We will grade them on the success of their own assignments, of course."

"I suppose," Bwagoln said slowly.

Zeemna smiled and pushed her dark goggles up her nose. "The sooner you finish the assignments and send them out, the sooner you can get under some water. Besides, I hate to see you working so hard and so late, my friend."

Bwagoln thought for a moment, turned back to his computer, and quickly started typing. He touched the screen and finished the assignments. He sent the assignment detail messages in bulk. "Done!" he exclaimed. "Thank you for the suggestion. It is much quicker when you don't have to peruse a candidate's file with years of classes and evaluations. Now if you will excuse me, I intend to go get wet." He started gathering his things.

"Think nothing of it," the Veetanho said as she turned to go. She looked back over her shoulder and said, "We should do lunch during the break sometime."

She walked out grinning to herself.

* * *

Chapter Three

Trindlark System
Trading Station

The two Peacemaker Candidates sat in the waiting area on the trading space station in the Trindlark System. Each waited for a system shuttle to take them to the planet of their assignment. The station was strategically located between the two planets in the star's habitable zone. One planet was sparsely populated, the center for system mining, and the other was like so many other colonies across the galaxy, home for the miners and the businesses that grew up in a new place.

This system was occupied mainly by Caroon, a race known for mining. The corporation owning most of the mining was not head-quartered in the system, so local business was managed by a subcontracted company of Veetanho which used Blevin for security. There was no further information in the mission brief.

Millzak looked over at his mission partner, a SleSha, and said. "You will go to one planet, and I will go to the other, right?" Their translators and ear-pieces handled the communication easily. Affixed to each of their coveralls, in the shoulder area, was a small speaker able to do the same should the situation warrant.

"Right, Millzak," Peacemaker Candidate Zerze answered. He reached up and touched the Peacemaker badge affixed to his uniform with the small pincers on his limb. It was almost identical to an actual Peacemaker's badge. He couldn't quite feel its weight through the clothes against his exoskeleton. That area of his body didn't have many nerves except inside. Sometimes he wondered if the wasps he resembled on Earth were made the same way, though so much smaller. "You will handle the issue on Trindlark while I take care of the problems on Gondlo. Our brief doesn't say exactly what the issues may be. Going in without a preconceived notion is part of the training but don't worry, though the request for Peacemaker intervention was made, those above us have determined a couple of candidates can handle it."

"That is good," said Millzak, "but we are not a couple. We are two. Wait, a couple is two. A few is three or more. We are a couple." He nodded his head after figuring it out.

"It will be fine," Zerze said. "We don't even have to go incognito."

"In what?" asked Millzak.

"It means 'in disguise,'" laughed Zerze. "Remember, sometimes a Peacemaker must conceal their identity on missions."

"I remember," Millzak said. "Something you are not."

"Exactly," Zerze grinned as well as his facial features would allow, imitating many other races when they were amused. Sometimes he was nearly as excited as his friend when the Lumar learned something new.

One thing Zerze was not, was frustrated. Far from it; he patiently answered Millzak's questions. He understood it took a little more for his partner to fully understand things. He did not mind.

In a way, Zerze envied Millzak. Sometimes he tended to overthink things. His friend, however, never did that. He studied whatever was at hand until he understood it, never more.

There had been many times over the last couple of years when Millzak had interrupted the SleSha's study to just talk or distract him otherwise. Millzak always told Zerze he felt he needed it. Zerze had to admit, many times he did need the brief break, even if it was to help Millzak study; it took his mind off the stress of trying to be number one, and it helped to ground him. Millzak had a way of easing his stress. It had been that way since they first met.

Once, during their freshman year, a group of upperclassmen had harassed Zerze. It stopped completely once Millzak cornered the four of them and let them know in no uncertain terms that he had four fists, as he counted them out slowly, and he would use them to defend anyone who needed it. He also counted the four of the upperclassmen and informed them the numbers were the same.

When Millzak said it to them, it came across as information he felt they needed to know. When they tried to shrug off what they had been doing, he told them they were lying. It *was* harassment and not just having a bit of fun. Confronted with a large, very strong Lumar, who seemed to not care about their hints at blackmail, or even acknowledge it, the Jeha acting as the group's ringleader backed off, and it never happened again.

Millzak watched the screen on the bulkhead. When he saw the shuttle number he was waiting on light up, he stood, gathered his gear, and turned to Zerze.

"My shuttle is here," he said. "If I complete my mission before it is time to go back to the Academy, I will find you. We can wait for our transport back to the Academy together. If not, I will see you here."

"You will complete it, my friend," Zerze said. "If I finish mine first, I will come to you. I would tell you to honor the threat and set the terms, but I don't think the missions we have been assigned will require it. Instead, I will wish you good fortunes."

Zerze watched Millzak leave the waiting area. He knew he would finish his own mission first. Afterward, he would find a way to help Millzak in a way it wouldn't count against his friend and his evaluation. They were supposed to complete their mission on their own unless specifically assigned to the same place. If he was caught, he would face the instructors and stand his ground for his friend, like Millzak had for him years ago, instructions be damned.

* * *

Sharvaton Mining Headquarters
Trindlark

"What do you mean you requested Peacemaker assistance?" demanded Korleego. She pushed her dark glasses back up her nose. The Veetanho was close to losing her temper, an undignified reaction from an executive in the mining industry.

"I-I thought it best," stammered Daylinn. She was confused at Korleego's reaction. "Credits have gone missing. It disappears. The Pangtol Company asked if I could assist. I can find no unauthorized entry into the account, by normal means or hacking. The recorded camera feed shows the hard credit being counted and the deposit slip going into the slot to direct the funds."

The Aposo wiped her face with her small paw and continued, bolstered by the facts. "All of the tellers at the credit exchange have been questioned locally. None show an increase in wealth. None have hidden accounts where the credit could have been transferred, even if one managed to slip by my searches. The credit disappears and never shows up anywhere else."

"You have been working for them, too? You work for Sharvaton Mining Control, not the companies we contract under us! We cannot be held accountable for the missing funds!" exclaimed the Veetanho. "If the contracted company cannot pay its wages fully, that is not our concern!"

"But, President Korleego, the miners need their credits," reasoned Daylinn. "Just because I work for you in accounting does not mean I don't feel for them. I volunteered my time. Someone is stealing from them…and their families."

"Feel!" screamed Korleego. "Feel! You don't feel for them. You just do your job for *my* company. You had no right to request assistance from anyone, much less Peacemakers. It's bad enough they are coming here; now I am told they will be on Gondlo as well."

"Yes, ma'am," Daylinn nodded. "The miners are threatening to strike. They did not receive wages for the fifth week in a row. Their families grow hungry. Many have had to move in together to cut expenses."

As an Aposo, Daylinn was rodent-like, as was her Veetanho boss, only smaller, but she didn't have dark glasses concealing her eyes so her genuine concern was easy to see in them. It sent the company president over the edge.

"Get out!" Korleego shouted. "You're fired! Don't even try and get a severance package. I'll see you in court for attempting to destroy my company. If you try and gain employment in a company contracted by me, you will be blamed for the losses, and I will see to it you never work in finance again!" She stormed out of the room.

Daylinn stood, quietly gathered her few belongings from the desk in her small office and left the building. She had no idea what she would do in the next few minutes, much less the rest of her life. She was too stunned to express emotions. She knew she had enough in her savings to return home but not enough to secure a place to stay and look for employment. She thought when she landed this job a year ago, it would be a company she could build a career with, somewhere to work happily with her numbers and computers until she retired.

It had seemed so promising. Now, because she tried to do the right thing, she had lost that dream. She walked slowly to her company provided home, gathered a few belongings and clothes to fill a bag, and went to the starport. There was no sense in hanging around. There was nothing left for her in this system.

* * *

Millzak walked past the customs area, a large bag slung over an upper shoulder and a small case in one of his hands. He nodded at the agent checking another passenger's belongings and kept going. The exposed Peacemaker Candidate badge and the well-known Peacemaker jumpsuit was obvious to the busy Veetanho. A few minutes after he passed, the agent made a quick call.

Millzak looked around in the waiting area. He saw the sliding doors leading out of the building. He knew there would be transport services outside. They were always at starports, and he knew how to use them. He would ask the operator to take him to the mining headquarters. He looked at the screen on the slate in his hand. *Sharvaton Mining Control.* He repeated it to himself several times before glancing around again.

At seven feet tall, the Lumar was an imposing figure, one most beings in the galaxy would avoid if possible. Everyone cleared a path for him as he walked toward the doors. All of them except one, a small Aposo. She was staring at her feet as she walked…right into Millzak.

She stumbled backward after running into his seemingly immovable bulk. "I am so sorry," she apologized and scrambled for her bag.

"It is all right," Millzak said with a small smile. "Are you injured?" he asked.

The Aposo looked up at hearing his deep voice. Her eyes went wide, likely thinking that Lumar were big, of low intelligence, usually rude, and nearly always mean, which made them perfect mercenaries.

She looked him over and seemed surprised at the pleasant expression on his face. It was then she noticed what he was wearing and the glint of his shining badge. His Peacemaker's badge.

"Peacemaker!" she exclaimed. "You came."

"I am not yet a Peacemaker," Millzak said. "I am a candidate. Yes, I came. I am here."

"My name is Daylinn," said the Aposo. "I requested Peacemaker intervention. I did not know they would send a candidate, but you have the same authority if you were assigned a mission. Don't you?"

"Yes, I am a candidate," Millzak said. "I have been assigned. Your name is listed as the contact for…" he paused a moment and thought. "Sharvaton Mining."

Daylinn's whole demeanor changed. She stared off in the distance, after a moment she looked up at him and said, "I *was* your contact. I am no longer the contact." She picked her bag up and turned to walk away.

Millzak studied her for a moment. "Stop. Come sit with me. Tell me what is wrong. Before I go, I will try and help you."

He guided her to a small sitting area. There were two tables. One was occupied by a pair of starport employees. The two occupants quickly gathered their belongings and left. The last thing they wanted was to get involved with whatever brought a Peacemaker to the planet, especially one as imposing as Millzak.

"Please tell me why you are so upset," Millzak said. "Sometimes talking about a problem helps." He could tell the small Aposo sitting across from him was close to falling apart. He felt her emotions strongly. This one was close to the edge. He felt this once before from a candidate, considering something drastic after the loss of his entire clan in a tragic accident. Now was the time to try and help. Now.

"I...I have been fired," said Daylinn. For some reason she felt she could open up to the large Peacemaker. The words came in a rush. "I have only enough credits to get home. I spent my savings on implants last year. I wouldn't have if I had known. I didn't know. I don't have anywhere to go when I get there. I have no family. There is no one left. I know a few others, but not many. I was always reclusive, stuck in my computers with my numbers and programs." The words coming from her slowed as she rambled. "I never made many friends. I don't know what I am going to do. I just don't know." The last came out as a whisper as she stared off again.

"Tell me little one, why are you fired?" Millzak prompted her.

Daylinn looked at Millzak, puzzled. "Because I asked for Peacemaker assistance."

"I do not pretend to be a smart Lumar," Millzak said, "but even I know that is no reason to lose your job. Did you do anything else to anger your boss?"

"I tried to help the Pangtol Mining Company find their missing credits," answered Daylinn. "I am an accountant, or I was, anyway. The president was not happy about it. I was only trying to help."

"So, credits are missing," Millzak said. He reached for his slate and slowly typed in a note. "Tell me, did you take it?"

"What? No," Daylinn answered. "I tried to help find it."

Millzak looked at here for a long moment, nodded, and took more notes. "Where did you look?" he asked.

"I searched their banking records, their account," Daylinn said. She appeared to be more comfortable with the change in the conversation. Numbers and computers were her life. "I ran several standard programs attempting to determine if there were authorized or unauthorized withdrawals or hacking attempts on the account. I found nothing."

Millzak put his slate down. "This case will have a lot of math...and use of computers, won't it?"

"Well, yes," Daylinn said. Confusion was evident in her voice. "Many credits are missing. The mining company cannot meet its payroll. The miners are threatening to strike, and my old company contracts a security force that will use intimidation and violence to make them go back to work. It will get bad at the mines."

"The mines are on the other planet, right?" Millzak asked.

"Yes," Daylinn said. "The rare elements are mined on Gondlo. They are shipped from there. A percentage of the profit goes to the company employing the miners. It is delivered here weekly, and several deposits are made simultaneously in the credit exchange. They use actual hard credits. The system buying the majority of the raw metals insist on paying in hard credits. I know it's very unusual, but some systems do not trust digital currency. It seems so old fashioned to me; it's almost impossible to believe it is still done that way anywhere in the galaxy."

"I understand," Millzak said. "An account with credits you cannot touch, where you can only see numbers, can be confusing."

Daylinn tilted her head slightly and her ears perked up at hearing this. "How will you determine where the missing credits are going? I could not figure it out. I have watched the video of the deposits being made—the deposit slips filled out, the credits being counted, and the deposit slips being fed into the slot on the computer. The next day a deposit is missing, sometimes completely."

"Deposit slip?" Millzak asked. "One is filled out for every deposit?"

"Well, yes," Daylinn answered. "I mean, the slips are preprinted with the account information, then the amount of the deposit is filled in and it goes into the slot. The credits are placed in the exchange's vault. I should tell you, the beings in the exchange have been very helpful, I feel they have allowed me access to more than they probably should. We could not determine where the credits are going. There have been no attempts to gain access to the account other than when the company itself does it. Every other account in the exchange has the proper amount of credits, coinciding with their own deposit slips."

"Co...what?" Millzak asked.

"Coinciding. It means their credits matches the amount they should have," explained Daylinn.

Millzak thought for a moment. *Math, computers, credits, accounts, unauthorized access.* These were things he knew he was not good at. He needed help. An idea came to him.

"You do not work for—" he consulted his slate, "—Sharvaton anymore. Correct?"

"No," Daylinn said, her shoulders slumped. Millzak knew the discussion of the missing credits had pulled her out of her depression for a while, but it was threatening to come back.

"Good," Millzak said. "I am authorized to contract help from the locals if it is needed. I need help. You will be my math and computer consultant. The Peacemaker Guild will pay you standard contract fees. I do not know what they are, but I can find out. Will you help me?"

"I—why yes, Peacemaker Candidate," Daylinn said, standing. "I will help in any way I can. There are Caroon families in desperate need. I have to help."

"Good. Thank you," Millzak said. "Since you do not work for them anymore, there will not be a...a..." He tried to think of the words.

"Conflict of interest?" Daylinn prompted.

"Yes! Those are the words," Millzak said. He grinned. "We will start at the credit exchange. Lead the way." He grabbed his case, adjusted the strap of his large bag across his shoulder, kept his slate in one hand, and reached down with his free hand and picked up her bag for her. Sometimes it was good to have four hands.

* * *

Chapter Four

The credit exchange was a local business owned by a Caroon, though it tied into the network of credit exchanges throughout the galaxy. The owner/president was more than relieved to see Millzak enter his establishment with the accountant who had been trying to determine where the missing credits had gone. As expected, the Peacemaker was given full access to the computer system.

This time Daylinn had access to much more than the account in question and the limited programs allowed before. It wasn't that the president hadn't wanted to give her more before, but there were regulations in the credit exchange industry that had to be adhered to. A Peacemaker on-sight requesting full access for his assistant was a completely different matter. The president was thrilled to have an excuse to allow unlimited access.

"Daylinn," Millzak said, "I am going to question everyone working here. I would like you to perform your searches again. I am told you will have greater access than you had before."

"Yes, Peacemaker Candidate," Daylinn said. "I have a question first. Before, I used standard programing. Am I authorized to use some of my own…um, personal programming? Or perhaps write what I may need to do a thorough search?"

Millzak looked at his new assistant and grinned. "You mean hack the system? I know what hacking is. I cannot do it. I use the standard programs available to Peacemakers. I am authorizing you, with the Peacemakers Guild's full backing, to use whatever means you feel are necessary to get the answers I need. Do not harm their system or leave a rear hatch. Or a door…or…?"

"You mean a back door?" Daylinn prodded.

"Yes, that. A back door," Millzak said. "Do not leave a back door or do anything dishonest. I trust you, Daylinn, but I must let you know that once my mission has been accomplished it may be followed up by the nearest Peacemaker. It is written in our mission guidelines. I remember."

"I understand," Daylinn said, nodding. "I would not dream of doing so. Thank you for your trust." She turned back to the console, cracked her fingers, hit a few keys, and got the faraway look indicating she had engaged her implants. Moments later she was lost in the system.

Millzak watched her work for a minute. As always, he was impressed by someone as intelligent as Daylinn. He was not jealous; he had long ago accepted his limitations. He was, however, smart enough to learn ways around them. *Use what you have, find what you need. There is always a way, look for the simple solution. Never learn to fail.* The big Lumar nodded his head as he recited his own personal motto in his mind and turned to find a room suitable for his interviews.

Three hours later, Daylinn walked into the conference-room-turned-interrogation-room. Millzak looked away from the Caroon he was glaring at. He could see the exhaustion on her face.

"What have you found?" Millzak asked.

"I used all my resources, Peacemaker Candidate," she said as she climbed up and flopped down into an empty chair. "The only thing I could find is a small blank section in the deposit timings. It is as if a slight hiccup occurred in the system."

"A hiccup?" Millzak asked. "Can a computer hiccup?"

"No, Peacemaker Candidate," she answered, smiling. "It is a figure of speech. There was a slight hesitation. It was deliberate. I found the embedded code that caused it. I removed it from the system. Peacemaker, it was uploaded here in the building."

Millzak looked back at the silent Caroon in front of him. "This one did it. She is lying to me."

Daylinn scooted to the front of her chair, excitement on her face. "What did she say?"

"Nothing," Millzak answered. "It doesn't matter. I know she is lying." He reached over with a pair of powered cuffs and locked the suspect to the chair she was sitting in.

"But…" Daylinn stammered. "Without an admission or the location of the missing credits, how will you arrest her? I still cannot find where they went. There have been no unauthorized system breaches. There are no extra credits in any account in this exchange. Every account has the balance attributed to deposits and withdrawals in it. Believe me, I looked at every one. I'm just thankful it is not a huge credit exchange or the branch of a large company."

"Daylinn, please explain again how the deposits are made here," Millzak asked for the second time since they walked into the exchange.

Starting to understand Millzak's thought process and realizing some things needed more explanation, Daylinn answered plainly. "The hard currency is brought in and counted in front of a teller. The teller re-counts the credits. The being making the deposit slides a preprinted deposit slip into the adding machine and the amount is entered. Both parties key in the amount. If it matches, it is printed on the top of the slip. That slip is then inserted into the slot on the deposit console and the credits are added to the account on the slip. Sometimes multiple deposits are made at once if the limit per deposit is reached."

Millzak stared off into space for a moment repeating to himself what Daylinn had said, over and over in his mind. Once he was sure he remembered it and understood the process he turned to his new assistant.

"I want to see the deposit slips," Millzak said. "Please notify your contact at the...the...?" He reached for his slate and his notes.

"Pangtol Company?" Daylinn prodded.

"Yes," Millzak said, "the Pangtol Company. Have the being responsible for depositing the credits bring the deposit slips here now."

With a look of slight confusion on her face, Daylinn made the call. Fifteen minutes later, an older Caroon walked in with a nervous-looking, younger version of himself. After the introductions were made, the young one handed Millzak the booklet of preprinted deposit slips. Daylinn shook her head at the archaic system of using actual deposit slips but she watched and waited.

Millzak flipped through the slips quickly, the print on them a blur as they made a steady flapping sound. He wasn't looking at them as he stared off. He turned to his assistant. "Write the deposit account number down please. I will read them."

"What?" Daylinn asked. "The account number? That is like, fifty digits. Do you want me to put them in my slate?"

"Yes," Millzak answered. "Can you write a program or something to tell me if every digit matches? That is a lot of numbers."

"I...I can, Peacemaker," said Daylinn, "Are you going to read each one? The slips are all the same, they are preprinted, but if you wish, it is only a few lines of programming. Just one moment." Her fingers flew over the screen of her slate. "Okay, I am ready."

Millzak read the digits slowly, one by one, to his assistant. Everyone in the room was silent. The exchange president was now in the room with the rest of them. None were brave enough to interrupt the large Peacemaker, though they all knew this was foolish. The slips were preprinted with the account number. It would not change.

Millzak flipped to the next deposit slip and read the digits. He did this three more times. On the fifth slip, he heard Daylinn inhale sharply. The fifth slip had one digit different in the thirty-second digit. The number was almost identical to the one it replaced.

Millzak looked at the suspect, now deflated and staring at the floor. He handed the deposit booklet to Daylinn. She flipped to the tenth slip, looked at the thirty-second digit, and nodded. The pre-printed slips had been printed like that on purpose, every fifth slip.

"That's it!" Daylinn exclaimed. "That is why I could not find it. That account's credit matched its deposit slips. There were no red flags. The gap in the system was there so no one could see when its deposits were made."

Millzak turned to the exchange president. "This one is in charge of opening accounts and providing the deposit books?"

"Yes," answered the president. He glared at the thief. "She is—or should I say, she *was*. Her console is used to print them."

"Transfer the missing amount to the correct account," Millzak ordered. "Contact the local authorities to have her picked up and charged for theft and any other law she may have broken on this planet and in this system.

"At once, Peacemaker," agreed the exchange president, clearly re-lieved. Several businesses had hinted at changing credit exchanges due to the rumors.

"From what Daylinn told me, there is trouble at the mines be-cause of her?"

"My mine supervisor informs me he has lost control," the head of the Pangtol Company agreed, his long nose bobbing up and down. "Things are getting out of control."

"I will notify the supervisor so he can let the miners know they will get paid as soon as it processes," the older Caroon said. He left with his son.

Later, standing outside the exchange, Daylinn turned to Millzak. "That was amazing. All my searching, the programs I used—some I wrote on the spot—the exchange's full cooperation, and I couldn't find the credit. You looked where no one, and I mean no one, would have thought. How did you know?"

"I am a simple Lumar. It is a fact," answered Millzak, shrugging all four shoulders. "I looked for a simple solution. All the knowledge and skills in the galaxy cannot help you if you can't see what is right there in front of you first."

Daylinn tilted her head and looked at Millzak in a new light. "I will remember that, Peacemaker. Thank you for the lesson. What will you do now?"

"I will go to Gondlo and help my partner," answered Millzak. "We will finish our missions in no time. We will get back to the Academy long before we are expected."

"I want to thank you," Daylinn said. "You barely knew me, yet you saw where I was...where I was headed. I have to be honest with you, I didn't even know where I was headed. Now, in a matter of hours, not only did you fix the problems for all those miners and their families, you fixed mine. I don't know how I can ever repay you."

"Little one," Millzak said, "there is no need to thank me. You helped a great deal. My first mission has been a success because of your help. Thank you.

"I will be honest with you. I still had doubts. I am not a smart Lumar. I wondered even with my determination, if would it be enough? Could I really do this?" He indicated his uniform, and his badge. "I knew I would not give up. But even in succeeding, am I good enough?" Millzak stared off in the distance. He turned back to her. "Can I do this? Yes. I can. I will be a Peacemaker."

"Yes," Daylinn agreed. "Yes, you will. I think you are one now. Only a Peacemaker could solve the problems of many...and of one at the same time. If I never see you again, be safe. Thank you for helping me with my new job at the exchange. The way you let the president know you would be my reference caused him to hire me on the spot. I am the first employee not of the Caroon race here." She wrapped her arms around his leg in a quick hug and ran inside, sniffing.

Millzak walked a little taller as he headed toward the starport. He decided to commandeer a shuttle to the sister planet and not wait for the scheduled flight.

* * *

Chapter Five

Millzak had the pilot land near the mines. As he walked down the ramp, he adjusted the belt of his holster, and shifted his pistol slightly. He decided during the day-long flight to take it out of its case. From the information the pilot could gather, the miners were still gathered outside the mines in a standoff with the security company.

He started jogging toward the mass of beings. As he got closer, he saw flashes of a Peacemaker uniform. Zerze was moving back and forth in front of the miners urging them to disband. Even after receiving the news about their pay, the miners had not gone back to work.

He forced his way to the front and called out. "Zerze!"

"Millzak!" Zerze exclaimed. "What are you doing here? Never mind. We have a major problem. The miners have been paid but security won't allow them back into the mines to go to work."

"Why?" Millzak asked.

"I don't know," Zerze said. Millzak could hear the exhaustion in his friend's voice. "They refuse to move, and the miners are now up in arms because they are losing credits because they can't work. It's a mad house. If it's not one thing it is another. No one will listen to reason. Diplomacy is not working. I can't get them to sit down and talk it out. I'm trying to tell them violence is not the answer."

Millzak looked across the open area between the miners and the security company. One of the Blevin was obviously the leader. He was larger than the rest and kept gesturing toward the miners, urging his troops.

Millzak turned to Zerze. "Tell me how a security contract works."

"What?" Zerze asked. "It's a contract. They get paid to be security. Guard the mines, the equipment, put down uprisings, too, I guess. Why?"

"Tell me about bonuses," Millzak said, still looking at the leader.

"Bonuses?" Zerze said, finally losing patience with his friend. "Look, Millzak, I don't have time for this. They…" Zerze paused as it dawned on him. "It's the bonus! They want the bonus for combat. Well, not really combat, but any type of action or fighting. They won't get it if there is a peaceful resolution to this, which, there is now. I don't know how you did it, but there is."

Millzak took off his holster and handed it to Zerze. He unzipped his jump suit to the waist, pulled his arms out and tied the top around his waist, hiding that it was a uniform and his badge.

He turned to Zerze and said, "Sometimes, violence *is* the answer." He started walking toward the guards. It took him a few minutes to get there.

Millzak walked up to the leader and said, "Move. Let them go back to work."

The Blevin sneered. "Make me."

Millzak shrugged all four shoulders, turned, and glanced back at Zerze. Quickly, he turned his body back and landed two punches with his left fists. One struck the large Blevin in his ribs the other in his face. The Blevin crumpled into a pile. He kicked a guard swinging a rifle butt at him from the other side and ended that threat. The next guard rushed him, his weapon forgotten. Millzak grabbed him, spun him around, and threw him with all four hands. The stunned guard landed more than six feet away.

Millzak stood ready. The remaining twenty or so guards let their rifles hang on their straps and raised their six fingered hands, backing up a step or two. When Millzak untied his jumpsuit and put it back on correctly, his Peacemaker's badge showed brightly. All of them looked up, down, and away. Anywhere but at him.

* * *

Epilogue

Peacemaker Academy
Ocono

A year later, the graduation ceremony was different. This year the candidates were called up in order of merit by their valedictorian. The entire auditorium was asked to hold their applause until the last candidate was commissioned as a Peacemaker.

The room was silent as newly graduated Peacemaker Zerze paused before calling out the last name. He looked slowly across the entire room and spoke into the microphone. "Do you know what they call the one who graduates last in his class at the Peacemaker Academy?"

The room remained silent. He glanced around. Puzzlement could be seen on every face.

After a long moment he leaned closer to the mic. "Peacemaker."

The room erupted, the class members cheering the loudest, when Millzak's name was called.

* * *

M ajor Bellgrund was the first to congratulate Peace-maker Millzak after the ceremony. She looked up at his badge and her eyes widened. She had wondered what tree from the Lumar home world Millzak would use. All Peacemakers were offered the opportunity to give input on the design of their individual badges.

The badge on Millzak's chest was of a barren tree. It appeared to be a tree in the middle of winter; there were no leaves on it. Suddenly, it dawned on her.

Millzak had chosen a tree he could see through.

* * * * *

Kevin Steverson Bio

Kevin Steverson is a retired veteran of the U.S. Army. Having written several Amazon bestsellers, he is a published songwriter as well as an author. When he is not on the road as the Tour Manager for the band Cypress Spring, he can be found in the foothills of the NE Georgia mountains writing in one fashion or another.

# # # # #

About the Editors

Mia R. Kleve has been an avid reader since high school, unless you count the cereal boxes during breakfast as she was growing up. She quickly became a huge fan of anything science fiction and fantasy, including authors like Robert A. Heinlein, Anne McCaffrey, Mercedes Lackey, Frank Herbert, and so many more.

She started proof editing on a volunteer basis with a couple small publishers, including Chris Kennedy Publishing (in an effort to get a jump on the Four Horsemen series). She currently does freelance content editing and proofing through her company MRK'd Up Editing.

Kevin Ikenberry is a life-long space geek and retired Army officer. As an adult, he managed the U.S. Space Camp program and served as a space operations officer before Space Force was a thing. He's an international bestselling author, award finalist, and a core author in the wildly successful Four Horsemen Universe. His eleven novels include *Sleeper Protocol*, *Vendetta Protocol*, *Runs in The Family*, *Peacemaker*, *Honor the Threat*, *Stand or Fall*, and *Deathangel*. He's co-written several novels with amazing authors. He is an Active Member of SFWA, International Thriller Writers, and SIGMA—the science fiction think tank.

* * * * *

Connect with Chris Kennedy Publishing Online

Website: http://chriskennedypublishing.com/

Facebook: https://www.facebook.com/chriskennedypublishing.biz

* * * * *

Do you have what it takes to be a Merc?

Take your VOWs and join the Merc Guild on Facebook!

Meet us at: https://www.facebook.com/groups/536506813392912/

* * * * *

The following is an

Excerpt from Book One of the Salvage Title Trilogy:

Salvage Title

Kevin Steverson

Available Now from Theogony Books

eBook, Paperback, and Audio Book

Excerpt from "Salvage Title:"

The first thing Clip did was get power to the door and the access panel. Two of his power cells did the trick once he had them wired to the container. He then pulled out his slate and connected it. It lit up, and his fingers flew across it. It took him a few minutes to establish a link, then he programmed it to search for the combination to the access panel.

"Is it from a human ship?" Harmon asked, curious.

"I don't think so, but it doesn't matter; ones and zeros are still ones and zeros when it comes to computers. It's universal. I mean, there are some things you have to know to get other races' computers to run right, but it's not that hard," Clip said.

Harmon shook his head. *Riiigghht,* he thought. He knew better. Clip's intelligence test results were completely off the charts. Clip opted to go to work at Rinto's right after secondary school because there was nothing for him to learn at the colleges and universities on either Tretra or Joth. He could have received academic scholarships for advanced degrees on a number of nearby systems. He could have even gone all the way to Earth and attended the University of Georgia if he wanted. The problem was getting there. The schools would have provided free tuition if he could just have paid to get there.

Secondary school had been rough on Clip. He was a small guy that made excellent grades without trying. It would have been worse if Harmon hadn't let everyone know that Clip was his brother. They lived in the same foster center, so it was mostly true. The first day of school, Harmon had laid down the law—if you messed with Clip, you messed up.

At the age of fourteen, he beat three seniors senseless for attempting to put Clip in a trash container. One of them was a Yalteen, a member of a race of large humanoids from two systems over. It wasn't a fair fight—they should have brought more people with them. Harmon hated bullies.

After the suspension ended, the school's Warball coach came to see him. He started that season as a freshman and worked on using it to earn a scholarship to the academy. By the time he graduated, he was six feet two inches with two hundred and twenty pounds of muscle. He got the scholarship and a shot at going into space. It was the longest time he'd ever spent away from his foster brother, but he couldn't turn it down.

Clip stayed on Joth and went to work for Rinto. He figured it was a job that would get him access to all kinds of technical stuff, servos, motors, and maybe even some alien computers. The first week he was there, he tweaked the equipment and increased the plant's recycled steel production by 12 percent. Rinto was eternally grateful, as it put him solidly into the profit column instead of toeing the line between profit and loss. When Harmon came back to the planet after the academy, Rinto hired him on the spot on Clip's recommendation. After he saw Harmon operate the grappler and got to know him, he was glad he did.

A steady beeping brought Harmon back to the present. Clip's program had succeeded in unlocking the container. "Right on!" Clip exclaimed. He was always using expressions hundreds or more years out of style. "Let's see what we have; I hope this one isn't empty, too." Last month they'd come across a smaller vault, but it had been empty.

Harmon stepped up and wedged his hands into the small opening the door had made when it disengaged the locks. There wasn't enough power in the small cells Clip used to open it any further. He put his weight into it, and the door opened enough for them to get inside. Before they went in, Harmon placed a piece of pipe in the doorway so it couldn't close and lock on them, baking them alive before anyone realized they were missing.

Daylight shone in through the doorway, and they both froze in place; the weapons vault was full.

* * * * *

Get "Salvage Title" now at:
https://www.amazon.com/dp/B07H8Q3HBV.

Find out more about Kevin Steverson and "Salvage Title" at:
http://chriskennedypublishing.com/.

* * * * *

The following is an

Excerpt from Devil Calls the Tune:

Devil Calls the Tune

Chris Maddox

Available from Theogony Books

eBook, Paperback, and (Soon) Audio

Excerpt from "Devil Calls the Tune:"

Kenyon shouted, "Flyer! Fast mover!"

Everyone grabbed their packs and started running. When McCarthy didn't, Devlin grabbed him by his uniform shirt and yelled, "Come on!"

The little outcropping they had weathered under was part of a larger set of hills. Devlin and McCarthy made for a sheer cliff face that was tall enough that it would make strafing difficult. They dove behind a few rocks, and Devlin peered over one. The flier had overshot the group and was circling.

McCarthy reached into his pack and pulled out a rail pistol and magazine. He slapped the magazine home into its well and charged the pistol.

"Where the fark did you get that!" Devlin panted. He reached over and took the pistol. McCarthy let him.

"This was the surprise," McCarthy said. "I found the pistol, then searched the wreckage for ammo. I found some and parts to a bunch of rifles. Most were in bad shape, but Pringle figured he might be able to cobble together a couple from the parts. He was going take the lot back to the camp so they would have something to defend the wounded with. He sent me with this for you. Best we could get together at the time. Sorry."

"Don't be sorry. This is pretty good. I won't beat the shit out of you now for the fire."

"The fire?" McCarthy looked blank for a moment, then realization hit. "Oh, you think that the fire attracted—"

"Our flying friend over there. Yeah, I just—get your head down!" He pulled at McCarthy as rounds from the flier dug into the earth. There was something odd about this one.

531

He took a quick look. This wasn't the same flier that had attacked the camp, this one was...

"Drone!" Devlin yelled. He watched the thing from the rocks, watched it circle around again. He braced the pistol on the rocks, steadied, and waited.

When the drone started its run again, Devlin sighted in, breathed out, and fired.

The drone disintegrated in a fiery cloud as the rail gun round entered its main capacitor bank. He watched it fall and then rose from behind the rocks. McCarthy joined him.

Devlin looked over at the tree line and waved his arm. A moment later, Kenyon appeared, followed by Gartlan and MacBain.

"Devlin!" Decker's voice came out of the tree line. Kenyon and the others started to where Decker's voice had come from. Devlin started to run.

He found the group gathered around Decker. She was holding Moran's head in her lap. Moran's uniform had a red stain in the abdomen that was growing larger by the moment.

"Got hit as I dived into the woods," Moran croaked. Her blond hair was already slick with sweat, her face pale.

"Sorry, Devlin. I...I..." her voice trailed off as her implant fed nanites and nighty-night into her system. A moment later she looked dead, which for all intents and purposes she was.

Devlin rubbed his scalp. He glared over at McCarthy, whose shocked face got even paler as he looked at the body, hibernating though it was, of Lisa Moran. He bowed his head and started to stammer, "I'm sorry, I didn't..."

"Shut up, Tom. Just shut up," Devlin said tiredly. "You didn't know; you had no way of knowing. This wasn't even the same flier that attacked the camp. Just a stupid mistake, but it's one that we have to deal with now. Is anybody else hurt?"

Arnette was sitting on the ground beside Decker with her legs crossed. She held one ankle in her hands. "Well, now that you mention it…" She looked at Devlin with pain-filled eyes. "I think my ankle is broken. I stepped straight into a hole as I came into the woods."

Decker moved her legs out from underneath Moran's head and laid it gently on the ground. She made her way to the other woman. Gartlan bent down as well and said, "Let's get your boot off."

Together, the two started trying to get the girl's boot off. When Arnette hissed once and nearly passed out, they realized they'd have to cut it off. Gartlan produced a tactical knife and used the monomolecular edge to slice down the side of the boot. His cut made, he handed the knife to Decker, who sliced down the foot portion of the boot, careful not to cut too deeply.

"Here you go, Wolf," she said handing the knife back to Gartlan, who folded it and put it back in his pocket. Together, he and Decker were finally able to peel the ruined boot off the injured girl's foot.

Her foot, already purple, immediately started to swell. They propped her leg up on a rock covered with Gartlan's tunic. Gartlan shook his head at Devlin. "She isn't likely to go nighty-night, but she might as well. She ain't going anywhere on that foot for a few days. And she's not going to like this, but we're going to have to set it and splint it so that the nanis don't knit it wrong. Probably still will, but the canker mechanics should be able to fix it without too much problem if we get home."

Sarah Arnette's eyes went wide as Gartlan's words hit home. "Oh Gods!" she moaned. "This is going to *suck!*"

"Do it," Devlin said. "Come on, guys. They don't need an audience, and we've got to get our shit together."

He turned to walk away as Gartlan bent back down, and Decker opened a med kit.

Another drone flier came to halt in front of them, and a voice came over its vocoder, "State your name and passcode."

* * * * *

"Devil Calls the Tune" now at:

https://www.amazon.com/dp/B0849QYWMJ.

Find out more about Chris Maddox and "Devil Calls the Tune" at:
https://chriskennedypublishing.com/imprints-authors/chris-maddox/.

* * * *

The following is an

Excerpt from Book One of the Earth Song Cycle:

Overture

Mark Wandrey

Now Available from Theogony Books

eBook and Paperback

Excerpt from "Overture:"

Dawn was still an hour away as Mindy Channely opened the roof access and stared in surprise at the crowd already assembled there. "Authorized Personnel Only" was printed in bold red letters on the door through which she and her husband, Jake, slipped onto the wide roof.

A few people standing nearby took notice of their arrival. Most had no reaction, a few nodded, and a couple waved tentatively. Mindy looked over the skyline of Portland and instinctively oriented herself before glancing to the east. The sky had an unnatural glow that had been growing steadily for hours, and as they watched, scintillating streamers of blue, white, and green radiated over the mountains like a strange, concentrated aurora borealis.

"You almost missed it," one man said. She let the door close, but saw someone had left a brick to keep it from closing completely. Mindy turned and saw the man who had spoken wore a security guard uniform. The easy access to the building made more sense.

"Ain't no one missin' this!" a drunk man slurred.

"We figured most people fled to the hills over the past week," Jake replied.

"I guess we were wrong," Mindy said.

"Might as well enjoy the show," the guard said and offered them a huge, hand-rolled cigarette that didn't smell like tobacco. She waved it off, and the two men shrugged before taking a puff.

"Here it comes!" someone yelled. Mindy looked to the east. There was a bright light coming over the Cascade Mountains, so intense it was like looking at a welder's torch. Asteroid LM-245 hit the atmosphere at over 300 miles per second. It seemed to move faster and faster, from east to west, and the people lifted their hands

537

to shield their eyes from the blinding light. It looked like a blazing comet or a science fiction laser blast.

"Maybe it will just pass over," someone said in a voice full of hope.

Mindy shook her head. She'd studied the asteroid's track many times.

In a matter of a few seconds, it shot by and fell toward the western horizon, disappearing below the mountains between Portland and the ocean. Out of view of the city, it slammed into the ocean.

The impact was unimaginable. The air around the hypersonic projectile turned to superheated plasma, creating a shockwave that generated 10 times the energy of the largest nuclear weapon ever detonated as it hit the ocean's surface.

The kinetic energy was more than 1,000 megatons; however, the object didn't slow as it flashed through a half mile of ocean and into the sea bed, then into the mantel, and beyond.

On the surface, the blast effect appeared as a thermal flash brighter than the sun. Everyone on the rooftop watched with wide-eyed terror as the Tualatin Mountains between Portland and the Pacific Ocean were outlined in blinding light. As the light began to dissipate, the outline of the mountains blurred as a dense bank of smoke climbed from the western range.

The flash had incinerated everything on the other side.

The physical blast, travelling much faster than any normal atmospheric shockwave, hit the mountains and tore them from the bedrock, adding them to the rolling wave of destruction traveling east at several thousand miles per hour. The people on the rooftops of Portland only had two seconds before the entire city was wiped away.

Ten seconds later, the asteroid reached the core of the planet, and another dozen seconds after that, the Earth's fate was sealed.

* * * * *

Get "Overture" now at:
https://www.amazon.com/dp/B077YMLRHM/

Find out more about Mark Wandrey and the Earth Song Cycle at:
https://chriskennedypublishing.com/

* * * * *

Made in the USA
Coppell, TX
22 May 2022

78065073R00295